"I spent a year in an overheated country where you couldn't drink the water, and if you trusted any of the people, you did it at your own risk. A bunch of my buddies got killed and more got wounded—hell, I got zapped there at the end myself. But what with us getting our brains half-fried from the heat, and going half-crazy in the godawful monsoons, and getting sliced up by elephant grass and having leeches try to drink us dry like they was Dracula, and having these strange little people running around trying to kill us, I'm proud to be able to say I was good enough to be a Marine and go off to fight in that crazy Asian war."

Also by David Sherman
Published by Ivy Books:

The Night Fighters

THERE
I WAS

David Sherman

IVY BOOKS • NEW YORK

Ivy Books
Published by Ballantine Books

Library of Congress Catalog Card Number: 89-91175

ISBN 0-8041-0498-0

Manufactured in the United States of America

First Edition: August 1989

For
My friends Dan Cragg and JB Post,
Who told me where to put my writing

"Can the foot soldier teach anything important about war, merely for having been there? I think not. He can tell war stories."

Tim O'Brien,
If I Die in a Combat Zone

"The only difference between fairy tales and war stories is the first line. Fairy tales begin with, 'Once upon a time . . .' War stories start out, 'There I was . . .' "
Military Aphorism

Acknowledgments

First, I wish to express my appreciation to my friends Linda Fischer and Tom Smith for their invaluable editorial and readerly assistance with this novel. No novel is truly the creation of one mind working in a vacuum, so after Tom and Linda, I want to convey thanks to the following people who provided the idea-germs that evolved (greatly changed) into some of the scenes and chapters in this novel: "Crazy" Higgins, who I never met because his war ended before mine began; my friend Jimmy Holland, former corporal, USMC; the lance corporal whose name I can't remember, but whose story I read in *Stars and Stripes*; Lance Corporal "Eggy," who I haven't seen since I left Ky Hoa; and the late Brigadier General S.L.A. Marshall, USA, Ret.

Note

Most men who have been in combat, I think, tell war stories. None of them tell their stories exactly the way they happened—except maybe once in a great while, when men who went through the same things sit quietly together, late at night when no one who wasn't there is around. Then maybe they'll tell each other their stories the way they actually happened. It's not that they lie. It's more that memory fails over time, and that there are things they don't want to remember, times when events were too confused to remember accurately, or men whose memory they want to honor. Here is the way one man might tell about his war—and the way it might have really happened. What he might say and what happened, they're different.

The unit in this novel is Company L, 3rd Battalion, 15th Marines. There was no 15th Marines during the Vietnam war. I used that unit designation to avoid any possible identification between my fictional characters and unit and real Marines or their unit. While some of the events in this novel are based on actual happenings, every one of them is the product of my mind; nothing in this novel happened in fact, none of the characters are based on any individual—except one minor character who is loosely based on me.

Have A Sit Down, Son

"Well, son, you've turned eighteen now. Have a sit down right there, it's time we had a little talk. You want a beer? I know your momma don't approve of you drinking yet, but drinking a beer with your old man at this time ain't gonna hurt none. Besides, it's traditional, and I don't think she should have a say in it.

"That's right, son, settle right in there. What's that you say? No, I'm not gonna tell you about the birds and the bees. That's what you get sex education in high school for—so's us old fogies don't steer you wrong with the same crap we learned on the streets when we was your age. No, this talk is about a family tradition.

"We have a history in this family—a birthright, an obligation, a by-damn tradition. And that's what I'm going to tell you about. You see, in our family each generation has a son who joins the United States Marine Corps and goes off to fight a war. And that son has a son who goes off and does the same thing.

"Have another swig of your brew, son. That's the way, sit easy. We have a tradition that goes all the way back to the Revolutionary War—that's what they probably taught you in school to call the 'War for Independence.'

" 'War for Independence.' Sure. Ever since our government started opposing revolutions against any right-wing dictator who

1

claimed to be our friend on the grounds the revolutions was communist-inspired, it hasn't liked to have people remember that this country started out by rebelling against a lawful government that just plain made life too miserable for the people. Oh, yes, they were some radicals, those old guys like Ben Franklin and Tommy Jefferson and Johnny Adams, they sure were. Bring them back around today and they'd likely find themselves getting put on 'enemies lists' and having their pictures taken by the police and getting tailed by the FBI out of some politician's fear they'd go upsetting somebody's apple cart. Yes, sir, they was rebels in those days, they was. Hardcase.

"Have another swig of your brew, son. Put some hair on your chest.

"But to what I'm telling you about now. You know I was a United States Marine in Vietnam, but you don't know much more'n that. Never did say much about my war experiences, did I? But like I say, we've got a tradition in this family.

"When I was eighteen my daddy sat me down just like I'm sitting you down and told me about his experiences in the Pacific war. He missed the big ones, my daddy did—the Canal, Tarawa, Iwo, Okinawa. But he was on Bougainville and Tinian and Kwajalien, and he was among the troops getting set to invade Japan. His daddy sat him down when he was eighteen and told him about how he was at Belleau Wood and Mont Blanc in the War to End All Wars.

"This tradition goes all the way back to the Revolution, when your great-granddaddy seven times removed was a Marine sharpshooter in the rigging of Navy ships. Family legend tells how it was that the first of our line was the very sharpshooter on the *Bon Homme Richard* who heard Captain Jones tell the British, 'I have not yet begun to fight,' and turned to another sharpshooter and said, 'There's always that ten percent that doesn't get the word.'

"Now, his son fought the Barbary pirates, and he had a son who went into the Everglades to fight the Seminole Indians with old Archibald Henderson, and he had a son who stormed the gates at Chapultepec in the Mexican War. Then the string was almost broke because the Civil War came too soon, but the son of our ancestor who was at the Halls of Montezuma managed to get to enlistment age in time to join the Marines before peace broke out at Appomattox. That not-quite-fighting Marine's son went up against the Apaches in the Southwest, and then his son, your great-granddaddy's daddy, liked to tell about how he went up San Juan Hill with Teddy Roosevelt, but that was a lie. The Marines didn't fight along with Teddy's Rough Riders.

"So here we are today, son. For ten generations the son of a fighting Marine in our family has gone out and fought in the next war. In every generation the son that got shot at in the last war sat his eighteen-year-old son down and told him what it was like, so the son was ready to go to his war.

"The way things are heating up all over the world right now, it might not be too long before your turn to fight in a war comes along. It wasn't that long ago we had a Marine battalion in Beruit and more than two hundred of them got themselves killed. Actually, I'm kind of surprised we never did get ourselves involved in that Afghan thing. Marines got sent to Grenada, and the way Ronnie kept going after that Colonel Kay-daffy in Libya, I right expected Marines would find themselves storming the walls of Tripoli again. Marine fighter-bomber aircraft were involved in the big raid, though. But mostly what each son tells his son about how to fight doesn't do the next son much good, because all the wars are different, but it tells him what it is like to fight.

"My daddy told me about island hopping and amphibious assaults against the Japanese. He told me about those crazy little people who fought to the death because they didn't believe in surrendering. That didn't do me much good in my war except that, just like the Japanese, those tough little bastards I fought didn't have enough sense to quit when we had their asses beat. I guess that's why they managed to hang around long enough to win after we finally got tired enough of it to go home and leave them to themselves.

"But the way things are going to hell in a handbasket in Central America, and the saber-rattling noises the White House and Pentagon are making about it, that's where we might go next. If it is, and you do go to war there, what I tell you about jungle fighting might help some. And the flatlands will be pretty much the same, too. Same crops, sugarcane and bananas. Same people, small and speaking a foreign language. Same climate, hot and humid. No monsoons, though—just a rainy season. 'Course, you won't have much in the way of rice paddies to slog through like I did, but that's probably for the best. Those paddies can get downright nasty.

"So you just sit there, son, and listen up. Listen up real good, because I'm going to tell you about my war. My war started with Operation Abilene Run, and ended with Operation Rockledge Manor.

"It was Christmastime, nineteen and sixty-four. My daddy sat me down less'n a year before, when I had just turned eighteen. That Vietnam thing just kept getting hotter and hotter, and it looked like things were about to blow up, so I dropped out of school in the middle of my senior year of high school and signed myself up. My momma tried to talk me into staying in school for a few more months and getting my diploma, but I told her it was better for me to get in uniform before the war started 'cause then I'd have more time for training and a better chance to survive. Daddy backed me up, so there wasn't much Momma could do about it.

"Two months after I got to Parris Island, the Ninth Marines landed at Da Nang. Some of the people in my recruit platoon got more gung ho than they were before, others suddenly got scared because they really didn't want to go to war. Shouldn't of joined the Marines, they didn't want to go to war.

"After boot camp and ITR—that's Infantry Training Regiment, son, all Marines used to go through it—they put me in the First Marines at Camp Pendleton in California for maybe three months, then pulled me and a bunch of other men out and shipped us off to Okinawa to where the Fifteenth Marines were forming. Being in a new regiment was a good thing for almost everybody who had been in the Corps for long enough to have some experience beyond ITR. That's 'cause half 'a the men in the Fifteenth were fresh outta training and there were plenty'a promotions to pass out. I didn't have my PFC stripe long enough then to get lance corporal's BB guns, but they made me an automatic rifleman anyhow and promised me a promotion soon's I had enough time in grade.

"My squad, third squad, third platoon, Company L, Third Battalion, Fifteenth Marines, had some good Marines in it. I'll tell you about them at the right time. Took about two months to form up the regiment and get us all to know each other. Then, at the end of November, Third Battalion shipped out for Vietnam. It was the damnest thing I ever did, eating Thanksgiving dinner on board ship in the South China Sea, but that's what we did.

"Once we got there, I want to tell you they didn't waste any time on us. We landed at Da Nang and transshipped right onto LSTs for a trip down to the Chu Lai peninsula. We made a dawn wet landing expecting all kinds of resistance, thinking we was storming the beach at Iwo Jima, or some such, but it wasn't that bad. Here's how we did it.

"Say what? Why am I talking like this when I all the time talk like the Yankee from the Northeastern Corridor that I am? That's almost the easiest thing in the world to answer, son. I'm talking like this because I'm talking about the Mo-reen Corps. When I got to Parris Island one of the first thoughts I had—other'n how scared I was—was, 'Am I the only Yankee here?' You see, son, in the Mo-reen Corps, everbody talks like they is from the South."

Abilene, Sweet Abilene

"JUST SETTLE YOURSELF IN RIGHT COMFORTABLE THERE, SON, this is gonna take a while. We got a cooler of beer sitting right here between us, and there's chips and pretzels on the table where we can get to 'em without hardly moving. Here, son, have a cee-gar. Puff on it for a while. Put some hair on your chest. That's right, light it right up there.

"Whoa, boy, don't inhale! Knock you right on your ass you inhale and you're not used to it. Just puff a mite, blow some smoke. Don't inhale if your lungs can't take it.

"Feeling better? I can start now? Good. Now, then, I'm gonna tell you about Operation Abilene Run. Abilene Run was the first operation I went on once I got myself to Veeceeland. Three Fifteen went on this operation almost the same day we got there. It was what they called a 'search and destroy.' What that meant was nobody knew for sure if someone was out there or not or, if they were, where they were. That's why it's a search—if they're there, we're supposed to find them. If we find them, we're supposed to kill them. That's why it's a destroy. At least that's sure the way it seemed to us.

"On those LSTs we boarded at Da Nang, we were issued ammunition, three hundred rounds per rifle, four-eighty for the ARs. Each sidearm got seventy, the M-60 machine guns had a couple thousand each, and every man in the company had to hump a sixty-millimeter mortar round unless he was carrying a LAW or a satchel charge. They also gave us four meals of C-rats to carry in our packs along with two pairs of socks.

"In the second squad was this little bitty private everybody called 'Mouse.' We called him Mouse on account of he was so small. The Marine Corps had a minimum height requirement that you had to be five-foot-four to get in. We had a standing bet in the platoon about if Mouse stood on a scale and they had the height bar set at five-foot-four, would the top of his head reach it or not if he was in his bare feet. No way he could have weighed much more than a hundred pounds.

"So Mouse straps his web belt round his waist with five magazines, a bayonet, two canteens, and a jungle kit on it, and it almost falls down over his hips because he can't close it tight enough to stay around his waist. Then he put on his pack with two pair of cushion-sole socks, shaving kit, and four meals of C-rations in it and an entrenching tool and mortar round hanging off it, slings three bandoleers over his shoulders, puts his piss pot on his head and picks up his M-14. Kind of looked like someone just stacked all that gear there and walked away from it.

"Then Mouse walks over to Lieutenant Haupt. Haupt the Kraut, we called him, was our platoon leader. Well, Mouse says, 'Sir, I just doubled my weight. Do I gotta wear the flak jacket and pants? If I put them on I don't believe I'll be able to walk.' Lieutenant Haupt was about six-foot-two and had played varsity football at Annapolis. He looks down at Mouse and says, 'Mouse, I'm gonna cut you some slack. You don't gotta wear the pants. Ain't no fragments gonna be able to fly that low to the ground. But you gotta wear the jacket.' Mouse looks down at hisself then cranes his head back to look at the lieutenant. 'You know, sir, I do believe you're right,' Mouse says, 'no frags gonna fly that low. But you just know a shitload of it's gonna be flying about six feet off the ground.' Then he turned around and went back and took off the bandoleers and his pack, put on the flak jacket and then pulled his pack and bandoleers back over the jacket. Everybody wondered how he was gonna move.

"Mouse wasn't known as a bad-assed gyrene before then, but everybody sure's hell admired him for what he said to the lieutenant.

"Mouse was an extreme example of how we were weighted down, but he's a good point to make for it. We were all carrying something like seventy or eighty pounds that day, except for the gun and mortar humpers. They were carrying more. A man can burn up a lot of energy carrying that much weight, work up a powerful sweat. Don't sound too bad, though, humping seventy, eighty pounds in November, does it? But this ain't November in New England. This is November in the tropics. By the time we got into them amtracks to hit the beach, it was already over eighty degrees hot and it was hardly past sunup. We just knew it was gonna get a lot hotter before it cooled off any.

"We crammed ourselves into the amtracks in the belly of that LST, and when they all revved up, the noise was like the end of the world. Thought those landing vehicles would shake that ship apart. The LST lowered its ramp and the amtracks put it in gear and rolled out. An amtrack looks sort of like a tank without a gun turret. According to some engineers it should float like one, too. It tries to. Soon as one hits the water coming off a landing ship, it drops almost to the bottom of the ocean before bobbing like a cork back to the surface. It only sticks high enough out of the water for the driver and gunner to see through their eye slits. Makes for a small target for shore defenders.

"We were all pretty nervous going ashore because nobody told us what to expect when we got there. For all we knew, it would be a hell like the Tarawa seawall. The amtracks rolled up onto the beach, dropped their beach gates, and we boiled out like John Wayne in the *Sands of Iwo Jima* and expecting all kinds of machine gun and artillery fire. Wasn't any, though. We got organized into company columns and marched northeast a couple klicks to a helicopter landing zone. The only resistance we had the whole way was some sniper fire. The whole battalion didn't have any more than a half-dozen casualties. After we secured the LZ, helicopters came in and picked us up to go somewhere else for the operation.

"The ride in the birds was nice. Those old Sikorsky UH-34s had doors on both sides, and both doors were open so the door gunners could aim their guns out and do any shooting they had to do. A nice breeze came in through those open doors and did a lot to cool us off. But we were only in the air for about twenty minutes before we dropped down between a couple of hills and scrambled off. Air wasn't moving between them hills and there was only low scrub, so there weren't much to talk about in the way of shade, and the sun just kept beating down on us. One dumb sum-bitch who didn't take his salt tabs that morning had his head half baked under his helmet and became a heat casualty before the whole company was down and the humping started. He was thrown back on the last bird dropping men in the LZ and got cooled off back in the hospital. They sent him back to us in the first resupply.

"Well, we sat there mostly in the sun, except for those people crawled under the bushes, getting hotter and hotter waiting for the entire company to come in and the skipper to give the marching orders to the platoon leaders and platoon sergeants. The four companies of the battalion were dropped down in different LZs all about a klick apart. The battalion CO was a couple, three klicks up in his command bird, watching us. There was also three or four gunships flying low over each LZ to help wipe out any resistance, but there wasn't any. Those LZs were what is called cold.

"Those LZs may have been cold, but they were hot. The temperature between them hills must have been over ninety by the time we were all there and got the word to saddle up. Good old third platoon got the point, with first and second following behind. There were trails around that we could've walked on, but Lieutenant Haupt was some kind of hard charger who believed the easiest way for an American in Vietnam to get himself wounded or killed was to walk on a trail. The Vee Cee and NVA believed that Americans all the time walked on trails, so they booby-trapped the hell out of them. They didn't put many booby traps in the middle of the brush because there's no way of telling where a man's gonna be walking there.

"So instead of taking it easy on ourselves and going on the trails, we had to break trails through that hard brush that was just full of them damn stayawhile vines. Stayawhile vines are these buggers that sort of grab ahold of you and don't want to let go again until after they've made you stop, or maybe tripped you. It was real ball-busting work breaking a trail. Most of the bushes was about half man height, but they were packed real close to each other. We had two machetes in the squad and both of them cut like they ain't seen a honing stone since Guadalcanal. We were so hot in that white sun beating down on us underneath our helmets and humping all that gear that it didn't take long at all before most of us didn't have much left to sweat out and started feeling the effects of the heat. Ain't nothing as bad as being that godawful hot and not being able to sweat. We had to change the pointman every fifteen minutes because nobody could go much longer than that without collapsing with heat exhaustion.

"We went on that way for about three hours before we got to the foot of this hill we had to climb to the top of. The squad leaders were telling everyone all the way about water discipline and how we should only take a small mouthful of water and hold it in our mouths before letting it trickle down our throats. 'Remember,' they said, 'you don't know when we're getting a re-supply, and what you got right now has to last until then because there ain't no more.' Some of us listened and still had some water left by the time we reached the foot of that hill. Others didn't listen and they were really hurting for some water when we got there. No matter. Now we had to climb that sucker. It was about two hundred and fifty meters high. Going up it, at least we didn't have to cut a trail. That hill'd been bombed out, and there weren't much bushes left standing on it, just some goddam stayawhile vines. It was steep enough we needed to grab on to what bushes there were to pull ourselves up with.

"At the top we all wanted to collapse and get our strength back from the hump, but we had to dig in because we were spending the night there and could expect to get hit. Also we had to clear an LZ so a supply chopper could come in and give us fresh water. The fighting holes were fairly easy to dig because we just finished off the craters from the bombing. Clearing the LZ was tougher because we had to fill in some bomb craters. By the time we were finished, only the old salts who had experience in tropical heat had any water left. The rest of us were all hurting pretty bad.

"When the bird with the water touched down it stayed longer than had been expected because we had to throw six men onto it for med-evac. They were heat casualties. Imagine this, son, we'd been in the field five, maybe six hours and had seven casualties already. They weren't from getting hit in a fire fight or from walking into a booby trap. They were from not knowing how to hump in that kind of heat.

"The chopper brought in enough water for us to all fill both canteens. A few of us, the ones who had the poorest water discipline and ran out of water first, almost got sick from guzzling a whole canteen right away. The squad leaders got on their cases about that pretty damn hurry-up quick. You gonna survive humping in a place like that, you got to learn how to conserve your water.

"So we dug in and got fresh water. That night we were put on a fifty-percent watch—that's half awake and half sleeping—but nobody came around to shoot at us. No snipers, no mortar rounds, nothing. Not even bugs.

"In the morning we were all awake before dawn and chowed down on Cs by the time the sun come up. Then each platoon sent out a patrol. The rest of us sat on that hill feeling glad it wasn't us humping out there. But the humping on the patrols wasn't as bad as the big hump because we didn't have to carry packs or mortar rounds on patrol. The only people on the patrols had a problem was the machine gunners and their ammo humpers. The gun is pretty heavy its ownself, and the humpers were each carrying a thousand rounds for it.

"Along about noon we pulled down off that hill and started humping again. We got to the bottom of the hill and found ourselves deep in paddy fields filled with more than three feet of water. This was some tough humping because the CO figured we was closer to where the Vee Cee were and the dikes were likely to be booby-trapped, so we went in the water and stayed off the dikes. Before we were in the paddies half an hour, near every man in the company had ten blood leeches hanging off of him. Third platoon got the rear and, wouldn't you know it, third squad, what had the point the first day, got the rear point the second day. At least we didn't have to cut a trail like we did the first day.

"The ground sloped downward for half a klick or more from the bottom of the hill to a small stream running through the paddies. About two hours after the column started moving we heard some shooting from up ahead and had to stand tight until we got some word about what we should do next. What we got the word to do was pull a flanking maneuver. While we were flanking this treeline the fire was coming from, a pair of A-4 Skyhawks came over and did some strafing and bombing runs that managed to keep Charlie's head down enough he didn't see us coming. When the A-4s were done with their runs, we charged through the side of that treeline shooting everything we had. We killed three Vee Cee in that place. Either they were all there was, or the rest managed to bug out before we got to the treeline.

"Then we waited to find out what came next. Word come to us the company's point squad stopped at this little stream to fill their canteens and got hit from those trees we were in now. Half the squad got itself zapped.

"While we were stopped the skipper called the platoon leaders and platoon sergeants together for a meeting. They came back and told the squad leaders that no-fucking-body gonna stop to fill a canteen from an exposed stream unless all possible ambush sites been reconned. This treeline was an ambush site, but it was cleared by fire, so we filled up with water.

"We humped the rest of the afternoon without any more contact, but to both flanks we heard fire fights a few times where Kilo and Mike companies ran into somebody. Then we reached another hill. Before we climbed onto the top of it a resupply bird came in with more water and Cs. It also took out three more heat casualties. Wasn't as many the second day because more of us understood about water discipline and nobody ran out of water as fast as the first day.

"This one wasn't a steep hill like the one we was on the first night, but it was high and didn't have any shade, so by the time we reached the top we were all pretty well hurting, so we crapped out a bit before we dug in again and settled down for the night. Charlie must have been watching and seen us climbing that hill because he hit us that night.

"Up till now, Abilene Run was just a hot walk in the sun, except for the one fire fight by the stream. Things were about to change, though. We were about to run into Charlie and kick some ass. He was gonna kill some good Marines, too.

"The company ringed the top of the second night's hill, and every platoon had a listening post out somewhere fifty or a hundred meters front of it. Just like the night before, we were on fifty-percent alert. First squad had a fire team out for our LP. About oh-two-hundred the LP calls in on the radio they're hearing some noise downslope from them and requests illume. The skipper says no illume yet, but passes the word for one-hundred-percent alert, so we all wake up and gets ready for a fight. Couple minutes after that is when we all became glad we dug in. There was the *whump whump* of mortar rounds being fired somewhere out there, and then those mortars came crashing inside our perimeter. No one got hurt by the barrage, but we had some empty water cans laying in the open and some of them got all blown to hell.

"By now it was after midnight, Charlie's favorite time of the day."

Chapter One

THE LSI HALF GROUNDED ITSELF AT THE CHU LAI BOAT RAMP opposite Ky Hoa Island and opened its bow to the night. All day long and into the darkness the thousand men of Three Fifteen had crowded themselves onto the too-small deck of the too-small troop transport ship, into its tiny troop holds, into whatever empty cargo bays it had. Now they stretched cramped muscles and, grumbling, let the ship's sailors escort them off the ship, onto the beach.

"Watch your step, people," an unseen Marine NCO from the base ordered. "Stay on the pathways between the tapes. We've got claymore mines in the wire outside the tapes. You set one off, you die."

"What this shit be?" PFC Malcolm Evans muttered. He was a slender, wiry man from the ghetto of Harlem.

"This is war, Malcolm X," replied Lance Cpl. Kim Chang, Evans's fire-team leader. "The idea is to kill anyone dumb enough to try and come through your wire."

"Shit, I gotta piss."

"Hold it, Malcolm X," said Sgt. Johnny Johnson. "You can piss by the numbers when I say to. Until then, hold it."

"Dumb-ass splib," PFC Henry J. Morris chuckled. "Needs to piss so bad he's willing to get his black ass killed to do it."

"Splib" was Marine slang for "nigger."

14

"Who you calling splib, chuck," Cpl. Buster Bahls growled. "Chuck" was Marine slang for "honkie."

"Just that bad-ass Malcolm X, Ball Buster." Morris grinned. "Sometimes he sure is dumb."

"Dumb enough to kill your chuck ass, Henry J. You be cool. Anybody in my fire team gets killed, I want it be by a fucking gook, not a Green Machine claymore, so shut that shit-eating mouth of yours." The big Marine emphasized his point by flexing his broad shoulders.

Morris laughed again. "You got it, Buster."

The battalion loaded onto the waiting trucks that moved out by the light of the stars. An indeterminate time later the trucks stopped and the Marines debarked from them and were crowded into thatch-roofed long houses whose lower walls were bamboo and upper walls were wire screening. There they lay on their equipment on the hard-packed dirt of the floor, trying to get some sleep before the approaching dawn. None of them got much.

No time for acclimation, none for learning the lay of the land or the ways of the people. There was a war going on, and the enemy was trying his hardest to win it. Third Battalion, 15th Marines, on its first full day in-country was armed and outfitted and sent on a week-long search and destroy mission, Operation Abilene Run. The average weight of weaponry and equipment carried by the men was close to eighty pounds.

The temperature at ten hundred hours on this late November morning when the first grunts of Lima Company boarded their helicopters for the short flight inland to the operation's line of departure was eighty-two degrees and rising. The grasshopper-like Sikorskys of the first wave lifted off their pads and twenty minutes later touched down between two hills and let off their cargoes of armed men. In fifteen more minutes Company L was together in a perimeter around the landing zone. India, Kilo, and Mike companies each had its own LZ. Kilo, Lima, and Mike companies would sweep areas about one kilometer apart; India Company was battalion reserve.

Captain Sarmiento, the company commander, issued the route orders to the lieutenants and staff NCOs, who relayed the orders to their squad leaders, who in turn passed them on to their men. Then third platoon led the company off the LZ.

"Hideaway, you've got the point," Sergeant Johnson, third squad leader, said to Cpl. Hernando Falalo, third squad's first fire-team leader. "See that skinny high point three fingers to the right of the broad high place? That's your aiming point. We're going around its right side."

Falalo turned to his three men. "Nutsy Nooncy, lead off. Then me and Salatu. Wegener brings up the rear. I'll direct you, Nutsy." Falalo's eyes scanned the unfamiliar terrain, densely covered with a low lying brush. "Ten-meter intervals and stagger it. Move out."

A nervous lick of his lips contradicted PFC Joseph Nuncio's grin as he stepped into the brush. "Any idea how soon I get to ding me some dinks?" he asked.

"When we find 'em, Nutsy," Falalo answered. "When we find 'em, and not before."

Nutsy Nooncy was Nuncio's nickname. He earned it in Boot Camp by being the most aggressive man in his training company during hand-to-hand and pugil-stick training. Nutsy Nooncy was the first recruit who ever managed to deck Staff Sergeant Wolufski, the hand-to-hand combat trainer. The name stuck through infantry training and the assembling of the 15th Marines. He kept his weapons in top shape and always talked about how he wanted to kill Viet Cong. He talked very convincingly.

The men of the third squad's first fire team broke parallel paths through the brush, their line staggered so they could all fire forward without hitting each other. The rest of the company followed in their paths.

The noonday sun beat down on dark helmets and unventilated flak jackets. Soon the one hundred eighty-three Marines in the company column were bathed in sweat. Most of them opened their jackets to allow some air to circulate near their bodies, evaporate the sweat, cool them. They started drinking from their canteens, some slowly sipping, others gulping. Heat buildup under the helmets dazed the Marines, made them less than alert. It wasn't long before word reached the point to hold up, a man in the first platoon had collapsed from heat exhaustion.

A few of the men stood still in the sunlight, gazing out over the brush through partly unseeing eyes. Most took advantage of the respite to drop down into the low shade provided by the scrub.

When the heat casualty was revived, the column moved again. This time the point team wielded machetes to help break through the brush. In its own way this was more brutal and punishing than breaking a path by force of leg had been.

Along the length of the column, squad leaders admonished their men to go easy on their water. No one knew when they would get more. It wouldn't do to have men collapsing from dehydration.

"Hideaway, you're drifting. Straighten it out," Johnson called to his point team.

Falalo shook his head and looked ahead. The heat was making him dizzy. "Nutsy, bear right," he called through a mouth that felt like it was filled with cotton.

Nuncio squinted at the high point they had been advancing toward and adjusted his angle of march.

The march was interrupted again when LCpl. Tony Salatu called, "Hold up, Wegener fell down."

Stumbling, Falalo and Johnson pushed their way to where the young Marine had fallen.

Johnson knelt over Wegener, saw his waxy complexion and rolled up eyes. "Corpsman up!" he called out. Then to Falalo, "Get his canteen and dribble some into his mouth."

Falalo pulled one canteen from its pouch on Wegener's belt and shook it. It was empty. Likewise the other one. "Shit," he swore. "I been saving some of this for myself." He pulled out one of his own canteens and let a slow trickle drip to Wegener's slightly parted lips.

"Let me in here." Doc Humbolt dropped to his knees next to Wegener. "Oh, shit. We gotta get him cooled off most ricky-tick." The corpsman stripped off Wegener's flak jacket and shirt and loosened his belt. "Pass the word, Johnny, we need a medevac," he said.

Johnson staggered to his feet and ran back along the column to where Lieutenant Haupt, the platoon leader, was coming forward to investigate.

"Wegener's down with heat, sir. Doc Humbolt says he's gotta be evacced."

"I'm going to see for myself." Haupt continued toward the downed man but was interrupted by his radioman.

"It's Six Actual, sir. Wants Three Actual." "Six" was the company commander's radio, "Three" was third platoon. "Actual" meant the unit commander himself.

Haupt took the radio handset. "Three Actual. Over." He listened. Then he said, "Six, Three. I have a heat casualty. Corpsman requests med-evac. I am investigating. Over." Again he listened. "That's an affirmative, Six. I will report in zero five. Out." He returned the handset to the radioman. "Skipper wants me to check it out and report back before requesting an evac bird. Let's take a look."

"He looks pretty bad, sir," Johnson said.

A grunt was Haupt's only reply.

Falalo and Doc Humbolt were fanning Wegener with their shirts when Haupt and Johnson reached them. Wegener was ghost-pale.

"We've got to get him out of here, sir," Humbolt said, "right now. He's going into shock and has to be cooled down in a hurry."

Haupt reached for the radio. "Lima Six Actual, this is Lima Three Actual. Over." A response came almost immediately.

"Six, Three. He's going into shock and needs an immediate med-evac. Over." The pause this time was longer.

"Six, that's a roger. Out." He handed the handset back, then said to the squad leader and corpsman, "There are two more, but not in such bad shape. The skipper is calling for a med-evac. First platoon is clearing an LZ for it." He looked down at Wegener. "Won't be long now."

Twenty-five minutes isn't long—unless you're going into shock or bleeding badly. Other corpsman worked with Humbolt to keep Wegener from going all the way into shock. If he did they might lose him. Twenty-five minutes. That's how long it took the med-evac to arrive and get the heat casualties aboard. Then it was gone and Lima Company was down to one hundred eighty men. No enemy had been encountered yet. No enemy but the heat. The company had been on the march for less than two hours.

Sergeant Johnson looked at his first fire team and decided they'd been up front long enough. "Ball Buster, you take the point. Move it," he said to the big man leading the second fire team.

"Chief, move it out," said Corporal Bahls. "Me next, then Henry J and Jeb. Ten-meter intervals and keep it staggered." The men of second fire team took the already dull machetes from the first fire team and set out.

PFC Michael Runningstar, better known to the men of his squad as "Chief," started breaking a path through the brush mainly by brute strength. The bronze-skinned man was short for a Marine and deceptively bulky. He carried a lot of fat, but that was the legacy of a childhood diet heavy in starches. Under the fat was muscle, a lot of muscle.

PFC Morris and Pvt. J.E.B. Casebolt used the machetes to chop through the brush. In minutes they were sweating worse than they had all day.

A half hour later the column stopped again. Back in second platoon a man had drunk all of his water too quickly. He no longer had any left to replace lost body fluids with and stopped sweating. The company was behind schedule and Captain Sarmiento was anxious to reach the objective, so he had second platoon leave a squad behind to wait for the med-evac. They could catch up after the bird came in.

Shortly after setting out again, the skinny high point was reached. Lieutenant Haupt sent Staff Sergeant Ortega, the platoon sergeant, around its left with first squad while the rest of the company continued on past its right side. Going around the left side of the point was harder work then going around the right side, and first squad had to move faster. By the time it rejoined the column, one of its men who had drunk all of his water had collapsed and was being carried. Doc Humbolt said he had to be med-evacked, too. The skipper had first squad stay with him until the evac came. They were to wait until the squad from second platoon reached them. The two squads would catch up with the rest of the company together.

A half kilometer beyond the skinny high point was a high,

bombed-out, steep-sided hill. It was the company's objective.
They would climb it, dig in, and spend the night on it.

"Hold up the point," came the order over the radio. Then
Captain Sarmiento called for a platoon leaders' and sergeants'
meeting.

"I don't want every Vee Cee in the area seeing helicopters
landing on that high place," Captain Sarmiento told them. "So
we'll resupply down here before going topside. Except for you,
Haupt. You take your platoon and the gun section and secure
that hilltop. I don't want us getting surprised when we get up
there. First and second platoons will hump your water up to you
when we get it. Questions?"

"How soon will the birds be here?" someone asked.

"They're on their way. If there are no more questions, Haupt,
secure that high place. Now." Sarmiento didn't wait for an answer. He turned away from the unit leaders.

"Aye aye, sir," Haupt replied to the captain's back. "Let's
go secure that high place," he added to Ortega.

It took third platoon and the company's six machine guns
fifteen minutes to scramble to the broad, level top of the dusty
hill.

"First squad, one o'clock to three o'clock. Second, eleven
o'clock to one o'clock. Third, nine o'clock to eleven o'clock.
One gun with each squad, the other guns, stay with me,"
Haupt's voice cried over the top of the hill, giving his squads
their areas of responsibility on the far side of the hilltop.
"Spread it out, get over the edge, off the skyline. Get down
there where you can see the sides of the hill, down where you
aren't silhouetted."

"Move it, people," Johnny Johnson called to his teams.
"First fire team, get down at eleven o'clock. Third, you're at
nine o'clock. Second, get between them. Spread it out, wide
intervals. We gotta cover a whole big chunk of this fucking
hilltop. Move it, keep it spread."

"Chief, you're too close, more to your left," Bahls shouted.
"Henry J, more to your right. Jeb, you in love with Henry J or
something? Get away from his ass, spread it out."

The Marines of third squad scattered across the hilltop, running toward the side unseen from where they had been. To the
far edge and over it, until Haupt stopped them some thirty me-

ters downslope. They were spaced close to twenty meters apart, too thinly spread for a defense against even a moderately determined enemy.

Lieutenant Haupt and Staff Sergeant Ortega scanned the lowland before them with their field glasses. There was no sign of an enemy, no sign of anyone.

"Squad leaders up," Haupt called.

The three squad leaders joined the platoon CP.

"We're going to spend the night here, maybe longer. I want you to go back and have your men dig out some bomb craters into fighting holes. And make damn sure they've got interlocking fields of fire. Questions?"

"Yes, sir," one of the squad leaders said. "We gonna stay in the holes we dig?"

Haupt stared at him. "How the hell do I know? The skipper might move us to the back slope of this hill when the rest of the company joins us."

The squad leader who asked the question spat and looked disgusted.

"Just remember, if we do wind up digging holes for another platoon, the other platoons are humping our water up this bad-assed sucker. Any other questions?" There weren't. "Go do it."

The squad leader shambled back to their men.

"Let's set a good example for the troops, sir," Ortega said. He drew his entrenching tool from its carrying cover and started reshaping a bomb crater into a fighting hole. Lieutenant Haupt and Sergeant Zimmerman, the platoon's right guide, joined him.

The squad leaders quickly divided their men, two to a hole, and had them start digging. One man out of four watched the lowland below. They had barely started when they heard the *whumpa whumpa* of approaching helicopters. Water was on its way, and welcome. Even the Marines with good water discipline had little more than a sip or two left in their canteens.

By sundown, shortly after eighteen hundred hours, the company was assembled on top of the hill, positions assigned, holes dug, and everyone was fed and watered. The resupply bird had brought in enough five-gallon water cans for every man to refill

both canteens and replenish one of the canteens the next morning.

Naturally, third platoon had to move to a different part of the
hill and dig new holes when the rest of the company came up.

"Think anything'll happen tonight, Henry J?"

"How the fuck I know that, Jeb? You been here long as I
have. What say you tell me?"

Jeb Casebolt's shrug went unseen in the night. "How'a fuck
do I know? I'm just a boot anna country boy besides. You wanna
first watch or I take it?" Eighteen years old, this Alabama country boy's blond hair had been bleached almost white by the
semitropical sun of Okinawa.

"Get some sleep, Jeb. I'll take the first watch. You got two
hours to cop some Zs, then it's my turn."

Silently the company settled down for the night. The last
cigarette was snubbed out just before the sun went down. There
would be no more smoking until dawn. About every fifteen
meters around the hill was a two-man fighting hole. One man
in each hole was awake at all times. Each squad leader checked
his men twice during the night. The only sounds heard during
the darkness other than the booming of the 105mm howitzers
back at Chu Lai and the crashing of their rounds on their harassment and interdiction firing missions, were a few distant fire
fights. None of the fire fights sounded close enough to involve
the other companies of the battalion.

Dawn broke and one hundred seventy-eight tired Marines
rose from their holes. They ate a breakfast of cold C-rations and
emptied their bowels and bladders in the open or not, according
to personal feelings. If they did not empty bowels and bladder
in the open, those bowels and bladders stayed filled, because
there was no hidden place to do it.

"Platoon leaders up." The word passed from company commander to radioman over the air to radioman to platoon leaders.
In minutes the three platoon leaders and their platoon sergeants
assembled around the company's CP hole, which was not far
from the middle of the hilltop.

"We're going to send out three patrols this morning," Captain Sarmiento said. "First platoon, send a squad and gun back

to that high narrow point, see if anybody's following us. Second platoon, take a squad and gun to this blue line on the map. Follow an azimuth of three-ten degrees. Third platoon, a squad and gun to the same blue line, only your azimuth is zero-ten degrees. Don't refill canteens there; we've still got clean water here, and I don't want anybody coming down with dysentery or any such happy horseshit. A hill beyond that blue line is probably our next objective when we leave this one. All patrols be back by eleven thirty hours. Questions?'' There were none. "Then do it.''

Soon after that three squads, each reinforced by a machine gun, were moving down off different sides of the hill for their morning patrol. For the men who stayed on the hilltop it was a welcome respite from the previous day's hump. They didn't have to spend their energy carrying a heavy load in the relentless heat, heading toward an unseen enemy. Their minds weren't being dimmed by the malevolent sun. It was even possible to create shade by erecting makeshift lean-tos from ponchos. Most managed to get a little more sleep.

Even the men on patrol felt life was easier than the first day. They only carried rifles and cartridge belts with canteens and magazines. Sure, they wore helmets and flak jackets, but they carried no bandoleers, mortar rounds, satchel charges, and only two men to a patrol had a LAW. Besides, the day hadn't reached full temperature yet. It was an easy hump for the men on patrol.

The patrols had no incidents and were back on the hill by the prescribed time. The men on the hill neither took incoming fire nor saw any sign of danger while the patrols were out. Everyone chowed down, and shortly after noon the company set out for the blue line the skipper had sent patrols toward. Grass grew on this side of the hill. Within a hundred meters of the foot of the hill it was six feet tall or deeper.

First platoon led off, followed by second. Third brought up the rear. Some members of third platoon's third squad thought it was sheer perversity that caused Lieutenant Haupt to give the same squad that had the first day's point the second day's rear point.

"Oh, shit, I don't like this, Hideaway," Sergeant Johnson said to Corporal Falalo.

Hernando Falalo looked up at the top of the grass. "Me neither, pano. Shit's too high to see over and too thick to see through."

Nutsy Nooncy grinned a stubbled grin at them. "Come on, you guys. Ain't you never heard the Vee Cee makes tunnels through this kind'a shit? We in the grass means we gonna get us some."

Johnny Johnson wanted to spit but didn't. He knew to conserve his fluids as much as possible. Three years in the peacetime infantry, going on operations of all kinds through all sorts of terrain and climatic conditions had taught him how to survive in the boonies. "Shit, pano, you hear this boot?" he said to Falalo. "He thinks we're on a fucking picnic."

Falalo shook his head. He didn't spit, either. "Dumbass. He gotta be learned, Johnny." Falalo had been a grunt as long as Johnson. They had gone through boot camp together and their Marine careers closely paralleled. The only reason Johnson was a sergeant and the squad leader rather than Falalo was the fact that he had arrived at the battalion's base on Okinawa before Falalo did.

"Thinks it's a fucking picnic."

"Charlie gonna die today." Nuncio grinned at them.

Johnson shook his head. "I'm gonna check the rear point, Hideaway," he said. "Keep this dumb-ass boot from getting someone killed until I get back, will you?"

"Sure 'nough, Honcho."

Johnson stepped aside to allow the rest of his squad to pass until the rear point reached him. When it didn't, he ran forward to Pvt. Nick Devoid, who had been the last man to pass him, eyes straight ahead.

"Where's the rear point, Empty Nick? I thought I saw everyone pass me," Johnson said.

Devoid looked around. "I do believe I'm the rear point."

"Then why the fuck ain't you watching where you been?"

"Huh?"

"Devoid, how are you supposed to walk rear point?" Johnson's jaw worked. He really wanted to spit now.

Devoid looked confused. "What d'ya mean?"

Johnson shook his head, then swiveled it through most of a three-sixty-degree circle, oriented toward his rear. "If we're following a Vee Cee patrol, how close are we going to follow it?''

Devoid still looked confused. ''Not close enough for them to see us before we're close enough to do something about it.''

''Why not? You think they gonna see us?''

''Yeah.''

''How they gonna see you if you behind them?''

''Look back.''

''Why ain't you looking back?''

''Ain't I looked back?''

''Not since the first time I seen you on this rear point.''

''Oh.''

''Oh, I'm gonna kick your ass, Empty Nick. You gotta look back.'' Johnson hawked deep in his throat but still didn't spit. ''As a matter of fact, the thing you gotta do is walk backward to keep Charlie from sneaking up behind us.''

Devoid looked at Johnson blankly. ''Walk backward?''

''That's what I said. Walk backward. Now do this thing.''

Devoid turned and started walking backward. ''How'm I supposed to keep contact with the man in front of me?''

''Don't worry about the man in front of you. I'll maintain contact for you.''

''Okay.'' Then Devoid tripped over a thick clump of grass.

''Boot, why don't'cha watch where you're going?''

''You told me to walk backward.''

''Can't you do both?''

''How?''

Johnson's shoulders slumped. ''Move ahead. I'll show you.'' As soon as Devoid passed, Johnson started moving, facing the rear, his head swiveling constantly, rifle always pointing where his eyes looked. After a few paces he turned his head all the way to check on his contact and path. Devoid was wandering ahead, not watching.

''Shit-for-brains, how can you learn what I'm trying to teach you if you don't watch me?''

A combat operation is not the right place to teach a man the subtleties of movement. It wasn't long before Hernando Falalo found himself walking rear point.

* * *

"What's happening?" Morris asked.

"Oh, shit," Runningstar said.

Gunfire erupted from the direction of the company's front. First the crack of a few small-caliber rounds, then the heavier boom of M-14s and rattle of an M-60 machine gun. Lima Company was making its first contact with the enemy.

"We be in it now," Evans said.

"We ain't in it yet, that's too far ahead," Bahls told them. "Wait for word."

"Everybody, get down and keep alert," Sergeant Johnson ordered. "Team leaders, face your people outboard."

The Marines squatted or knelt in the high grass, trying to penetrate it with their eyes. Stifling heat settled on them: the air couldn't move in the grass.

Two A-4 Skyhawks screamed overhead and swooped down somewhere ahead of the company's point. The guns of the small, delta-wing attack bombers stuttered and their bombs exploded. Twice more they swooped down, strafing, then they gained altitude and flew away. A few minutes later two helicopters fluttered by. One was a gunship, the other seemed to touch down for a moment. Then the two birds fluttered off the way they had come.

A platoon leaders' meeting was called, then the platoon leaders and sergeants returned and met with their squad leaders.

"There's a small stream with open paddies on its far side up ahead," Lieutenant Haupt told his squad leaders. "Second platoon's point squad stopped to fill canteens from it and they got ambushed from a treeline. They didn't set any kind of security, so by the time they could start returning fire, they had taken four casualties. Skipper says from now on nobody stops to fill a canteen unless all possible ambush sites have been checked and cleared. Understood?"

The squad leaders nodded.

"Good. Tell your people and get ready to move again. That treeline has already been reconned the hard way, so canteens can be refilled when we get there. Have two men from each of your squads gather all empty canteens. They can fill them all at the same time." He looked in each of their eyes, hard. "And don't forget to put halazone tablets in the canteens. Go."

Slowly, in bits and pieces and jerks, the column started moving again. When third platoon neared the stream, Haupt sent the six canteen fillers ahead. A few bloodstains on the bank of the stream were the only sign of the men wounded by the Viet Cong ambush. The company wouldn't stop to wait for canteens to be filled, and Haupt didn't want any of his men to be left behind. He hurried the canteen fillers.

Several hours after setting out on its hump, the column stopped at the foot of another hill. Lima hadn't had any more contact though there had been the sound of fire fights involving the companies to both flanks. There was a short wait until a resupply chopper came with fresh water and more C-rations. The bird brought back Wegener and three of the other men who had been evacuated on the first day, then carried out three more heat casualties. Resupplied, the company climbed the hill and formed a defensive perimeter around it.

"Okay, people, Charlie knows we're in the area and we know he's around here. Dig your holes and make 'em good," Johnson said.

"Aw, come on, Sergeant Johnny," Casebolt complained. "We been busting ass all afternoon and just climbed this fucking hill. Cut us some slack, huh?"

"Put that ass in gear, shithead. You take a break after you dig your fucking hole."

"Ain't no good bomb craters on this hill. We gotta dig the holes from the top down."

"Tough titty. More reason to start digging now. This was an easy hill to climb. That means Charlie can climb it easy, too. So start digging."

There was more grumbling around the perimeter, but everyone started digging two-man fighting holes, just like the day before. All had finished eating by the time the sun set. Once more there was a fifty-percent watch in the holes. After dark each platoon sent a fire team out about seventy-five meters to be a listening post. No holes were dug for the LPs. If any unfriendlies were watching, no one wanted to give away the LPs' positions.

High clouds had come in with the setting of the sun on this last day of November, making the night darkness complete. The men on watch didn't bother looking down the hillsides, they turned their heads and listened. For three two-hour watches nothing was heard nearby, the only sounds were distant artillery and someone else's fire fights.

Abilene, Deadly Abilene

"AFTER MIDNIGHT, SON! THEM LITTLE PEOPLE SURE LOVED THE late night. They figured no American was gonna be moving around in the boonies after dark, and they were just about right. Got dark, we set in and waited for them to come to us.

"Soon as those mortar rounds came in, first squad's LP started shooting and calling for support because there was a whole shit-load of gooks hitting them. Lieutenant Haupt didn't want to risk us shooting our own people, so he had the M-79 bloopers lob some HEs to the front of the LP's position. The skipper decided this was a good time for illumination, and had the three mortars drop some down that slope. Slope, that's a good word here. That illume popped and three flares started floating down on their parachutes, showing us what looked like a hundred slopes running up that slope toward us. They was the first real live Vee-Cee-type gooks any of us seen, and they were already almost to the LP and those four guys were shooting as fast as they could, trying to keep from getting overrun. There wasn't a hundred of those gooks, but there must have been at least forty of them. Well, thirty, anyway.

"Now that we could see, Lieutenant Haupt started shouting for us to open fire but to pick our targets. He still didn't want any risk of us shooting our own people. Now I want to tell you, Marines get some good marksmanship training. Took about ten, maybe fifteen seconds, and all the Vee Cee that wasn't d⋅wn was running the other way. The skipper gave us more illume to keep shooting with and had the mortars drop HEs farther downslope. The LP came back in then and the squad leaders took a head count, and we didn't have any casualties.

"Haupt the Kraut was getting ready to put out another fire team in an LZ not too close to where the first one was when whistles started blowing down at the foot of the hill and what seemed like all the Vietnamese in the world were charging back up at us, shooting as they came. The skipper had the mortars lay out more illume and we cut loose with everything we had, now that we didn't have to worry about hitting our own people anymore. We mowed them right down and they retreated again. They did that twice more before we could put out another LP.

"The second LP was out for maybe fifteen minutes before they radioed back they was hearing dragging sounds. The mortars popped some more illume and we saw the Vee Cee dragging bodies off the hillside. We opened fire on them and they bugged—the ones we didn't shoot down.

"That's how it went for the rest of the night. We put out a new LP, it hears bodies being dragged, throws grenades, the Skipper puts out illume, and we have a turkey shoot and the LP gets pulled back in. About a half hour before dawn they stopped trying to get their wounded and bodies. In the morning we found seven bodies on the slope, two more who were wounded, and twelve blood trails. We kicked some ass and that made us feel damn good.

"What we couldn't understand was how come Charlie didn't use his mortars to cover the body removal. Must have run out of rounds. We also didn't understand why the other companies got hit so much harder than we did when the Vee Cee did the same thing to them they did to us. Maybe they didn't have LPs out in the right place like we did.

"Next morning we started doing things differently. This was a search and destroy, and the battalion CO decided we'd found them, so the search part of the operation was over. Now was the time for the destroy part of Abilene Run. We didn't do any humping the next day, just sent out patrols, since this is where we knew they were. This day we got resupplied with water, Cs, and ammo on top of the hill. They even brought in an eighty-one-millimeter squad from battalion, so we knew we were gonna be there for at least one more night. But the best thing they brought us was mail. Mine was the best of the mail we got in third platoon. My daddy sent me a bottle of SVO. Other mail in the platoon was a birth announcement and a bunch of love letters.

"The company put out two ambushes that night. One was at the foot of the hill along the right side of third platoon's line, close to where we was up against first platoon. First platoon put out another past their middle, toward the right side of their line. Third squad got third platoon's ambush. Being at the foot of the hill had us about three hundred meters out. We actually went out a little farther than that because at the foot of the hill we would've been in the open at the edge of the paddies. Fifty meters farther out was a treeline. Third squad and a gun team set up in it.

"Johnny Johnson was kind of nervous because he figured this treeline was a place Charlie used to assemble the night before and he'd probably want to use it again if they wanted to hit us tonight, so he put us on a seventy-five-percent alert. That's tough. We went out there at twenty hundred hours and was gonna stay until about oh-five-hundred or so. That means most of us could get two hours sleep, some of us less than that.

"On an ambush you don't dig in, you just hide as good as you can and hope there's something to hide behind that'll keep you from getting hit when the shooting starts. So we went in there and settled down just as flat on that ground inside the treeline as we could, every one of us looking for a place where maybe the earth was an inch or so lower than other places. Johnny Johnson had us facing half toward the paddies away from the hill, half toward the hill.

"Everything was quiet until close to oh-two-hundred, then Chief Runningstar saw some shadows moving out on the paddies. No doubt about it, Chief had the best eyes in the platoon, maybe the whole company. He saw the shadows far enough out that we were all alerted and turned toward the paddies before they were close enough to hear any small noises we made. Johnny Johnson was right. Charlie was coming here to get ready for another assault on our hill.

"We all hunkered down real low until Johnny Johnson set off

the ambush by having Lance Corporal Boyd, the machine gunner, open up. Soon as we opened up we heard one of the sixty-millimeter mortars on our hill go *whumpa*, and a few seconds later a flare burst open and started floating down in front of our position. I guess there were about ten Vee Cee caught in the killing zone to the front of us. They all dropped, some were dead, others wounded.

"Then someone beyond the illume's area started firing at us. They must have been filtering in by squads. So we lay return fire on them, and their bullets were just zipping and nipping through the trees above us. We couldn't tell if we were hitting any of them, or even getting close to them. Johnny Johnson called in for some mortar fire and tried to direct it onto the top of Charlie, but nobody could tell if it was having any effect.

"Now we started taking fire from our left bank. Another Vee Cee squad entered the treeline from that side and tried to roll us up. Kim Chang turned his team to meet them, and Frenchy Lafleur jumped from his position in the middle of the line to go help out. Chang's automatic rifleman was this bad-assed black dude name of Malcolm Evans. We all called him Malcolm X. Malcolm X was one hell of a good ARman, and his piece was taking that squad out so bad he didn't need much help from the rest of his team or from Frenchy. Least that's what it seemed like at first.

"There must have been some kind of retreat signal given to Charlie because all of a sudden the fire from our front stopped and the Vee Cee on the left flank pulled back. Sergeant Johnny got us all on a line and we pursued those gooks that flanked us along that treeline, trying to get all of their asses.

"We were making so much noise yelling we didn't hear the Vee Cee mortars firing. The first thing we knew was when the rounds started landing in the treeline. Chang and Frenchy went down right away when a round hit on the edge of the trees next to them. About eight or ten mortar rounds hit in the treeline, but none of them come near where the rest of us were, so the only casualties we had was Kim Chang and Frenchy. Neither one was too bad hit, but bad enough to be med-evacked all the way back to The World. Then we went out into the paddies to check out the kills we had. There was plenty of 'em, and not all were whole.

''The morning before, I'd seen dead gooks on the hillside in front of our positions, so I knew what people looked like when they were dead from combat wounds. But this was different. It's pretty rugged looking at a man shot dead clean through the heart; it's something altogether different to see a man blown into pieces from a mortar round. I felt like somebody kicked me right in the gut, looking at those body parts.

''Our ambush did what it was supposed to do, it broke up the Vee Cee attack before it started. Also, now Charlie knew where the ambush was, so Captain Sarmiento called us back in instead of making us stay out the rest of the night. I want to tell you, that was one happy squad that walked back up the hill. We had to carry both Kim Chang and Frenchy, but they was whooping and hollering right along with the rest of us because of the hurting we put on Charlie. Next day when we looked again, there weren't any bodies in the paddies where we ambushed those squads, but a few blood trails on the dikes. Spooky, that was.

''Battalion thought we were putting a hurting on Charlie being where we were, so the word come down for us to stay on that hill for another day. First and second platoons went out on patrols that day and third platoon stayed to hold the hill. We got cut the slack because we were the ones had the contact both nights and we were the only ones took any casualties since we got to the hill. Didn't last, though, us being the only ones making contact and getting casualties. First platoon took sniper fire all day long and got three men wounded. Second platoon's point hit a booby trap that killed two men and wounded another. Neither platoon was able to make any real contact with the enemy. They just went out and a few Marines got killed or wounded.

''That night each platoon put out an ambush and about oh-two-hundred all three made contact. Each of the ambushes lost at least one man. No Vee Cee made it to the hill, so those of us who were on top of it just had to sit back and watch the tracers flying. Red tracers were ours, green were theirs. All three ambushes came back after their contacts, but first the skipper had our mortars put out some illume so they could go into the paddies and get a body count. Then a half hour later Charlie's mortar starts working again and twenty or so rounds hit on top of the hill, but all they did was give people headaches.

''Next day third platoon went out on a patrol. We skipped

over the paddies and into the hills behind them. Battalion thought that's where Charlie was hiding during the day, and Captain Sarmiento agreed. Those hills were more like high rolling prairie than what you think of when you think of hills, and none of them were near as high as the hill we were staying on. There was a low kind of scrub brush on them, but very lush and full. It was anywhere from knee to waist high, and didn't give no relief from the sun. We felt naked most of the time because there wasn't no way we could walk around without being seen. We'd of had to crawl on the ground for that brush to give us any concealment.

"Before we turned to go back to our hill, Lieutenant Haupt got word on the radio the company was moving to a different hill and we were gonna be the first ones there. Turns out battalion didn't think we was making enough good contact during the day and thought Charlie was deeper in the hills than we could make it on our day patrols, so we had to go deeper into the hills so we could be closer to where he was hiding, to find him in the daytime and kick the everloving shit out of him.

"We stayed on that next hill for two nights and a day, running patrols and putting out ambushes. During that time none of the companies in the battalion had any kind of contact, so the order come down to withdraw to Highway One, where we'd get picked up by trucks and ride back to Chu Lai.

"Highway One was about three miles off when we started humping. Halfway there we found out why we ain't seen any sign of Vee Cee for so long. Looks like Charlie figured sooner or later we were gonna hump back to Highway One, so they pulled together what must have been every Vee Cee in the area and laid an ambush. We walked right into that ambush.

"Just like when we went in, all the companies were coming out independent from each other. Lima was crossing this large area of rice paddies with treelines all over the place. No kind of air support was overhead, nobody thought we needed it. We were on our own. Then all of a sudden we were taking incoming from three directions. A mortar was in a treeline on our left flank and machine guns were in front and on the right flank. None of them were closer than three hundred meters away. There was also a lot of rifles shooting at us from those three places. About the only thing we could do was get down behind the dikes and call for help. First platoon was on the point and deployed to return fire to the front. Second was in the rear and lay down fire to the left flank. Third shot back at the mortar. Don't matter. We were pinned down good.

"The mortar walked rounds from the point of the company to the rear and back again. All of us were down in the paddies, hoping water could stop mortar fragments. It must have just been dumb luck, but those rounds only wounded four men in the company. The machine guns are what hurt us. Second platoon got about one out of three men killed or wounded by them. After maybe fifteen minutes a couple of helicopter gunships showed up and started peppering them treelines and the fire slacked off a bit, but it wasn't until Mike Company showed up and took on the Vee Cee in the treeline on the left flank that we got cut any kind of break. Then the two gunships concentrated on Charlie's other two positions. That's when the shooting at us stopped. Charlie was shooting at those birds.

"Charlie got his ass wiped. They couldn't bug from those treelines because that'd put them in the open paddies where they'd get blown away complete. Poor old Charlie had to do something he never liked to do, he had to stand and fight. It was like a turkey shoot, except the turkeys did some shooting back. There were just about ninety bodies got brought out of there. We hit them about four times as bad as they did us, and it was their ambush.

"After the med-evac came for our wounded and dead we humped the rest of the way to Highway One and boarded the trucks for the ride back to Chu Lai. We were bloodied and shook up, but now we knew for sure we was Marines and anybody come up against us was gonna get hurt worse than we were.

"That was Operation Abilene Run, Three Fifteen's first combat operation."

Chapter Two

===============

SOME TIME AFTER MIDNIGHT, IN THE MORNING HOURS OF December first, first squad's Private Harrison nudged Lance Corporal Zinny, his team leader, and tugged on his own ear. Zinny tipped his helmet back from the right side of his head, raised up and pointed that ear downslope. Third platoon's LP was in an old bomb crater.

"Whoa shit," Zinny whispered. "Wake Carmichael and Wynn." Then he picked up the groundwire phone and clicked the lever on the handset three times.

"LP Three, this is Six, go," a quiet voice said over the handset.

Speaking as softly as he could, Zinny said, "Six, I have mucho voices downslope to my front. Put out some illume. Yours."

At two other points around the perimeter the other LPs heard the transmission and went to one-hundred-percent alert.

"Wait one, Three," came the reply.

A moment later a new voice spoke on the handset. "Three, this is Six Actual. What do you have? Go."

"Lotta gook voices down below. Request illume, over."

"Are they moving toward you?"

"Negative that, but I think they're gonna."

"Stand by on the line. If they start moving uphill, I want to know immediately. Six Actual out."

"God-fucking-damn shit," Zinny whispered to his men. "We gotta sit tight until they come to us."

Making as little noise as possible, the four men made sure their rifle safeties were off, magazines firmly set in their wells, and grenades close at hand. PFC Carmichael turned his selector to full automatic and anchored his automatic rifle's bipod past the crater's edge. Higher on the hill word was passed for a full alert and all sleepers were awakened. Illumination and high explosive rounds were readied next to the mortars.

The voices at the foot of the hill faded to silence and ten minutes passed. Then a stone was kicked near the LP's position and a voice swore in Vietnamese.

Zinny squeezed the clicker on his handset and screamed into it, "They're here, gimme some light!"

The four men in the crater started firing blindly into the dark. On the hilltop behind them three illumination rounds spiraled from their tubes, arched high overhead, dropped down until their parachutes popped open. Three flares drifted down, fizzing eerie blue light over the hillside and exposing a VC platoon moving up it.

"Pick your targets!" Lieutenant Haupt screamed at third platoon. "Use aimed fire. Now."

The command was echoed by the squad leaders, and carefully placed M-14 rounds started their flights of death at the charging Viet Cong. Several dropped, dead or wounded, then the others turned and ran back down. The advance had already passed the crater with the listening post by the time they turned around. Three more flares opened above the hillside and high explosive mortar rounds crashed to earth among the retreating VC.

Somewhere on a distant hill a mortar *carumped* several times, then six rounds exploded ineffectively on Lima Company's hill.

First and second platoons made no contact, and their LPs didn't hear any sounds from below. When the last flare sputtered out, Lieutenant Haupt withdrew first squad's LP and had second squad put one out in a different location.

Twenty minutes later the new LP phoned in. "Noise on the hillside. I think they're retrieving bodies."

An answer came almost immediately. "Do not fire, you'll give away your position. Throw grenades at the sounds."

The exploding grenades masked the whumps of the mortars

firing more illumination rounds. The VC were caught in the blue light as they tried to pull away the bodies of their wounded and dead.

"Pick your targets, use aimed fire!" Haupt shouted again. More VC fell under the Marines' withering fire.

The last flare died and the LP pulled back to the line. It was replaced downslope by a team from the third squad which set an LP in yet a third spot. If Charlie had any ideas of pinpointing and wiping out the LP, he was out of luck. A half hour later they reported dragging noises and threw grenades at the sounds. The mortars lit the night again and the VC were caught once more and more of them dropped. When the flares went out, the LP returned to its upslope holes and first squad sent out another team.

So it went until shortly before dawn. Third platoon would change its LP, the LP would hear dragging noises and throw grenades at them, the mortars threw out flare rounds, third platoon fired and the VC died. The platoon suffered no casualties during the night.

At daybreak third platoon swept downward on the slope to recover bodies and equipment. They returned to the top of the hill with seven dead bodies, two badly wounded prisoners, and fifteen rifles. They reported at least a dozen blood trails leading to the paddies at the foot of the hill.

A med-evac was called in for the prisoners. It didn't arrive quite soon enough; one of the VC died before the helicopter reached the hill.

For the next hour the Marines of Lima Company went about slapping each other on the back and throwing high fives, third platoon more than the others. "They ambushed our point yesterday, but we kicked their asses last night," the Marines told each other. And in the slang of the combat Marine, "Payback is a motherfucker."

The search part of the operation seemed to have found its objective. This was where the VC were, this was where the Marines would remain to destroy them. No hump was called for the third day of the operation. Patrols went out and possible ambush sites were examined. Before noon a resupply chopper came in with water, food, ammunition, and mail. Another bird delivered an 81mm mortar squad from the battalion HQ.

Third squad's mail ran the gamut from a bottle of Crown Royal received by PFC Morris and Buster Bahl's latest issue of *Playboy*, to love letters from girlfriends and notes from parents or brothers and sisters, to a "Dear John" for Renee Lafleur.

"I'm gonna kill some-fucking-body," Lafleur said after he read the letter. "Somebody gonna fucking die for this."

After reading their letters, everyone in the squad except for Lafleur gathered around Bahls and Morris to ogle the centerfold and sip from the purple-velvet-covered Seagram's bottle.

Shortly before seventeen hundred hours, Staff Sergeant Ortega, Johnny Johnson, the three team leaders of third squad, and Lance Corporal Boyd, a machine gunner, sat in a dusty circle to review third squad's activities for this night.

"You all know where you're going to spend the night, you reconned it today," Ortega said. "It'll be easy. You go down at twenty hundred hours, cross the paddies to that treeline and set your ambush on its far side." A stick held in his hand sketched a rough map in the dirt. A rough map was more than was necessary, everyone could see the treeline, he drew it only to keep his hands occupied. "The forecast is for another cloudy night, so nobody should see you going down. You'll have a prick twenty for communications. That won't be any problem, either. The mortars are zeroed in on the paddies to your front so you can get instant support if you need it. Keep alert, and if anyone gets within twenty-five meters of you, blow him away. Sergeant Johnson knows what to do, do what he says. You come back in at oh-five-hundred. Any questions?"

"What are the chances of friendlies walking into our ambush?" Buster Bahls asked.

"No one in the battalion will have patrols out tonight. Ambushes only."

"What do we do if more Vee Cee than we can handle come in?" asked Lance Cpl. Kim Chang. Chang never called the enemy gooks, always Vee Cee or Viet Cong. Never gooks.

"We've got three sixties, an eight-one, and an entire company up here. There won't be more than we can handle." Ortega looked around the circle. "Anybody else?" There were no other questions. "Sergeant Johnson, it's all yours." Ortega rose to his feet, slapped at the dust on his trousers, and returned to the platoon CP.

Johnson rose also. "Pass the word to your men and have them chow down," he told his team leaders. "I'll distribute ammunition before sunset. Then we can all cop some Zs before going out. Once we get into position I don't want more than one man in a team asleep at any time. That treeline's got to be where Charlie grouped last night. If he wants to hit us again tonight, that's where he'll be going. We've got to be ready when he gets there."

Sixteen Marines huddled together in the deep night below the skyline of the hill.

"Unless somebody steps on you, I'll set off the ambush by firing a red star cluster," Johnson told the others. "If he steps on you, you set if off by shooting his dumb gook ass. The red star cluster will also be the signal for illume in the direction I fire it in. Hideaway, lead it out, followed by Frenchy and me. Then gun, second, and third teams. Move it."

Silently, the squad and its attached machine-gun team rose to their feet and started shuffling down the hill to the paddies. Soundlessly they padded along dikes until they reached the treeline. Johnson took the point and the ambush patrol melted into the trees. Stepping softly, Johnson led the way to the far edge and set his men into their positions, then returned to his own spot on the line. To his right was the gun team, and beyond it lay first team. Frenchy Lafleur with the M-79 grenade launcher, second and third teams completed the line to his left. Each man in the line settled to the ground and wiggled his body until he found a comfortable position he could sleep in, one he also hoped would give him some protection from enemy fire if they got into a fight. They stared sightlessly into the night and waited.

"I see movement, pass it," Michael Runningstar softly whispered to the men on his sides.

"Everybody wake up, pass it," came the word back from Runningstar's right.

"What'cha got, Chief?" Johnson dropped down beside the Indian.

"Shadows fifty, sixty meters out."

Johnson squinted across the paddies. He didn't try to look directly at anything. Shadows moved in the edge of his vision. "I do believe you're right, Chief." He raised the cluster tube and fired it.

The red star burst over the paddies. Its brief light showed ten or twelve armed men on the dikes coming toward the treeline. Every man in the ambush fired at the newcomers. On the hill a mortar *whumpa'*d, and seconds later a flare burst overhead and drifted down on its parachute. More fire poured from the ambush into the lit area. Then there was no one left standing in the paddies and no fire being returned.

"Cease fire, cease fire!" Johnson called, then radioed for another illumination round.

A second flare cast its light over the paddies to the ambush's front, but showed no movement. But before the second flare hit the water and sputtered out, several automatic rifles opened up from beyond the lit area.

"Return fire, people," Johnson called. "Keep your fire low and you might hit something. Watch for muzzle flashes and shoot at them." He radioed for the mortars to drop high-explosive rounds.

Several minutes of returning fire with mortar rounds exploding in the muddy water didn't seem to have any effect on the bullets cracking overhead. Then new fire came from the left flank of the ambush.

"Chang, get your team turned," Johnson bellowed.

"I'm gonna help 'em! Charlie gonna fucking die." Lafleur leaped to his feet, ran toward the new assault and started dropping high-explosive rounds on the advancing VC.

Malcolm Evans laid out effective fire with his automatic rifle, killing or wounding several in the VC squad advancing toward the ambush's flank. Suddenly the VC broke and ran back into the night. The fire from the front ceased.

"I want me some more!" Lafleur roared and set out in pursuit of the fleeing shadows.

Chang followed him. "Them fucking gooks giving all us Orientals a bad name," he shouted.

"Get your dumb asses outta my way," Evans yelled at Lafleur and Chang. "I wanna get me some more." But he stopped firing to avoid hitting his own men.

"Get down, dammit!" Johnson yelled. "Chang, Frenchy, get your asses back to your positions."

But they didn't. Chang and Lafleur didn't stop until they reached the edge of the trees where the VC had gone into the paddies. They stood firing into the darkness. A mortar *whumpa*'d three times on another hill. Three rounds barely missed hitting in the treeline.

Chang and Lafleur stopped shooting at the night. Minutes later Sergeant Johnson and the other two men from Chang's team were kneeling over them. One of the mortar rounds had landed a few meters away. Both men were dead.

"Shit," Johnson swore. "God-fucking-damn shit. They should of done what I told 'em to." Then he returned to his position and radioed in a report.

The ambush was successful in breaking up another VC assault on the hill, but the squad's position was now known to the enemy, so it was ordered back up the hill. A sobered group of Marines carried their dead back with them. They agreed it was one thing to see dead enemy, like they had that morning. Seeing dead friends was another matter altogether.

Aside from an occasional mortar round on the hill, Lima Company had no more contact that night.

Third platoon went back to the treeline and into the paddies beyond them in the morning, but they found no bodies or weapons. A few blood trails in the trees and blood trails on some dikes gave the only evidence that any VC had been hit.

The battalion CO decided that Charlie was being hurt, so he ordered the companies to stay on their hills for another day. Each company sent two platoons out on patrol that day and left one platoon along with the mortars to hold the hills. One of India's patrols found a rice cache it was able to destroy, and Mike killed two snipers. Kilo had no contact. Lima's first platoon lost three men wounded by snipers, and the second platoon had its point man killed by a booby trap. But there was no major contact.

That night each platoon set another squad-size ambush. All three ambushes made contact shortly after oh-two-hundred and repelled the VC. Captain Sarmiento had the mortars fire illumination rounds over the paddies so the ambushes could make a body count before returning to the hill with their own casualties. Six more Marines were killed or wounded that night.

Twenty-two VC bodies were found in the paddies and one wounded man was taken prisoner.

Everyone was satisfied with the night's activity except for those who had lost a friend.

An hour later the VC mortar dropped a few rounds on the hill, but that was the only other action Lima Company had that night.

"Third herd, saddle up. We're going for a walk in the sun." Lieutenant Haupt walked briskly along his platoon's line. "Your squad leaders have told you what we're doing, so get on the stick." He ignored the low-pitched grumblings about ". . . the Kraut gonna hump our asses too hard some day . . ."

The platoon route marched down the hill and into the low hills behind the paddies. Thickly packed thigh-high brush covered with brilliant green leaves carpeted the gently rolling hills and constantly threatened to trip the men pushing their way through it. There was no shade from the sun. Visibility, except looking back toward the paddies, was limited to less than two or three hundred meters because of the closeness of the hills.

"Sergeant Johnny, can I be a flanker?" Nutsy Nooncy asked. "Flankers get a better chance to kill gooks. Let me and Wegener take a flank. He's over the heat now." A broad grin split his pale face, which was just beginning to turn pink from the sun.

"Can it, Nutsy," Johnson said. "Stay in line. Flankers get a better chance of getting killed, too. The only effective way we can put flankers out is on the other side of the hill."

"Other side of the hill? Whatever you say, Honcho. Let's go, Wegener." Nuncio started walking rapidly away from the platoon column.

Wegener looked at Corporal Falalo for direction.

"Nuncio, get your ass back here," Johnson called after him.

"Back in line, Nutsy," said Falalo. "You ain't going nowhere."

Nuncio slowed his pace but continued moving away from the column. "You shitting me, right? I'm really going over this hill to be a flanker, right?"

"You don't get back in line, Nutsy, I'm going to kick your ass for you," Johnson said.

"After I do," Falalo added.

Nuncio stopped and leaned forward slightly, eyes moving from his squad leader to his team leader and back again. "I gotta get back in line. That what you saying?"

"That's what we're saying, Nutsy."

"Shit, why didn't you say so? I didn't wanna go on the other side of no fucking hill no how." Twisting his way through the brush, Nuncio returned to his place in the column.

The temperature rose to ninety degrees and then climbed some more. An occasional waft of breeze was a big relief in the still air between the hills. Men conditioned by two long humps with heavy loads to conserve water on the march sipped cautiously from their canteens. Brains tried to stay alert, not to daze from the heat. Then shots rang out.

"Hit the deck!" someone screamed.

Everyone dropped into the brush and waited for more fire to come. A few looked over the brush, trying to see where they had been fired on from. Nothing moved. No more rounds were fired.

"Where is he? Anybody see where that sniper is?" Ortega called.

No one had seen anything. No one could say where the sniper fire came from. After a few minutes Haupt ordered the platoon back to its feet.

"Look sharp," Haupt ordered. "Next time, let's know where this sniper's shooting from and take him out."

Of course, no one could tell quite where the sniper fired from when he opened up again fifteen minutes later. Once more the Marines dropped into the brush. They returned no fire at the unseen sniper.

"Move it out, look sharp," Haupt ordered when it was clear the sniper had stopped sniping.

There was more sniper fire. Every time, the Marines dropped for cover. No one saw where the sniper was. Two or three more incidents made the Marines realize the snipers weren't hitting anyone, and they stopped going for cover when they got sniped at.

That's the way the patrol went. A tiring but otherwise unnotable walk in the afternoon sun, occasionally punctuated by entirely ignorable sniper fire. The snipers were the only sign of the Viet Cong, and they were never located. Dull. Nearly everybody on the patrol wished he was back on the hill, where at least he could crap out and not have to waste energy on the stinking hills.

The patrol's path seemed to meander at random through the hills, but it did, in fact, follow a rough route. Very rough. "Go out about a klick on an azimuth of something like three thirty degrees, then turn right about one hundred degrees for another klick and a half, then come back in. Cover as much ground as you can. Call in when you reach the two checkpoints where you change direction. Be back in four hours," is what Captain Sarmiento told Lieutenant Haupt. So even though the patrol didn't seem to be going anywhere in particular, it did have a general direction to follow.

At the second checkpoint call-in, Haupt was given new directions. The platoon was to go three klicks deeper into the hills to another high hill. The rest of the company would join it there. Battalion thought they had chased Charlie farther into the hills and all the companies were moving deeper into them. Third platoon turned left instead of right. Another hour's hump brought them in sight of what Haupt thought must be the objective hill. Certainly, it was higher than its neighbors, and it was about the right distance along approximately the right azimuth.

An explosion rent the air and shook the ground. Men hit the deck, those who weren't knocked down by the blast. A cloud of dust erupted around the center of the explosion and hung in the still air.

"Corpsman up!" The yells for assistance came almost immediately. The screaming had started even before the noise of the explosion died down. "Corpsman up! Both corpsmen up!" Some of the voices were at the edge of hysteria.

The platoon's two corpsmen grabbed their medkits and bolted toward the head of the column, where Lieutenant Haupt was already assessing the damage. Someone in the point team had hit a booby trap trip wire. It might have been attached to a two-hundred-fifty-pound bomb, the explosion was that big.

"Ortega, get on the horn and call for a med-evac most rickytick," Haupt called.

Staff Sergeant Ortega ran to the lieutenant's radioman and almost yanked the handset away from him. Ortega spoke into it urgently, listened, then called out, "How many down, sir?" and tugging on the radioman's arm, started in the direction of the wounded.

"We're still counting," Haupt answered. "Tell 'em ten." He turned back to supervising the men helping the corpsmen sort the dead and wounded.

"Second squad, get some people up here pretty chop-chop quick," Haupt ordered.

A team from second squad moved forward and two men were assigned to assist each corpsman. Sergeant Zimmerman took charge of the rest of the platoon and got the men into defensive positions. If Charlie wanted to hit third platoon while it was disorganized, Zimmerman didn't want to be disorganized.

"They wanna know how many dead and how many wounded, sir," Ortega said. "I told them we're not under fire."

"Give me that," Haupt snapped, and jerked the handset from Ortega's hand. "This is Lima Three Actual," he said into it. "I have three KIAs and at least six WIAs here. I want a med-evac and I want it now. Over."

He waited for a reply, then said, "Those are minimum figures, there may be more. Get me that med-evac now. I want it before any of the wounded die. We are at wait one." He turned to Ortega. "Give 'em our coordinates," he said, and returned to the wounded.

After giving the numbers, Ortega waited to listen again, then said, "That's an affirmative. I will have men on the high ground and will signal with green smoke. Out." He returned the handset to the radio.

Five minutes later third squad's first fire team was on top of a nearby hill watching for the med-evac birds. The rest of the platoon, those not wounded or working on the wounded, was busy clearing a landing zone.

Soon five helicopters were circling overhead. Two sped close to the ground looking for enemy, firing machine guns into tree-lines and thick patches of brush. One of the higher choppers came down to the cleared patch of earth, received its load of wounded, and left, to be followed by a second and finally a third.

Haupt looked hollow-eyed at his remaining men. He had just lost an entire squad to one booby trap. "Third squad, take the point and make goddam sure you don't hit any trip wires," he said. "Charlie's ready for us here. Let's not give him any more. Move it out."

Charlie's work was done. Lima Company had suffered more than twenty casualties on this part of Operation Abilene Run, and the other companies in the battalion were similarly hit. Two more nights of ambushes and LPs and two days of patrols made no more contact. So the operation was called to an end and ordered to go east, where the battalion would be met on Highway One by trucks for transit back to Chu Lai.

The hills fell down to the coastal plains where broad paddy lands sparkled their emerald brilliance under the sun. The companies would form into one column going through the paddies with Lima leading the way. Because the other companies had a greater distance to go before entering the paddies, a gap grew between the end of Lima and the beginning of Mike Company. Air cover was not felt to be immediately necessary, though two gunships were on standby if needed.

The joking started soon after the Marines entered the paddies from the hills. "Hey, man, you think they gonna give us paddy water to shower with when we get back?"

"Hey, no, bro'. They gonna send us down to the landing ramp and let us swim inna water the landing craft dumped oil in."

The farther each man got from the hills the higher his spirits rose. In only a little while they would get off their feet, get to stop humping and start riding, then have a break back at the big air base. They were truly combat Marines now. All they had to do was get through the paddies alive.

A long, wooded finger protruding more than a kilometer into the paddies from the hills rose to its low height three hundred meters to the right of Lima Company's route. A treeline was an equal distance to the left. Three kilometers into the paddies another treeline stood perpendicular to their path.

Lima had lost close to thirty men to enemy action and the heat on Abilene Run. With nearly twenty-meter intervals between men, Lima was strung out on a line nearly three kilometers long. First platoon's point man was less than three hundred meters from the treeline the company had to cross when the last man in second platoon entered the paddies. He got nearly fifty meters from the edge of the hills before the Viet Cong sprung their ambush.

Two mortars started popping rounds from the ridge on the right. Three machine guns fired from the left flank and a fourth enfiladed the company from its front. Automatic and semiautomatic rifle fire also rained from all three sides.

"Hit the deck!" "Get down!" "Take cover!" "Down behind the dikes!" The officers and sergeants screamed their orders up and down the lines.

Cries of, "Corpsman up!" also started being heard.

"Where are they?" "They're all around us." "Fire on that treeline." "Who's got a LAW? Put it on that ridge." "Keep your fire down. Shoot into the trees, not over them." "Get those mortars up. Everybody with a mortar round, pass it along." "Corpsman up." The voices started in a babel, but quickly order took over and disciplined fire began to be returned. And always the wounded were cared for.

The VC mortars walked their rounds from the ends of the column to the middle and back to the ends. If their sighting had been better, they could have inflicted heavy casualties on the Marines. But most of them kept hitting a paddy too short or a paddy too long to do much damage.

"Second squad, put your fire in the treeline on the left," Lieutenant Haupt shouted. "Third squad, fire into that ridge."

Sergeant Johnson called to his team leaders, "Hideaway, Buster, see that puff of smoke? That must be the mortar. Put your fire below it. Try to take that sucker out."

Third squad concentrated its fire where Johnson thought the mortar was. It didn't seem to have any effect.

"Report! Is everyone all right?" Johnson wanted to know.

Falalo and Bahls looked to their sides. "All here," Falalo said.

"All cocks in second team shooting," said Bahls.

Johnson himself was acting as third team leader since the death of Kim Chang.

"Slow fire, conserve your ammo," the lieutenants ordered. "Ten seconds between rounds and move them around."

Lima Company had reacted quickly to the ambush by taking cover behind the dikes and laying down disciplined return fire.

Charlie's fire had little effect after the opening salvos. But the Marines' fire was too dispersed and seemed to have little effect on the enemy. The company was pinned down. At least the cries of "Corpsman up" had stopped.

Then heavier fire struck in the back of the treeline on the left. Mike Company had reached the paddies and was sweeping through and behind that treeline. Two helicopter gunships *whumpa*'d overhead, colored smoke was popped, and the gunships guided on it, swooping onto the ridgeline and the front treeline.

Fire at Lima Company from those two directions eased; Charlie was shooting at the birds. On the other flank the firing also eased, as Mike worked its way along the trees.

"First platoon, get into those trees," Captain Sarmiento ordered. "Second platoon, hit that ridge. Third platoon, fire into that treeline, lead Mike Company."

First platoon reformed into a line and advanced on the treeline by fire and maneuver. Second platoon also fired and maneuvered. Third platoon's fire aided Mike Company. The Viet Cong on the ridge retreated into the hills. The ones in the treelines had a much harder time—they had counted on withdrawing through the trees on the left, and didn't really have anywhere to go.

The gunships pulled back and looked for clear targets when the Marines reached the ridge and the treeline. The fighting in the treelines grew furious as the Marines and Viet Cong closed. Charlie didn't believe in standing and fighting. But this time he couldn't run. Then the fight was over.

Med-evac birds came in to take out Lima's fifteen or twenty casualties and the few more from Mike. The two companies pulled nearly a hundred VC bodies out of the trees. They also captured four machine guns, eighty-one rifles, twelve sidearms, and a few thousand rounds of ammunition.

"Payback's a med-evac," somebody said as he watched the birds fly out the dead and wounded.

"Yeah," someone else answered him. "But their payback wasn't even a Pyrrhic victory."

"What's a Pyrrhic victory?" the first speaker wanted to know.

* * *

India and Kilo companies, which had not been involved in the fight, made a final sweep through the treelines and the ridge, looking for anyone who had been missed. Lima and Mike resumed their march to Highway One, where they boarded the trucks and waited for the rest of the battalion.

Spirits had fallen at the ambush. They stayed low on the ride back to Chu Lai; everyone was watching for another ambush.

The battalion had lost a hundred forty men killed or wounded on Operation Abilene Run. It had accounted for more than two hundred confirmed kills and at least that many more unconfirmed. Additionally, nearly two hundred weapons were captured along with fifteen thousand rounds of ammunition. Several tons of rice had been destroyed. Operation Abilene Run was declared a resounding success.

Nutsy Nooncy,
The Killing Machine

"LOTS OF MARINES ARE CRAZY IN COMBAT—THAT'S ONE OF the reasons Marines usually win fights. But once in a while there's one who's crazy all the time and gets to liking to kill people and lives, eats, breathes, shits, and sleeps killing gooks. That's the kind you never cross or get on his bad side, but you always want him on your side when a fight starts.

"We had one like that in my squad. He was PFC Joseph Nuncio and we all called him Nutsy Nooncy. When we weren't out in the bush, Nutsy Nooncy'd sit around kind of caressing his rifle and always sharpening his bayonet. He'd just hunker down there and croon to that weapon of his. Anybody'd get close enough to hear what he was saying to that piece always heard him saying about how his baby shouldn't worry, they was gonna go back out soon and kill more gooks. When he wasn't like that he was pacing nervous like, as close as he could get to the wire and looking out toward where he thought some Vee Cee might be.

"Nobody liked being with him on a daytime security patrol because he'd keep pointing his piece at civilians and going, 'You Vee Cee. I bang bang you, you dead Vee Cee.' That made the locals a skosh bit upset and made us wonder when some of them might turn out to be real Vee Cee who would set more booby traps for us on account of because Nutsy Nooncy scared them.

51

He was good on a night ambush or LP, though. You just knew he'd be awake all night long listening real hard because he just plain wanted someone to walk into our killing zone so's he could zap himself some more gooks.

"Nutsy Nooncy was a dangerous man in a fight, and he loved to fight. That's why everybody tried to stay away from him when he got to drinking a little brew or some of that white lightning the gooks sold us in bottles with Seagram's Seven labels. Especially when he had some of that white lightning. And he was the only grunt I ever knew who actually liked Vietnamese Tiger beer. That crap tasted more like tiger piss than beer. Some pogue types claimed they liked it, but I think that was just so we'd think they were macho and bad-assed like us real Marines. The rest of us only drank Tiger when we really had to drink something and Tiger was the only thing there was. Tiger beer is brewed in just about every country in the Far East, and it's different from country to country, some being good and some not so good. But that Tiger in Vietnam, well, that was some bad crap. Ba Moui Ba was the premium Vietnamese beer. It wasn't a good brew, but it was a damn sight better than Tiger. Nutsy Nooncy liked that Tiger. Maybe it helped him be so crazy.

"In the bush, Nutsy Nooncy was the best man in the platoon. Maybe in the whole company or even the whole battalion. He always wanted the point if our squad had it, or he wanted the flank if we didn't. When I say he was good, don't mistake me, now. He wasn't good like he'd be a good leader—a corporal or a sergeant, nothing like that. If he was an NCO his men would never know what they were supposed to do 'cause he could never tell anyone what he wanted them to do, just what *he* was gonna do. So Hernando Falalo, who was his fire-team leader, and Johnny Johnson, pretty much let him do what he wanted. The main thing he wanted to do was to kill gooks. Hated them little suckers.

"It must have been about January, we were on this operation somewhere with two Arvin battalions sweeping through this ocean of elephant grass looking for a Vee Cee main camp, when Nutsy Nooncy proved just how crazy he really was. I don't know how many square miles or hundreds of square klicks this grass covered, but there wasn't nowhere you could look and not see it. Even if it was only covering a little area, you couldn't look anywhere and not see it. This grass was mostly about eight feet high, and none of us was tall enough to see over it no how. What we were told was somewhere in it, or just on the other side of it, was a big Vee Cee main camp, and we were to find and destroy that main camp.

"We went in there, one Marine battalion flanked by two Arvin battalions. Every company was in column, more or less, but the companies were all on line abreast of each other. That way we could cover the most territory, but headquarters could have control over our movement without anybody having to worry about how to keep everybody on a line when nobody could see more than a few feet in any direction. It was only an hour or so before noon by the time all the companies got lifted in and in proper formation, so we got a late start on the sweep.

"I mean to tell you it can get bodacious hot in high grass where the wind can't blow and you're wearing a flak jacket and helmet and carrying fifty pounds of weapons, ammo, and gear, and the temperature is maybe ninety degrees. I'm powerful surprised we didn't lose half our men from heat stroke. We did lose a few, though. Not many, just a few.

"The operation CO was topside about five klicks in his helicopter watching the progress of the companies, and kept radioing down to us when any company was turning and twisting too much or if somebody was moving too far ahead or dropping behind. So there was a lot of stopping and starting and a lot of just standing in that goddam grass that can make a man go bugfuck. From as high as the CO was, we must've looked like ten pencil lines snaking our way through that grass.

" 'Long about seventeen thirty—ah, that's five-thirty P.M., son—we reached the far side of that grass where it butted right up against a forest, and stopped to dig in for the night. May sound kind of early, but night comes fast there and we only had time to scrape shallow slits in the dirt, have a quick smoke, and locate our Cs and John Wayne can openers before the sun dropped behind the mountains and it was night. Most of us finished eating by feel. None of our platoons had time to set out LPs before the sun went down, so we wound up not setting any out.

"All day long sweating our way through all that high grass we didn't make a single contact. I didn't hear a single shot fired, and it seemed like every booby trap in our way was spotted by the point man. So far this operation was a drag. Had us all on edge because we figured the longer it took us to run into Charlie, the readier he'd be for us.

"For the first couple or three hours that night all of us were awake. It was a long day's walk in the sun but nobody was sleepy. We knew Charlie had to be somewhere nearby. By twenty-one hundred we were dropping off to a fifty-percent alert on our own, and about the time the two-hour watches had just changed, both flanks of the battalion starting picking up some sniper fire. What most of us didn't know until a skosh bit later was the fire was coming directly from the flanks, where the Arvins was supposed to be.

"That's right. Where they were *supposed* to be. But they weren't there anymore. Those little gooners done bugged out as soon as they thought we wasn't paying them any attention. They must have been right about us not paying them attention because the first thing our flanks knew about them being gone was when old Charlie started dinging a few in from where the Arvins were supposed to be. Later in the war the Arvins got to be good soldiers, but when I was there, Marines hated them little gooks because you couldn't depend on them to stand and fight.

"Most of us, except the ones getting it, of course, ignored the snipers. There's most always snipers out there someplace. But they didn't let us ignore them long. Next thing we knew the middle of our line was getting overrun and calling for all kinds of help from everyone else.

"Well, we laid down heavy fire toward the middle of the line like they asked for, and that broke the Vee Cee attack there just as what seemed like half the Vee Cee in all of Eye Corps opened up on the rest of the battalion. The stuff they threw at us, it seemed like every one of them that wasn't armed with B-40 rockets, mortars, or machine guns had an AK-47. Most of us had scratched lines in the dirt less than a foot deep to spend the night in. All of a sudden we were all wishing we had bunkers.

"Well, this assault lasted about fifteen minutes before we got them kicked back into the woods, and all they did there was hit us with a shitload of sniper fire. But that was just a diversion while they pulled themselves around to the sides and assaulted both flanks at the same time. The platoons on the flanks pulled themselves around mighty fast and started fighting off the hell what was coming at them and gave better than they took, but they sure as shit took some hell. By the time the flanks beat off their attacks, the word been passed to saddle up because we were pulling back away from the trees as soon as only the snipers were shooting at us.

"That pullback was a bitch. Every platoon in the battalion had to get in line and go back on its own while maintaining contact with the platoons on both sides—remember, we were Marines, and we took all of our dead and wounded with us. Marines don't leave no-fucking-body behind. It's tradition, just like us Morris men being Marines. Took us more than two hours to move about a klick, then another hour getting back on line and oriented toward where Charlie was following and sniping at us.

"That's when Johnny Johnson finally took a head count and found out Nutsy Nooncy was missing. All the time along we thought he was pulling rear point dinging a few back at the gooks that was following us. Both Johnson and Falalo was pissed at themselves for not knowing he was missing, and the rest of us were pissed, too, because we figured we'd need that sum-bitch before the night was over. We were also pissed because we figured the next morning we'd have to go back and spend boo-coo time trying to find his dead ass.

"Well, it's like the preacherman say, 'O ye of little faith.' We had us some LPs maybe twenty-five meters out in front of every platoon. Couple or so hours after we set in, the LP in front of the first platoon's LP, which was in front of the squad next to third platoon, heard a rustling in the grass coming toward it. Well, the men in that LP knew some Marines were still out there, so instead of shooting at the noise, one of them called out a challenge. When Nutsy Nooncy answered, the LP told him the whole platoon was looking for him and come on in.

"Seems that when the Vee Cee hit us right after we broke the assault on the middle of the line, a B-40 exploded right near Nutsy Nooncy. It tore him up real bad. A shitload of shrapnel hit him in the left leg and arm, broke his leg in about three places, busted up his M-14 something fierce, and a piece hit him upside his head and knocked him out. If his flak jacket hadn't done what it was supposed to do, which is to stop rocket, mortar, and grenade fragments, he would have been killed. When he came to, he crawled all around looking for the rest of the platoon, and when we weren't there he figured out what we had done. Not having a corpsman to patch him up, he did it his ownself. His rifle was broke to hell, so he stripped it down and cut up his belt and some strips from his shirt and strapped his rifle stock to his leg just like a splint.

"The only working weapon Nutsy Nooncy had was his bayonet, so he pulled it out into his right hand and started crawling away from the trees. As bad shot up as he was, and with all those gooks moving through the grass, too, it took more than five hours for him to go the thousand meters to where we were. Along the way he fell into a machine-gun position and killed its four-man crew with his bayonet. Also, he killed a couple of other gooks he ran into, as well as a sniper who was sighting in on that LP that challenged him.

"We were all glad to have old Nutsy Nooncy back, but he was shot up bad and became a priority med-evac. His leg wounds were bad enough they had to send him back to The World to fix him. Before I left Veeceeland we got the word he was let go with a medical discharge and got a disability pension.

"Anyway, there he was in a hospital bed in Da Nang a couple days later, waiting to get sent back to The World, and a reporter from some TV network was going through the ward interviewing the men being sent back and he came to good old Nutsy. 'Son, I'll bet you're damn glad to be going home, aren't you?' the reporter asked him. 'Fuck no,' Nutsy Nooncy answered. 'I wanna go back out there and kill me some more gooks.'

"While he was with us, Nutsy Nooncy was our main man. He was the man we wanted on our side in a fight. When we heard what he told that reporter, we knew exactly what he meant."

Chapter Three

THE HELICOPTERS HOVERED LOW OVER THE ELEPHANT GRASS, the wash from their rotors bending the thick stalks almost to the ground. Anxiously, their cargoes of Marine infantrymen disgorged themselves, dropped the few feet to earth, and scattered into the almost man-high grass, more than man high in some places, setting a defensive perimeter around the landing zone. As the last man jumped from each bird, it flew upward and another took its place over the grass, until the entire company had been landed. The scene was repeated a half kilometer north and south and yet another half kilometer farther to the south.

Even farther north and south, truck convoys bumped over secondary roads on their way into the grass from Highway One. These trucks carried two battalions of the Army of the Republic of Vietnam's 37th Infantry Regiment.

Five kilometers straight up, the Marine colonel commanding the operation circled in his command helicopter. From there he would be able to see the trails in the grass that all ten companies would make through the eight-kilometer width of grass. Somewhere in that grass, or inside the forest it bordered to the west, was a Viet Cong main base. Operation Scythe's mission was to locate that main base, capture or destroy all weapons, munitions, medical supplies, and food in it, to kill or capture all Viet Cong personnel found.

Many other helicopters circled above the grass. Most of them flew relatively low—they were gunships supporting the grunts. Three of them were high above the grass; they carried the battalion commanders.

"Yo, Skipper! Give third platoon the point. I wanna be the first swinging dick on this here operation to zap a zip."

Captain Sarmiento looked toward the speaker, then shook his head at one of the other men in the small group huddled around him. "Nutsy Nooncy! I hate having him around in garrison, but I'm damn glad he's with us when the shit hits. Well, Haupt, he's in your platoon. If you want to put him on the point, you've got it."

Second Lt. Rudolph Haupt shrugged. Even hunched over in the huddle, he stood taller than the other officers and staff sergeants in the company. "May as well." He grinned. "Nutsy ain't going to walk us into any booby traps. And he might find Charlie before Charlie finds us."

The man identified as Nutsy Nooncy stood a few meters away from the command huddle, waiting for an answer. His normally fair face had turned a bright red from the sun. He had the kind of complexion that never burnt or tanned, it just turned red and stayed red, contrasting sharply with his shock of coal black hair. A crooked grin split his face while his hands nervously caressed their way around his M-14. The seven bandoleers that weighted down his shoulders added four hundred twenty rounds to the one hundred forty in his magazines. He also carried six fragmentation and two white phosphorus grenades.

Joseph Nuncio intended to use all of it on the VC.

"We got it, Nutsy," Haupt called to him. "You'll get your chance to zap some Vee Cee."

"Thanks, Lieutenant. Thanks, Skipper," Nuncio said gleefully. "I'll go give Sergeant Johnny the good news."

A stocky Mexican staff sergeant who glistened with sweat spat into the mashed-down grass. "Good news, shit. The only good news I want to hear on this op is we're going back to Chu Lai."

Lieutenant Haupt slapped his platoon sergeant on the shoulder. "No sweat, Ortega. We gonna find Charlie and kick his ass."

"Right." Staff Sergeant Ortega spat into the grass again. "No sweat." The moving edge of his beefy hand runneled perspiration from his eyes.

The ten companies, four Marine and six ARVN, assembled themselves and set off into the grass. They moved in parallel columns at half-kilometer intervals. Each company sent a squad out one hundred meters to each flank so that the wide front was more completely covered. High overhead the command bird watched and gave directions. If a company got too far ahead of the others, the colonel would order it to stop until the others caught up with it. If one fell too far behind, he would halt the others until the laggard made up the distance. He could redirect companies that wandered off their assigned paths. During this operation the colonel spent a lot of time on his radio giving the companies directions.

"Hurry up and wait, hurry up and wait, hurry the fuck up and fucking wait. That's all this goddam Green Machine ever does," Nutsy Nooncy complained to Corporal Falalo.

Falalo removed his helmet and fanned himself with it. "Shut up, Nutsy. Nobody's shooting at us."

"I wish somebody would. I wanna kill me a gook." Nuncio peered eagerly through the eight-foot-high grass they waited in.

The early afternoon temperature was in the mid-eighties, but with no air movement possible through the grass, it may as well have been over a hundred. Falalo, Nuncio, Salatu, and Wegener had taken turns on the point, every fifteen minutes handing off the machete they used to chop a path through the grass. When Nuncio wasn't chopping—chopping with one hand, M-14 ready in the other—he was right behind the man who was, eyes ever on the move. Eyes moving, muzzle moving with the eyes, ready to fire at the first sign of enemy presence. Nuncio's eagerness to make contact had pulled the company two hundred meters ahead of the rest of the battalions, and it was ordered to sit and wait for the others to catch up. So the men of Lima sat. They sat in the high grass with the tropical sun beating almost directly down on them.

The ten companies had been on the move through the stifling grass for three hours. The heat had taken its toll. Already more than fifty of the eighteen hundred Marines and Arvins on the operation had had to be med-evacked because of heat exhaustion. Probably several hundred more were suffering from the effects of the heat. Heat exhaustion leads to heat stroke. Heat stroke can bring on shock and death.

"Hideaway, move out." Sergeant Johnson's voice came to the point team.

"On your feet, people," Falalo ordered. "Wegener, you got the chopper."

"Negative that," Nuncio interrupted him. "I had me a break, I'll take it." He grinned crookedly at his fire-team leader. "Remember, Honcho, I wanna be the first swinging dick on this operation to kill a gook."

Falalo shook his head and allowed Nuncio to take the machete.

Nuncio grasped the pistol grip of his M-14 in his right hand, index finger curled through the trigger guard, hefted the machete in his left hand and started swinging.

So it went throughout the long hot afternoon. More men collapsed from heat exhaustion and had to be med-evacked. An ever larger percentage of the remainder suffered from the heat. Canteens were emptied into sweat-parched bodies and refilled from five-gallon cans brought in by the med-evac birds. The point squads of each company rotated teams on the point; the teams rotated men on the machete. Except for third platoon. Sergeant Johnson never rotated his teams. Joseph Nuncio wouldn't have accepted that. Wegener and Salatu grumbled about it.

And there was no contact. If the VC main camp existed in the grass, it was well hidden. There was no sign of it from the air, and the men on the ground found nothing, not even a booby trap to tell them Charlie had ever been there.

At seventeen-thirty hours the three battalions reached the far side of the grass and found themselves facing a broad sward of low grass fronting a forest.

The colonel commanding Operation Scythe radioed an order to the battalion commanders to have their men halt at the edge of the high grass and dig in for the night. Then he flew back to his headquarters at Chu Lai. The battalion commanders in turn radioed down to their company commanders on the ground that they were to dig in for the night and hold until dawn. Then they likewise flew back to the safety of their headquarters.

In effect, each of the ten companies on the ground now became an independent unit. No one on the scene was truly in charge of the entire operation, or even in charge of any of the battalions. Of course, the companies would be in radio contact with headquarters throughout the night. A lieutenant would be on duty in the radio room. He would decide whether or not to wake the colonel commanding or one of the battalion commanders if the companies made contact with the VC during the night.

Captain Sarmiento, like the other three Marine company commanders and, supposedly, the six Arvin company commanders, held a brief meeting with his platoon leaders and platoon sergeants. He told them to have their men dig fighting positions along the edge of the grass before chowing down, and to set out two listening posts in front of each of their platoons. The LPs were to carry a PRC-6 walkie-talkie radio and check in every half hour. There would be a fifty-percent watch, half the men awake at all times, and the smoking lamp was out at sundown. Maintain strict fire discipline, don't shoot unless you have a definite target. Charlie's out there someplace, no need to give away your position to him unless absolutely necessary.

The platoon leaders and platoon sergeants then met even more briefly with their squad leaders and passed the same orders on to them. The squad leaders told their fire-team leaders, who told their men.

Naturally, third squad got one of the LPs in front of third platoon and, just as naturally, it was the first fire team that got it. Nobody wanted to have to deal with Nutsy Nooncy if he didn't get to be on an LP. If there was contact with Charlie overnight, an LP would probably make it before the main line would.

Joseph Nuncio was getting pissed. He was still carrying all that damn ammo.

The LPs waited until dark before moving into the trees. Not far into the trees, just far enough that they wouldn't be silhouetted against the night sky if someone was watching from deeper in the woods. They didn't dig in.

"Damn l'il fuckers're pissing me off," Nuncio whispered to Salatu. They were lying side by side behind a fallen tree with only the tops of their heads and their rifles poking over it. Falalo and Wegener were sleeping on their spread-out ponchos a couple of meters to their rear.

Salatu grunted softly. He didn't want to be on an LP in the first place. He wanted even less to be on watch with Nutsy Nooncy when Nutsy wanted to talk.

"I humped all this fucking ammo and all these grenades and ain't seen a gook all goddam day."

Salatu grunted again. "Grass too high. Couldn't see a gook five feet away nohow."

"If there was a gook five feet away I'd'a smelled him."

Salatu grunted.

Nuncio twisted his wrist around to where he could see the face of his watch and held it close to his face. "Twenty-three hundred. Time to check in."

Salatu picked up the PRC-6 radio, held it to his head and whispered into it. A response came back and he whispered again, then put the radio back down by his left shoulder.

The minutes dragged by and Nuncio fidgeted silently with his M-14, wishing someone would appear to his front. But the night was silent and still. Until the quiet was broken by the distant sound of sporadic sniper fire.

"Shit," Nuncio swore. "Some'un else gets all the fucking luck. Why can't we get the snipers?"

Salatu shushed at him and listened to the tinny voice coming over the radio. "Wake up Falalo," he said.

"Why for?"

"Do it."

Nuncio shimmied back to where his team leader was sleeping and laid a gentle hand on his shoulder. Falalo's body tensed as he became alert.

"Salatu's listening on the radio and said to wake you up."

"Waz'up?" Falalo said.

"Donno."

"Wake Wegener." Falalo crawled to Salatu and put his ear next to the radio. "What the fuck?" he asked. The radio was reporting that the two Marine companies on the flanks were taking sniper fire from the Arvin positions.

All four of the men in the LP were alert now. The sniper fire on the flanks continued for a half hour before petering out. Eventually word came on the radio that the Arvins were no longer in their positions, they had bugged out earlier, leaving the Marines facing the forest alone. Facing the forest and the VC main base.

"I don't like this," Falalo whispered. "Only one man asleep at a time now. Who's been awake the longest?" he asked Nuncio and Salatu.

"Let Salatu cop some Zs," Nuncio said. "Charlie comes through here, I wanna be awake to ding his dink ass."

Salatu shrugged his shoulders and closed his eyes. No sounds came from the other side of the fallen tree. Absolute silence. Not even normal night noises.

Then the forest erupted twenty meters in front of the LP. Erupted, exploded, tore, rent with light and sound.

"Holy shit!" Falalo grabbed the radio and called for help. "We're about to get overrun," he said. He was in the center of the short line of Marines.

"Hot damn. Gonna get me some." Nuncio started firing at the flashes of light. He was on Falalo's left.

Wegener ducked down behind the fallen tree and held his rifle above it, firing without looking. He was on the far right of the line. Salatu snapped awake and added the rattle of his automatic to the cacophony. He was between Falalo and Wegener.

Hornets started zipping through the forest to the sides of the LP. Angry hornets with death in their hearts, death to the VC who were shooting at the LP.

"Let's go," Falalo shouted. "Pull back under this cover."

The four started to rise to their feet when a rocket exploded on their left. Falalo and Nuncio were knocked from their feet by the blast. Struggling to hands and knees, Falalo shouted, "Let's go! Move it, move it, move, move, move!" Three

Marines ran and scrambled from the forest, back to the safety of their line. One Marine remained on the ground, unconscious.

All along the Marine line, listening posts were withdrawing under heavy assault. Not all of the Marines made it alive or unhurt. Rockets, mortars, machine guns, and automatic rifles rained fire into the companies' fronts. The company commanders radioed their headquarters for instructions and assistance. After listening to fifteen minutes of chaotic shouts and fire on the radios, the lieutenant on duty in the regimental radio room decided that someone above him should be alerted to the fact that Operation Scythe had made contact with the enemy. It was another fifteen minutes before two orderlies managed to wake the colonel commanding and the Marine battalion commander. The Arvin orderlies didn't bother waking their bosses. They knew their battalions weren't involved.

By the time the colonel commanding and the battalion commander reached the radio room, the companies had beaten off the first assault and were only taking sniper fire. The colonel and the battalion commander each talked with two of the company commanders, getting situation reports, then conferred between themselves. They decided the companies should stay in position and maintain full alert.

They had already started to return to their quarters for more sleep when chaotic voices and heavy fire started coming over the radios again. Both flanks of the battalion were coming under heavy assault. The colonel commanding and the battalion commander conferred again and agreed that the companies should pull back away from the forest as soon as the current assault was ended. It was obvious that the VC could use the forest's cover to regroup for more assaults. Then they decided to remain in the radio room until the companies were in their new positions. Their orders were duly passed on to the company commanders, who then carried them out.

Nuncio was lying on his back under a bush where the rocket explosion had thrown him. He was in pain. His left arm and leg were on fire and felt like a maniacal steam-roller operator had tried to pave them. The granddaddy of all toothaches had found a home in his left jaw. Groping with his right hand, he found his M-14. Gingerly he sat up and found he could use his left arm as long as he was careful about it.

The rifle was broken. Its flash suppressor was bent at a crazy angle and the barrel was twisted. Setting the rifle aside, he examined his left leg. It was broken, too.

Further examination showed several wounds in his left arm and leg and another in his left jaw. Three teeth were missing on that side. The left side of his flak jacket was shredded. Maybe he'd be dead if he hadn't been wearing it.

Nuncio used the two compress bandages in his jungle kit to bind the worst of his wounds, then stripped off his flak jacket and shirt, tore the shirt into strips and bandaged the rest of his wounds. At least the ones that were still bleeding. Two deft motions and his rifle was broken down into its three basic parts, and he used the remaining strips torn from his shirt to tie the rifle stock to his leg as a makeshift splint.

Carefully, Nuncio hung his grenades on his web belt and drew his bayonet. Orienting himself on the fallen tree the LP had hidden behind, he started crawling toward the high grass where the rest of the battalion waited. But when he got there, the rest of the battalion wasn't there anymore.

"All right, buddy, what do you do now?" he asked himself.

"You figure out where the fuck they went to and you go there, that's what you do, shitface.

"Then do it, numbnuts."

"Aye aye, dipshit."

Nuncio never had a problem finding someone to talk to. He could always talk to himself if no one else was available.

Nuncio started crawling through the high grass. Boris Karloff would have appreciated the way Nuncio dragged his broken leg. "Just like I did it in *The Mummy's Curse*, kid," he would have said.

Walking through the grass during the day had been a bitch. Swinging the machete, pushing aside the stalks of grass, sweating under the baking sun, drinking too much water and getting a bloated feeling from it. Constantly having to stop or start again, time and again changing direction, all on someone else's order. Crawling through the grass at night was even worse. None of the stalks where Nuncio moved were cut, they were all standing.

Down near the ground where he was, the stalks were thicker, tougher, more reluctant to move out of his way. Every few meters, or even every few feet, he had to stop to disengage a grenade or something else on his belt from where it got hung up on the grass. When his makeshift splint got hung up, it was all he could do to keep from screaming in agony. Sweat beaded on his forehead.

"Hold up there, champ," Nuncio said to himself.

"What'za madda, chief," he asked back.

"Listen up."

He listened. The soft swishing of other bodies easing their way through the grass told Nuncio he wasn't alone in his quest to find the Marines' new line. VC were moving along with him. Nuncio's movement suddenly became slower, more painful. He couldn't make any noise now. If he did they'd hear him and he'd die.

Crawling, crawling. Moving forever onward. The night seemed to be lasting a lifetime. Maybe he had died and this was his hell.

"Wait a minute," he said to himself. "If I was in hell would I be smelling *nuoc mam*?

"Have you ever tasted *nuoc mam*?" he replied.

"Yeah. Tastes like rotten fish.

"Why do you think they call it hell?

"Good point."

Inch by inch he eased forward and found an open area in the grass. Hardly breathing, he looked into it. The starlight showed a small cleared space a little more than two meters in diameter. A 60mm mortar was set up in the middle of it. Next to the mortar sat a VC chewing betel nut. Two others lay sleeping fetally nearby.

"Mo-dicker. If I try'n crawl around, that sum-bitch'll hear and that's it for old Nutsy Nooncy. Good night, Charlie."

Still barely breathing, Nuncio slid across the flattened grass, reached up for the watching VC's chin with his left hand and plunged his bayonet upward under the man's rib cage. A slight gurgling came from the VC's mouth and he slumped, dead. Nuncio slid to the side and quickly slit the throats of the sleepers. Then he left the open space from the other side.

Another eternity of crawling later the sound of sniper fire from up ahead came to Nuncio. The VC had found the Marines' new line. The occasional boom of an M-14 punctuated the sharper cracks of the VCs' AKs, and once in a while the roar of a grenade added emphasis. Slowly, the sounds of fire came closer as Nuncio crawled toward it.

A small cough only a few feet away froze Nuncio. Sweat drained down his face, dripped off the tip of his nose, made him feel like sneezing. Without making any noise he brought his hand to his face and brushed water from it.

The cough came again, closer. It was followed by the sound of a man walking through the grass, coming nearer. Nuncio tensed, prepared to fight, to die. A sandal-shod foot brushed over his left arm and came to earth in front of his face. Ignoring the pain in his left leg, Nuncio lurched to his knees and jabbed upward with the bayonet. The blade caught the VC under the chin, drove up, sliced through his tongue, burst through his palate, penetrated his brain. He crumbled to the ground and Nuncio collapsed on top of him, writhing in agony from the pain in his leg.

It took a little while, but eventually the pain ebbed. When it did, Nuncio started crawling again. The sniper fire was closer.

"Squad leaders report," Lieutenant Haupt ordered. "I want to know the status of every man in this platoon."

The squad leaders called for their fire-team leaders to report.

"Salatu, you okay?" Fernando Falalo asked.

"Five by, Honcho."

"How 'bout you, Nuncio?"

Silence.

"Where the fuck's Nuncio? You see him, Wegener?"

"That's a negative."

"Shit. Where the fuck'd Nutsy Nooncy get off to?" Falalo turned to his squad leader. "Hey, Johnny, I don't have Nutsy Nooncy. Pass the word for him to get his ass over here."

Of course, Nutsy Nooncy wasn't anywhere on the line. Johnny Johnson had to report a man missing.

"Halt! Who goes there?" The unexpected voice seemed to be the sweetest thing Nuncio had ever heard. He had reached his line. In minutes a corpsman would be tending his wounds, giving him morphine for the pain.

"Nuncio, and man I'm glad as shit to hear your voice."

"What's the password?"

Nuncio froze in his crawling. "Say what?" That's a crazy question, he thought.

"Give me the fucking password or I'll blow your slope ass away," the challenge came again.

"Slope my left testicle." Nuncio was getting upset. This wasn't the reception he expected. "You forget this happy password horseshit or I'll come in there and cut your dumb ass like I did those gooks that wouldn't stay out of my way back there."

"You better let him in," called a second voice. "That's Nutsy Nooncy, all right. You keep fucking with him, he'll do exactly what he says."

"Thank you, whoever you are," Nuncio called to the second voice. "I got a fucking broken leg. What say somebody come and give me a hand?"

A half hour later Nuncio was adrift in a wash of morphine. Fresh dressings were on all of his wounds. At dawn a med-evac would take him away from the war.

Two days passed. Nuncio was in the hospital in Da Nang following the surgery that set his broken leg and sewed up his other injuries or opened them for drainage. A CBS reporter walking through the ward with a camera crew stopped at Nuncio's bedside to interview him.

"What's your name, Marine?"

"PFC Joseph Nuncio. But they call me Nutsy Nooncy."

"Why do they call you Nutsy Nooncy?"

" 'Cause I'm a real bad ass-kicker and I love to kill Charlie. I hate them fucking gooks."

That can be edited out later, the reporter thought. "According to the doctors," he said out loud, "you are going home now. Won't that feel a lot better than killing Viet Cong?"

"Well," Nuncio hesitated in his answer, "maybe."

"What do you mean, maybe?"

"If I get laid a lot. Maybe fucking round-eye tail is better than killing gooks. If it ain't, I wanna go back to my platoon. Ding me some more dinks. I *know* that's fun."

Somehow, that interview never got used on TV. But word of it did get back to third platoon. Everybody there loved it.

Mister Peacetime Grunt, Meet Mister War

"THIS MUST HAVE BEEN LONG ABOUT FEBRUARY OR SOMETIME. We'd been through a bunch of operations. Kim Chang got himself killed, I told you about that, and Salatu and Jeb Casebolt got wounded on Operation Braxton Hill, which I ain't told you about but maybe will some day, and they weren't back from the hospital yet and Nutsy Nooncy wasn't coming back at all. And Buster Bahls and Empty Nick Devoid was wounded and they were still out, too. So the squad was kind of shorthanded and needed some new people. Oh, yeah, Frenchy got killed same time Kim Chang did.

"There were thirteen of us in the squad when we got there, but now we were down to six. Johnny Johnson was carrying the blooper his ownself because there wasn't nobody else to do it, and he had me for radioman because I was the only one in the squad knew how to use it. That left one fire team. Hernando Falalo was the team leader, and he had Malcolm X for his automatic rifleman and Chief Runningstar and Wegener were his riflemen. Nowhere near enough for a squad.

"Then a big replacement draft arrived, a whole shipload of Marines. Mostly they was boots, and this was their first duty assignment. Some of them never got to a second duty station. But there were a few that had grunt experience from before the war. My squad got three of these new men. Two of them were

70

a skinny redheaded kid named Hunter and a street-tough black dude called Gant. Both of them were real good-looking Marines, even if they didn't have any kind of grunt experience, and Hunter never heard a shot fired in anger. Gant started off not wanting to wait to get into the bush and kick some ass. He claimed he killed someone in a gang fight in Brooklyn, but Malcolm X was a Brooklyn gang member from before he joined up and he said he never heard of the gang Gant claimed to be a member of, so you can take what Gant said for whatever you want to.

"But the real prize we got was this short-timer by the name of Corporal Doyle. That's all anybody ever called him, either Corporal Doyle or just plain Doyle. Poor sum-bitch only had seven months to go before he got out, and if it wasn't for that four-month extension the entire Marine Corps got hit with the year before, he'd have been getting out in May. Doyle came in feeling sorry for himself because the day the ship he came over on crossed the international date line was his twenty-second birthday and he felt cheated. It might be his last birthday, and it only lasted twelve hours because they changed to the next day at noon.

"Anyone ever tell you he ain't scared going into combat, you know you're talking to a liar. Corporal Doyle was scared shitless. He came to Vietnam from a stint as an MP at the Marine Corps Air Station at Cherry Point, North Carolina. Before that he was with the Fourth Marines at Kay Bay. Ah, Kay Bay, that's what Marines call Kaneohe Bay, the Marine Air Station in Hawaii. Anyway, he rotated back to CONUS right about the same time Three Nine and One Three landed at Da Nang. He followed the war in the news and just didn't like what he heard about the way it was being fought.

"Let me give you a little historical background here. The top honcho of the FMFPAC, that means Fleet Marine Force Pacific, was this Lieutenant General Victor Krulak. When he took over in 'sixty-four he saw the Vietnam war coming. Now Krulak knew it was a guerrilla war, and he studied the French Indochinese war and knew what the Frenchies did that made them lose. He didn't want us to do the same, so he started training his troops in counterinsurgency warfare. What this meant was a lot of small-unit operations, platoons and squads mostly, but even a lot of fire-team patrols and ambushes. Go out, be quiet about it, kill the enemy if you can find him, and make friends with the people. That last is so you take support away from the guerrilla. Guerrillas can't keep operating too long without grass-roots support. Basically what he was teaching was, fight the guerrilla like a guerrilla.

"Remember, Billy Westmoreland was running the war, and he firmly believed in gadgets and large-unit actions. We never knew if this was true or not, but the way we heard it was that Krulak disagreed with Westmoreland and wasn't too chicken to say so to his face. Then we heard that Krulak told Westmoreland he could do whatever he wanted to do with the Army in the rest of the country, but Eye Corps was a Marine Corps show, and he was going to run the war there his own way. So Westmoreland ordered Krulak to get his ass back to his headquarters in Hawaii and stay there because he, Westmoreland, was running the whole war. Whatever the truth about that was, I know Krulak didn't go back to Hawaii and stay there because I seen him my ownself sometime in May after he was supposed to be ordered not to come back. We was told not to tell anybody we seen him, either.

"So Corporal Doyle learned all this junk about small-unit actions and how anytime you put big units out there trying to find guerrillas, all you do is let them find you and they put more of a hurting on you than you do on them. We were doing battalion and regiment operations and taking a lot of casualties without knowing exactly what kind of hurting we put on the Vee Cee and NVA, except we knew we was killing a lot more of them than they were of us, but Corporal Doyle didn't understand that, and he had the crap scared out of him by battalion operations.

"With Doyle, Hunter, and Gant added to the squad, we were up to nine men, and Sergeant Johnson made two fire teams. Falalo kept Malcolm X and Chief Runningstar and got Gant. Doyle was made the other team leader and got me and Wegener and Hunter. He'd been out of the grunts for about a year and said he'd forgotten more about being a grunt than I learned yet. On Corporal Doyle's first day in-country he was given a security patrol to take out. The patrol was Hunter and me and Doyle. That same day Wegener got sent on R and R, so Doyle only had me and Hunter.

"Corporal Doyle got his patrol order from Staff Sergeant Ortega. Then Sergeant Zimmerman gave Doyle the ammo for the patrol. Doyle was a-quaking and a-shaking from fear because he wasn't sure of what to do. All he had to do was ask me for help and I would of given him all the straight scoop he needed, but Doyle never did ask anyone for help. We had a hundred and twenty rounds and two frags each. In addition I got an extra bandoleer on account of I had the AR, and Zimmerman also gave Doyle a Willie Peter grenade. When Doyle gave us the ammo for the patrol, Hunter saw the Willie Peter and says right away he should carry it. 'Willie Peter's bad shit to carry unless you have a good arm,' he said. 'I had scouts from half a dozen major league teams coming around to my high school to time my fastball and get a look at the motion on my slider.' So Doyle handed him the phosphorus. Glad Hunter wanted it, 'cause I hated carrying Willie Peter.

"We also had a prick twenty, which is a backpack radio. He looked at Hunter and said, 'You know how to use a radio?' and Hunter nods his head. That man may have been a boot, but he seemed to know just about everthing there was to know about being a field grunt. Doyle had Hunter carry the radio, and he sounded like he'd been to communications school when he talked on it. Good man, Hunter. I was sure glad he was in my fire team.

"Then we went out. Son, I want to tell you, Corporal Doyle was scared. I mean that man was almost crapping himself. We went about four or five hundred meters down this trail that was wide enough for a Mighty-Mite to drive on, until we walked right into this ville with a lot of shade because it's got trees all in it. Doyle is standing there looking around at all the people, and all he can think to ask me is how many of them are Vee Cee and how can we tell. I tell him I don't know how many of them are Vee Cee but if any of them pull out guns and start shooting at us, it's a pretty good guess they're Vee Cee.

"Then the little kids start running around us wanting to play and wanting us to give them candy and cigarettes. Doyle's kind of nervous about them because he's heard too many stories about little kids with grenades strapped to their backs killing Marines, but Hunter got down on his knees, and next thing you know, them little kids was crawling all over the three of us and we all had a good time for maybe a half hour with them. When they saw how good we was with the little ones, the teenagers started giving us Coca-Colas and beer and Doyle insisted we pay them for it instead of taking it for free. Spoilsport. Not often you get things for free; you should take them when someone offers.

"After a while we started patrolling through the ville like we're supposed to, and then we came to the edge of the trees and were looking out over about a klick of open rice paddies and Doyle stops us and looks at the map he's carrying. 'Don't seem like we've gone as far as we're supposed to,' he says, 'but nobody told me anything about having to cross all that open area. What do you think?' he asked me, and I said, 'I don't know, you're the patrol leader, you tell us what to do,' because he'd already made it clear he didn't want nobody telling him anything. Hunter said he was ready to go anywhere the Marine Corps wanted him to go—he wasn't afraid of no gooks. He took a peek at the map and told Corporal Doyle it looked to him like the green area was the paddies we were looking at and he pointed out on the map where the pagoda was we was supposed to go to.

"Well, Doyle chews on this for a while, and when he didn't make up his mind fast enough, Hunter said he was ready and stepped off onto one of the dikes and led the way. He was a real take-charge type, Hunter was. Corporal Doyle couldn't do anything but follow. When we got to that pagoda Doyle had to shit so bad he didn't even take time to dig a cat hole, just dropped trou and squatted. Then we went back to the other end of where we was supposed to patrol.

"When we got there we run into two other patrols third platoon put out and they were sitting in the shade drinking Coca-Colas they bought from the teenagers and they're playing with the little kids. We sat there with them for a while shooting the shit and drinking Coca-Cola, until it was time for us to go back in. Doyle was nervous all the time and kept eyeballing the farmers in the paddies like he was waiting for one of them to come up with a rifle and start zinging at us.

"After that we went back behind the wire at Chu Lai, and Doyle was sure glad to be there except that now he knew how close to the wire our company area was so he was still pretty nervous. Nobody ever did tell him Marines had been at Chu Lai for six months and the villes right outside the wire were secure and the people there liked us. Corporal Doyle never did get over being scared shitless, but it was more or less okay. When Buster Bahls and the others came back from the hospital the squad was shuffled around again and Doyle got Malcolm X and Empty Nick Devoid. They had to work harder than the rest of us did when we were on operations because Doyle was so scared he never pulled his fair share. But to be fair to the man, he never got anybody killed or wounded. Later he was sent to a Combined Action Platoon, which scared him even more because he saw the CAP program as a suicide operation.

"Nobody missed him when he left us."

Chapter Four

"YO, DOYLE! THAT REALLY YOU, MAN?"

The diminutive, rounded Marine turned to the familiar voice. "Hey, Sergeant Zimmerman! Yeah, it sure is me. Where the fuck am I?"

"You're in Chu Lai, man, and I gotta say I'm glad to see you." Hard and muscular, Grady Zimmerman was average height with a receding hairline that was normally hidden by his helmet. Zimmerman reached Doyle and grasped his hand. "Doyle, we've been getting shot to shit here and I need some good NCOs. When did you get here? You been assigned to a company yet?"

"No, I haven't been assigned. Got here sometime in the middle of the night. This time yesterday I was on board ship pulling into Da Nang harbor to switch to an LSI that brought me here. What the fuck's going on? Nobody's said diddly-shit to me." Doyle's normally fair skin paled even more when Zimmerman said the battalion was taking heavy casualties. "What do you mean, you've been getting shot to shit?"

"I'll talk to someone and get you assigned to my company. Then I can get the Top to give you to my platoon—the platoon I'm right guide of. We really need some fire-team leaders. You still a corporal?" Zimmerman had clamped his hand on Doyle's shoulder and was leading him toward a master ser-

76

geant who stood puzzling over a clipboard clutched in a beefy paw.

"Yah. I was in the PMO, the Provost Marshal's Office, at Cherry Point. We came under the base headquarters battalion and they didn't believe in promoting the MPs, so I haven't gotten my third stripe. What do you mean about getting shot to shit?" There was almost a tremble in Doyle's voice.

"You was an MP? No shit. Didn't you try for that when we were at Kay Bay?" He abruptly stopped walking. "Stay right here, don't move. I'll be back in a mo." Zimmerman left Doyle standing where he was and walked to the master sergeant. After a brief conference in which the master sergeant made a mark on his clipboard, Zimmerman returned to Doyle and started leading him off in a different direction. "Where's your seabag? Let's get it, you're in my company now. I'll get you a weapon and gear when we get to the company area."

"My seabag's in that shack over there. What do you mean, you've been getting shot to shit?"

"Your seabag's in the battalion supply hootch?" Zimmerman shook his head. "Hope we can pry it loose. Those pogues who work in there are mostly grunts that got wounded bad enough they don't have to return to their units yet but not bad enough to go back to The World, and they're pissed about it. They don't want to have to do diddly-squat."

Zimmerman had a firm grip on Doyle's shoulder, so he almost lost his balance when Doyle halted. "Wait just a fucking minute, Grady," Doyle snapped. "What's this you're saying about getting shot to shit?"

Sergeant Zimmerman looked steadily down into Doyle's eyes. "What I mean is, when my platoon got here three months ago there was a lieutenant and forty-two NCOs and men. We're down to not much more than half that now. If we wanted to make fire teams we could field two under-strength squads, that's what I mean. The squad leaders are carrying their squad's bloopers because they don't have enough men to give it to one of them. Third squad only has six men. I'm gonna put you in it because I want to build it up to where I can make fire teams in it again, and I need another corporal in third squad so it'll have the NCOs to be able to make two fire teams. Do you understand now?"

Doyle spun wide-eyed from Zimmerman. "Goddam fucking shit. I ever see that sergeant major again I'm gonna kill his fucking ass. I'm too damn short for the Marine fucking Corps to send me here in the first place, and what do they do? Some goddam sergeant major gets a wild hair up his ass about me and cuts my orders and I wind up in a unit that's lost half its fucking men in three months?" He turned back to Zimmerman. "Grady, I only got seven months left before my EAS. What you're telling me is this platoon is losing three or four men a week. Man, that's too many for anybody to be able to make it for seven months."

Zimmerman grinned. "That's why I need you in my platoon, Doyle. You're so short you've got your civvies airing out. I bet you even talk like a sloppy civilian now. You were a good fire-team leader at Kay Bay, and you'll be one here, too. And no way you're going to do something dumb that'll get people killed. You're too short for any John Wayne shit. I need you. Now let's get that seabag of yours." Zimmerman grasped Doyle's shoulder again and pulled him to the supply hootch.

Two hours later Doyle and two other new men, both boots, were outfitted and assigned to third squad, third platoon. The third squad had been reorganized into two fire teams and one of them was getting ready to go on a patrol. Corporal Doyle was the patrol leader. His men were PFCs Henry J. Morris and Richard Wegener, both of whom had been in-country for the entire three months, and Private Hunter. Hunter had arrived in Vietnam with Doyle. Wegener didn't go on this patrol because he left for R&R in Taipei the day before.

Staff Sergeant Ortega gave Corporal Doyle his patrol orders and a map, then sent him to Zimmerman for ammo. Zimmerman gave him seven bandoleers—two for himself and each of his men and an extra for Morris, who had the AR—six fragmentation grenades, a Willie Peter, a PRC-20 radio, and told him not to sweat the patrol; it would be a cakewalk with no problems.

Before distributing the ammunition, Doyle took Morris aside. "Mister Morris," he started.

Morris's face screwed up. "Wha'jou call me?" he asked and hawked onto the ground.

Doyle started. "Mister Morris, why?"

"I'm PFC Morris, or I'm Henry J, or just Morris. None of this 'Mister' shit. I ain't no sloppy civilian."

"In the MPs at Cherry Point we called each other Mister," Doyle said. He managed not to stammer saying it.

"This ain't no MPs, Corporal Doyle. This is the fucking grunts. We're real Marines here and we call each other like it. You better learn about the grunts in a hurry if you want to live."

Doyle's jaw locked. "Listen, PFC, I spent more than two years in a line company in the Fourth Marines. In the past year I've forgotten more about being a grunt than you've had time to learn. Don't you tell me about learning to be a goddam grunt."

Morris shrugged disdainfully. "Whatever you say, Corporal Doyle. You're the honcho." He spat again and looked away.

"You got it, Morris. I'm the honcho. Remember that." Doyle stared up at Morris for a moment. "Now, what I wanted to talk about. I've been out of the grunts for about a year now and I don't understand how things are done here. You've been through three months of this shit. Hunter's a fucking boot who don't know diddly-wop about what's going on. Until I got the feel of what gives here I gotta rely on you. You know what's happening, so you advise me. Got it?"

Morris looked surly. "Wha'dya mean 'advise'?"

"If you see something I don't but I should, tell me. If I'm doing something that is dangerous, or not doing something I should, tell me. Man, we gotta work together if we both expect to get out of here alive. Now do you understand what I mean?"

Morris spat again. "Yeah. Advise." He still didn't look at his fire-team leader.

Morris went to see Sergeant Johnson before going out on the patrol. "I really gotta go on this patrol? Wazza madda, Sergeant Johnny, you don't like me no more? You want old Henry J should get killed? This dip corporal you gave me thinks he's some kind of fucking sloppy civilian. He called me Mister Morris, Jesus H fucking Christ, what kind of thing is that to say to a grunt? And the other man on the patrol is so boot he smells like Lincoln shoe polish, he don't even look like he knows what end of his rifle the bullets come out of." Lincoln shoe polish was the only shoe polish available in the recruit PXs in Marine boot camp. Many Marines firmly believed this distinctive-smelling concoction was available nowhere else in the world.

Johnny Johnson turned a bloodshot eye to Morris. "You gotta go. I never did like you. And Sergeant Zimmerman said him and Doyle were in the same platoon before and Doyle's a good fire-team leader. You wanna call Grady a liar? Then you do it to his face, don't bitch to me about it."

Morris grimaced, spat, and stomped away shaking his head.

Doyle looked at his two men and the PRC-20 radio, trying to decide who should carry it. "I can't give you the radio, Morris," he said, "you're going to be the point. Besides, I need to keep you fresh. You know how to talk on a field radio, Hunter?"

The thin redhead stopped gawking around the company area long enough to shake his head, then continued his rubbernecking.

Doyle stared at the radio as though demanding that it tell him who was to carry it. "I'm not carrying you," he told the radio. "I've been out of the grunts too long, I'm not in that kind of shape anymore. I'd get so beat carrying you, if we ran into some shit I wouldn't know what the hell to do." This was only the first time his men heard Doyle talk to his equipment.

Morris spat and looked surly.

Hunter was still looking around with a bewildered expression. He seemed to have been suddenly transported to a strange place without anybody having told him he was going anywhere.

Corporal Doyle made his decision and gave his first command in a combat zone. "Hunter, you got the prick twenty. Put it on. When we need to use it I'll take the handset from you." Then he prepared to give his second command. "Either of you men throw good?"

Morris dipped his head and, from under his lowered brow, looked at Hunter, who was staring at the radio. "I do," he said at length.

"Great. You carry this." Doyle handed Morris the white phosphorus grenade.

Morris stood looking at the canister like it was a helping of the watery scrambled eggs they got served for morning chow when they were on base. A particularly runny helping that had been dumped straight into his hand. "Shit," Morris said. "I hate fucking Willie Peter."

"All right, if we're saddled up, let's move it out. Morris, the gate's in that direction." Doyle started walking in the direction he indicated, then stopped, looking back at Hunter. "You're carrying the radio," he said. "Pick it up."

"How do I carry it?" Hunter was still looking at the pack arrangement.

"You put your arms through the straps, just like a haversack."

"Oh." Hunter picked up the radio and slipped his arms through the shoulder straps. The radio hung crookedly. He started looking around again.

"Adjust the straps, Hunter."

"Huh? How do I do that?" He pawed feebly at the straps.

"Shit. Didn't they teach you anything?" Doyle showed Hunter how to adjust the radio and hung the handset from the rubber tubing around his helmet so he could hear any transmissions to come over it. "Now let's move it out. Ten-meter intervals."

Morris spat and started walking.

The three-man patrol passed through a narrow opening in the concertina wire fence. At night a plug of concertina filled the opening. During the day it was open and watched over by two bored riflemen. The two guarding it now recognized Doyle and Hunter as being brand new in-country. Doyle and Hunter had to be new. Their uniforms were clean, their boots weren't caked red from the dirt and mud, and their skin hadn't been baked bronze by the relentless sun. The two guards grinned at each other and shook their heads.

"Sorry to see more good Marines have to get wasted out there," one of them said.

"You got it," the other answered. "Lost five patrols that came through here in the last two days."

"No we didn't," said the first. "It was six went out and got carried back in body bags."

"Fuck you and the horse you rode in on," Morris muttered at them.

"Oh, shit." Doyle's eyes widened. "I'm gonna kill that sergeant major if I live through this. I'm gonna find his ass wherever he is and blow him the fuck away. I'm too goddam short, I don't need this shit."

The broad path they followed meandered through four hundred meters of lush vegetation before emptying into a densely packed dirt path and a grass-shack village that was deeply shaded by high trees. The three Marines were immediately surrounded by a pack of small children who pulled on them and shouted, "Hey, Ma'dine, you souvenir me can'y." "I want ciga'det." "You want boom-boom my sista? She numba one fuck."

"Di-di mau, di-di mau," Doyle shouted at the children; get away from here. He danced a sidestep, avoiding them, and pushed on the ones who strayed too near. "Don't let 'em get close to you," he shouted at the other men.

The children scattered, shouting, "Hey, Ma'dine, you numba ten." "You jive-ass dumb fuck." "Me sista no boom-boom you."

"What'cha doing?" Morris asked. "They're just little kids. I'd of give 'em candy."

"Bullshit. Haven't you heard about these gook kids being booby-trapped and blowing Marines away?"

Morris screwed up his face and spat into a patch of undergrowth. Hunter looked around. He still didn't seem to have any idea where he was or what he was supposed to do there.

Five meters away two teenage girls and an old woman sat behind a table in front of a thatch-roofed hootch with corrugated tin sides. They were giggling. On their table sat rows of Coca-Cola and beer bottles side by side with cartons of black-market cigarettes and dolls dressed in *ao dais*, the traditional Vietnamese formal dress. One of the girls stopped giggling and called to them, "Hey, Ma'dine, you want buy Co-Cola, beer, ciga'det, geisha doll?"

Morris and Hunter wandered over to the table to examine the merchandise. "How much?" Morris asked, pointing at a bottle of Ba Moui Ba, the premium Vietnamese beer. "I'm thirsty."

"Get away from there," shouted Doyle.

"Say what?"

"Get the fuck away from that table," Doyle shouted. "If you're thirsty, drink from your canteen."

Morris leaned toward Doyle. "You got a problem, man?"

"I don't, but you will if you drink a Coke that has battery acid in it, or a beer with ground glass."

Hunter picked up one of the dolls.

"Put that down, boot," Doyle shrieked at him. "Sometimes the Vee Cee put explosives in them."

Hunter looked up quizzically.

"We're not buying anything," Doyle snapped at the old lady and the two girls. "Move it out," he said to his men. "We're going to the left."

Morris spat again. He was disgusted.

Hunter simply walked in the direction he was told to. All he understood was that a corporal told him to do something, so he did it.

One of the duties of daytime security patrols in the Chu Lai, Tam Ky area was to check the ID cards of all men, regardless of age, and all women between late teens and middle age. Anyone without an ID card was presumed to be VC and would be taken prisoner and returned to Chu Lai. Neither Ortega nor Zimmerman had told Doyle how he was to accomplish this. They hadn't told him what a South Vietnamese ID card looked like, either. They did tell him, though, that *can couc* was Vietnamese for ID card. The next person the patrol saw was an elderly Vietnamese man walking toward them.

"Cover him, Morris," Doyle ordered. He signaled the elderly man closer and clearly enunciated, *"Can couc."*

The elderly man grinned through the stumps of betel-nut-blackened teeth, bowed and pointed with his wrists at a plastic laminated card suspended from a cord around his neck and started bobbing his head. He didn't gesture with his hands because he didn't have any.

"Huh," Doyle huhed. "He's probably not Vee Cee, is he?" he asked Morris. Looking closer at the card, he asked, "Is this a South Vietnamese ID card?"

Morris looked at the card. "I think so." He paused before continuing, "I've seen this old man before. He used to be a Vee Cee. When he told them he wanted out, they chopped off his hands so he could never bear arms against them. That's what I heard."

"Oh." Doyle bowed sheepishly to the elderly Vietnamese. "Okay, papa-san, sorry to bother you. So long."

The man continued grinning around his black tooth stumps and bobbing his head.

"How do I tell him he can go?"

"You don't. We go."

"Oh. All right. Move it out."

The old man stood where he was, grinning and nodding at the Marines' receding backs.

During the next twenty minutes the patrol examined twelve more IDs. So far as they could tell, all were legitimate. Every villager they stopped grinned and bowed, and most of them giggled as well. Then the Marines reached the end of the village.

Just like that. No "You are now leaving . . ." signs, no petering out of hootches. The hootches and trees simply stopped. They didn't go any farther. A kilometer or more of open rice paddies stretched to a distant treeline. Morris started following the trail into the paddies.

"Hold up, Morris. I want to check the map again." Doyle drew the topological map from the inside pocket of his shirt and stared first at it then at the paddies. "This don't look right. Look at the map, it shows green at the end of the village." He held the map out for Morris's examination. "That means trees. Paddies are water, they should show up blue. Think we took a wrong turn someplace?" His eyes carefully swept the open land.

"I don't think so. This looks like the same place we ran a patrol a week ago."

"You crossed these paddies?"

Morris nodded.

"How big was the patrol?"

"Squad."

"Squad." Doyle's eyes continued sweeping the paddies.

"There's only three of us. I don't think we should cross these paddies with only three men. We get hit out there we're fucked."

Morris looked at the open area. Map reading had not been one of his best subjects in Infantry Training Regiment, but he understood open area. "I think the pagoda we're supposed to go to is in those trees over there."

Hunter waited quietly while Doyle and Morris talked. Hunter looked disoriented.

Doyle shook his head. "I still think it's too dangerous for a three-man patrol to cross those paddies. What do you think, Morris?"

"I donno. What do you think?"

"What do you think, Hunter?"

Hunter was staring up into the tops of the tall trees at the edge of the village.

"Hunter, what are you looking at?" Doyle and Morris looked up into the trees.

"They're so tall."

"What?"

"The trees. They're so tall."

Doyle's head slowly dropped until his eyes met Morris's.

Morris's head had to drop a little farther until his eyes met Doyle's.

Slowly, they shook their heads. For once they understood each other. Where was Hunter's mind, anyway? Where did he think he was?

So Doyle made another command decision. He was not going to risk his life leading a three-man patrol across a kilometer of open paddies. His patrol would stay in the village and conduct a search for VC and weapons.

The village, whose name Doyle never did learn, was long and narrow, hemmed between the high ground on that side of Chu Lai and the paddy lands. One main path ran along its length, and smaller paths feeding off the main path led to hootches that were mostly two or three deep away from the main path. Most of the hootches were bamboo and thatch, though some were old adobe brick. Some of the brick hootches were fronted with something like stucco. A few of them had Vietnamese slogans stenciled on them. Some had dragons or Buddhas painted on their sides. As rice villages went, it was prosperous. Of course, Doyle didn't know that.

Everywhere the Marines went the people grinned, bowed, and nodded. Some of them giggled. Everyone deferred to the Marines—as soon as they figured out what they wanted. Unlike when the patrol entered the village, the children did not mob them. These Marines were acting strangely. No one else had wandered through the village like this, looking into people's houses and storage bunkers. No one else kicked through the straw thatching laid out to dry, looking for hidden weapons.

Doyle heard the children use a strange expression, one he hadn't heard before. Some of them whispered to each other something that sounded like "dinky dau." Later he learned that *dien dau* means crazy.

After a couple of hours shambling through the village and mildly disrupting the lives of the people—it was only a mild disruption because even though they were visited in a suspicious manner by warriors, the villagers didn't have to put up with any of the real nuisances of war like murder, rape, and pillage— Doyle looked at his watch and decided it was time to start heading back to Chu Lai.

About time, thought Morris.

Hunter just did as he was told.

I hate having to go back by the same trails we came out on, thought Doyle. They had taught him in the 4th Marines that guerrillas would set an ambush on a trail you'd used, hoping you'd be dumb enough to return that way.

Neither Doyle nor Morris even considered asking Hunter what he thought.

The old woman and two teenage girls were still seated at the table in front of the tin-sided hootch. The small children started to mob the three Marines again, then recognized them and wandered away, chattering to each other and making angry gestures at the Marines.

Doyle signaled Morris to turn onto the wide trail leading back to the gate. Morris did as he was told.

"Who'zat?" Hunter suddenly asked, animated for the first time.

"Where?" Doyle turned back to Hunter, then looked where the redhead was looking.

Maybe three hundred meters farther along the main village trail, past a treeless area, several armed, green-clad men were gathered in the shade of a lonely tree.

"I don't know," Doyle said. "Who do you think they are, Morris?"

"I donno. Looks like another one of our patrols."

"Think they're not Vee Cee?"

"Don't look like gooks to me."

Doyle stared at the others for a moment. "Guess they don't. Let's get closer for a better look, anyway. Spread out and stagger it."

Morris grimaced and spat, then led off in the new direction.

Doyle let Morris get farther ahead and more to his left than he had earlier and positioned Hunter to his own left rear. One mortar round couldn't get all three of them, and if they had to, they could all fire straight ahead without worrying about hitting each other.

The several men clarified into six. Two of them languidly watched the approaching patrol. None of them were wearing helmets, though helmets were visible. They were drinking from bottles. By the time Doyle and his men were halfway to the sextet, the strangers were recognizable as Marines.

"Second squad," Morris said a little later.

"What?"

"They're from second squad. Another patrol from our platoon."

"What the fuck they doing there?"

"Taking a break. Drinking beer," Morris said dryly.

It *was* a patrol from second squad and they were indeed taking a break and drinking beer. Morris introduced Doyle and Hunter to them.

"New guys, huh," said the one identified as "Smiff." He was a huge man, six-foot-four and close to two hundred forty pounds, none of it fat. A corporal, he was the squad leader. Smith had decided to take out his squad's patrol himself, leaving behind only his two men who were in the worst shape.

A second man from the squad stepped up to Doyle and looked straight into his eyes. He didn't have to look down. "And you people call me fucking Mouse," he said and shook his head. "See this, Smiff?" he said over his shoulder. "They do too make Marines as small as me."

Smith looked at the two short Marines. "He's from the Old Corps, Mouse. Nobody grew as big as me when he enlisted."

"Bullshit, Smiff. The Gunny's almost as big as you, and I'll bet he signed up before Doyle did."

"Almost as big as me, but he ain't as big as me." Smith looked away and took another pull at his Ba Moui Ba.

The other four Marines in Smith's patrol ignored all of this. They were more interested in napping or drinking their beer. Or both.

"Where'd you get the beer?" Morris asked.

"Old papa-san over there." Smith jerked a thumb toward an old man who was partly hidden by a small masonry structure thirty meters distant.

"I'm gonna get a beer. Anybody else?"

"Is it safe?" Doyle asked Smith.

Hunter was gawking around like a sightseer.

Smith shrugged. "I guess so."

"What if there's battery acid in it?"

Smith held the bottle in front of his eyes and looked through it. "Wrong color. Anyway, before you open it you hold the bottle upside down. Then if the cork in the cap is eaten away when you open it, you don't drink it, you kill whoever sold it to you instead."

"What about ground glass?"

"Then you die." Smith shook his head. "At least you ain't humping out in the fucking bush no more."

Morris came back with three open bottles. He held one out to Doyle and another to Hunter.

"Did you check the corks?" Doyle asked.

Morris looked at Doyle like he didn't understand. "No."

"I don't want it."

Hunter grinned a lopsided grin, took the offered beer and drank from it.

Mouse tossed his empty. "He don't want it, I'll take it."

"It's yours." Morris handed the bottle over.

"Much obliged, pano. Where'd you find him?" Mouse jerked his head toward Doyle.

"New guy. Came over by ship, landed at Da Nang yesterday. Old peacetime grunt. Been an MP the last year."

Mouse studied Doyle for a moment. "Man's been an MP for longer'n I been in this bad Green Machine, before that he was a grunt? He shook his head. "Good luck, pano."

Nine Marines, mostly sitting but a few standing, in the shade of a lone tree. Only one looked around alertly.

"You got any observation posts?" Doyle asked Smith.

Smith sat leaning back against the tree trunk. His soft cover was hanging low over his eyes. He didn't bother looking up. "Don't need 'em. Anybody come at us here, we can see 'em a long way off."

"But nobody's watching."

"You are."

Corporal Doyle chewed on his lower lip for a moment, his head continually swiveling, eyes taking in everything. He didn't know where he was or who the black-pajama-clad little people dotting the landscape were. All he knew was he didn't think it was safe where he was.

"Morris, Hunter, saddle up," Doyle said when his men finished their beer. "See you back in the company area, Smiff."

Smith waved a desultory hand at Doyle.

Soon the three were back at the narrow gate in the wire. The same two bored grunts were sitting in the shade above it.

"Hey, my man, you superstitious?" asked one.

"Nah," the other answered. He was laying back with an arm over his eyes. "Never me. Why?"

" 'Cause we got ghosts coming by."

"Boo-shee-ick."

"No shit, man. Look. It's that patrol what went out a few hours ago. They coming back in on their own feet 'stead of in body bags. Gotta be ghosts."

The second Marine uncovered his eyes and turned his head toward the trail. "You dreaming, man. I don't see nobody. Ain't no ghosts there."

"I see 'em, you don't see 'em. Gotta be ghosts."

"Fuck you and the horse you rode in on," Morris muttered at the two as he passed them.

Doyle glared at the guards. "Fuck off, screws," he snarled.

Hunter didn't seem to hear any of this. He simply looked like he was wondering where he was.

But that's the way it was early in that war. Nobody told the grunts anything. Nothing except, ''Go here, do that.'' Never why or what the circumstances were. Just get off the ship or the airplane and go to work at the war.

Good Morning, Vietnam!

"NORMALLY, SON, WARS ARE RUN BY GENERALS, WHO ADMIN-
ister them and do the strategic planning. Below them are colonels and lieutenant colonels, who see to the managing and
tactical planning. Next comes lieutenants and sergeants, who
are like the foremen doing the actual supervising of the workers,
who are the privates and PFCs doing the fighting.

"Vietnam wasn't like that, though. In Vietnam, most of the
generals were trying to run the war like they were graduates of
the Harvard Business School or the Wharton School. They were
being entrepreneurs and big-time spenders who had an unshak-
able belief that if they walked in like Texas oil millionaires,
they'd just blow the pants off those half-primitive Vietnamese
and get them to surrender most ricky-tick. From the level of the
foot soldier, the colonels and lieutenant colonels looked like
they were trying to rack up as many operations on their records
as they could get with no regard for the effect that it had on the
progress of the war and the continued living of the troops. The
more successful operations a colonel or lieutenant colonel had
on his record, the more likely he was to become a general.

"Most of the time, the actual war in Vietnam was run by the
lieutenants and sergeants, who should have been straw-bossing.
The captains were in charge on big operations and company-
size patrols. But this was such a screwy war, not having any

front lines or secure rear areas, fighting an enemy who was almost too hard to tell from the civilians, that we had to do a lot of small-unit actions. This is where the lieutenants and sergeants had to be in charge. You send out a platoon, there ain't no captain or colonel with it. A squad goes out, the top man is a sergeant—or maybe a corporal or maybe even a lower-ranking man.

"This ain't too hard for the Marines to deal with, because Marines all the time get trained to function in units as small as four-man fire teams, and a lot of those four-man teams are only three men. But the lieutenants are like the colonels—they want to get promoted. Sergeants and corporals that are lifers want to get promoted, too. The rest of us just want to stay alive. It's a truth of war that the best way for you to stay alive is to make the man on the other side die.

"But killing and dying ain't always what war is about. Sometimes the idea is to keep someone alive so you can get information from him that'll help you keep your ownself alive. Third platoon got one of them assignments one day. We were in a fire base a few klicks outside of Chu Lai and spent some time working with a Popular Forces platoon—not that we liked them or wanted to work with them; we were ordered to. Well, the PF lieutenant came to the skipper one day and gave him a list of people in a different ville from the one he lived in and said they were all Vee Cee or Vee Cee sympathizers. The skipper passed that list up to battalion, and three days later they called him and Haupt the Kraut and the PF lieutenant in for a meeting. They came back down from that meeting with orders for third platoon to pull a dawn raid on that ville and bring back the people on the list.

"The plan was for us to leave the fire base about oh-three-hundred in the morning and get in position to walk in right at sunrise, catch some of the people in it when they were waking up, and wake up the rest of them. This way it was pretty certain we'd get all the people on the list. Any of them we didn't get were probably Vee Cee that ain't got back from whatever they were doing that night they shouldn't have been doing. If we were real sharp about it, none of them would have a chance to escape before we got them.

"Haupt the Kraut took the squad leaders and most of the team leaders on a recon partway to the ville that afternoon. They didn't go all the way, and the whole platoon didn't go, because Haupt and the skipper didn't want to do nothing that might make the people in that ville suspicious. When they came back, the squad leaders got together with their men and gave us the scoop on the terrain and the route we'd be following in the morning. After that we all had a hard time getting any sleep because we knew we were gonna be out in the bush a couple hours before dawn. That was a time we knew Charlie liked to be out there setting ambushes and booby traps and sniping at our lines.

"At oh-three-hundred we were all putting camouflage paint on our faces and the backs of our hands and making sure all of our gear was secured down tight so we wouldn't make any noise going through the bush. We were wearing soft hats for this one because helmets cut down on your hearing and make noises of their own. At oh-three-thirty the squad leaders lined us all up and gave us a final checkout in the dark, including making each man jump up and down to see if he made any noise. Then we moved out into the night.

"Our movement was slow and easy. We had close to two hours to go a couple klicks and get into position. No need to rush ourselves. There wasn't any moon that night, but the sky was clear and the stars were shining down bright. Ain't no air pollution or smog in that part of the tropics, and the sky is clearer than anything you ever see up here in the industrial Northeast. The stars were giving us plenty of light to see by— almost like the full moon does here. The land we moved through was fairly open and we could see a good piece. If anybody was out there with us, they weren't moving—we'd have seen them if they were. Closer to the ville the brush started growing a bit higher and thicker, and we had to start picking our way more carefully and going slower. Even so, at the end, when we settled down to wait, we still had maybe fifteen, twenty minutes before dawn. The false dawn was already up and past.

"The ville we were raiding had a hedgerow fence with two openings in it. There was the main gate and a back one. Haupt was at the main gate with second squad and a machine-gun team. Staff Sergeant Ortega and third squad was at the back gate. First was in reserve with Sergeant Zimmerman. Second and third squads were in contact with Haupt by prick-six radios.

When the lieutenant gave the word, the two squads were to go in by the different gates, preventing anyone from getting out them. The gun team'd stay at the main gate while the rest of the platoon made the sweep.

"When Haupt gave the order to go in, it was still a little dark. By the time we reached the first hootches the sun was edging over the horizon. It was weird, walking into a ville at dawn like that. Nobody was up yet and the place looked deserted—for about a minute. Those people used the sun for their alarm clocks. All of a sudden surprised-looking villagers was coming out of their hootches. Some of them tried to ignore us and go about their morning business, but we wouldn't let them go out of the gates to the riverbank to take their morning craps, so some of the men just went to the hedgerow fence and took a piss right there. The women were screwed—they weren't gonna drop trou with us standing there, so they had to hold it.

"Each squad had a sector of the ville to search. The squad leaders broke us into fire teams and the teams checked into each hootch as they went by them. Every person got stopped and asked for *can couc*. Wasn't long before Buster Bahls said, 'This is one of them,' and I grabbed the gook whose ID card Buster was looking at. Chief Runningstar looped a piece of rope around his wrists and tied the gook's hands together real tight. Ortega looped a come-along cord around the prisoner's neck and dragged him along behind us. Over in Smiff's second squad, Mouse caught another one of the suspects. Every fire team caught at least one of the people on the list, except for Corporal Doyle's team. Doyle acted like he was trying to avoid all contact. Nobody was surprised at Doyle doing that, but he had Malcolm X and Gant and they were a couple bad-assed grunts and they should have wanted to kick some ass. But it was okay. Everybody was a bit worried that Doyle being so scared of being where he was, he might try to waste anyone he found who was on the list instead of taking them prisoner like he was supposed'a do and accidentally zap one of us doing it.

"When we got the prisoners all together and were about to leave the ville, the headman got into a shouting match with the PF lieutenant about what was we doing with his people. Our gook outshouted the ville's gook, which had to be easy because our gook had a whole platoon of Marines backing him up and all the local guy had was a bunch of old people and women—weren't many men of military age there.

"The five men we took had their hands tied behind their backs and were strung together by come-along cords around their necks. When we left that place, we were feeling mighty good about taking five prisoners without having to do any shooting or getting any of us shot up.

"Halfway back to the fire base we had us some real excitement. The point passed through some trees and started shouting about they see some people running away from us across the cane fields. We all scrambled through the trees pretty hurry-up quick and we saw a half-dozen armed gooks about two hundred meters away running like the devil was on their tails. Haupt yells for us to fire over their heads to make them stop.

"The whole platoon started firing around them gooks, but all they did was duck low and run even harder. By now they were more than halfway to a treeline five hundred meters from us. If they reached it, they were home free, so some of us lowered our sights and zinged some rounds right into them. We did that and half of the bunch dropped like they been hit, even though only two of them were. The rest of them kept going until the machine gun laid a string of tracers right in front of them. Then they screeched to a halt, dropped their weapons and stood with their hands on top of their heads.

"When we got the new people in, they all started crying about how they were PFs from another ville and they were running because they were late for their formation and their lieutenant was going to have their asses if we didn't let them go right now so they could make it on time. Bullshit. Our gook didn't believe him because he said he knew all the PFs in the area. So instead of five prisoners, we went back to the fire base with eleven, two of whom were wounded.

"Back at the fire base a helicopter came in and we threw the prisoners on it. Then they were handed over to the Arvins for questioning and we never did hear what was learned from them or if they were Vee Cee or what happened to them after the questioning. All I can do is guess, and what I heard of the way Arvins treated prisoners, probably none of them ever made it back to that ville. At least they didn't make it back whole and unharmed. The Arvin interrogators presumed anybody brought to them was guilty until proved innocent.''

Chapter Five

Half an hour before nightfall four Vietnamese dressed in olive-drab shirts and black silk trousers squatted in their tire-soled Ho Chi Minh sandals apart from the two Marines inside the barbed-wire compound. Three of the Vietnamese cradled M-1 carbines in their arms, the fourth struggled to balance a Browning Automatic Rifle. The Marines were discussing them, and the Vietnamese knew it, even though they couldn't understand the words being used.

"Goddammit, Staff Sergeant Ortega, it's bad enough I got to take a patrol out tonight. Why do I have to take these gooks with me?" Sergeant Johnson asked.

"They're not gooks, Sergeant Johnson," Ortega said, "they're Vietnamese Popular Forces. We're working with them to train them how to defend their own homes. This is part of our 'Hearts and Minds' program."

Johnson hawked into the dirt. "I don't give a good goddam who they are. They're Vietnamese civilians and they're armed. I don't want to take them on my fucking patrol."

"They're militia, kind of like the National Guard." Ortega's voice was patient. "Think of them that way."

"Right, the National Guard. All right, they're the reservists. We saw on Operation Scythe how dependable the regulars are—

the fucking Arvins ran on us. Why should I think the reservists are any better?''

"They're defending their own villes, that's why." Ortega's patience was beginning to wear.

"There's Vee Cee in these villes, Ortega. How do we know these gooks aren't Vee Cee?" Johnson demanded.

Rapid singsong words came from the Vietnamese when they heard "Vee Cee."

"Cool it, Johnson," Ortega snapped. "You're upsetting them."

"Upsetting *them*? How the fuck do you think *I* feel?" Johnson waved his arms.

"They aren't Charlie. They're Popular Forces and they're going on your patrol."

Johnson shook his head. "I've heard too damn many stories about these PFs being Vee Cee in disguise and turning on the Marines they were patrolling with."

"I've heard those tales, too, but I haven't heard any official confirmation of them and I don't believe those stories. They go with you."

"I don't want them."

Ortega punched his hands onto his hips and leaned slightly forward, staring into Johnson's eyes. "Do I have a rocker under my stripes, Sergeant Johnson?"

"Yes, you do, Staff Sergeant Ortega." Johnson stared back.

"Do you have a rocker under your stripes, Sergeant?"

"No, I don't, Staff Sergeant."

"That means I have rank on you, doesn't it, Sergeant?"

"Yes, it does, Staff Sergeant."

"Then you're going to do what I say, aren't you, Sergeant?"

Johnson swallowed before answering. "Yes, I am, Staff Sergeant. And you just remember whose orders I was following if these gooks turn on my patrol out there."

"I'll remember that, Sergeant. And you remember whose orders you were following if you run into some shit and they save your dumb ass for you." The two stared at each other for a moment longer. "You've got your patrol orders, Sergeant Johnson. Now do this thing."

"Aye aye, Staff Sergeant Ortega." Johnson spun on his heel and stomped to where his squad awaited its orders.

"Third squad up!" Johnson shouted to his men. Third squad gathered in a half circle in front of him. "We've got a night patrol and we've got some company. A PF squad is going with us."

"The hell you say," Buster Bahls muttered.

"Bullshit. I don't be going on no fucking night patrol with a bunch of goddam gooks," Malcolm Evans swore.

"Hey, man, you dinky dau or something?" Tony Salatu asked.

"Oh, shit," Corporal Doyle said, and shivered.

"No shit, we're taking the gooks with us," Johnson said. "Patrol order is first team with Hunter on the point, second team is next with the gooks behind Runningstar and in front of Morris. Third team brings up the rear." He looked closely at Morris and lowered his voice. "You keep your piece on full auto and aimed straight ahead of you. If we run into any shit out there the first thing I want you to do is blow them the fuck away. Do not return fire at anyone until you've wasted those PFs. Do you understand me? I don't want to take any chance of those little fuckers turning on us in a fire fight."

Morris grinned. "Keep my piece on full auto and aimed straight ahead. If we run into any shit, I zap me four zips before I return fire at anybody. I got'cha, Honcho. We run into any shit, those PFs is dead."

"Good man, Morris." Johnson slapped Morris on the helmet. "I know I can depend on you. Everybody," he turned to the rest of the squad, "check your weapons and gear, paint your faces, tie everything down, soft covers. Then get ready to saddle up. We move out in half an hour."

Not long after sunset a fifteen-man patrol moved quietly out of the compound. In the middle of it was a four-man Popular Forces squad that was tagged for death in event of trouble. When the Marines didn't know who they could trust with their lives, they didn't trust anybody.

"Squad leaders up!" Sergeant Zimmerman called from near third platoon's CP bunker. "Bring your team leaders with you."

Lieutenant Haupt and Staff Sergeant Ortega, the platoon sergeant, sat on folding chairs at a small camp table standing next to the bunker. They were bent over a map spread on the table. Zimmerman joined them in studying the map. In minutes they were joined by the three squad leaders and seven of the platoon's eight fire-team leaders. Haupt looked at them.

"Where's the Womper, Smiff?" Haupt asked. Corporal Wompole, "the Womper," was second squad's first-team leader.

"Out there on a patrol with his team." Sergeant Smith waved his arm toward the hidden paddy land to the east.

Haupt grunted. "Right. You'll have to fill him in on this later. Everyone take a look at the map. Here's our fire base." He tapped the map. "Over here two grid squares is Cam Ty village." His finger moved. "Lieutenant Nguyen of the Popular Forces says five people living in it are known Vee Cee or Vee Cee sympathizers. Battalion wants us to pull a dawn raid on Cam Ty tomorrow and bring them in. Squad leaders and one team leader per squad will go with Sergeant Zimmerman and me on a recon. Squad leaders, pick your team leader, then get your helmets, rifles, and cartridge belts. Be back here in ten minutes. We're going for a short walk in the sun and scope the situation out. Dismissed."

Those ten minutes passed and Haupt led an eight-man recon patrol out of the compound. Ortega stayed behind in charge of the remainder of the platoon. The patrol went west through the low, lightly forested hills that overlooked the treelines separating the paddies. They watched closely for booby traps but had little concern about ambushes—the Marines owned the days in that area. Somewhat more than a kilometer from the fire base they turned north until they reached a hill higher than its neighbors. Haupt stopped the patrol near the hill's top.

"There it is, people," the lieutenant said, "Cam Ty. Sit down and observe. This is as close as we go for now. I don't want anybody down there seeing us and guessing what we're doing here."

Four hundred meters to the northwest was a small hamlet containing maybe fifteen thatch hootches. A few women and children could be seen moving about in it over the hedgerow fence surrounding the hootches. A large opening in the fence facing to the south was the main entrance to the hamlet. Smaller openings in the northern corners made secondary entrances. Beyond these secondary gates a lower hedgerow surrounded the mounds dotting the hamlet's graveyard.

Haupt and the others watched for a few minutes, examining the land between their hill and the hedgerow with the eyes of experienced infantry.

"At the crack of dawn, first squad will go through the main gate," Haupt said. "Second will take the small entrance on the northeast, and third will enter through the other one. Sergeant Zimmerman is drawing a layout of where the hootches are. We'll gather all the villagers in one place and first squad will check their *can coucs*. Second and third squads will then search the hootches for anyone hiding from us. Each team leader will be carrying a list of names to match against the *can coucs*. Hopefully, nobody down there will be armed and we can gather our prisoners without any trouble."

He looked at the platoon guide. Zimmerman nodded back and held up a sheet of paper.

"Gather around Grady and take a look at his layout, then match it with what you see down below. The better we know what we're doing down there tomorrow morning, the less chance of anybody getting away or any of us getting hurt."

Soon the six squad NCOs were confident they knew where they would be going in the morning, and Haupt led them back to the fire base by a different route.

At a quarter to three the following morning the squad leaders were checking their men for the night movement that would bring them to Cam Ty. Rifle straps were removed and swivels taped to stocks to eliminate noise. Bayonet and knife scabbards were tied tightly to thighs. All gear hung on cartridge belts was snug. Most of the men wore rain hats, though some had on bush hats. No bandoleers were slung over shoulders. Grenades were tucked into the inside pockets of shirts. Three shades of dull green greasepaint daubed faces and necks, backs of hands and exposed forearms, breaking outlines and dulling shiny skin. Each man in turn jumped in place for his squad leader, demonstrating that he made no metallic noises.

"First squad ready," the reports started. "Second squad all okay." "Third squad ready to go."

Haupt peered through the starlit darkness at his platoon. "Got your radios?" he asked the squad leaders. They replied in the affirmative. He turned to Lieutenant Nguyen. "This is a good platoon. We'll get those people if they're there."

Haupt looked over his platoon again, and when he was satisfied that everyone was ready, said, "Corporal Smith, move it out."

"Mouse, take the point," Smith said. "I'll be right behind you if you get lost. Go."

Mouse turned toward the machine-gun guarded, zigzag opening in the barbed wire and took his rifle off safety.

Second squad headed out of the compound, followed by Haupt, Ortega, Nguyen, and the platoon radioman. Third followed them, then a machine-gun team. Zimmerman and first squad brought up the rear.

The route through the wooded hills paralleled the previous afternoon's. If anybody had seen them then and placed booby traps along that route, Haupt didn't want to walk into them. The movement was slow and easy. No hurry—they had two and a half hours to cover two kilometers and get into position before sunup. Downhill, through the trees, starlight sparkled on the rice paddies. None of the men liked the night movement or going through the trees, but they felt it would be far worse to be in the paddies where they could be easily seen. And being able to see the paddies were empty of people gave the Marines a sense of confidence.

The platoon stopped on the high hill where some of them had watched Cam Ty during the day. Haupt had everyone observe the open land between the hill and the hamlet before giving the signal to move on. Crouched low and stepping carefully, they moved swiftly along the paddy dikes to the northeast opening in the hedgerow. Ortega and second squad stopped there while the rest of the platoon moved between the hamlet and its graveyard to the northwest gate. Zimmerman and third squad stopped there, and Haupt led first squad, the gun team, and the Popular Forces lieutenant, to the main entrance.

At three places around Cam Ty the Marines lay down and the squad leaders waited with their radios next to their ears for Haupt's signal. Third platoon had moved quietly enough that none of the dogs in the hamlet heard them and set off an alarm. The night was silent.

The lieutenant had his watch set carefully and knew the moment the sun would appear over the horizon. That moment was when the Marines would enter the sleeping hamlet.

Haupt watched the sweep hand on his wristwatch. To his right the sky was lightening. Three minutes before the sun peeked over the horizon he depressed the clicker on his radio handset. "Red Apple, all Red Apples, this is Actual," he said into the handset. "On your feet, prepare to move in."

At three places around the hedgerow, tense squads rose to their feet and edged toward the openings in the hedge.

Haupt stared at his watch face. "Red Apples, go," he finally said.

The squads rushed inside the hedgerow and lined up along it. The top edge of the sun appeared on the horizon, and they started moving toward the nearest hootches. The noise of awakening people came out of the hootches and people began emerging from them. These first risers started at the sight of the Marines, then attempted to go about their morning routines, but the Marines stopped them and herded them together in the center of the hamlet. Other Marines stood at the sides of hootch doorways and yelled into them *"Lai dai, lai dai,"*—come here, come here. Reluctantly, looking confused, the villagers moved out of their homes and assembled in the area the Marines indicated. They were lined up and made to present their identification cards to first squad. Second and third were going through the hootches, searching them for weapons and making certain everyone was rousted from them.

"What we got here?" Buster Bahls stood inside the door of the second hootch his team was searching. A middle-aged man cowered half hidden behind a chest in a corner. *"Lai dai*, papa-san, *lai dai*. Henry J, cover him. Chief, poke behind everything, see if anybody else is hiding in here."

Morris moved to the back wall of the hootch and pointed his rifle at the man. Runningstar rummaged through the small room that was the interior of the hut.

The middle-aged man didn't move from his hiding place. The muzzle of Morris's rifle gestured.

"Lai dai," Bahls repeated more harshly.

Slowly, hands held high, the man stood, then he scampered to Bahls with his hands behind his head.

"Can couc," Bahls demanded.

Bobbing slightly, in a bowing motion, the middle-aged Viet-namese moved one hand from his head to his shirt pocket, with-drew a laminated card, and handed it over. Bahls looked at the name on the card and checked the list he carried.

Bahls leveled his M-14 at the man. "He's on the list. Henry J, frisk him. Chief, help me cover this son of a bitch."

Runningstar turned from the search to point his rifle from the hip while Morris ran his hands over the Vietnamese's body. The prisoner was unarmed.

Handing a cord over, Bahls said, "Tie his hands behind his back."

Morris tied them so tightly the man grimaced in pain. He grimaced again when Bahls grabbed him and roughly threw him out of the hootch to Sergeant Zimmerman, who was standing nearby.

"Got one, Grady," Bahls said.

"Good," Zimmerman replied, "and I got a come-along just for him." He pulled a noosed cord from his shirt pocket, and looping it around the short man's neck, drew it snug. A jerk on the cord and the prisoner followed Zimmerman to the middle of the hamlet.

Another of the five people on the list, a young woman, had been found among the people gathered there. The come-along cord on the one prisoner was tied to the cord around the other's neck.

The hamlet chief was arguing with Lieutenant Nguyen and both men were shouting and waving their arms. The only words they used the Marines could understand were "Vee Cee," which were repeated frequently; the headman shook his head vehe-mently every time he said it, Nguyen nodded vigorously when-ever he did. The argument was interrupted by a loud voice from the side.

"Yo, Grady, what you disappear for, man? You take these three and we'll go find the other two."

All heads turned toward the voice of PFC Evans. He was walking toward the group, prodding a bound man with his fixed bayonet. Doyle and Gant were with him. Each of them was also escorting a bound, frightened prisoner—one of the prisoners was a middle-aged woman. The villagers chattered nervously among themselves at the sight. The Marines grinned and yelled at Doyle and his men.

"Two of 'em was hiding in one hootch we searched, Grady," Doyle beamed at Zimmerman. "We caught the other one when she was trying to sneak out the side gate we came in."

Zimmerman stared at Doyle for a moment, then grinned at the other members of the squad. "What'd I say? Didn't I tell you he was a good Marine?" Then he looped come-alongs around the newcomers' necks and linked them with the other two.

All of the platoon's wounded except Casebolt were back from the hospital, and no one was on R&R, so Sergeant Johnson had reorganized his squad. He reunited Bahls and Morris, and giving the two black former gang members to the timid Corporal Doyle appealed to his sense of humor. Also, he thought they would have the best chance of surviving Doyle's leadership. But now he thought maybe Doyle wouldn't be so bad, after all.

"Should'a seen this dude," Evans crowed. "We goed into this hootch where them two gooks was holding hands and hiding, and Doyle just slammed 'em up against the wall and frisked their asses like he be Jack Webb or Sergeant Friday or somebody."

"I think he would of wasted their asses without even thinking about it if they blinked the wrong fucking way when we was tying 'em up," Gant added. "Real bad-fucking-ass back there."

"What about the split-tail?" Morris asked.

"We seen her sneaking along the hedgerow, and Doyle locked and loaded on her ass and told her, "*Lai dai* or fucking die, gook,' " Evans said. "Her eyes got big as goddam milk saucers and she froze where she stood. Doyle let me frisk her—uh, she don't got nice tits—and had me tie her hands before checking her *can couc*."

"If she was trying to get away, she might be Vee Cee even if she's not on the list," Doyle interjected.

"But she is onna list," Gant said. "Hey, my honcho's a real bad-ass when it comes to capturing unarmed suspects."

Doyle shot a look at Gant.

"Be cool, Gant," Haupt said. "Third team got the prisoners. You Marines did a good job."

Nguyen turned to yell at the headman some more, but the

man had backed into the mass of villagers, so he yelled at all of them. "I say them these people Vee Cee, we take them tiger cage, tell who other Vee Cee," he explained to the Marines when he stopped yelling.

Third platoon formed in a column with the prisoners in the middle for the walk back to its fire base and moved out through the main gate of Cam Ty hamlet.

"Hey, they're running," the voice shouted from the platoon's point, just outside the hamlet gate.

"Who's running?" Haupt pounded forward, twisted past the Marines going through the gate.

"Over there." Someone pointed to where a half-dozen people were running across the paddy dikes to the west. Most of them appeared to be women. A man in the middle of the group looked like he was carrying a rifle.

"Put a few warning rounds over their heads," Haupt ordered. "We don't know who they are, so don't shoot them. We'll make them stop with warning shots."

First squad started firing at the running people. The rest of the platoon rushed out of the hamlet, their prisoners forgotten for the moment, and joined in the fire. The fleeing people kept running.

"Where's the gun?" Haupt asked. "Put a burst in front of them."

The gunner put his bipods down and lay behind his gun. One short burst went past the running people, who were now not much more than a hundred meters from a distant treeline. All of them except the man with the rifle dropped into the paddies.

"Everybody cease fire," Haupt ordered. "Put a burst next to him," he told the machine gunner in the momentary silence when the rifles stopped shooting.

The gunner fired a burst that seemed louder than before in the relative silence, and the last runner dropped his rifle and stood with his hands high in the air.

"Second squad, round 'em up and bring 'em in," the tall lieutenant ordered. "You go with them, Nguyen, give orders to the prisoners."

The Vietnamese irregular grinned through deep red betel-nut-stained teeth. "I go with them, yes. Bring back more Vee Cee."

Corporal Smith led his squad and the PF lieutenant across

the paddies at a trot. The other squads and the gun team moved to the sides to be able to give second squad covering fire without having to fire over them. The people in the paddies stayed there, and the lone man stood quietly with his hands above his head.

When second squad reached the cowering women, they bound their hands. They were crying and insisted on showing their ID cards. "We no Vee Cee," one of them kept saying. One fire team continued to where the man stood waiting. He wasn't able to produce a *can couc* and was belligerent.

Following Haupt's directions, Nguyen questioned the women.

"They say man with rifle make them run with him or he shoot them," Nguyen said after the first round of questions. "They say they no know him, he stranger."

Haupt stared harshly at the women. "You Vee Cee," he snapped at them. "You run from Marine, you Vee Cee."

They cried more loudly, and the one who had the English phrase insisted again, "We no Vee Cee, we no Vee Cee."

"Hold them with the others," Haupt said to Ortega. The platoon sergeant motioned for a few Marines to put the women with the other prisoners.

"Ask him why he ran," Haupt told Nguyen.

Nguyen exchanged rapid Vietnamese with the man with the rifle, then said in English, "He say he run because he forgot carry *can couc*."

"Bullshit," Haupt said to the bound man. "You Vee Cee." To Nguyen he said, "Ask him where his *can couc* is."

Another rapid exchange, then Hien said, "He say it at home. He say home Ky Hoa. I say he lie."

"Ask him why he's carrying a carbine."

More Vietnamese words were exchanged, and Nguyen spat in the prisoner's face. "He say he Ky Hoa fay epp. Boo-shee-ick. I know all Ky Hoa fay epp. Ky Hoa fay epp like me, work with Ma-deen. He no fay epp, he Vee Cee."

"Grady, put a come-along on him and link him with the other prisoners," Haupt told Zimmerman. "Take the women's names and let them go." To Nguyen he added, "Tell the women we have their names. If we ever think they lied to us, we can get them."

* * *

The Marines' spirits were high on the way back to their base. They had captured six prisoners without receiving any injuries themselves. The hump wasn't even very bad because they traveled light and would be back long before the full heat of day slammed down. Some of them, the ones with the biggest grudges or the most macho, took turns roughing up the prisoners on the way to the fire base. Others talked.

"Know what pissed me off the most, Buster?" Evans asked.

"Nah, what pissed you off the most, Malcolm X?" Bahls said.

"I don't be shooting over their fucking heads. I tried to hit them and I be missing, that's what pissed me."

Bahls laughed. "I shot over their heads and came closer than you did, boot." Then he became serious. "But if I'd tried to shoot their asses, some of 'em would be dead now."

Behind them, Doyle spat. "I wanted to," he said. "I really wanted to see if I could hit a running target at three hundred and fifty yards." He shook his head. "I'm a fucking Marine rifle expert, I really wanted to see if I could do it, but the Kraut said to shoot over their fucking heads. I had that sucker right in my sights and I raised them."

"You'd have missed them just like the rest of us did," Gant said.

"I don't know." Doyle shook his head again. "Maybe I'm glad I didn't try. I'd be pissed if I tried and missed. Then, we don't know they're Vee Cee, and I'd always wonder if I killed an innocent person."

"Don't sweat the small shit, Doyle," Johnson said. "Ain't nobody in this fucking country innocent. If they ain't Vee Cee, they're sympathizers. If they ain't sympathizers, they don't like us. If it's not that they don't like us, they don't give a good goddam." He shook his head. "Ain't nobody in this stinking country innocent."

Lonely Island Day

"THERE'S THIS BIG RIVER THAT RUNS INTO THE SOUTH CHINA
Sea on the north side of that peninsula the Chu Lai Marine base
was on, the Song something or other, but all Vietnamese rivers
are the Song something or other; *song* is the Vietnamese word
for river. It's a fat-assed river and sort of formed its own delta
of overgrown sand-spit islands and tidal flats. This is in addition
to the regular barrier islands you find along that part of the coast.
Kind of like you find off South Jersey, Maryland, or the Caro-
linas. When you get on them, they even look like that part of
the U.S. east coast, except it's bodacious hot.

"One day when we were between operations, third platoon
got itself sent out on a patrol on one of those islands. Those
islands are sand, and you know what wet sand's like, it sticks
to you. Didn't take long before it felt like we were carrying five
pounds extra on each boot. Made humping harder. The sun was
beating down real hot and evaporating the moisture from the
sand, so we must have been slogged through something like
eighty-five, ninety percent humidity, too. Only good thing about
this patrol is battalion was so sure Charlie wasn't where we were
going, we didn't have to wear flak jackets.

"Remember that time we were in the South Jersey Pine Barrens and I told you to remember what it looked like because one
day I'd tell you about it? This is what I was talking about. We

got into the Pine Barrens and I almost freaked out. Thought I was back in Veeceeland. Looked just like the coastal strip and islands around Chu Lai, except there's no paddy land in South Jersey.

"Anyway, we were humping along whatever island we were on and going in a more or less straight line, following along on paths sometimes and off them when they weren't going the same direction we were, when Lieutenant Haupt ordered the point to change directions and go to the right. He went up front with his map and compass after the point got out of the woods and checked out where we were and where he wanted us to go, then the point set off in another direction and the rest of us followed. It was now about thirteen hundred hours.

"Now we were walking across really wet, hard-packed ground. It was gray and was very fine sand, full of water. We didn't sink into it but did indent it slightly with every step and leave a little puddle in each footprint. At least it wasn't caking to our boots like the inland sand did. All around was treelines. Don't think I said this before, those treelines were like the hedgerows in Europe in World War Two. A ridge of earth sits there anywhere from two feet to seven feet tall with trees growing on top of it, so you don't just walk through it, you have to climb over it. That's what makes treelines good places for ambushes, you got good cover behind them as well as concealment. I felt real shaky walking in the open with all those treelines around and we wasn't checking them out.

"So we came to another treeline and went through it and found ourselves in something that'd make a good set for a Fellini movie. The ground was the same that we had just walked over, but it had stuff growing in it. Clumps of real high reedy-looking grass popped up every here and there, and the place was dotted with these stunty trees. Wasn't real wide, maybe two, three hundred meters from the treeline we came through to the waterline, but I couldn't see how far it went north and south. It was spooky-looking, wouldn't have surprised me too much to see Boris Karloff or Peter Lorre step out of the thin air and say, 'Welcome to my home, gentlemen. Please make yourselves uncomfortable.'

"No one from a fright flick showed up, but there was something else there that jarred us. Sitting in the middle of all this muck was an A-4 Skyhawk. The A-4 was a small attack bomber the Marines loved. It was a real nasty little bugger that could come in real low and slow and put its cannon rounds or bombs right where the grunts needed them. When we got in bad fire fights, sometimes we was happier to see Skyhawks than helicopter gunships.

"So there was this Skyhawk sitting there and there were four Marines sitting on it. I don't know for sure, but later someone told me they were from Three One, so maybe they were. Staff Sergeant Ortega put the platoon into a defensive perimeter around that broken bird while the lieutenant and Sergeant Zimmerman went over to talk to the Marines on the bird. Soon as we were in position, Ortega joined them at the Skyhawk, listened for a minute, then he called, 'Squad leaders up.'

"Johnny Johnson went to the bird with the other squad leaders for the meeting, then called Buster Bahls over. The Ball Buster was back with us. The shrapnel wounds he took all up and down his left side from that mortar round on Braxton Hill healed up real nice in that hospital. Now I stopped watching outboard and turned to see what was happening there because anything that involved the old Ball Buster was sure as hell gonna involve me. I liked what I saw. The way Haupt and Ortega were talking and pointing at that A-4 in the water kind of made me think we would be staying there for a while, and I could use a break. Well, I was right. Sort of.

"Buster Bahls called second team up, so Chief Runningstar and Jeb Casebolt and me got up and walked over to where he was standing next to the Skyhawk with Sergeant Johnny and Ortega. Haupt and Zimmerman was already walking away with the Marines who were there when we arrived. 'Give them the word, Sergeant Johnson,' Ortega said, then left his ownself. Buster Bahls was looking kind of smug.

"The word was Buster volunteered us sit on that bird until we got relieved, and nobody knew when that'd be, but we'd get to ride back on a helicopter instead of humping. Sergeant Johnny went back to the squad and the platoon got up and left the four of us alone with that Skyhawk. We were going to lay around and sandbag until someone came with a bird to fly us out of there.

"Old Jeb, he couldn't wait. The platoon wasn't hardly out of sight and he got himself into the cockpit of that A-4, grabbed hold of the joystick and pretended he was flying around shoot-ing gooks. Buster Bahls told him to get out of there, but Jeb just said he couldn't abort the mission yet and kept on playing. He pulled on this red handle Buster didn't think he should, so the Ball Buster grabbed him by the stacking swivel and yanked his ass out of there. It was a whole half hour before he let anybody get in that cockpit again, and then we had to swear we wouldn't touch that red handle.

"Then Buster swore and pointed to the waterline. It was half the distance away it was when we got there. Jeb whistled and pointed inland. Between where we was and that last treeline was water that wasn't there before. Then Chief grunted and pointed at a line going around the Skyhawk just below the cockpit top. The tide was coming in and that line showed how high the tide was coming.

"Right about then I looked back at the water and there was a Navy river-patrol boat coming in toward us. Buster called them on the radio to let them know we saw them. There was a master sergeant on that boat from the Airedale unit that owned the Skyhawk we was sitting on, and he was coming out to eyeball the situation.

"He gave us some C-rats and told us he'd be back in the morning to remove the bird and we'd get a ride back to Chu Lai with him. In the meantime the Navy patrol boat would come back before dark to help us guard the Skyhawk overnight, and we could spend the night on it if we wanted to so we wouldn't have to get wet. We didn't like them going away so soon like that because we were stuck there and the tide was coming in.

"Before the master sergeant left, Buster Bahls asked him about the red handle. He said it was for the ejection seat, but it was okay 'cause it was disarmed.

"That tide did come as high as the line on the A-4, and we had just enough room to stand on the top of it without getting our feet wet. Then the tide went out and it started getting dark. Now we understood why that gray sand left puddles when we walked on it. It was tidal flats and got covered with water twice a day.

"The patrol boat came back right after the sun went down, and we got on it before the tide had a chance to start coming back in. The coxswain maneuvered his boat into a position where it could watch over the A-4, see the river, and was backed against trees where it didn't have a silhouette to show against the sky. With the engines off, someone would have to come within a few feet to spot us. That boat carried two Starlight night-vision scopes so we could see the river and the boat at the same time.

"The night watch was set with two Marines and two sailors up at all times. Everything was quiet until oh-three-thirty hours. All we could see through the scopes was fishermen out in midstream, and we didn't need the scopes to see them with because their sampans were carrying lit torches. But I was on watch at oh-three-thirty and I looked out and there were five unlit sampans coming our way. Sampans at night without lights was bad news. Everybody that had legitimate business on the river at night, which was only fishermen, carried lit torches so the river patrol boats would see them and not shoot their asses out of the water.

"We woke everyone up, and the sailors manned their fifty-caliber machine gun and their M-60, and the coxswain got ready to start that boat up to chase the Vee Cee if any of them got away, and Buster, Chief, Jeb, and me got along the side of the boat with our M-14s. We waited until the Vee Cee opened up on the A-4. They knew there was a Marine fire team guarding it, but they didn't know about the patrol boat. They was really shooting the hell out of that bird, blowing these big chunks right off of it and, son, they had the shit surprised out of them when we opened up on their flank.

"The fifty almost disintegrated one of those sampans, and the M-60 tore the shit out of another one. Us Marines knocked down everyone on all of the other sampans. One drifted close to us, and Jeb lobbed a grenade into it and it sunk right to the bottom. The coxswain revved his boat up and we checked out both the sampans still floating, then hauled all the bodies we could find out of the water. We got fourteen bodies and don't know how many we couldn't find, but it wasn't likely any got away alive.

"The sailors waited a while longer until the tide started going out before making us get off their boat and going back to the A-4 to wait for the master sergeant.

"One last thing to tell about happened. That Airedale master sergeant came back on a helicopter in the morning with some more Cs for us and a team of engineers and an aircraft mechanic. Them engineers and the mechanic looked over that Skyhawk while we chowed down, then decided it got too shot up in our fire fight to be worth trying to salvage anymore. They put a couple thermite grenades in it and we all moved back about a hundred meters to watch the pretty fire. Pissed us off because we spent so much time and had a fire fight guarding a bird that just got blown up after all.

"Then the Airedale told us there wasn't enough room in his bird to carry us, but there'd be another patrol coming along later in the day and we could join them for the hump back to Chu Lai. That platoon we was waiting for didn't show up until about fourteen hundred hours. By then they'd already had their noon chow so's we had to wait until we got back to Chu Lai before we could eat again. All told, we spent twenty-five hours guarding that A-4."

Chapter Six

IN AN EARLIER GEOLOGICAL PERIOD THE ISLAND HAD BEEN A small sand bar, but millennia of the river's silt meeting the sand carried by the South China Sea's waves made the sandbar grow until it became an island. Wind- and bird-borne seeds germinated, rooted, and grew. A few of them did, anyway. The sandiness of the soil combined with the oceanic salts percolating through it to make the soil inhospitable to most growing things.

Third platoon humped through the scrub-pine forest that grew on the island's low spine. Some areas of the forest were clear of undergrowth, other parts were almost impenetrably overgrown with weeds and grasses between the trees. The day was hot and the sun was doing its best to cook the water from the soil, greatly raising the humidity. Sweat flowed from bodies suffering from too frequent, too complete, fluid exchanges. Little air moved through the trees, and the sweat puddled on the men, soaked their uniforms. They had been humping for one hour and had three more to go before the end of this patrol. Hopefully, two canteens of water per man would hold them until they returned to Chu Lai.

"Wait one," the Marine with the platoon's radio said into its handset. He turned to the tall, lanky lieutenant commanding the platoon, "It's Six Actual, sir. He wants to talk to the Actual," and passed the handset over.

Lieutenant Haupt took the handset and walked as far from his radioman as the cable would stretch. He went through the I-talk, you-talk procedure of radio communications, returned the handset to the radioman, then walked rapidly forward to the first squad leader. First squad had the point.

In another minute the column turned to the right from its southward path, heading downslope from the island's high spine toward the forest edge. When open areas of out-of-season peanut-farming land and tidal flats were reached, the column stopped.

Haupt consulted his map and used his compass, then called the platoon sergeant and guide forward. They were joined by the first squad leader and his point-team leader.

"About three quarters of a klick from here, over in that direction," he pointed a long arm, "is a downed A-4 Skyhawk. That's where we're going. The word is there are no Vee Cee in this area so we can make a beeline across the flats without having to worry about ambushes. So move it out. Just remember to watch for booby traps when going through treelines."

The island dropped only a few feet from the forest's edge to the river channel, some 450 meters to the west. A narrow band of dike-protected peanut patches and rice paddies lay between the woods and the mud of the tidal flats. At two- to three-hundred-meter intervals a treeline stretched from the forest almost to the water. Occasional treelines interrupted the clear vista between island and water's edge. The cultivated areas and flats were checkerboarded into a quiltwork pattern.

Tension grew in the column as it moved into the openness of the flats. Marines nervously checked the seating of magazines in their rifles and worked the bolts to be sure a round was in the chamber. Carefully, they eyed the surrounding treelines.

"You sure there ain't no Vee Cee around here?" Wegener asked. He still limped from the leg wound he had suffered two and a half months before.

"That's what the big honcho says," Corporal Falalo answered.

"Then why're we humping here?"

Falalo shrugged. "We're letting them know we can come through anywhere we want any time we want." He looked back at Wegener. "But just because there's no Vee Cee doesn't mean there's no snakes, so watch your step."

"Snakes? What snakes? I ain't seen a snake in the five months I been in-country. Besides, snakes don't live on this kind of island."

"Alpha Company sent a platoon through this island last week, just before you got back from the hospital," Hunter said. "They lost three men to snake bite."

"What kind'a snakes?"

"Don't matter. There's ninety-two species of snake in Vietnam, and ninety-one of 'em are poisonous," Falalo said.

"And the ninety-second one's a man-eating python," Hunter finished.

"Shit, I hate fucking snakes."

"Watch your step."

The point fire team spread out when it reached the treeline it had to cross. The four Marines cautiously peered into it, looking for enemy, searching for telltales that would indicate booby traps. All seemed clear, and the team entered the trees single file. Third platoon followed.

The gray sand on the one side of the treeline was bare. On the other its bareness gave way to small clumps of grass and scattered, stunted trees. Less than two hundred meters distant, the river flowed. Slightly more than midway between the trees and the water, a delta-wing A-4 Skyhawk attack bomber had bellied into the sand. Four Marines lounged around it, waiting. They waved when they saw third platoon.

"Staff Sergeant Ortega, set a perimeter, then join me at the bird," Lieutenant Haupt said. "Sergeant Zimmerman, come along."

Haupt, Zimmerman, and the radioman walked to the A-4 while Ortega set the squads in nearby treelines. Then Ortega joined the others by the downed aircraft.

After a brief consultation Ortega called, "Sergeant Johnson up."

Johnny Johnson disengaged himself from his squad, leaving Hernando Falalo in charge, and trotted to the command unit. "What'cha got, Honcho?" he asked. After being told, he rubbed his chin then turned back to the treeline and called, "Bahls up."

Buster Bahls rolled over and eyed the group at the Skyhawk. "Oh shit, Henry J," he said. "I do believe we got us a problem." With less enthusiasm than Johnson had displayed, Bahls sauntered over to the group.

"Bahls, I got a nice sit-down job for you," Ortega said. "Real pogue duty." He was grinning.

"Thanks, Staff Sergeant Ortega," Bahls said, "but I'm a grunt and don't want any pogue job." He had never seen Ortega grin before, and didn't like the look.

"Nah, you'll like this one, Bahls. You'll even get to ride back to Chu Lai instead of humping with the rest of us. Look at it this way, your shoulder is still pretty stiff from that AK wound. I'm cutting you a hus by not making you hump with the rest of us. I know that pack has to be killing your shoulder. Get your fire team over here on the double."

"My shoulder's okay; you don't need to cut me a hus because of it." Bahls looked to Johnson for help, but all his squad leader did was shrug his shoulders and shake his head.

The four Marines sitting on the Skyhawk were going back with third platoon, leaving Bahls and his fire team to guard the downed bird.

"How long are we going to be here?" Bahls asked Ortega.

"Until you get relieved."

"When will that be?"

"In a few hours."

"It better be. We don't have any chow with us."

"No sweat. We'll get some to you."

"What do I do if Charlie comes with more men than the three of us can handle?" Bahls wanted to know.

"He won't."

"Yeah, but what if he does anyway?"

"I'll leave a prick six with you. You need help, call in for it. I'll get help to you."

"Is anybody going to be close enough to pick me up on a six?"

"Don't sweat it. You won't need to use the radio, anyway." Somehow, the way Ortega said that didn't reassure Bahls.

Bahls turned to Johnson. "Johnny, you got to give me another man. Three men don't stand a chance against no one."

Johnson gazed blank-eyed at his squad lying against the treeline. "I'll give you Gant. He don't like being with Doyle, anyhow."

Bahls spat. "Shit. Can't you give me Malcolm X, or somebody?"

Johnson's eyes didn't move from the treeline. "Gant." Without another word he returned to the squad. Bahls watched as the big black Marine rose to his feet and walked toward him.

"Everything's cool here," the strangers' fire-team leader said. "You just have to be careful you don't drown when the tide comes in."

"What do you mean, when the tide comes in?" Bahls asked suspiciously, looking at the waterline seventy-five meters away.

"See those marks on the trees?" The stranger pointed to dirt caked in rings about three feet up the trunks of the spindly trees around them.

"What about them?" Bahls asked.

"That's how high the water gets."

Bahls looked at the rings and back at the water. "You're shitting me."

"When the tide comes in, make sure the bottoms of your boots are dry." The stranger shrugged. "There's just about enough room on top of that bird for the four of you to stand on."

"And when is this miracle supposed to happen?"

"About sixteen hundred. The water covers all this mud." He pointed to the treeline third platoon had come through after crossing the open fields.

Buster Bahls stood quietly on the starboard wing of the A-4. Henry J. Morris and Chief Runningstar leaned against its fuselage. They watched their platoon drift away, leaving them alone with the broken bird. They didn't know where they were, how close other Marines were if they needed help, or how long they would be stuck where they were. For all they knew, a VC company had been dodging third platoon and was just waiting for the patrol to get far enough away to not be able to give any help before coming in to wipe out the fire team.

But Gangland Gant didn't give a damn. Nothing ever seemed to bother him, except for being put in Corporal Doyle's fire team. The platoon wasn't even out of sight before he squeezed himself into that Skyhawk's cockpit and started playing with the joystick. "Brrrripp!" he went. "Tat-ta-ta-tat! And another Charlie bites the dust, victim of MAG Forty-three! Hey, Chief, do I get to paint a cone hat on my bird for that?"

"Nope." Runningstar was taciturn and didn't often use more words than were absolutely necessary. Sometimes he didn't even use as many words as were necessary.

"Gangland, get out of there. You don't know what you're playing with," Bahls ordered.

"Yeah, Gangland, get out of there. I want a turn," Morris said.

"No can do. I'm flying over the Song Bonh River and have a Vee Cee sampan in my bombsights. Look out, Charlie!" Gant's shoulders dipped and swayed as though he was flying through the sky. "Bombs away!" He jerked at a lever on the port side of the cockpit and pulled back on the joystick. "Yahoo, I got me a sampan! Now I go back to zap any Charlies who think they know how to swim."

Gant hunched over the stick, twisted it to the left and pushed it forward. "Goners, you goners!" he shouted. "Tat-ta-ta-ta-tat!" Suddenly, he sat straight up, "Aargh, they got me!" reached back over his shoulder and yanked at a red handle.

"Don't pull on that!" Bahls shouted and grabbed Gant's wrist. "I believe that activates the ejection seat."

Gant looked up at Bahls with wide, innocent eyes. "No shit. They just shot me down. I gotta get out of this sucker before it crashes." Fortunately, the handle didn't budge. Reluctantly, Gant dismounted. "Chief, do I get to paint a sampan on my plane?"

"Nope. You got shot down." Gant looked dejected.

"Gangland, you such an asshole I can't understand how you got into this Green Machine in the first place," Bahls said. "What the fuck you enlist for?"

Gant stared east, toward the interior of the island. He seemed to be looking through the treelines that hid the island's spine from the mud flats the aircraft lay on. His eyes unfocused, staring beyond the island, past the South China Sea, across the Pacific Ocean, halfway around the earth to where The World lay waiting for him. "You see," he half mumbled, the words coming slowly as though reluctant to be formed, "there was this judge. He told me I could do three to seven the hard way or I could do four in the Corps.'' A long moment passed before he spoke again. ''Sometimes I think I guessed wrong.''

For the next couple of hours the men played pilot in the Skyhawk, peering at the dials, twisting the joystick and jerking on everything that looked like a moving part. They even managed to get Bahls into it, although he was far more interested in watching for relief or bad company.

Then Bahls noticed the waterline was less than half the distance it had been earlier. ''Oh, shit,'' he said. ''Maybe that Marine was giving us straight scoop.''

''Look.'' Runningstar pointed inland. An arm of water had reached halfway across the mud flats between them and the treeline.

''Is this what I think it is?'' Morris wanted to know. There was a line around the fuselage of the Skyhawk. If it was the high-water mark, they would have barely enough room to stand on the top of the aircraft without getting their feet wet, just like the men they relieved said they would have.

An hour later that's exactly what they were doing.

In a couple more hours the water was ebbing back to where it had been when they arrived. Out on the river a half-dozen sampans were approaching the A-4. They saw that some of the black pajamaed figures in the boats were armed.

''Oh, hell,'' Bahls said.

They ducked down behind the aircraft and made sure their M-14s were ready to fire. Then the PRC-6 said its first words since the platoon had left them behind.

''Hello, Marines on the A-4. We are friends coming in. Do you hear me? Over.'' It was an American voice.

Bahls held the six to his head and depressed the speak button. ''Sampans, this is A-4. Identify yourself. Over.''

A taller man they hadn't noticed before stood and waved. He was dressed in Marine utilities and soft cover. A .45 holster hung from his web belt. He held the handset of a PRC-20 to his mouth and spoke into it.

''Advance and be recognized,'' Bahls told the radio.

The tall man stepped into the shallow water and splashed toward them. He turned out to be a master sergeant from the Marine Air Group that owned the A-4. He had been sent to eyeball the situation and bring some C-rats to the grunts watching over his bird.

"These men are from the local Popular Forces platoon," he said, indicating the Vietnamese he had come with. "They'll come back at sunset to help you guard the bird, and you can spend the night on their boats so you won't have to get wet. I'll be back in the morning to get this bird out of here and then you can go back to your unit."

Before he left, Bahls asked the master sergeant about the red handle in the back of the cockpit. The master sergeant confirmed that it was for the ejection mechanism but said, "No sweat. Its charge was removed earlier. There's nothing there to go off." Then he left with the Vietnamese, and second fire team got lonesome again, knowing where they were going to spend the night.

At sunset Bahls started getting tense and insisted that his men keep alert. If I was Charlie, Bahls thought, and wanted to hit us, this is when I'd do it.

When the sky had grown dark, four boats with their orange lights burning approached and set up as near to the Skyhawk as they could get. Their leader came and talked to Bahls in a form of pidgin English. It was a bit hard for the Marines and Vietnamese to understand each other in the pidgin none of them spoke very well, but in the end they decided that the boats would come in as close as the tide allowed them to, and the Americans would stay with the bird until the water was almost at it before boarding the boats. At dawn the Marines would debark and be left to wait for the Airedale on their own.

In the meantime the Popular Forces would leave their lights lit all night so they wouldn't be mistaken for Vee Cee by any passing river-patrol boat.

Not fully trusting the PFs, Bahls set the watch at fifty percent. Two of the Marines stayed awake for two hours while the others slept. Then they switched.

Around three-thirty in the morning all four Marines got into the boats for the remainder of a dry night. Bahls and Morris got on one boat and Runningstar and Gant boarded another. This late, Bahls decided that they should all stay awake.

It was maybe an hour later when the Popular Forces leader

started nudging Bahls. "Di-di, di-di," he said. "We go now. You off."

Bahls had no idea why the Vietnamese was trying to get rid of the Marines so early; sunup was still at least a half hour away. The false dawn wasn't even glowing on the horizon yet. But they rolled over the sides of the boats into two and a half feet of water. The sampans glided silently off while the Marines climbed onto the jet. Just because they were already wet didn't mean they wanted to stay in the water.

Not until Runningstar spoke, that is. "I think we've got bad company," he said.

Bahls and the others peered through the night to where Runningstar was pointing, and saw them. Two unlit sampans were drifting silently over the water toward the aircraft and the four Marines.

"Oh, shit," Bahls said, "now we really get to find out how bulletproof this bird is."

Hardly raising a ripple, they slid into the water behind the jet and checked their M-14s again. The newcomers couldn't be anybody but VC.

Just to be on the safe side, Bahls tried to raise the new boats on the radio. "Sampans approaching the A-4, identify yourselves. Over."

Static was the only answer.

"Henry J, full auto," Bahls whispered. "On my command, take the starboard sampan. Chief, Gangland, you've got the one portside."

Through the darkness they could make out at least three figures in each boat. They saw the poles being boated.

"Pick your targets," Bahls whispered, then shouted, "Fire!"

Bahls's command was almost drowned out by the VC opening up at the same time. Their bullets splashed into the water all around the A-4 and banged off the hull of the aircraft. The boat on the right shuddered from the impact of Morris's automatic fire and a body dropped overboard. Maybe more than one of them was hit or maybe the unexpected fire caught the VC by surprise, because their shooting dropped off.

Gant hopped to his feet shouting, "Bombs away!" and started lobbing grenades at the boat on the left. His first two grenades dropped in the water and didn't do any more damage than rock the boats and throw off the VCs' aim. But the third had a short fuse and exploded in the air next to a sampan, sinking it. Some splashing around the boat indicated that the grenade hadn't killed everyone aboard it.

Then the crew of the other boat decided to bug out and someone started poling it away. Their fire ceased and the sampan picked up speed. The Marines poured everything they had at that boat and thought they hit at least one more VC. Bahls called cease fire when the sampan was too far out to be seen anymore. Then he took Runningstar to check for bodies while Morris and Gant covered them.

No bodies were found then or when they looked again after dawn. With the fight in the water that way, they couldn't even come up with a blood trail. If it hadn't been for the boat that Gant's grenade sank, and the new hits on the A-4, nobody would have believed them about the fire fight. At that, some people from their platoon later thought they had scavenged an old boat to sink and shot up the bird themselves just to relieve the boredom of sitting there.

Of course, the locals never admitted that they left the Marines alone before dawn to face Charlie by themselves.

The Airedale master sergeant came back around oh-nine-hundred with some more chow for the team and said the MAG had decided to destroy the Skyhawk rather than try to retrieve it. He came in a helicopter which dropped him off and left on another mission. Second team was to remain with him while he waited for the engineers to show up, then provide security for the engineers while they did their job.

The engineers arrived in another chopper about two hours later and spent a half hour looking over the bird, deciding what to do to it before setting two thermite grenades in it. Then everyone stood back in a treeline nearly a hundred meters away and watched the fire.

Suddenly, a small explosion ripped through the air and the ejection seat from the Skyhawk shot about a hundred feet straight up.

The men of the second fire team stood in stunned silence. "Why did it do that?" Bahls asked the master sergeant.

"The charge went off," the master sergeant said laconically.

"I thought you said the charge was removed."

"It was supposed to be." He shrugged; nobody had gotten injured.

Bahls turned to Gant. "See why I told you not to pull on that handle? What if it had done that with you in it?"

Gant's face turned the color of his shirt and he grinned weakly. "I told you I had to get out of that sucker."

Bahls slapped a hand on the back of Gant's neck. "Man, when I tell you do something, do it. Maybe that way you won't get yourself killed."

The master sergeant examined the hull of the aircraft, and satisfied there was nothing of any value remaining, said to Bahls, "We're going to leave now, Corporal. Another patrol will be coming along here in an hour or so. They've been alerted that you're here, and you can go back to Chu Lai with them." He turned to board the engineers' chopper.

"Wait one, Top," Bahls said. "We're supposed to fly back with you."

"No can do," the master sergeant said. "Between me and the engineers there's no room in this bird for a grunt fire team. Just hang loose. Someone's going to pick you up soon." He boarded the chopper and it lifted off and flew away.

Bahls, Morris, Runningstar, and Gant stood looking after it.

"Fucking shit Airedales." Bahls spat into the mud. "We sit here and do their guarding for them, then they make us hump back on our own instead of giving us a ride after we took care of their asses for them." He spat again and turned to stare at the burnt out Skyhawk. "Fucking shit."

At fourteen hundred hours, twenty-five hours after third platoon had dropped them off, a platoon from India Company diverted from its patrol route along the wooded spine of the island and located second team. Three hours and a little more later, the four Marines strolled back into their own company area.

Staff Sergeant Ortega ignored them. Sergeant Johnson looked apologetic. "Sorry, pano," he said. "The Kraut told me it would only be for a couple hours. He said you'd get a ride and probably be waiting for us when we humped back here. I was thinking of your shoulder. Thought I was doing you a favor by letting you take your pack off for a while and giving you a chance to ride back to Chu Lai."

"Don't do me no more favors, Sergeant Johnny," Bahls told him. "Cut somebody else a hus next time. I'm a grunt and I want to stay with the platoon."

Sniper, Sniper, in the Night

"IN THE LATE SPRING OF 'SIXTY-SIX, AFTER A COUPLE MONTHS slack time when we ran patrols outside of Chu Lai, the Fifteenth Marines was mostly running battalion operations. We went out for anywhere from three days to a week and a half at a time. Come in for showers, hot food, and a few days' rest, then go back out again. Charlie was getting hard to find, and we had to go farther and farther out every time.

"I'm not really sure what operation this was on, but we'd been out in the field without a break for a week or so and we were beat to the bones. We'd seen all kinds of strange things on this one. One of the strangest was when we ran into this Combined Action Platoon. We'd all heard about CAPs and figured they were candy duty, sitting in safe villes right outside the barbed wire of big combat and fire bases with all kinds of help close to hand. Marines in the CAPs, though, they figured they were doing the same job the Army's Green Berets were without the rank the green beanies had.

"We'd been humping maybe a hundred klicks or more and were lots of miles from any fire base when we ran into a small farming ville. We got one hell of a surprise when we walked into it. Marines were already there.

"It was a Combined Action Platoon. About a dozen Marines living in a little barbed-wire compound a hundred meters from the edge of the ville and working with the local Popular Forces platoon. We thought this was strange as all get out because Marines pretty much universally distrusted the PFs. Half of them were probably Vee Cee and the other half were either sympathizers or would run if there was trouble. PFs were the civilian militia, local guys that got out of military service by 'protecting' their own villages. But during the war a few thousand Marines lived in the villes and worked with the PFs in the pacification program that seemed to work out all right.

"These Marines all used to be grunts and were glad to be out of the line companies. They had a fifty-five-gallon drum rigged up for a shower in their compound and got to wash regularly, and someone in the village worked as a laundry boy for them so they always had clean utes to wear. None of them had any gook sores, and they all seemed well-fed and pretty happy. Every day they had a hot meal flown out to them from someplace, and all they had to do was run patrols and ambushes every night. What the hell was Marines doing running night patrols, we wanted to know. Ain't nobody told these people Charlie owned the night? Only thing scared me worse than night patrol was a tunnel rat. They just grinned and said *they* owned the night around there. It was the daytime they had to sweat. When we got to thinking about it serious, we freaked out a bit. This was a dozen Marines a lot of klicks away from any other Marines, and the only help they had on hand was a platoon of armed civilians. They could get wiped out easy before help came if Charlie decided to do it. They said they'd rather take that chance than have to hump like regular grunts.

"After we left that ville we humped on until we was near the edge of this forest when night fell. My fire team got sent into the trees to be an LP. We had the luck to find and set up in some old Vee Cee fighting positions. Not bunkers, mind you, just little holes in the ground. Each one was about big enough for two Americans to kind of hunker down in and have some cover if any shooting started. Those little fucking gooks probably could have stood straight up in one of them and still had to stand on their tippy-toes in order to see over the top.

"The sun crashed down behind the mountains and there it was the dead of night, just like that. There wasn't no moon out yet and it was black as a coal miner's ass where we were under the edge of the trees, but you could look the other way out over the rice paddies and see the stars was making it as bright as it ever gets here under a full moon.

"Anyhow, there we was in those holes and the clouds came over kind of sudden like, the way it sometimes does when it's getting near monsoon season, and it started raining like a mo-dicker. Ah, son, I just said 'mo-dicker.' That's 'cause your momma don't like me saying 'motherfucker,' but it's really the same word. Anyhow, that rain's coming down in honey buckets and we were already filthy and miserable as well as dead tired, and didn't feel too much like adding to our misery. And I'm not saying a goddam thing about the jungle rot half of us was suf-fering with or the immersion foot and gook sores most of us had.

"Ever notice how I don't like to take off my shoes and go barefoot after I've been walking around in shoes for a while? You're old enough now that you probably know some people like to mess around with feet in sexual foreplay. I don't. Both of them things are from having immersion foot. My feet's got scars all over them from that, and they just plain stink after they've been sweating inside shoes.

"So there we were in those holes with the water coming down in honey buckets, like I said, and the holes start filling up with water and the next thing you know we're hunkering down in water up over the tops of our boots. Remember, this is still the first half of 'sixty-six, and even though the Army'd been wearing jungle boots for more than a year, the Marines were still in the old high-top black leathers that didn't let water drain.

"Old Jeb Casebolt had spent near two months in the hospital after Operation Braxton Hill, recovering from his leg wound, but what with the heat and humidity and bugs and who knows whatever kind of germs floating around, the middle of that wound was still infected with pus and kept threatening to get worse. And he had immersion foot. So he says, 'Hell with this shit,' in that Tennessee twang of his that I was just about the only one who could understand, and got out of the hole he was in with me and stomped to a few yards away where water was just flowing across the ground instead of puddling on it and sat him-self down and took off his boots and socks. 'Bad enough Ah have to be out here and get wet with my leg pussing up like this,' Jeb says. 'Ah'll be goddam if Ah'm gonna sit thar in a fucking gook pond and have leeches eatin' on ma leg, too.'

"Now, we already spread our ponchos on the ground in front and behind the holes to keep our rifles out of the dirt and have something to lay on for sleeping when we were off watch, and Jeb left his piece right where it was.

"Buster Bahls sort of swore under his breath and yelled at Jeb to get his ass back in his hole where he'd have some cover if Charlie hit us, and Jeb answered that Buster should come on out with him and wouldn't have to worry about getting hit because no gook had eyes good enough to see his black ass in the dark like it was, and anyhow, no dumb-ass gook was dumb enough to come out on a rainy night like that.

"Now Buster was starting to get a mite pissed at this when all of a sudden the clouds scuttled out of there just as fast as they came on, chased by a dry wind what started right off drying the rain off our skin wherever it touched. The next thing we knew, all four of us were all out over by Jeb with our feet bare, giving them a chance to dry out for the first time in a couple weeks or so.

"Once our feet got dry we got dry socks out of our packs, put them on and got back in the holes. And not a minute too soon. We were hardly back in them when some gook started dinging some rounds at us. Remember, it was pitch black under those trees, but that gook sniper had us right down. The rounds just kept barely missing us. He had a dead lock on where we were. And he varied his rhythm enough we couldn't figure out where or when he'd shoot next. Sometimes he'd alternate his shots from one hole to the other and sometimes he'd wait as much as fifteen seconds between rounds. Then, sometimes he'd put two so close together at the same spot, anybody sticking his head up after the first shot would get his head blown off by the second shot. We were pinned down good. Later we found out he was hitting so close because he was using an infrared sight.

"After a little while Malcolm X started laughing at Charlie hitting so close and never hitting any of us. That started us all off laughing and giggling.

"Of course, the laughing told Charlie we weren't getting hit and maybe weren't taking him as serious as he wanted, so he started trying to ding us even harder. His rounds was going all

over the damn place. Real close, mind you, but everywhere
except hitting us.

"After a little while Buster just says to all of us, 'How's about
some-fucking-body go flank that Charlie and chase his ass away
from here?' "

" 'No way, José,' Jeb said back. 'That sucker keeps hitting too
close. Not a chance I'm going to put my young ass out where
he can see it.'

"That set us on another round of laughing, and poor Charlie
started getting real frustrated because he knew he was missing
us and he started laying out more rounds and still never hit any
of us because we wasn't showing him anything to hit.

"After a while he slowed down his shooting and I nudged
Malcolm X in the ribs and he understood what I was telling him
even without me using words. Off to our right front the ground
dropped almost straight down ten feet into some bushes. I patted
his shoulder three times and on the third pat we dove out of the
hole we was in and right down that drop into the bushes. The
gook sniper must have been looking through his sight at the hole
Buster and Jeb were in, because he didn't seem to realize what
we did.

"It didn't take us more than two or three minutes to get into
a position where we could see that sniper's muzzle flash. I made
sure my piece was on full automatic, and the next time he fired,
Malcolm X and I blew his gook ass away.

"Malcolm X got the infrared sight as a souvenir and I took
the Swedish K that sniper was using. Later I sold that rifle to a
sailor boy for five hundred in greenbacks. That money paid for
my R and R in Bangkok. I never did know what Malcolm X did
with that sight, probably sold it like I did the rifle. That was one
Vee Cee sniper who never shot at Marines again.

"It was after that operation something funny happened. Corporal Doyle, who thought CAPs were crazy and just too damn
dangerous, he got transferred to one. Nobody missed him when
he went."

Chapter Seven

DURING THE SPRING, 1ST MARINE DIVISION INTELLIGENCE KEPT getting reports of Viet Cong buildups in the Chu Lai–Tam Ky area, buildups in preparation for a major assault against either the Marine base or the city. Three Fifteen was assigned to aggressively patrol the area—combat patrols, platoon- and company-size patrols. The men were told it was a search and clear operation. They weren't told about the reported buildup. They'd heard too often of buildups and pending assaults that never came about; the brass was concerned the troops might not take the word seriously if they knew what the operation was about. The men didn't know they never got more than five or ten kilometers away from Chu Lai or Tam Ky, no matter how long they were in the field at a stretch.

On the point, PFC Gant held one hand back and dropped to his knee, peering through the brush to his front. Corporal Doyle scurried to him.

"What'cha got, Gangland?" Doyle whispered.

"Ville. Some people moving in it."

They were at the edge of a scrub forest with cane fields and rice paddies beyond it. Two hundred meters from the edge of the brush stood a cluster of hootches shaded by trees. Half-naked children ran the ville's paths and a few adults were visible cooking or lounging about.

"What's the problem, Doyle?" Sergeant Johnson dropped to his knees by the point.

"Scoping out a ville, Honcho."

Johnson held his radio to his face and spoke into it. "Stand tight," he said to Doyle and Gant. Doyle gestured to Lance Corporal Evans to join them. In another minute Lieutenant Haupt and Sergeant Zimmerman dropped to the ground alongside the waiting Marines.

Haupt studied his map while the others watched the quiet scene to their front. "It's all right," Haupt said when his study was finished. "There's a CAP here. Let's move it out. Pass the word, don't fire at any armed civilians unless they open on us first."

"Excuse me, Mister Haupt," Doyle interrupted Haupt's leaving. "What'd you say there?"

The tall lieutenant looked down at his smallest NCO. "A CAP, a Combined Action Platoon. There's a reinforced Marine rifle squad in there with a Popular Forces platoon."

Doyle looked like he didn't believe Haupt.

"On your feet, Doyle," Johnson said. "Move it out."

Slowly, Doyle rose to his feet and motioned Gant forward. "I don't believe this shit," he muttered. "What the fuck is a Marine rifle squad doing alone out here in the middle of fucking nowhere?"

By the time the column was halfway to the ville, children were running through the lead squads, begging for candy and cigarettes, clinging to the Marines' trousers, offering to carry their packs and rifles. Most of the Marines tried to ignore the children; a few gave them candy and cigarettes. None accepted their offers to be gun bearers. Some nervously tried to shoo them away.

When three armed men in camouflage bush hats and green uniforms strolled toward them from the ville, Gant fell to the ground and put his rifle in his shoulder. All the other Marines in the open spread out and dropped without waiting for orders. The three stopped and held up their hands when the Marines hit the deck.

"Hold your fire," Doyle shouted at his men. "They're walking funny," he said in a voice so low he might have been talking to himself, "more like Americans than gooks."

As if in answer to him, one of the armed strangers yelled, "Yo, Marines, friendlies here! We're Marines coming toward you." The trio resumed walking toward the column.

Haupt and Staff Sergeant Ortega rose to their feet and moved toward the strangers. The strangers were members of the CAP.

Lima Company took a half-hour break at the CAP compound. Members of the PF platoon milled among them but didn't get a warm welcome from the grunts. The grunts were more interested in how the Marines of the CAP could live out there.

"How do you people know these gooks won't turn on you in a fire fight?" Corporal Doyle shuddered when he asked one of the CAP's patrol leaders the question.

"They haven't yet," the well-washed Marine in a patched but clean uniform said. "And we ambush Charlie a couple times a week. These little fuckers even stand with us when we get ambushed."

"You saying they never lead you into an ambush?" Gant wanted to know.

"Shit, no. They did, they'd get killed, too. If anything, they know where Charlie has his ambushes set and they'll lead us away from them."

Evans sat quietly and stared around the compound.

In another place Johnson asked another CAP patrol leader, "What happens if Charlie decides to come in hard and take your asses out?"

The Marine shrugged. "We'd find out about it up front and have a grunt company on standby to help." He nodded to himself. "Charlie tried it once. Sent two companies after us. Out there's a mass grave with thirty-five Vee Cee in it." He waved a hand to the west.

Bahls shuddered. "But what if you don't find out in advance?"

"We die." He wrinkled his nose and stared at Bahls. "But, man, I spent four months in a line company before I got this assignment. I want to tell you I'd rather do this any day than go humping all over the fucking place like you do and never get to take a shower, wear clean uniforms, or have a hot meal every day. Let me go on my patrols and ambushes every goddam night. Life's a damn sight easier here. Even if I do run the risk of Charlie coming in with more than I can handle.''

''Saddle up!'' the cry rang out.

''Saddle up! Saddle up! Saddle up!'' It was repeated in every platoon. ''Saddle up! Saddle up! Saddle up!'' Each squad leader echoed the command. Lima Company rose to its collective feet and shuffled out of the CAP compound, back to its life of the never-ending hump.

The endless paddies trudged past the slowly moving column. The point slid cautiously through the treelines and hedgerows the company crossed. To the Marines' left the sun was dropping rapidly toward the Annamese mountains, far beyond the forest that was slowly edging toward them from the west. Soon it would be dark and time to stop for the night.

A signal, unheard and unseen by most of the men in the column, was passed, and then by platoons, by squads and fire teams, the column choo-choo-trained to a halt. The fifteen-meter interval they had maintained closed slightly within squads, increased between them. More signals and messages, again unseen and unheard by most, passed through the company. By platoons they would scatter and set in to wait anxiously for dawn's light. Exhausted, the men sat or lay on the paddy dike. Some of them used a little of their remaining energy to remove their packs.

''Bahls up,'' the word passed down the platoon line.

''Morris, take over,'' Bahls said before hiking his pack to a less uncomfortable position on his back and walking along the dike in the direction the order had come from. Along the way he was joined by Sergeant Johnson.

''Your turn for listening post, you ballsy bastard,'' Johnson joked at Bahls.

''Shee-it.'' Bahls hawked into the water. ''Where that dumbass wetback going put me tonight, in the middle of a fucking paddy or something?'' Then they were at the platoon CP.

Lieutenant Haupt was squatting down, bent over his map, murmuring into the handset of his radio. Staff Sergeant Ortega stood glowering at the forest's edge, now not much more than two hundred meters distant. He didn't look at Johnson and Bahls when they closed on him.

"Johnson, I want you to put four men fifty meters inside that wood over there," Ortega said through clenched teeth. "Give 'em a prick six and tell 'em to check in every half hour. Fifty-percent alert. Call sign's Red Fox here, you're Blue Hen Two, LP gets Blue Hen Two Alpha. I don't want 'em shooting at nothing unless they got positive targets. Any questions?" Ortega continued staring at the trees the whole time.

Johnson shook his head. "No questions."

"Get 'em out there."

Johnson and Bahls turned back to their men. Ortega hadn't looked at them the whole time he was giving the orders.

"Don't like going fifty meters inside the woods with only one team," Bahls said. "Lot of gooks can get between me and you."

"No sweat, Ball Buster. I'll go along and help you find a good spot," Johnson replied. He didn't want any of his men getting cut off, either. "Doyle, I'm taking Malcolm X with me for a little walk," he said when he and Bahls passed the third fire-team leader. "Malcolm, drop your pack and come along. We'll be back in a skosh bit."

"Second team, saddle up," Bahls ordered when he and Johnson reached his men. "Rifles, cartridge belts, grenades, bandoleers. One meal of Cs. Leave your packs here." He shrugged his own pack off his shoulders and dropped it onto the dike, where it joined his men's.

Morris, Runningstar, and Casebolt struggled to their feet. They had semicollapsed on the dike, half keeping a wary eye cocked at the forest edge.

"What'cha got for us, Ballsy?" Morris asked.

"LP inna fucking woods with the big bad wolf," Bahls answered.

"Bullshit. I ain't gonna do it." Casebolt spat into the water, glaring at the trees. He sat back down.

"Sure you are," Johnson said. " 'Cause if you don't I'm gonna sit you in a fucking paddy and let the leeches eat on your leg."

Casebolt swore, looking out over the paddies to the forest. Then he slowly levered himself to his feet again and checked the action of his M-14 and stood staring at the trees.

"Let's go," Johnson said and started along the dike until he found one heading toward the trees. Bahls and his fire team followed, all eyes searching into the trees for sign of an enemy.

Ortega still stood glowering at the trees. He hadn't moved since the column halted.

The dikes angled and turned in a mazelike manner, so that it took more than three hundred meters to walk the two hundred plus to the forest edge. No one spoke during the approach. Then the ground abruptly sloped upward for a few meters between the paddies and the trees. Rifle held high, Johnson broke through the densely packed underbrush under the edge of the trees. Scant meters inside the forest, where the sun seldom shone, the undergrowth thinned. The ground continued to rise for about twenty-five meters before dropping slightly. From this height they could look back and see the paddies over the top of the brush.

Johnson stopped where the ground fell and looked around. "I'm not putting you any deeper than this," he said in a soft voice. "Everybody spread out and let's find a good place for your LP."

The six Marines moved laterally over the high ground, one eye on the land's lay, the other looking deeper, peeled for trouble.

"Oo-ee, lookee what I found," Runningstar whistled from the far right of the line. He was standing waist deep in an old fighting hole.

A quick inspection uncovered enough holes to accommodate a VC platoon facing the paddies and another facing into the woods.

"Looks like someone was expecting company here some time," Bahls said.

"And long ago enough they moved away," said Morris.

"You got that right," Johnson said. "Ballsy, let's find two good holes and you got some cover for the night." Minutes later Bahls and his team were settling in two adjacent holes near the south end of the lines facing into the forest.

"Remember, CP is Red Fox, I'm Blue Hen Two, you're Blue Hen Two Alpha," Johnson told them. "Check in every half hour and maintain fire discipline. See you in the morning. Malcolm X,

let's go." He turned back to the paddies and the relative safety
of the rest of the company.

"In the morning, Honcho," Bahls said to his squad leader's
receding back.

Bahls and Morris shared one hole, Runningstar and Casebolt
had the other. A poncho was spread in front of each hole to lay
weapons on to keep them off the damp earth, and another lay
behind the holes for the men off watch to sleep on. They had
time to open Cs and start eating before the sun fell behind the
mountains and brought about an abrupt darkness. They finished
their chow by touch.

After eating, Morris stood up and looked in the direction they
had come from. "Goddam," he whispered, "Charlie had himself a great ambush site here."

Under the trees the night was so deep a man couldn't see his
own hand held in front of his face. The stars shone brightly
enough on the paddies that even without a moon the water,
rippling with the slight breeze, sparkled and nearly showed color.
The rest of the platoon was visible as irregularities along a distant dike.

The others looked out over the paddies, and everyone knew
they would have to be particularly alert. If there was a VC unit
in the area, they would probably want to come back to the old
holes and open up on the Marines in the paddies. All four tuned
their ears to the night's noises, listening for anything out of
place, any sudden silences that could give evidence of someone
moving to their front. No matches were struck to light hidden
cigarettes, no words were passed except for the half hourly,
"Red Fox, Blue Hen Two Alpha. Situation remains the same,"
that Bahls murmured into the radio.

After three hours the light on the paddies dimmed. Unexpected rain clouds scuttled overhead and a large-dropped torrent
fell on the Marines in the open. They rose from their prone
positions and fumbled into their ponchos to try to salvage some
of their dryness. Under the trees the rain took a few minutes
longer to come crashing down, waking the off-watch sleepers.
The four men in the holes pulled their ponchos over their heads
and spread the ends out over the edges of the holes in an attempt
to keep the rain from pooling around their feet. But there was

too much rain, it forced its way under the edges of the ponchos, ran down through neck holes, weighted the rubber down and, finally, crashed into the holes.

In less than an hour the water was several inches deep in the bottom of the holes and threatening to go higher. Casebolt suddenly jumped out of his hole.

"Fuck this shit," he said, making the first words of the night other than Bahls's radio reports. "My god-fucking-damn leg still ain't healed. I'll be goddam if I'm gonna spend the night sitting in a stupid-ass gook pond letting leeches suck on it." He stomped to the top of the rise, spread his poncho on the ground and plopped to a sitting position on it. He took off his boots and socks and rolled up his trouser legs, letting the rain rinse the accumulated crud off his feet and calves. His rifle lay where he left it at the front of his hole.

"Jeb, get your stupid red-necked ass back in your hole before Charlie sees it and blows it away," Bahls ordered harshly.

"Fuck you and the horse you rode in on, Ballsy," Casebolt shot back. "I can't go sitting in no fucking pond like that until my leg heals up." Then, almost as an afterthought, he added, " 'Stead of worrying about Charlie seeing my red-necked ass, you should haul your black ass out here with me. Ain't no gook got eyes good enough to see you on a night like this. Anyways, no gook is fucking dumb enough to come out on a rainy-assed night like this just to snipe at an LP."

"Listen, you cock-sucking sum-bitch, I told you get your dumb ass back in your hole, and I expect you to do that thing right fucking now! You hear me?" Anger put an edge to Bahls's voice.

Casebolt ignored him and sat letting the rain rinse over his feet.

"Casebolt, you don't get your red-necked ass back in that fucking hole right now I'm gonna put it back for you."

A "Fuck you, splib" from Casebolt brought Bahls to his feet just as the stars reappeared over the paddies, bringing a quarter moon with them. Bahls froze, one foot standing in the pool in the bottom of the hole, the other on its lip. He held his head up and pushed back the hood of his poncho, letting the warm dry wind that had chased away the clouds evaporate the water from his face.

"Hot damn, that feels good," he exclaimed, and put his rifle down to shuck his poncho. In ten seconds he was spreading his poncho on the ground next to Casebolt and shedding his clothes to dry his soaked body in the wind. His rifle was forgotten at the side of his hole.

In another half minute all four Marines from the LP were on the top, standing naked on their ponchos, letting the wind dry them off, wringing the water from their clothes, waving their garments in the wind to dry them as well. At least their holes were well-armed with rifles and grenades, even if the Marines didn't have anything more than a bayonet among them.

The warm breeze quickly dried their skin, and Bahls started dressing and ordered his men to do likewise. They didn't want to put their still-wet uniforms back on, but reluctantly did when Bahls agreed they could remain barefoot. So there they sat, facing the deep woods, partway dry, with the wind working on their clothes, and their weapons more than five meters away at the holes, when Runningstar suddenly said, "Listen, what do you hear?"

They listened.

"I don't hear a goddam thing," Bahls said shortly.

"Right," said Runningstar, "the forest noises are gone."

"Oh, shit," Bahls whispered. "Someone must be coming our way. Let's get back to our holes."

They were interrupted in putting their socks and boots back on by a shot hitting near one of their holes. Before any of them could move, a second round hit next to the other hole. They froze. Seconds later a third round hit near the first hole. Then a fourth bullet hit by the second. A sniper was zeroed in on the two fighting holes the Marines had abandoned.

"Shee-it, will you look at that," Morris whispered. "What the fuck's he using? That's the brightest goddam muzzle flash I ever seen."

"Bright enough to sight on easy," Bahls whispered. "Take him out, Henry J. Easy shot, he's only about fifty meters off."

"Can't." Morris's head shake went unseen in the darkness.

"Why not?"

"Same reason you can't."

"Shee-it," Bahls swore softly. "What kind'a Mo-rine you call yourself, you ain't got your weapon?"

"A dry one. Samee-same you."

"Chief, Jeb, what about you?"

"Mine's guarding my hole."

"So's mine."

"Mo-dicker."

Several more rounds crashed into the ground near the holes. Mostly they alternated between the holes and were spaced several seconds apart, but the sniper fired two in a row at the same hole a couple of times and rapid-fired once or twice, so the Marines weren't able to pick up his rhythm. They sat huddled and tense, wondering if the sniper wondered why they weren't returning his fire. They watched the muzzle flash, each knowing that he could probably kill the sniper with one shot—if he had his weapon.

A few minutes passed, then Runningstar let out a war whoop. "Aiyy-eee! Sum-bitch don't know we ain't in the holes!" and started laughing.

The next round hit near them.

"He do now," Bahls said, laughing, and they all started giggling almost hysterically.

Another round tore into the dirt on their other side. Then came more. All of them near the Marines, to the sides and in front of them and a couple through the air over their heads, but none close enough to hit anyone. Every miss raised another gale of nervous laughter and giggling.

Every laugh and giggle also told the sniper he was missing, and he must have become frustrated, because his shots started coming faster.

"Someone go get his piece and take that fucking gook out before he gets lucky and hits one of us," Bahls finally said between laughs.

"Not on your fucking life, Honcho," Morris said. "That gook's been hitting all around the holes and all around us. He's hitting everywhere but where we are. No way I'm going to where I know he can hit. I'm staying right here where it's safe."

"You got it, Henry J," Casebolt said.

"I'm with you, pano," Runningstar agreed.

"Shee-it." Bahls giggled and squeegeed the sweat from his forehead with the edge of his hand.

The sniper's continuing fire at the giggles only caused more nervous giggling from the Marines, who were now hugging the ground as closely as they could. But still the sniper hadn't located them.

The heavier booming of an automatic M-14 suddenly crashed to the right of the sniper and he stopped shooting.

"Yo, LP. You alive over there?" Corporal Doyle's voice came from the sniper's location.

"All present and accounted for, Short Round," Bahls called back.

The four could hear Doyle and someone else approaching.

"Dinged me that dink," Evans exclaimed.

"Where are you?" Doyle asked from just in front of the holes.

"Topside," Bahls answered and sat up with his arms around his legs.

"Why didn't you people return his fire? With that fucking muzzle flash you should've taken him right the fuck out." Doyle started walking toward the top of the rise when he almost tripped. "What the fuck?" He bent over to feel what he had kicked. "What?" His hand fell on an M-14.

Almost running, Doyle stormed to where the others waited for him. "Whose goddam weapon is this?" he demanded, shaking it in the darkness no one could see through.

"One of ours," Bahls said. "Probably mine from where your voice was."

"What the fuck's your piece doing there and you here?"

"I had to get my leg out of the fucking pond was growing in that hole, so I just left everthing where it was and came up here," Casebolt said.

"Then the rain stopped and we all joined him," Bahls explained.

"And you left your weapons behind?"

Casebolt shrugged an unseen shrug. "Somebody had to guard the holes."

"You dumb fucking shits!" Doyle exploded. "Don't you know any goddam better'n that? All of you people been in this war for more than a half a year. You've seen too many of your buddies get killed by making dumb mistakes, and then you go and make one of the dumbest I've ever heard of."

Evans stood quietly nearby. He didn't like Corporal Doyle

and he didn't like Doyle chewing out his buddies, but when the man was right there was no way he could object.

Doyle dropped to all fours and pressed his face near where he could hear Bahls breathing. His voice had a freezing chill in it. "You called me 'Short Round,' motherfucker. Well, I'm shorter than you'll ever know. All I have to do is survive two or three more months of this shit and I catch a freedom bird back to The World and become a sloppy civilian most ricky-tick. You're still gonna be here when I leave—if you haven't got your stupid ass killed by some dumb fucking stunt like this one, shit-for-brains."

Doyle stopped for a moment to catch his breath. "I'll be goddammed if I'm gonna die because some asshole on an LP got careless. You pull shit like this again and I'll waste you myself if Charlie can't do the job." He swiveled his head to include all of the men in the LP. "You're supposed to be Marines. Act like it. Be professional, not like the fucking doggies."

He jerked to his feet and snapped, "Come on, Malcolm X. Let's get away from here before these whale turds do something else stupid."

Bahls and his men sat listening to Doyle and Evans pushing their way through the thickening undergrowth.

"Listen to them," Casebolt said. "Much noise as they're making, no way I want them on any kind of night move with me."

"Shuddap," Bahls snarled. "If they's so fucking noisy all the time how'd they get so close to Charlie a little while ago to ding him before he knew they was there?"

Casebolt was silent.

After a while longer they got to their feet, picked up their ponchos, and returned to the holes where they stayed through the rest of the no longer eventful night.

At dawn the four stepped out of the holes and returned across the paddies to the platoon. Ortega was standing on the dike staring at the trees. He looked like he hadn't moved all night.

When they reached the platoon, Bahls took Doyle aside and told him, "Hey, man, that was ballsy, what you and Malcolm X did last night, killing that sniper. Thanks a shitload. That sucker might have got lucky and hit one of us." He hesitated before continuing, like he couldn't find the right words. "You were right in what you said to me, I won't do it again. You okay in my book." He started to return to his place in the column, then turned back to Doyle. "But if you tell anybody I said that, I'll kick your ass from here to Hanoi."

Rain, Rain, Go Away.
Come Again Another Day
(but not until after
I've left this place)

"SON, WHEN YOU LISTEN TO OLD GRUNTS WHO FOUGHT IN Asia, no matter what war they fought in, you hear all kinds of stories about those little yellow people we always seem to fight and how tough they are. It's true, they are mighty tough little bastards. The way they fight, any American or European is gonna think they don't have no regard for their own lives; all they care about is how many of us they can take with them when they go. They're resourceful, too. You leave anything behind on the field, they're gonna pick it up and find a use for it. Maybe even a use that'll kill you.

"Grunts who fought there'll tell you about the gawdawful heat, too, and how it's an enemy near as bad as them yellow people. No, no, no, don't tell me about how Korea is cold. Sure is in the winter, but ask anybody who's been there in the summer. Hot as the inside of a lit oven.

"There's another thing about the Orient, though. Something most grunts who fought there probably won't tell you about—leastways not much. I think maybe the reason we don't talk much about it is because we don't believe it our ownselves, even though we lived through it. When we talk about it among ourselves it's like in a whisper with code words. Mostly we just ask each other, 'Do you remember?' What I'm talking about's a monster sum-bitch drives a man just plain crazy. It makes the yellow folk harder to find and gives you one hell of a time trying to keep your weapon working and your gear from rotting. What I'm talking about is the monsoon.

"In coastal Vietnam it was hot and dry during March and April. The ground in lots of places was cracking open because there wasn't no wet left in it. Where it wasn't cracked it was mostly red dust, except where it had green stuff growing on it to keep it from cracking or turning to dust. Or maybe we just couldn't see through the green to see the cracks and the dust.

"Then in May we started getting some bodacious bad thunderstorms. Shee-it! I want to tell you that was some kind of wind with them storms, too. Any kind of tent you had, it better be guyed down hard and staked deep or it was gonna blow over and get clean away from you. And a small man had best keep himself weighted down with gear and hunched over so's not to expose too much of himself to the wind or he's liable to get blown away with the tents. Hell, even a big man'd have trouble staying on his feet when that wind came hard. Aside from the wind, the rain came hard, too. Only took about a day before just about everybody stopped trying to keep himself dry and started worrying about keeping his rifle from rusting away complete and his gear from rotting.

"We didn't do much for about the first week or so of the monsoon except daytime patrols, pull some all-night ambushes, and sit in foxholes the rest of the nights. Well, we were supposed to sit in those holes. Mostly they were half flooded, so we sat outside them and hoped if Charlie hit we'd have time to dive in before getting shot.

"Then the thunderstorms stopped. While they were going on there were breaks between storms and times the sun come out to give us a chance to wring some of the water out of us. When the thunderstorms stopped, though, the rain kept on going. Seemed almost like what the thunderstorms were doing was trying to stop the rain from getting started up good in the first place. This rain just came down all the time. It was like being under a waterfall. The word 'dry' didn't have meaning no more. We were wet all the way through and so was everything we had.

Inside a tent it wasn't raining on you except where there were drips coming through the canvas, but there was too much water in the air for anything to ever dry out. That goddam rain seemed to last forever.

"Lima Company had to go on a three-day patrol in that steady rain. We were all saying how Charlie had enough sense to stay inside and the only problem we'd have from him was maybe a few snipers that got cabin fever and needed to get out of their hootches for a while. The way it was raining, we knew it wasn't no use going on no operations or big patrols, because we wouldn't find nobody. Big brass didn't think that way. So we started thinking maybe they wanted us to take some showers with more water than had been available for us before the rain started. Nobody was going and taking showers during the monsoon, that's for sure. No point to it when water's falling on you all the time anyway.

"They trucked us up Highway One about twenty klicks or so, then the trucks turned inland a couple more klicks before dropping us off. Then we had to hump a zigzag course back to the fire base. That was a tough hump. We weren't much worried about Charlie—not drowning while crossing flood streams or when we were sleeping were more immediate problems. All the water in our utes and gear must have made them weigh more'n twenty pounds extra. The dirt'd turned into greasy mud and we were slipping and falling down all the time. Made us real glad, knowing we weren't going to run into Vee Cee in this shit. Smelled like shit, too.

"So we humped all that first day, three klicks one way, then make a turn and go four klicks in another. Clouds were so thick in the sky and the rain came down so hard it looked almost like night, couldn't hardly see the next man in front of us if we let him get the twenty meters ahead we were supposed to maintain. That first day all we did was try and stay on our feet and not get lost. About eighteen hundred hours we pulled up for the night. Opened up our Cs and tried to eat them down before the rain washed them away. Then we settled into our night defensive positions. First platoon put out an ambush and the other two platoons each put out two LPs. We were supposed to be on a one-third alert, but for the most part there were only two men in a squad awake.

"Second day was samee-same as the first day, only difference was when it ended we were only six klicks and less than twenty-four hours from our fire base and the end of the patrol. Third platoon put out the ambush. Had to be third squad, wouldn't you know. Lieutenant Haupt sent a gun team with us, so we were twelve men out there. The ambush was at a bend in a trail on a bushy hillside above the paddies. Johnny Johnson set the gun at the corner of the trail, where it could fire down either leg of it and the squad along one of the legs. Instead of only two or three men being awake out of this group like they would have been the night before, we were one sleeping, one watching.

"Some time after midnight Sergeant Johnny got one of those feelings experienced combat sometimes get and decided to go on one-hundred-percent alert. His feeling was right on the money. We wasn't all awake there for ten minutes when a Vee Cee squad come walking down a trail right into our killing zone.

"We were all laying on our ponchos except for the machine gunner, who was sitting on account of his gun was on its tripod instead of its bipod because of all the mud. It was so dark none of us could see old Charlie coming through the rain until he was almost right in front of us. Johnny set the ambush off by popping a red star cluster when he thought enough of them were in the killing zone. They didn't have no idea anybody was out waiting for them, and were bunched up real bad, close enough to each other they could have hung onto the man in front of them, which they probably were doing so none of them would get lost in the dark. The squad opened up on their flank and the gun fired down the length of the column. Thanks to the star cluster, we could see a little bit and got some good shots off. Them buggers didn't even try to return fire. The ones that didn't get wasted by the first bursts tried to bug out through the bushes but we chopped them all down, too.

"That was a real effective ambush. We didn't get any casualties ourselves but we killed six of them and one more was wounded but alive enough to take prisoner. Johnny got on the radio and called in his report. The skipper told him to bring us in along with the wounded man and all the weapons and gear we could find, but leave the dead for the Vee Cee to worry about later. We couldn't have been any wetter than we was if we was ten feet deep in the South China Sea, but we were so happy going back to the company carrying that wounded gook, seven rifles, and cartridge belts, and knowing there was six dead Charlies back on the trail, we could have been hanging on the beach at Malibu with three blonde sun bunnies for each of us. Haupt and the skipper met us when we came in and they was mighty happy, too.

"The Kit Carson scout the skipper had with him questioned the prisoner while the corpsmen patched him up, but he didn't know anything he could tell before he died from loss of blood.

"In the morning we ate another meal of wet Cs and started humping back to the fire base. We were to go three klicks at an angle to it, then turn straight on in. Our route took us through some old sugarcane fields. Three Vee Cee platoons and an NVA company were waiting for us to come there.

"Two of our platoons were in the fields, and the point was almost to the other side of them when one Vee Cee platoon opened up from the front. We all dropped down into the mud of that field and second platoon, which was on the point, spread out to fire back. The skipper thought there was only the one unit facing us, so he radioed for the first platoon, which wasn't in the fields yet, to go around them and flank the gooks in front of us. First platoon got about two hundred meters when they ran into the other two Vee Cee platoons and got pinned down. Now the skipper told third platoon to maneuver through the fields to the other side of second and help out that way. We started the maneuver and that's when the NVA company opened up on us.

"This was some kind of bad place we were in. Vee Cee and NVA units were smaller than Marine platoons and companies, but an NVA company and three Vee Cee platoons were almost two hundred men. In Lima Company there was maybe a hundred and twenty of us out there pinned down in them fields and on that flanking movement. Also the rain made us hard for the Charlies and NVAs to see. And anyhow the NVA company was too far away to lay really effective fire on us.

"They must have been expecting us to come in farther to that side of the cane fields, where they could get us good from three sides. Us not coming in where they thought we would really saved our asses. Through this whole shit we only took a few casualties when each of the gook units opened on us. I think maybe ten men in the company got hit, and none of the hits was real serious. Nobody was away from the company for more than two weeks from their wounds in this fight.

"We stayed down and returned fire while the FO—that's Forward Observer, he's the artillery liaison—called in for the big guns to give us some help. So happened we were the only unit that needed the guns just then. All they were doing were some harassment and interdiction fire, called H and I, so all the big guns in range wanted to help us. The FO called in one battery on the NVAs first, then directed another one on the two platoons that had first platoon pinned down.

"By the time he was able to get a battery on the position of the platoon in front of us, the gooks decided to di-di and bugged out of there. Because of the rain and some atmospheric conditions I don't know nothing about, it took more than the three or four spotting rounds normal to zero in on each gook position. But when the batteries got on target, it was all over except for the screaming. Those bad bastards laid everything they could on the targets once the FO told 'em 'Fire for effect.'

"Then we spread out and swept through the areas the gook units had been in. There were lots of bits and pieces of bodies on the flanks, but damn little sign of any hurting put on the Vee Cee platoon that opened on us first. The weather was too bad for any aircraft to come in to med-evac our wounded, since none of them were that bad off. So we collected the weapons and other shit we found, and souvenired what we could and used some thermite and Willie Peter grenades to try and destroy the rest of it. When this was finished we started humping again and got ourselves and the wounded back to the fire base in about another three hours.

"Nothing much in the way of action happened for the next five weeks. Most of what we did was trying to keep our bodies from turning into prunes and our weapons and gear from rusting or rotting away. That damn endless rain. Nobody who ain't been in a monsoon can imagine what it's like. Most of us who've been through it sometimes doubts anything can possibly be that miserable. Fighting only made it a little bit worse, but Charlie didn't want much of fighting in the monsoon no how—he wanted to try and not turn into a prune, either.''

Chapter Eight

RAIN.

Rain, rain, rain-rain, rainrain. There are many kinds of rain. There is the soft spring rain that sort of drifts down out of the sky for hours or days, giving seeds the moisture they need to germinate. There is the wind-driven, crashing rain of thunderstorms that soaks everything at once, then dies abruptly. Hurricanes bring torrential, destructive, flooding rains. Then there is the just plain rain kind of rain that drops out of the sky and makes things wet and keeps them wet until after it ends and the air has a chance to dry it all off again.

Those are the rains of the Western Hemisphere. The East has all those rains and another one that is a stranger to the West. It is a rain that starts in India below the Himalayas. It floods that subcontinent before sweeping eastward along the underbelly of Asia and inundating the Indo-Chinese peninsula. Then it turns northward, half-drowning the East Asia mainland and the massive archipelagoes of the western Pacific before petering itself out north and east of the main islands of Japan.

This rain is the monsoon, an everlasting rain that starts fitfully with violent storms and settles into an unending torrent that lasts what seems for all eternity. It is the rain that brings the floods needed by the millions of acres of rice paddies that feed more than half the human population of the world. It gives the water

152

needed by the jungle for it to grow high and huge, tangled and matted. It provides the humidity that rusts metal to a red powder and rots wood and leather, destroying anything made by man that is not continually cared for. The monsoon is the deadly life-giving rain that kills the spirit.

Continual flashes of lightning kept the night sky brighter than daytime. One after another the bolts and sheets broke through the atmosphere, each flashing before the previous one had a chance to dim.

"Goddam, who ordered this shit," Buster Bahls shouted to make himself heard above the thunder. "Henry J, what'd you do to piss off the Okinawa Rain God so bad?"

"Weren't me," Morris shouted back. "Malcolm X did it."

The muscular PFC with his hands covering his ears to protect them from the din of the thunder curled down three fingers of one hand and wagged the remaining—middle, of course—finger at his companions.

Bahls and Morris laughed at Evans's gesture and slapped hands. Then they ducked low at an even louder clap of thunder.

"Goddam, you think this is what artillery sounds like to Charlie?" Morris asked.

"Probably." Bahls nodded.

The thunder boomed, crashed, rolled, exploded around them. It was a bedlam that made conversation impossible. As abruptly as it had begun, it ended. The unexpected silence at first sounded as loud as the storm. Numbed ears gradually stopped ringing and hearing slowly returned. The rain continued, but not as heavily.

"How long before the next one?" Morris asked when he recovered his speaking voice.

Bahls and Evans widened their eyes. "You think there's gonna be more of this shit?"

Morris shrugged. "Thunderstorms don't come one at a time."

"But we already had three of them sons'a bitches this morning."

"And they been going on for two days now."

"There's more thunderstorms in the afternoon than in the morning."

"Goddam shit."

"I don't be doing it, Buster. This ain't my fault," Evans insisted again.

"Shut the fuck up, Malcolm X. You caused enough trouble already, and lying about it ain't gonna make things any better."

"Shee-it. I don't even do nothing and it be my fault."

The three turned to cleaning their rifles and other gear. Rust was trying to make inroads, and mildew was settling in for a long visit.

Elsewhere in the company area, men were reerecting flattened tents, driving stakes deeper into the earth, gathering belongings scattered by the winds, wringing what water they could from sodden fabric, wiping and oiling metal. The war against the monsoon had begun.

In a few more days the storms were over, then began the *endless* rain. Squad and platoon patrols, small ambushes, and perimeter duty were the order of the day. Until regiment got word of an NVA company lurking nearby. Three companies were sent on separate patrols to find that NVA company, fix it, and kill it.

"Just like a battalion op," Staff Sergeant Ortega told his squad leaders. "Five magazines and four bandoleers per rifleman, two extra magazines and bandoleers for the ARs. Eight frags, a Willie Peter, and two smokes per fire team. Two LAWs per squad. Six rations per man. Make sure your men have their halazone tablets, because we've got little or no chance of any water resupply in this rain. Any questions?"

The squad leaders made faces but said nothing.

"Get 'em ready now. We move out in"—Ortega checked his watch—"twenty-eight minutes. Go."

"Why the fuck we gotta do this shit?" Morris asked. "Mister Charles ain't gonna be nowhere we can find his ass in this kinda rain."

"You be right as shit, man," Evans answered him. "That dink staying dry in his hootch, keeping hisself warm by dorking his old lady."

"He gets tired dorking her, I'll relieve his gook ass." Runningstar laughed.

Four six-by trucks, two of them with mounted fifty-caliber

machine guns, splashed up Highway One escorted by two jeeps
and a tank-killing Ontos with its six 106mm recoilless rifles
mounted three on a side. The jeeps were also armed with fifties.
Lima Company's one hundred forty effectives rode the trucks
through the rain. They didn't bother putting their ponchos on in
the uncovered truck beds. They were already as wet as they
could get.

"You hear that shit they talking, Grady, about why the fuck
we doing this?"

"I hear it, Ball Buster. What about it?"

"Why the fuck *are* we doing this?"

Zimmerman's pale eyes drifted vacantly over the passing
landscape. He wanted to spit but didn't. "Regiment thinks
there's a new NVA unit in the area and wants 'em found."

Bahls squinted at the platoon guide. "You shitting me. NVA
try coming down here in this shit, he's gonna turn into a prune
and get flushed away in the *song* before he gets this far."

Zimmerman slowly shook his head. "Ol' man river ain't rolling these damn gooks nowhere. They live in this shit every goddam year of their lives. They're not like normal people; they're
used to this kind of rain."

Bahls looked doubtful, but checked that his magazine was
properly seated. His eyes searched the treelines in the surrounding paddy land more carefully.

Ten kilometers up Highway One the convoy slowed while the
point jeep searched for a roadway leading inland. The side road
was found, and the convoy proceeded more cautiously along it
for another four kilometers. On a low hill that hadn't been ter-
raced for paddies, the vehicles circled. The grunts dismounted
and formed a route-march column. Captain Sarmiento gathered
his platoon leaders and staff NCOs for a final briefing and the
column moved out. The convoy with its fifties stayed on the hill
until the company was far enough away that the guns couldn't
give them covering fire.

Splash, slip, slide, slew, slog. Anything but fall. The rain
soaked the earth. Battered it, churned it, mixed with it. The
more the rain fell, the muddier the earth became, until it could
hold no more water. But still more rain came down, settling on
the saturated earth, making slender pockets of mostly water in

it, giving the surface the texture and consistency of a plaster of paris slurry. The mud sucked at boots, tried to hold them, clutched like glue. No one wanted to fall. The men were too afraid that if they did, the mud would grab them and refuse to give them up.

Pull a boot caked thick with mud out of this earth stew, swing it forward through the rain, see the mud start rinsing off, put the foot back down before all of the mud is washed away. Pick the boot up again with more mud on it. Put it back down. Repeat several hundred times. The mud becomes very thick and heavy on the boot.

Several thousand steps after Lima Company left the convoy at the hill, the dark day grew darker. Night was falling. The column halted on the dikes. Watch rotations were set and each platoon sent a fire team LP out one hundred meters on each side of the column. First platoon sent a squad out for an ambush. The men struggled to eat their evening meal of Cs before the rain washed the food away. The men who weren't assigned to the first watch huddled under their ponchos and tried to get some sleep. No one drowned that night, though a few woke in a start, spitting and snorting water from their noses.

At length the utter blackness of the night eased to the sodden darkness of the morning. The men relieved themselves into the paddies and puddles and slurped down another cold C-ration meal. Captain Sarmiento quickly briefed his officers and platoon sergeants on the second day's objective, and the column moved out once more.

Day two was a carbon copy of day one. Except that twice as many thousand steps were taken through the ever thinner, ever slicker mud. The first day's march didn't start until well past noon. The second started not long after the unseen sunrise and continued until the darkness nearly dimmed into full night. Morale was lifted slightly by the men's knowledge that this would be their last night trying to sleep in the rain. The next day they would return to their fire base and the relative dryness of their tents and bunkers.

The company was no longer in the paddies, but in the low hills overlooking them. This night no one had to worry about rolling into the flooded paddies during his sleep. Each platoon put out two LPs again, and third platoon sent its third squad forward along the trail to set an ambush.

"Three hundred meters farther up this trail is a fork," Lieutenant Haupt said to Sergeant Johnson.

Johnson looked at the map in its waterproof, transparent cover that Haupt was drawing on with a grease pencil.

"Take Marsden and his gun team, set him where he can cover both tines of the fork, and place the rest of your men where they've got the best cover. Questions?"

Johnson stared at the map a few seconds longer before shaking his head. "No, sir."

"Then do it, Sergeant. I'll see you in the morning."

"Aye aye, sir." Johnson gave the map one more look, committing it to memory, then turned and sloshed through the rain, back to his squad. "Third squad, team leaders up," he called when he reached it.

Falalo and Bahls rose grumbling to their feet and half waded to Johnson's side.

"We got a 'bush tonight," Johnson told his fire-team leaders. "Marsden and his gun are joining us. It's an all-nighter three hundred meters up the trail at a fork. Get your men saddled up and let's move out. We'll pick Marsden up when we pass him."

"Shit," Bahls swore. "Why we gotta do this thing?"

"Your mama told you there'd be nights like this," Falalo answered.

"Nope. My mama didn't know there was nights like this."

"Saddle up," Johnson repeated.

Falalo and Bahls walked back to their teams. In little more than a minute third squad was moving toward the front of the column. Marsden and his gun team were waiting for them, having already been alerted by Sergeant Zimmerman. The ambush patrol moved slowly along the trail, first team, blooper, squad leader, gun team, second team. The incessant rain disguised the sound of their passage, washed away their sign.

A short while later the squad huddled watchfully in the rain while Johnson and Marsden scouted the ambush site for the best location for the gun. They decided to emplace it on the low side of the trail, where it might be below grazing fire. In this position it was pointed directly along the right fork and could sweep the left fork. Because of the soft mud, Marsden decided to spread his poncho and mount the gun on its tripod on the poncho. Johnson set the rest of his men in the brush on the high side of the trail, where they could fire along the left fork and flank the right one.

The men spread their ponchos on the ground to keep themselves out of the mud. One man out of three slept at a time. Johnson would try to stay awake all night.

Around midnight the rain eased to a heavy drizzle and the clouds looked like they might break up, but it was a false hope; the rain continued to drift down. The sleepers shivered; the men who were awake shook them to stop their groaning.

Not long after two in the morning, Johnson was snapped to full awareness by the sound of sniper fire coming from the other end of the company's column. There weren't many shots fired and none were returned. Johnson listened intently for a few minutes before making up his mind.

"Everyone awake," he whispered to the men at his sides, "pass the word and bring it back." That sniper fire might have been a diversion. Other VC could be coming from a different direction.

Moments later the men to his sides said, "Everyone awake." The word had been passed to the ends of the line and back. Johnson crossed the trail and made sure the gun team was alert.

"If someone comes, a red star cluster will set us off. Pass it." Now the signal for the ambush was set.

A star appeared low on the horizon, along the line of the left fork, twinkling dimly where none had been seen before. The Marines who could see the star tensed and tried to melt into the ground. They nudged each other and pointed until they were all watching the moving star. One machine gun, the blooper, and nine rifles were lined up on the light. The star came closer and resolved itself into a shielded flashlight. Muffled voices plodded through the rain, and the clank of a rifle butt banging rhythmically against metal followed the voices.

The light reached the juncture of the fork. Johnson pointed his flare gun toward it at a high angle and fired. The flashlight stood still at the sound of the flare's firing, and the muffled voices stopped. Then the red star burst over ten frozen Viet Cong and the ambush opened fire on it.

The VC moved. Some of them dropped to the trail, the others spun and ran screaming. Two more fell to the Marines' fire before they disappeared into the concealing brush.

"Cease fire! Cease fire!" Johnson bellowed. The firing stopped. "Team leaders, report."

Low calls passed among the men in the ambush.

"First team, all okay," Falalo called out.

"Second team, we all right," Bahls answered.

"Gun team's okay," Marsden reported.

"Oo-ee," Johnson breathed. Several VC had fallen, but none of his men were wounded. Then he reported the contact to the company CP on his radio and requested mortar illumination so he could check the enemy casualties.

The illume request was granted and a minute later a flare's parachute popped open above the fork.

"Second team, let's check 'em out," Johnson ordered. "First team, gun team, cover us." Johnson led Bahls and his two men onto the left fork. "Spread it out, people. Move easy. We don't have any casualties yet, and I want to keep it that way."

Keeping their eyes and M-14s pointed at the bodies on the trail, the four Marines hurried toward them.

"Get their weapons," Johnson said.

One of the VC moaned when his rifle was yanked from him. The other two made no protest. Johnson grabbed the feet of the one who moaned and twisted, rolling him onto his back, and shined his flashlight into the man's face. The wounded Viet Cong blinked and closed his eyes against the light. His hands waved feebly, pushing at the light. He mumbled. Johnson panned the light down the man's front. He bled from the lower chest, and a loop of intestine protruded from a hole in his abdomen. Johnson stripped the VC's knife and grenades from his body and stood over him.

"Hideaway," Johnson called, "this one's still alive. Keep an eye on him while we check out the others." Then he spoke into his radio again. Half a minute later a second flare opened overhead.

A fourth body lay in the mud twenty meters farther back, and a fifth less than ten yards beyond it. The fifth body was alive. Johnson looked into the brush where the rest of the VC squad had run and shook his head. His ambush was successful; he didn't want to give someone else a chance to successfully ambush him.

Again Johnson called the CP. He reported three Charlies KIA and two more WIA. He got his instructions.

"Third squad, saddle up," Johnson called. "We've got two wounded prisoners there. We'll carry them back in their ponchos and leave the dead for their buddies to take care of. Gather up all their weapons and ammo. Move." His grinning teeth glistened in the rain.

Everyone else was grinning while they collected the VC armament and made litters from two ponchos to carry the wounded.

"Got some," Casebolt crowed.

"You see that sucker flip backward when Marsden hit him a burst?" asked Morris.

"Yeah," PFC Wegener answered. "And he looked surprised as shit."

"Surprised as shit, hell. He looked like he just be biting into a shit sandwich," Evans said.

"Got 'em good," Runningstar laughed.

"Yeah."

Back at the company CP a corpsman patched up the prisoners while the Kit Carson scout, a former Viet Cong who had turned to the government side and acted as a scout and interrogater for the Americans in exchange for a pardon, questioned them. When the prisoners refused to answer him, he made the corpsman stop treating them and tore off their battle dressings. "You can bleed to death if you won't talk," he told them. A half hour later one of the prisoners decided to save his life. The other seemed to prefer death, or else he didn't understand that he was bleeding to death.

"There are only a few Viet Cong squads in the area," the wounded man said. "All you can expect tomorrow is some sniping."

The Kit Carson questioned him some more, but that was all the man claimed to know. The Kit Carson stepped away from the man and motioned the corpsman to treat him. The other was left to die. Unfortunately for the talker, he had waited too long before speaking and he died as well.

* * *

Dawn somewhat eased the darkness of the night. But only somewhat, as the rain increased from a drizzle to a near torrent. The Marines of Lima Company cut their morning Cs open and ate the soup the rain turned the field rations into. Then they were humping again, trying to maintain their balance, listening for sniper rounds, looking forward to reaching their bunkers at the end of the day's hump. Second platoon had the point, third dropped back to the middle, and first took up the rear. The VC bodies from third squad's ambush were gone from the trail where they had been left. The march was uneventful for two and a half hours until the company reached an expanse of paddies—not even the snipers the dying VC had said were there made an appearance.

"Oh, shit," Morris said. "Know what this place reminds me of?"

"Tell me," Bahls answered.

"Them paddies we crossed on the last day of Abilene Run."

Bahls looked around more. Treelines were to their front and both flanks. "You got it, Henry J, looks just like it."

In the dim light filtering through the clouds and rain, the company had closed to five-meter intervals walking through the brush. On the paddies they opened to ten meters between men. There was about three-quarters of a kilometer of open land to cross before the company reached the next treeline. The point closed into little more than a hundred meters of the trees, and two of third platoon's three squads were in the paddies when fire started from the front. It started light.

"Fucking snipers," Casebolt swore.

"Dead gook told it like it is," Runningstar said.

"Straight scoop," Devoid agreed.

"Second platoon, hit the deck," the second platoon's lieutenant called. "Squad leaders, control your fire, fire only at targets." Second platoon couldn't locate targets to return fire at.

"Third platoon, move forward and get down behind the dikes," Haupt shouted, waving his arms. "We don't need any damn casualties from snipers." Third platoon grumbled, but the men moved forward and got into the water.

First platoon pulled back out of the paddies and squatted in the brush, waiting for the orders that soon came.

The fire from the front slowly increased, but the snipers were too far back in the trees for their muzzle flashes to be seen from the paddies.

"Radio, tell Lima One to go the long way around to the right and flank those snipers," Captain Sarmiento said to his radioman. Lima One was the designation of first platoon.

Sarmiento's order was relayed and first platoon headed through the brush to another treeline half a kilometer to its right. Moving quickly, it would take fifteen minutes to reach the trees where the snipers were hiding. Second and third platoons settled down in the paddy water to wait. On this day Sarmiento would rather take his time in the paddies than risk pointlessly losing men to sniper fire.

First platoon had covered about half the distance to the parallel treeline when two things happened so close together as to be simultaneous. One was that a machine gun and several automatic rifles joined the fire coming from the trees in front of the company. The other was first platoon plunging into an L-shaped ambush formed by two Viet Cong platoons.

Sarmiento swore when he realized the position he had let himself be maneuvered into. His company was divided, with the smaller part under assault from a superior force and the main body pinned down in the open by a smaller unit.

"Radio, tell Lima Three to move forward on the left and help Lima Two fire on this blocking force," Sarmiento told his radioman. This order also was relayed.

Haupt started maneuvering his platoon one half at a time. Run crouched over two paddies to the front and left, then wait for the rest to come up. Do it again. When third platoon reached the middle of the paddies, another thing happened. Heavy machine-gun and automatic-rifle fire erupted from a treeline more than a half kilometer to its left.

Sarmiento swore again. He thought this new fire must be coming from the NVA company Lima Company was looking for. Lima wasn't receiving any casualties, but the surrounding fire was so heavy the company couldn't move, either. This was almost embarrassing.

"FO," Sarmiento said to the artillery observer, "can you get me some big guns in here?" He hated to do it this way because he saw calling in massive artillery to break an ambush as an Army tactic, not as a Marinely thing to do. On the other hand, anything else would bring serious risk of unacceptably heavy casualties.

"Sure can, Skipper," answered the second lieutenant who was the FO.

"All right, then. Start with the ones to the left. That's the heaviest concentration and gives you the greatest margin of error."

Eagerly, the young lieutenant hunched over his map, finding his position. He sighted through his compass on the distant NVA position and talked on his radio. He gave his position in map grid coordinates, the direction to the target in azimuth degrees, its approximate distance to the nearest fifty meters. The numbers were repeated to him by the artillery battery's radioman.

"Fire one HE spotter round," he ordered. A minute later a high explosive 105mm howitzer round splashed into the paddies close to the NVA position.

"On my azimuth, left one hundred, up one hundred. Fire one spotter." Another round blossomed in the paddies. A third spotter, more finely adjusted, dropped in the treeline. It was on target, so the FO told the battery to fire for effect. "Fire for effect" means just dump the rounds in, scatter them around the area near where the final spotter hit.

A second battery came on the net. It was free and volunteered to take on any other targets Lima had. Sarmiento told the FO to fire them on the treeline to the front.

Same position, different azimuth, different range. "Fire one HE spotter round." Adjust the aim, adjust once more and "Fire for effect."

Now a third battery wanted part of the action. Sarmiento conferred with the commander of the first platoon over the radio, passed on to the FO the necessary information, and the numbers process was repeated. "Fire one spotter." Adjust. "Fire one spotter." Adjust again. "Fire for effect."

Somewhere along the line, nobody ever found out for sure where, although there were strong suspicions—a young and promising lieutenant's career is a terrible thing to waste—an adjustment was made from first platoon's position instead of the FO's. A six-round salvo landed in the paddies among second and third platoons.

"Cease fire! All batteries, cease fire!" the FO shouted into his radio. Unfortunately, a second salvo was already descending from the apex of its arc by the time he called to the battery radiomen on the net. The gunners were already yanking on their lanyards, firing the third salvo when the message was relayed to them—one was slow, his gun hadn't fired yet.

The last five rounds of seventeen that landed in the paddies drowned out the cries of "corpsman up" from the wounded and the men near them. Silence, interrupted only by the moaning of the wounded and the hushed-rushed voices of the corpsmen attending them, descended over the paddies and surrounding treelines and brush. The enemy had left the field of battle.

While he waited for the casualty reports from his two injured platoons, Sarmiento ordered first platoon to sweep through the ambush site and then return to the company. The numbers came in. Five men in second platoon were wounded, four from third. No one, miraculously, was killed.

Everyone from second platoon who wasn't needed to tend the wounded was sent forward to the trees to look for VC casualties and equipment. The body pieces they found smeared on the sides of shell craters and hanging from tree branches told a grisly tale. No whole bodies were found, nor was any equipment.

When first platoon returned to the paddies, it went with third to check out the NVA position. More body parts were found—feet, arms, entrails, an intact thorax, legs. A mangled head or two. One broken machine gun and three AK-47s were retrieved. No whole bodies or wounded.

Battalion HQ ordered Lima to leave one squad with the casualties to await med-evac while the rest of the company pursued the NVA company on its probable line of march. Kilo Company was in that direction and would set a blocking force.

Two hours later Lima passed through Kilo's line without either company having made any more contact with the NVA. The enemy had made good his escape. No one knew how many there had been in the company at the beginning of the fight, how many had gotten away, how many later died of their wounds.

A very depressed Lima Company trudged into its fire base in time for a hot evening meal.

"Goddam, Honcho, that artillery sounded worse than the most bodacious thunderstorm I've ever been in," Morris said, dumping his gear onto a wooden pallet in his team's bunker.

"I do believe you're right, Henry J," Bahls replied from where he stood slumped over inside the entrance to the bunker.

"Don't know how Charlie can take it."

"He's a crazy little fucker, that's how. I'm gonna find Grady." Bahls left the bunker in search of the platoon guide. Now he knew why they had gone on that patrol. What he wanted now was to understand why they'd had to be the ones to do it.

Night of the Sapper

"WHEN THREE FIFTEEN FIRST ARRIVED IN EYE CORPS AND WAS shipped to Chu Lai, we did all of our operating out of that main Marine air base. Most everybody there did, like the First Marines and the Fifth Marines and all of them. Vee Cee were all over the place then and we had to keep good watch on the perimeter every night we weren't out on an operation. There were a few times we were all put on one-hundred-percent alert because we were expecting an assault. Patrols went right outside the wire, they had to be prepared for some crap and lots of times got it. In the beginning we usually didn't have to go more than maybe ten klicks from Chu Lai on an operation to find plenty of Charlies to kick ass with. By the time July came along, though, most Vee Cee that close to Chu Lai had their asses kicked too bad to want to hang around anymore, so we were going farther out on operations.

"You heard of the Army's First Cavalry Division, Airmobile, and how they perfected what's called vertical assault. That's where the attacking unit comes in by helicopter instead of by truck or humping. The Marines pioneered vertical assault and were already using it by the time the First Cav got to Vietnam. But we ran into tough luck. See, we didn't have enough birds to keep all of us in operation, so instead of staying in main bases and flying out to find Charlie when we went on operations, we

166

had to move into forward fire bases where we were close enough to Charlie that we could hump to him without having to wear ourselves out for a couple of days before we found his ass. The Green Machine started up the concept of riding into combat in choppers, but the Army was the ones that mostly got to do it.

"That's how come Lima Company was living about twelve klicks northwest from Chu Lai by late July. The four companies of the battalion was sitting on a line of little hills out there in the middle of these huge rice-paddy fields near the foothills Charlie liked to hide himself in. Each company was on its own hill, and there was maybe a half klick to a whole klick between hills. Each of them fire bases had an eighty-one-millimeter mortar and two 106-millimeter recoilless rifles from battalion on its hill. From where we were, we sent out patrols every day and ambushes every night. None of the patrols went out for more than two days. When we had to go on an operation, either three companies went out and left the other one to hold all four hills, or we all went and another battalion came in and held the hills and ran our patrols and ambushes for us.

"Every day when we were on the hills we ran into some kind of crap from the Vee Cee. The pointman on a patrol had to be real careful where he stepped because Charlie put booby traps all over the place. Good thing he had to mark where the booby traps were so the civilians and other Charlies wouldn't trip them off. We learned in a hurry what to look for, and after the first two weeks when we lost ten point men to booby traps we dropped back to only about one casualty a week from them. There were snipers all over the place and they zinged at our patrols every day and our lines every night. Seemed like the Vee Cee was always using sniping to teach new men how to shoot, because they didn't hit anybody very often. Almost every day and always every night Charlie'd pop a few mortar rounds on our hills.

"Marines'd been at Chu Lai since August the year before, and in that time put a bad hurting on Charlie, so he wasn't putting up much of a fight against us anymore and we were all beginning to think we were gonna go up north to the DMZ pretty soon and invade the North. Either that or we just about had the war won and we might be going home for Christmas. That'd sure be nice.

"What we didn't know was that up North Uncle Ho and

General Giap were getting worried about how we were winning. They decided to do some new stuff and started sending more cadre and NVA regulars down through Laos and into southern Eye Corps. Charlie was building up right in our front yard and we didn't know it.

"Am I surprising you talking about how we were winning? You better believe it, son. We lost a lot of men in that war, but our dead was not much more than one percent of the men we had over there. Charlie and the NVA lost close to ten percent of their countries' populations. Hell, Hanoi admits they lost, NVA and Vee Cee combined, 400,000 men in the war. Don't even try to tell me we lost that war. Nobody in this country understood why we were there in the first place—even most of the men we had fighting that war didn't understand why. We didn't lose. We gave up. Anybody tells you different don't know what he's talking about. Every time we could get old Charlie to stand and fight, we put his ass so deep in the hurt locker we figured he'd never get out.

"Enough editorializing for now. Anyway, we settled ourselves in one night near the end of July. First platoon had two squads out about a half klick on an ambush and there was a fireteam LP out in front of each platoon. On the perimeter we were on one-third alert, one man awake and two sleeping. Nobody thought we'd have any kind of trouble at all. Nobody but Charlie, that is.

"It'd been a quiet night. No sniper rounds were zinging in at us and there ain't been no mortar rounds popping in, bugging us and keeping people awake that should have been sleeping. We should have known it was too quiet. Little after oh-three-hundred, I just got off my watch and was starting to cop me some Zs, there was this bodacious explosion right in the middle of the compound. Rocked the whole damn hill. Thought we were having an earthquake.

"Sappers came in and blew the eighty-one's ammo bunker. Those greasy little gooks slipped right under the perimeter wire and sneaked between our fighting holes. They knifed the eighty-one's crew to death where they were sleeping—even the one who was supposed to be awake watching—then threw a satchel charge in the the bunker and blew it all to hell. The explosion killed three more men and wounded a couple others, including some-one on the perimeter more'n a hundred meters away.

"That explosion was the signal for the Vee Cee mortars. They started popping all the rounds they weren't sending in earlier. All those rounds and then some. Usually the rounds just hit random inside the wire and didn't cause much damage. This time they had our range. Some of the rounds landed right in holes with men and we lost a bunch of casualties that way. They also landed in the perimeter wire, poking holes in it that allowed the main assault force to come through. There were secondary explosions from our claymore mines set off by the mortar rounds. What made that even worse was that the sappers turned them around so they faced at us. Maybe four more men got zapped by our own mines.

"Next thing any of us knew there was a hundred Vee Cee charging in through each place the wire'd been breached. Char-lie was tired of us having this hill in the middle of his turf. He wanted to overrun and kick us the hell off it. And remember, there were sappers inside the perimeter already. The hole near-est to me in the wire was fifty meters to my left. I turned my M-14 to full auto and started firing short bursts at them.

"At first there was nothing but confusion in Lima. People were waking up not knowing what the hell was going on. The officers and platoon sergeants were trying to find out how their people were doing and if they had any casualties, squad leaders were trying to make sure their squads were awake, and fire-team leaders were looking to see where Charlie was. Nobody knew what was what. It was almost like one by one we pulled our-selves together and started making a defense.

"In the hole with me was Richard Wegener. Chief Running-star was on R and R, Nick Devoid was in a hospital with his second wound, Corporal Doyle'd just been transferred to a CAP, and Malcolm X was carrying the blooper. So Johnny Johnson reorganized the squad again. Hernando Falalo had Salatu, Hunter, and Gant. That left Buster Bahls with me, Jeb Casebolt, and Wegener. Wegener was laying on the ground behind the hole. The first time I changed magazines I wapped him upside the head on account of all this noise ain't woke him up and I told him to get his ass in the hole with me and start cranking them out at the gooks coming through that hole in the wire.

"For a half minute he just straightened out where he was laying and kind of bug-eyed at all them Vee Cee. This was even worse than that night they tried to overrun that hill we was on back in Operation Abilene Run. Then he rolled into that hole next to me and started putting out some nice-aimed slow fire just like they taught him back in ITR.

"Vee Cee were dropping in their tracks coming through the wire, but more of them was getting through. We weren't organized enough yet to stop them, and it was too dark to make every round aimed. By the time the sixties got themselves together and started putting some illume out where we could see, most of the Charlies was inside the wire. That made it real tough for the mortars to fire on any concentrations of them. It also meant we had to keep our heads low in our holes because fire was going all over our fire base. Squad leaders started calling out to stay in our holes and shoot anybody we saw standing up because only Vee Cee would be standing above ground.

"American voices was yelling all over the damn place and we could hear Vee Cee voices jabbering all around us. Wounded men were screaming for corpsmen. Squad leaders were yelling, trying to coordinate their men's firing. Hand grenades were exploding. There were shadows flitting everywhere.

"Then Wegener just buckled next to me and collapsed into the bottom of our hole. I spun around and saw three Vee Cee running at me with fixed bayonets. One of them was still shooting at Wegener and hitting him. I turned my rifle on its side and held the trigger back until it stopped shooting. Two of the Vee Cee went down, including the one shooting Wegener, but the other one kept coming straight at me and lunged with his bayonet.

"I flinched out of the way and rose halfway to my feet, then I gave him an upper butt stroke with all the muscle I had. Caught him right in the solar plexus and flipped him all the way over to the other side of the hole. He just laid there rolled up in a ball, moaning, so I brought the butt plate of my rifle down on his head with everything I could. He stopped moaning and I wiped my butt plate dry on his shirt.

"Then I didn't see no more shadows to shoot at. I don't mean the fight was over, just that there didn't seem to be any more Vee Cee near where I was. There was still firing going on in other parts of the compound. I called for a corpsman and bent over to check Wegener out. Then I called out to belay the corpsman because I could tell Wegener was dead. He'd been hit at least six times in the middle of the back and once through the middle of his neck, which was broken by that bullet.

"Then Johnny Johnson rolled into my hole, saw the two Vee Cee on one side of it, the other one on the other side, and what'd happened to Wegener. He swore, and after I told him what'd happened, said the gooks must have run out of ammo and I should check the piece the Charlie with the broken head tried to bayonet me with. I did and it was empty. Then I checked all three bodies and didn't find no ammo on them, either. Sergeant Johnny swore again and said if Charlie was running out of ammo we had to watch real careful because he'd be sneaking around trying to knife us and steal our weapons.

"Johnny didn't want to leave me alone, but he had to check the rest of the holes, so he grabbed Wegener's rifle and ammo and took me with him. Buster Bahls and Jeb Casebolt were in the next hole. Johnny left me there and went on after telling Buster what he figured out.

"By now the mortars had stopped putting out illume. We didn't find out until later that was because they'd been overrun. Buster, Jeb, and me just lay there as quiet as we could and listened.

"After a while we heard something over by the hole I'd been in with Wegener and then a grenade exploded in it. Then we heard the noise again, only closer. Silently, Buster signed us to aim at the noise and fire. We did. I fired half a magazine in three-round bursts, Buster and Jeb let out with about five rounds of rapid fire and we heard something fall almost in front of us. Then a grenade rolled into that hole with us and we bailed out most ricky-tick. The grenade went off, but didn't do any damage to us.

"We crawled to where we heard something fall and found a sapper laying with a bunch of bullet holes in him. He had a bayonet in his left hand, a bag of grenades around his waist, and three M-14s and cartridge belts slung over his shoulders. He was naked except for Ho Chi Minh sandals and a loincloth, and his skin was covered with grease to help him slip through barbed wire. He must have been crawling on all fours because all the hits on him were in his face and on the top of his shoulders and chest.

"This showed Johnny Johnson was right about Charlie trying to knife us and steal our rifles to rearm himself with. We went back to the hole and waited some more.

"A few minutes later an artillery battery popped some illume over us and we could see beaucoup Vee Cee trying to sneak out of the perimeter. Seemed like boo-coo Charlies because they were on our side of the wire instead of the other, but wasn't near as many as came in in the first place. Everybody opened fire on them and a whole shitload of them dropped, but bunches managed to get away anyhow.

"Not all of them tried to get out. For the rest of the night a few were sneaking around, and every now and then a grenade'd go off or someone would fire at a shadow. All of us stayed in our holes except for the corpsmen who were going around patching up the wounded. Nobody wanted to get mistaken for a gook and get shot by his own men.

"After sunup we were able to take stock. Lima had about a hundred and thirty men inside the perimeter when the sappers hit. We lost about thirty-five or forty dead and wounded. Maybe one-third of our strength. There was more than a hundred dead Charlies inside the wire and a bunch more bodies hung up in the wire where they got killed either trying to get in or trying to get out at the end. The best estimate is we got hit by an entire battalion that night.

"We got hurt bad, but it wasn't nowhere near as bad as the hurting we put on Charlie. He was so deep in the hurt locker we didn't get no sniper fire or incoming mortars for the remaining three days we was there before being taken back to Chu Lai for a flight up to Da Nang for some in-country R and R after that fight."

Chapter Nine

Phuc Binh was a sixteen-year-old Viet Minh when he helped dig trenches and saw a French Foreign Legioneer fall in his rifle sights at Dien Bien Phu in 1954. Earlier, his father had fought the Japanese during World War II, and then the French until they killed him in 1951. Phuc Binh had fought the French at the end of their time in his country, then he battled the Southerners to reunite his country. Now he fought the American invaders. War had been his entire life.

Twelve years after Dien Bien Phu, Phuc Binh was a sergeant leading the first squad, 24th Sapper Platoon. A card-carrying member of the Communist Party, he was high on the list for promotion to lieutenant. If successful, this raid could secure that promotion for him.

The five men who would set the torpedoes and slip through the wire with him were very good sappers. Phuc Binh had trained them himself. The night's raid would be a great success. He could feel it in the deepest depths of his being.

Tan Duc's father had been fighting the French for several years by the time he commanded a Viet Minh platoon at Dien Bien Phu. Retired now from combat, the old man had passed on his hatred of the Saigon regime and all foreigners to his eldest son. Tan Duc fought the minions of the Army of South Vietnam with greater ferocity than his father had fought the French. Tonight he would make combat with the American devils for the first time. His entire life had also been devoted to war.

The Americans would be made to pay. They would die for being foreigners on his soil and for supporting the corrupt Saigon regime. There was one more thing for which the Americans would die. Tan Duc's youngest brother had joined the Saigon army and become a lieutenant leading an infantry platoon. This defection within his own family had cast doubt on Tan Duc. Instead of being promoted to a position of leadership within his Viet Cong unit, Tan Duc had remained a private, a follower. He should have been a leader. Many Americans would die because of his brother's defection.

Lima Company hadn't had much contact with the Viet Cong in the past few days, mostly harassing sniper fire during the day and an occasional mortar round dropped inside the fire base at night. The other companies of Three Fifteen had similar limited contact with the elusive enemy. The six-hundred-odd Marines on the four small hills in the paddies at the edge of the foothills were growing complacent. Battalion headquarters was concerned. Part of this concern was because the men were easing their watchfulness. Another part was because of unconfirmed reports of the arrival of a new NVA regiment in the area. Unfortunately, this concern about a new NVA regiment hadn't yet filtered down to the platoons and squads of Lima Company, and alertness continued to decline.

The sun fell and three listening posts were put out around Lima Company's perimeter. A two-squad ambush patrol had left a couple of hours earlier. Watch on the perimeter was set at fifty percent, though some squad and fire-team leaders took it upon themselves to reduce it to one-third. Dawn would come early, then some of the watchers could get a little sleep before going on the day's patrols.

Starlight glinting harshly on the water betrayed no movement in the surrounding paddy land. The night was calm and silent. After a few hours most of the squad and fire team leaders who had enforced the fifty-percent watch relented and let more of their men sleep.

High-flying clouds drifted in shortly after midnight, cutting down the light on the paddies. Tired watchers behind the barbed wire rubbed tired eyes and made time checks. Charlie ain't coming tonight, they assured themselves.

The ambush patrol had been properly reconned and its location marked. It would cause no problems tonight, would be avoided until it could be dealt with after the main battle. One of the listening posts was in the way and would be silently eliminated before the assault, but Phuc Binh's sappers could do that easily enough before penetrating the wire. The 159th Infantry Battalion of the North Vietnamese Army's 84th Infantry Regiment, newly arrived in I Corps, filtered in by companies to group slightly more than a kilometer from Lima Company's perimeter. One company was to the north, another to the east, and a third to the south. The high clouds came in and the North Vietnamese entered the paddy water. Led by an indigenous Viet Cong guide, each platoon would cross the paddies, neck deep in the water. At the foot of the hill they would reform and wait for the sappers' strike. Then guides would set off the tubular bangalore torpedoes the sappers had put in the wire, opening breeches in the Americans' defensive perimeter, and the NVA would pour through the holes. Many Americans would die tonight, and the world would see the justice of the communist cause.

On the silent signal, Tan Duc slid from the dike into the water of the paddy. He sank down until his hands nearly touched the bottom and only his head showed above the surface. By twos and threes the members of an NVA platoon followed. Each man carried four potato-masher grenades and fifty rounds for his rifle. If more was needed to wipe out the Americans, weapons and ammunition could be taken from the bodies of enemy dead. Stealth was mandatory for this movement. No sound could be allowed to drift to the Americans on the hill, no ripple would be allowed to show itself on the water's surface. Regimental headquarters allowed three hours for the companies to move the kilometer-plus from their staging areas to the foot of the hill. The sappers, of course, would need to get there much earlier to do their preliminary work.

* * *

Six sappers, led by Sergeant Phuc Binh, took advantage of every shadow cast by the clouds. They walked nearly upright on the dikes, yet were unseen by anyone who happened to look in their direction. In this war the Viet Cong and NVA usually owned the night because the Americans and their Saigon-led puppets *believed* they could move unseen through the darkness. Some Viet Cong and NVA actually *could* move unseen through the night. It meant nothing to most of the Americans that some of their own men could also move unseen in the night.

It took Phuc Binh and his men only an hour to reach the foot of the American hill. Wraithlike, they moved about, removing from their hiding places the sections of bangalore torpedoes they would use to blow openings in the concertina wire surrounding the hill.

Working methodically, the six sappers, clad only in loincloths and thick layers of skin oil, placed the torpedoes under the wire. Five torpedoes were placed and the claymore mines along their paths turned to face inward, then an American listening post had to be destroyed before the sixth could be installed. Phuc Binh did not know the Americans' check-in pattern for these LPs. He only knew there had to be a pattern. If the listening post was destroyed too early, the Americans would be alerted when the LP failed to report. Phuc Binh and his men settled down to wait until their own people arrived. The guides would be shown where the torpedo fuses were, then the listening post would be overrun.

Installing the bangalores and turning the claymores had taken enough time that the sapper squad had only a short wait before the lead elements of the 159th Battalion reached the foot of the hill. The sappers showed the Viet Cong guides the locations of the bangalores, then assembled to destroy the LP.

Phuc Binh took one man with him to do this job. More than two men moving through the darkness might alert the Americans. Most likely two of the four Americans in the LP would be sleeping, therefore two men could do the job with no undue danger to themselves.

Armed only with their knives, Phuc Binh and his companion slithered to the rear of the LP. They lay quietly for three minutes, observing the four Marines from a distance of less than five meters. As Phuc Binh had believed, two of them were asleep. The other two were intently looking toward the paddies, yet not seeing the large number of North Vietnamese soldiers who were settled in it.

Phuc Binh touched his companion on the shoulder. The two men rose to a low crouch—like sprinters on the blocks—then burst into the LP in two strides. The two awake Marines barely had time to turn before strong hands at the ends of sinewy arms grabbed their chins and forced their heads back. Knives plunged upward under the Marines' rib cages, rupturing lungs, piercing hearts. The bodies shuddered, sagged, and were lowered to the ground. Then the sleepers' throats were slit.

A third sapper watched from nearby. As soon as the LP was neutralized he crawled to the edge of the wire and slid the bangalore underneath it. On fingers and toes he carefully picked his way through the banks of concertina wire. The others followed him. Each man carried a knife and a pack. One of the packs contained a satchel charge, the others held various small explosives.

As the sappers traveled they reversed all the claymore mines they encountered. Not one pebble-filled tin can in the wire made a noise during the ten minutes it took the sappers to traverse the area. Six of the most dangerous men in the North Vietnamese Army had arrived undetected inside Lima Company's perimeter.

Belly down, the six slipped through the line of fighting holes guarding the perimeter. Past the main line of defense they rose to their feet and trotted to the 81mm mortar position in the center of the compound.

One man "on watch" sat with his back against a pile of mortar rounds. He was asleep. Five other men lying on their ponchos were asleep nearby. None of them wished to sleep in the stifling bunker in the night's heat. Each sapper looped a cord around a sleeping man's neck and jerked the loop closed. Six mortarmen died.

On Phuc Binh's signal one of his men pulled the fuse pin from a satchel charge and tossed it into eighty-one's ammunition bunker. The six sappers bolted for the shelter of the mortarmen's sleeping bunker.

At six points around the perimeter a Viet Cong guide waited for the signal to set off his bangalore torpedo. Behind each VC waited two twenty-five-man platoons of the 159th Infantry Battalion. The hill rocked with the explosion of eighty-one's ammo bunker. The six VC set the fuses and ducked behind cover. As soon as the torpedoes went off, fifty NVA rose to their feet and ran through each gap. Tan Duc was the first man through the gap he had made.

No one spoke until through the wire and past the ring of fighting holes. Battalion headquarters decreed that the Americans might be so disoriented by explosion of their mortar bunker they might not immediately notice the holes in their wire, the men pouring through. The order was to maintain silence until within the compound. Then make noise.

The NVA ran through scattered resistance at the wire. Some of them fell dead or wounded making the top of the hill, but most reached the interior of the fire base unharmed. Then they made noise. "Ma'deen you die!" "What you say now, GI?" "Yankee go home!" they screamed once they were inside the lines. "You mother cry for you, Ma'deen!" "Another man fuck you girlfriend, GI."

Inside they spread out and broke into small groups that ran toward the center of the defended hilltop. The fire base would be destroyed from the middle to its edges. Kill the command post and supporting arms before the main defenses. Make the Americans on the perimeter shoot across their own area, shoot at each other from one side to the other. The Americans' fire would help the NVA destroy the heart of their base. The NVA cocked their grenades and tossed them into fighting holes as they ran past them. Beyond the holes they threw their grenades at noises, shot their rifles at flitting shadows.

While the main assault force was running, screaming, and firing, toward the middle of the fire base, the first squad of the 24th Sapper Platoon moved invisibly about that center setting booby traps. The water truck would kill the next American to open a certain tap on it. A 60mm mortar would detonate a block of plastic explosive underneath it the next time it was fired. Two cases of rifle ammunition would erupt when either one was moved. Other booby traps were set.

The sounds of the bangalores went unheard under the explosion of the 81mm mortar's ammo dump. Confused Marines were jarred from sleep. Men on watch snapped around to see what was happening to their rear. Someone saw an opening in the wire in front of him and masses of troops pouring through it. He screamed a warning. A potato-masher grenade landed in his hole, killing him and his no-longer-sleeping partner before either could fire at the invaders.

The company commander started to wakefulness. Everyone around him seemed to be saying, "What the fuck's going on?" or, "Where are we being hit from?" So far nobody in the CP realized they were being overrun. The nearby crack of an AK settled that. "Call battalion, tell them we're being overrun," Captain Sarmiento ordered his watch radioman. All the radioman had time to transmit was this basic message before a grenade killed him and his radios. Lima Company was now isolated from the outside world. They could not talk to anyone else except on the platoon band.

The company commander realized the seriousness of the situation and started passing an order on the ground-line phones to his platoon leaders. "Everybody stay down, stay in your holes. The Vee Cee are inside the compound. Assume anyone above ground is an unfriendly and kill him."

Most of this message reached all three platoon CPs before any of the phone lines was cut. Enough of it was received for nearly everyone in the company to get the word to stay down. Most of them did, and they started firing at higher than grazing level. It would be much longer before Lima knew its enemy was not a small Viet Cong unit but most of an NVA battalion.

Another command had the 60mm mortars pointing almost straight up and they started popping illumination rounds over the compound. The first flares had barely died before the survivors of the mortar section had the five mortars that weren't booby-trapped firing again. Only one man other than the gunner of the booby-trapped mortar was injured when it exploded.

Phuc Binh's part of the main operation was finished. From this point on, all he needed to do was stay alive. There was no way he could join the main battle without a rifle. He signaled his men to leave the compound. "Don't use the openings in the wire," he told them. "Go through the wire and turn more of the claymores around as you pass them." They went to do as he ordered. Phuc Binh stayed to arm himself and kill more Americans. It didn't take him long to find an American who wasn't watching his rear. That American's throat grinned widely and he gave up his rifle and grenades to the sergeant leading the first squad of the 24th Sapper Platoon.

Running with the pack, Tan Duc fired his carbine randomly. He had no assignment on this phase of the operation; his duties ended when he set off the bangalore. But his family had been disgraced by the younger brother who had changed sides, so Tan Duc ran with the Northerners and fired at flickering shadows and threw grenades at noises. Once, when stopping to change magazines, he fixed his bayonet. The thing Tan Duc most wanted was to kill Americans up close so he could retrieve their dog tags. Captured dog tags would prove he had been in this battle and give evidence that he had killed Americans. An M-14 would make a wonderful prize as well as offer further proof.

But something was not going right. Tan Duc joined in with his North Vietnamese brothers in shouting taunts at the Americans, but the Americans were not yelling back. The Americans didn't seem to be panicking. Why did they seem to be staying in their holes instead of trying to group or attempting to escape?

Tan Duc tripped over an unseen obstacle and fell heavily. His rifle flew from his hands and skittered away into the darkness. He scrabbled forward, groping madly, trying to find his weapon. Without it he might have no chance of killing any Americans. It came under his hand and he breathed a sigh of relief. "Kill an American, kill an American," the refrain ran through his mind.

Voices rang out in the night. Familiar voices rallying the attackers. The voices said the middle of the compound was clear. Assault to the perimeter. Tan Duc picked a direction and ran that way. His ammunition was getting low; he would not fire again until he had a clear target.

Two strangers appeared. Tan Duc did not know them. This was not a surprise; he did not know most of the men in the platoons he led through the wire. These two strangers had expended all of their bullets and grenades without being able to replenish their weapons from dead Americans. "I have bullets," Tan Duc said to them. "We will find Americans and I will kill them so you can take their weapons. We will work together.''

The strangers thanked Tan Duc for his help. They fixed their bayonets and ran with him to a place where they saw M-14 muzzles flashing away from them.

Backlighted by their muzzle flashes, two huge Americans became visible in a hole. Tan Duc pointed his carbine at one of the images and started pulling the trigger. The huge man sagged and crumpled, fell to the bottom of his hole. Tan Duc was so excited at killing an American he forgot to point his rifle at the other man in the hole; he kept shooting the one he had already killed.

The second American twisted around in the hole and fired a long burst from his rifle. Suddenly his companions were down, and Tan Duc ran alone toward the American. It was too late for Tan Duc to shoot this second American, he had fired his last bullet into the dead man. He would kill the second American with his bayonet.

Then a giant kicked Tan Duc in the stomach, drove all the air from his lungs and tossed him to the far side of the hole. This was the greatest pain Tan Duc had ever felt. He curled on his side, clutching his bruised belly, trying to gasp air into his chest. Out of the corner of his eye he had a fleeting glimpse of the second American's rifle stock descending toward his head an instant before his head exploded with an even greater pain than the giant's kick. Then he felt nothing more.

Phuc Binh saw clearly what the Americans were doing. Even though they were being overrun by a superior force, they stayed in their holes to fight rather than trying to run. This gave the Americans an advantage in the fight. It also gave Phuc Binh an advantage. If the Americans were not getting up and running, that meant simply that they stayed in one position and that they could be easily found.

The sapper sergeant lay quietly, watching for a moment. Orange machine-gun tracer rounds and the muzzle flashes around the perimeter showed him the Americans were firing high enough to avoid shooting each other. A man crawling on his hands and knees would be in little danger of being shot. Near the middle of the fire base a short man could walk crouched over with little danger. Near the fighting holes he could slither on his belly and allow bullets to bite the air above him.

Phuc Binh started crawling toward the nearest muzzle flashes.

The mortars in the middle of the fire base stopped sending out their illumination. They had been silenced by an NVA platoon. Rallying voices sang out, telling the men the middle of the fire base was secure, directing them toward its edges. Phuc Binh knew this was not totally the truth, but agreed it was true enough. The small amount of resistance remaining in the headquarters bunker in the middle of the compound could be more easily cleared once the fight at the perimeter was reduced.

Running feet pounded past the sapper. Let them go, he told himself. The Americans will waste much ammunition trying to kill them. They will not be watching for me.

Close to the hole he was crawling toward, Phuc Binh lowered himself all the way to the ground and slid between two holes before turning toward the one he wanted. He pulled the pin from an American grenade and eased the spoon off it, then rolled the grenade into the hole and hugged the good earth.

Brief screams answered the explosion in the hole—then silence. Phuc Binh crawled to the hole's lip and rolled over it. Two Americans were in the hole. They were both dead. Phuc Binh checked their rifles. One was jammed but the other seemed to be in good condition. Working quickly, the sapper slung it over his back and stripped both bodies of their cartridge belts. The belts joined the rifle around his chest. The first rifle he had taken was also slung.

These M-14s and their ammunition, so heavy, he thought. It is no wonder the Americans tire so quickly in battle. With their arms and the other equipment they carry, they are overburdened.

In one fluid move Phuc Binh was out of the hole and crawling toward the next one in line. He drew another grenade from his loincloth, pulled its pin and eased off the spoon. The grenade rolled into the hole and one more American died. The other American in the hole was already dead from bullet wounds.

The rifle and cartridge belt from one man joined those already on Phuc Binh's body. The other man had an M-79 grenade launcher. The sapper left it behind because it was out of ammunition. It could be retrieved later if ammunition was found for it. He did take the hand-grenade pouch with its dozen deadly eggs and strapped it around his waist.

No firing was coming from the next hole, but Phuc Binh rolled a grenade into it anyway. No need to take chances. One man was in this hole. He was already dead and someone had already taken his weapon and ammunition.

Most of the fight had moved elsewhere. There was little firing in this sector of the fire base now. Phuc Binh would have to move more carefully. One more hole here, then I go to where there is heavier fighting so it can mask my movements, he decided.

A few feet from the next hole the sapper half rose to his knees, bent sharply over. At the same instant that he rolled a grenade toward the hole, a wall of white, orange, and red erupted from it. Phuc Binh's body and head shuddered from the impact of several bullets and he pitched forward, dead.

The North Vietnamese had never been able to properly organize themselves after breaking into the Lima Company's base. Individually and in twos and threes they had run amuck, trying to find Americans to kill. But the Americans remained in their holes and fought with good discipline. Too many NVA officers and sergeants gave voice to their commands and rallying cries. Too many of them made themselves clear targets for Marine riflemen and died for it. The 159th NVA Infantry Battalion was turning into a reduced mob without leaders. Too many of its fighters had seen comrades fall to the Marines' fire. Individually and in twos and threes, they started running from the fire base. Most of them found the openings in the wire they had used to come in. Others tried to go over the wire and were hung up on it to die.

The battle on the nameless hill was ending, not in the expected rout of the Americans, but in the disintegration of a once-proud battalion. Some few brave soldiers stayed to fight on. Nearly all of them died before the sun rose. The remainder were captured. Their gesture had been futile. The Marines maintained their discipline, sat in their holes, and waited for a target to shoot or to throw a grenade at.

The morning mood on the hill was somber as thirty-nine dead Marines were flown away on helicopters. Another fifty had to be evacuated for medical attention. The remaining Marines, hardly more than enough to form a complete platoon, were reinforced by men from the battalion headquarters company. They had to dispose of the bodies of one hundred forty-seven North Vietnamese Army soldiers and one indigenous Viet Cong.

Eventually a mud-and-blood-encrusted Marine looked over the battle-ravaged hilltop, raised his head to the heavens and shouted to the world, "Payback's a motherfucker, Charlie, and don't you forget it."

This Is Rest and Recreation?

"WELL NOW, SON, I'M HERE TO TELL YOU THERE'S R AND R and there's R and R. One's in-country and the other's out of country. In the one case they send you to a place where there's no shooting going on today. In the other they send you to a country that don't have a shooting war going on at the minute they cut your orders. In either case they pay your air fare in both directions. What they really got in common, though, is on R and R you pays for everything—except transit to and from—yourself, and you're unarmed. Unarmed, son. That's important.

"What you do when you come out of a shooting war, even for just a few days, is you get as drunk as you can and you pig out on as much good civilian food as you can wolf down and you screw out as much of your brains as you can find women to screw them into.

"Can you imagine going from a place where every day people are trying to kill you and you're doing your damnedest to kill them back first, and then you get yourself drunk and someone crosses you the wrong way? What you think you gonna do if you're armed? You gonna kill that sum-bitch, that's what. That's why it's important grunts on R and R are unarmed. Believe me when I tell you we had us plenty of reasons to kill people when Lima Company was on R and R in Da Nang, too.

"Less than a week after that NVA battalion tried to overrun

us on that hill out in the paddies, the few of us that were left after the battle got pulled back to Chu Lai for a few days. While we were there the men who'd been out-of-country on a real R and R when the NVA hit rejoined us, and some of the guys that were in the hospital then came back and a few of the ones that weren't badly wounded in that big fight also came back from the hospital, so we were back up to about seventy-five, eighty men in the company. Remember, a TO Marine company—TO means full strength—at that time was about two hundred men including officers and corpsmen. Wait a mo there, I'm forgetting the first sergeant, the supply sergeant, and a couple of clerks was at Chu Lai waiting for us. Maybe we got up to eighty-five men left in the company.

"Anyway, we held a chunk of the Chu Lai perimeter for a few days while getting a few people back, then they saddled us up and flew the company up to Da Nang for five days in-country R and R. Even the Top, the supply sergeant, the clerks, and the men that just come in off of out-of-country R and R got to go.

"Da Nang. First thing you got to remember about Da Nang is it's a huge mixed-service military base. The Air Force was there real big and so were the Marines. It was also the largest seaport in Eye Corps, so it was also a big Navy base. What's more, Da Nang was the second biggest city in South Vietnam.

"Next thing you got to remember about Da Nang is it's more French than a lot of places that really are French cities. Those parts of it that aren't totally Vietnamese or basic U.S. military town.

"Soon as we got to Da Nang they put us in a barracks, made us put our rifles in racks and locked them goddam racks. You should have seen us when they locked them racks. We all looked like we'd just seen our best friend killed, or maybe like we were two-year-olds that just had our candy taken from us. We just came in out of the field where we never—well, almost never—had our weapons out of arm's reach. Most of us'd just been through one bodacious fight a few nights before, too. But they knew what they was doing, disarming us like that. If we had to have our weapons they were there, and so was somebody with a key so we could get them. If we didn't have to have them, we couldn't get to them.

"I don't know about later on, but in the summer of 1966 Da

Nang was real rank conscious. There were PXs all over the place and they were divided according to rank. Officers shopped in one place, staff NCOs in another, junior NCOs someplace else, and us peons had our own crappy little PX.

"Coming in like we did, we was out of a lot of basic amenities such as toothpaste, soap, cigarettes, lighter fluid, shaving cream, razor blades, talc. All the kind of garbage you normally take for granted because whenever you're getting short of them you just go to your favorite store and buy some more. In the boonies there ain't no such thing as your favorite store. You get these things when and where you can and you go without a lot.

"The Da Nang PXs had everything you could ever imagine wanting. Some of them were huge buildings looked like department stores with display windows, central air-conditioning, and everything. You could go into one of those places and buy a color TV for less than a black and white cost back in The World, deep-sea fishing gear, sports cars, wedding bands, and all kinds of jewelry. Big brass beds and all the bedding to go on them— hell, for all I know, you could buy a woman to go on that bed, too. But us grunts in out of the field for a few days couldn't use the main PXs, nossir. We had to use this little small PX that didn't even have any air-conditioning and was hotter inside than out in the sun.

"To make a bad matter worse, the shelves in that little PX were half empty and it didn't have but half of what we needed, much less any of that other happy horseshit I told you was in the big PXs. You had to search hard to find anything you could use in there and then you had to stand in a long line to pay for it. There were lots of little gook Vietnamese at the doors of all the big PXs to keep field grunts out. And all kinds of MPs, Air Force, Marine, and Navy, were around to back up the doormen if a grunt gave him any shit.

"Most of the time MPs was around more than we wanted them. They gave us liberty in Da Nang city, but privates, PFCs, and lance corporals had to be back on base by twenty-two hundred hours, that's ten P.M. Me, Chief Runningstar, Jeb Casebolt, and Malcolm X went into the city together with Lance Corporal Humphry Donnot. Donnot was base personnel, a clerk in the

Three MAF headquarters who we met in the E-club and offered to show us the big city.

"Don't never let nobody tell you combat don't bring people together or that being a Marine don't cancel out just about all other differences. We were a white city boy, an American Indian, a country redneck, and a ghetto black going out drinking together; four grunts fresh out of a big fight plus a desk jockey who never fired a shot except on the rifle range. We were all Marine Corps Green, and that's the only thing that mattered the most. Besides, Donnot knew all kinds of places we wanted to go to and he felt safer going to them with four grunts who could take care of any kind of crap if we ran into trouble.

"We took the liberty bus into town and grabbed a quick drink at the first bar we could get into. That's the first one didn't check our ID to make sure we were over twenty-one. Then we slipped out a side door and followed Donnot through some bad-looking alleys into a part of Da Nang he said was off limits to Americans. We could see why it was off limits. The people there looked like half of them were Vee Cee and the other half were sympathizers. And we were all unarmed and real uncomfortable.

"Then Donnot opened an unmarked door in a pink and blue stucco house and walked in. We followed him and got the biggest surprise we'd ever had. One side of the room had a polished teak bar running its length with a mirror behind it. The walls were covered with a plush red wallpaper and had paintings of willing-looking naked women on them. Away from the bar were comfy-looking overstuffed chairs and love seats with little tables next to or in front of them. Oriental carpets covered the floor. Stained-glass chandeliers hanging from the ceiling gave the place a private kind of light.

"Wasn't many customers in sight, but the sound of voices drifting into the room from behind a couple beaded curtains at the other end of the room suggested there was more than we could see. The customers were all Americans in uniforms.

"Thing surprised us the most, though, was the women in the chairs and love seats. They were the most beautiful Asian women I ever saw and they were all wearing lingerie or just wisps of sexy underwear.

"A white woman in a Dragon Lady dress came over and introduced herself to us and took us to the bar. We sat at the bar sipping our drinks and looking at the women in the chairs until finally one of them got up and slinky-walked over to Donnot and slipped her arm around his waist. She whispered something to him and he grinned ear to ear, turned red as a beet and winked at us. Then she led him through one of the beaded curtains.

"Jeb, Malcolm X, Chief, and me just looked at each other for a second or two, then we grinned like Donnot grinned and walked over to the ladies in the chairs and took our pick.

"No, son, I ain't gonna tell you what came next, except I did go through a beaded curtain with one of those women. The room we went into was decorated kind of like the main room, only it didn't have a bar and didn't much need chairs.

"Later on we were sitting there, just starting to get drunk, when a kid came running into the place and says something quick in Vietnamese to the white woman. The place had kind of filled up by now—must have been twenty-five, thirty Americans in it. After listening to the kid, the white woman says out loud in a clear voice, 'MPs.'

"You never saw so many people fly out so many doors and windows so fast in your entire life. It was like somebody shouted 'grenade' in a bunker. All the Americans in the place split except Malcolm X, Chief, Jeb, and me. Our first reaction was to stand and fight, not run away. By the time we realized we were unarmed and it was MPs coming to arrest us, not Vee Cee coming to fight, it was too late.

"Five MPs walked in the door before we could run out of it. We ran the other way and slammed right into four more MPs that were standing outside the back door. I think they were more surprised than we were. We knocked them right over and kept going, except Jeb wanted to stop and take their rifles. Funny-looking things they were carrying. Later on we learned they were carrying M-16s, which the Marines didn't have yet. Glad we didn't have them when the NVA tried to overrun that hill, we might not've made it because they were always jamming too much. Chief grabbed Jeb before he could stop and we ran like the devil was after us. Nobody likes MPs anyhow, but in the combat zone they're really hated.

"Problem was, we didn't know where we were. Where's a cop when you need one, right? We needed one for directions, but if we found one, we'd get arrested for being in an off-limits zone. And we were unarmed and half these gooks we were running past looked like they wished they were armed so they could shoot us. Fortunately, we came across some other Marines who weren't supposed to be where they was and they gave us directions to someplace we could be.

"Then we had another problem. The last enlisted liberty bus already went back to the base. There was one for sergeants in another hour, but we were all PFCs except me, who was a lance corporal. We were gonna have to bluff our way onto the liberty bus.

"Having an hour to kill, we went into a bar to do a little drinking. Wouldn't you know it, after a while three MPs came and stood inside the door to keep people from getting out while four others walked around checking ID. We were about to be screwed, blued, and tatooed.

"Until Malcolm X took over. When the MPs got to us he good evening'ed them and introduced us to them. Sergeant Bluedeer, Sergeant Humbold, Sergeant Cranberry, and Sergeant Fogel of Hotel, Two Five. That's what he told them. They didn't care, they just wanted to see our ID. Damn cards all said PFC, even mine. Not to mention gave our right names. Somehow the MPs didn't notice the names were different from what Malcolm X said. Malcolm X stayed cool, though. Explained how as we just come in from six months in the field and ain't had a chance to get new ID cards yet. MPs didn't care diddly-squat. They were all for arresting us. Malcolm X told them if they'd take us to our company area the company first sergeant could identify us for them. Now the MPs started taking him serious like. Then one of them got the bright idea of going to a phone and calling Hotel, Two Five, and asking.

"Screwed, blued, and tatooed. Jeb excused himself to go to the head. To go there, though, he had to pass this table full of swabbies. Old Jeb said something and them swabbies come up swinging. All of a sudden the MPs forgot about us because they had a riot on their hands. Jeb got back to us in a hurry and we bugged out of there. When the liberty bus came by, the MPs were so busy hustling the guys they busted in the riot they didn't have time to check anybody getting on the bus, so we didn't have no more problem getting back to base.

"No problem except Staff Sergeant Ortega did a roll call earlier and we weren't there to answer it. We told him we were at the E-Club on base and didn't think the same curfew as shore liberty applied, so he let us skate on that one. But we didn't get any liberty the next day.

"Later we heard that Hotel, Two Five, had a muster and the MPs went through their ranks looking for the sergeants that started a riot in a bar in Da Nang city. Didn't find them.

"R and R and MPs just don't mix too good."

Chapter Ten

THE SUN ROSE OVER THE SOUTH CHINA SEA, SPREADING ITS light over Animal Land, the grunt area of the sprawling American air base at Da Nang. One large Quonset hut held the remnants of Lima, Three Fifteen.

"I need some razor blades and lighter fluid," Johnny Johnson said to Hernando Falalo when they returned from morning chow. "Do a hump to the PX with me."

Falalo nodded. "I need some shit, too."

"You two ain't going nowhere without me," said Buster Bahls. "I'm the only one of us knows where the NCO PX is."

"Then get your ass in gear and let's go," Johnson told him, rising to his feet.

The sergeant and two corporals checked their uniforms, reached for the rifles and the cartridge belts that weren't there, hesitated at being unarmed, looked wistfully at the locked weapons room, then swaggered out of the Quonset hut into the blazing sun.

"Gonna be a hot one."

"You got it."

"Steam-bath city."

Fifteen minutes' walking brought them to a one-story building that looked like half an entire shopping center back in The World. A massive air-conditioning unit squatted on its roof. They grinned at each other, hungrily thinking of the coolness waiting to greet them inside. But first they stopped to rubberneck at the goodies in the show windows.

"Oo-eee, do you believe this shit?" Arms akimbo, Buster Bahls rocked back and forth on the balls of his feet.

Hernando Falalo's face screwed up as he leaned his forehead against the window for a closer look. "Washing machines?"

"Sure could use something like that back in the bush," said Johnny Johnson. "Be nice to have clean utes to wear."

"The refrigerator'd cut a real hus, too," said Bahls.

"If we could hump 'em out there," said Falalo.

"If we could plug them in someplace," said Johnson.

"No sweat," said Bahls. "They got this kind of shit here, you just know they gonna have extension cords that'll reach that far."

Laughing, the trio moved to the next window.

"I'm in heaven."

"I'm in love."

"I'm uncommitted. Just let me get to her, she'll be in heaven and fall in love."

An elegantly posed mannequin stared glassy-eyed at them. She wore a low-cut silk brocade evening gown. Next to her stood a rigid male figure in a tuxedo.

"Where you think they going?" Bahls asked.

"They come out of that window, she's going with me," Johnson answered. "He ain't going nowhere."

"You can have her, Johnny," said Falalo, "I'll take that one. She's already almost naked." He nodded at a bikini-clad third figure in the window.

"Jesus H fucking Christ." Bahls whistled. "That what we busting hump for? Let me go kill more gooks, get my quota and let me go back to The World."

"Ain't no quota, you dumb-assed splib," Falalo said. "You gotta live through four more months of this shit."

"You don't know what you talking about, spic," Bahls said. "Us bros got a special deal. We stay here until we dings so many dinks. Then we go back to The World. No time limit."

"What's in the next window?" Johnson asked and side-stepped to it. The next window was filled with stereo equipment.

Johnson stared at it for a moment. "When I get back to The World I'm going to get me an apartment big enough to put that sucker in."

"You want it, you better get to the store before me 'cause I'm gonna buy it all," Bahls said.

"Too late, bro'," said Falalo, "mine's already on order."

Wordlessly, they gazed at the jewelry in the fourth window, each wondering what luxury items that a man could never use in a combat zone were doing in the PX.

Johnson finally broke the spell. "Let's go in. See if they got the shit we need."

A Vietnamese man in the doorway stopped them. "ID please," he said.

"Say what?" Johnson asked.

"ID please," the small man repeated. "This NCO PX. No can go inside not NCO."

"You supposed to be doing this?" Falalo asked him.

"Yes. Doorman." He puffed up and proudly patted his chest. "ID please."

Johnson shrugged. "Your IDs up to date?" he asked the other two, and drew his own from his shirt pocket.

The doorman examined it and the IDs of the others. "What unit you?" he asked suspiciously.

"Lima, Three Fifteen," Johnson told him.

"Lima, Three Fifteen," the doorman repeated, "who that?"

"Bad-ass grunts, man," Bahls snarled.

"You grunt?" The Vietnamese darted a look at each of them.

"That's right," said Falalo. "We kill boo-coo Vee Cee. Kill 'em dead."

The doorman shook his head. "You no go in."

"What do you mean, we don't go in? This is the NCO PX, right?" Johnson asked.

"NCO PX, yes." The little man nodded vigorously.

"I'm a sergeant, they're corporals. We are NCOs. We go in."

"You grunt. You no go in."

"Say what?" Falalo said.

"Grunt no go in NCO PX. Grunt go E-man PX. Down street." He pointed the way.

"Bullshit," Bahls snapped. "We're NCOs, we're going in,

and you can't stop us." He started to push his way past the little doorman.

"Maybe he can't stop you, Marine, but I can," a voice said from behind them.

The three turned toward the new voice. An Air Force sergeant wearing a Military Police armband stood facing them. His arms were crossed over his chest. A nightstick dangled loosely from one hand, and the flap on his holster was unsnapped. Three more MPs stood behind him with nightsticks in their hands.

Johnson walked over to the Air Force sergeant. "What the fuck is going on here, Sergeant? Why is this civilian trying to stop us from going into the PX?" he asked politely.

"Base personnel only," the MP said. His steel blue eyes held unwavering on Johnson.

"Why? It's the NCO PX. We're NCOs. Why can't we go in?"

"There's been a big problem with grunts buying things in there and selling them on the black market, so grunts don't get in anymore, that's why." He grinned.

Johnson waved an arm at the show windows. "Major appliances?" he asked. "Evening clothes? Stereos? Jewelry? Sergeant, where we go, people don't have the money to buy that kind of shit. Even if they did, they don't have electricity or running water. We couldn't sell it if we had it."

The MP shook his head. "Tough luck, Marine. You're grunts below E-six, you go to the E-men's PX. You don't get in here."

The other MPs twisted their nightsticks between their hands.

"I think you had best leave now," the sergeant said, and his eyes glinted.

"I don't believe it. I don't fucking believe it," Johnson said.

One of the MPs slapped his palm with his nightstick.

"Shit," Johnson swore and turned to his companions. "Let's get away from this fucking bullshit." He stomped off.

"You stay away, you're off duty, sucker," Bahls snapped at the MP sergeant. "You come my way when you're off duty, you're ass is mine."

The sergeant unfolded his arms and rested his hand on his holster. "Don't try it, Marine," he said softly. "Don't even think it." The smile never left his face.

The enlisted PX was a few short blocks away. Where the NCO PX was large, like a small department store, the enlisted PX was small, like a large drugstore. The big PX had a wide variety of unusable luxury items, the small PX carried a small selection of necessities. Base personnel got to shop in air-conditioned comfort. The grunts sweltered in the poorly venti-lated enlisted PX.

"What is this shit?" Johnson wanted to know.

The place was crowded. Marines, airmen, and sailors jammed its narrow aisles, probing and searching for what they wanted. Johnson, Falalo, and Bahls decided to split up and each look for different items of what they needed.

The toothpaste section was empty, though mouthwash was available next to it. Only one brand of razor blades could be found, and the shaving cream was almost gone. Towels and perfumed hand soap were there, but not washcloths. Cigarettes were on the floor in their cut-open shipping cases, but most of the cases were empty. No lighter fluid, cigars, or pipe tobacco. Perfumed talcum powder, but no after-shave. The only things that seemed plentiful were potato chips and cases of canned soda.

"Exactly what grunts in from the boonies need," Falalo ob-served when he joined the other two in the long checkout line. "Junk food and hot soda."

"How am I supposed to light my cigarettes without fluid for my lighter?" Johnson asked.

"It's a government plot to get you to quit smoking," Falalo told him.

"I'm gonna get me an MP," said Bahls.

"No, you're not," Johnson said. "They don't make the rules, they only enforce them."

"That's a shit rule."

"Bet we'll be in this shit line long enough to miss noon chow," Falalo said.

After depositing their few purchases in the company's Quon-set hut, they found an NCO club in the transient grunt area and settled in to get drunk. Housed in another Quonset hut, the club

was furnished with long tables and benches. Along one side of
the room were two bars and a food counter. The beer and soda
served in cans was cool, not cold. No mixed drinks. If a drunk
decided to throw his empty drink container, a can would cause
less of an injury to someone than a glass would—and wouldn't
have to be replaced. The food counter served hamburgers, french
fries, and potato chips. Occasionally, but not now, other food
was available. The place was more crowded than the enlisted
PX had been. Three large window air conditioners labored un-
successfully to cool the interior.

"Grab us a space at a table while I get some brew," Falalo
said.

Johnson and Bahls found enough room for three men at a
table not too far from the entrance and one of the bars.

Falalo came back with six beers. They drank quietly, brood-
ing about their situation. The beers were disposed of in less than
fifteen minutes.

"My turn," said Johnson, who went to the bar for another
six.

When the second half-dozen beers were gone, Bahls asked,
"Who wants chow?"

All three did. Johnson went to get food while Bahls bought
the third double round. Falalo saved their place at the table.

Several hours and far too many beers later, Buster Bahls announced, "I'm gonna get me an MP," rose to his feet, and
staggered out of the club.

Johnny Johnson tapped the beer can Bahls left on the table,
turned bloodshot eyes at Hernando Falalo and said, "Go bring
him back. Man ain't finished his brew."

Falalo leaned forward to hold his eyes steady on Johnson.
"No can do."

"Why the fuck not?"

"He's bigger 'an me and he's drunker 'an me."

"Kick your ass, huh?"

"Kick my ass."

Johnson chugged the last of his beer. "Let's go get him together."

"You got it, pano."

The two staggered out of the club and almost tripped over

Bahls's body. He had lost his balance a few feet outside the door and passed out as soon as his body hit the ground.

Bleary-eyed, Johnson looked around for an MP. "Never a cop when you want one," he said. His chin dropped to his chest and he gazed at the prostrate form of his unconscious buddy. "We gonna have to haul that dumb black ass our ownselves. Should be an MP around, give us a hand."

"Better'n me having to carry both of you suckers," Falalo said.

"Let's get him."

A while later, but not too much of a while, Johnny Johnson and Hernando Falalo dumped Buster Bahls's body across his rack. They then collapsed unceremoniously onto their own and passed out.

"You people have shore liberty." Sergeant Johnson spoke softly the next morning so as not to jar his hangover headache too badly. "Where you get off the liberty bus is where it will pick you up again. The last bus back is nineteen hundred hours. You will be on that bus. Do I make myself clear?"

"You shore do, Sergeant Johnny," Henry J. Morris punned. "How soon does the liberty bus leave?"

Johnson examined his Omega for a moment before answering. "Fifteen minutes. Any other questions?"

Michael Runningstar cleared his throat. "What happens if we miss that last liberty bus back?"

Moving carefully, Johnson looked around at corporals Falalo and Bahls. "They're your people. You tell 'em."

Falalo peered out of bloodshot eyes at the four men standing before him. "You miss that bus, you gonna wish you was back on Abilene Run or getting overrun by the NVA on that hill again."

"But what if we get drunk as Corporal Bahls did last night and can't make it back without help?" Malcolm Evans wanted to know.

"Listen up, you!" Bahls barked. He emitted a low moan, and held his head between his hands for a few seconds before continuing in a quieter voice, "You get as drunk as I did last night, it won't matter, 'cause you gonna die before you get that drunk. No excuse."

"Get out of here before you miss your bus," Johnson ordered. When the four had left he turned to his comrades in agony. "Let's go find a mess hall that'll give a dying man a cup of coffee, or maybe a slop chute or some such place."

"I'm dead. I gonna need a hearse to get there," Bahls said.

"Come on, Buster, you ain't dead yet," Falalo said.

"Not close enough to dead. You just should be, that's all," Johnson added.

When they left the Quonset hut, the three walked like they were treading on uncooked eggs.

Moments before the liberty bus reached its Da Nang city terminal, a lance corporal in starched and pressed utilities poked J.E.B. Casebolt's shoulder. "Hey, you guys grunts?" he asked eagerly.

Casebolt grinned sharklike at the pogue. "Yah. Lima, Three Fifteen. The baddest of the bad."

"No shit!" The pogue's eyes were wide with excitement. "You know your way around Da Nang? I know a great place, but it's off limits for Americans so I don't get there often." His head darted around to see if anyone was listening. Dropping his voice, he continued, "Four bad-assed grunts should be able to handle any shit that comes down, though. What do you say?"

Casebolt had nudged Evans, Morris, and Runningstar. The four listened carefully to the pogue.

"You want us to go into Indian Country, huh?" Runningstar asked. "What's in it for you, paleface?"

"I get to go. Man, no way I'm going off limits alone. I'm not going without someone bad to cover my ass."

"Paleface." Evans laughed. "I be knowing there was a reason I like you, Chief. We gotta same picture 'a them chuck dudes."

"You ain't no more Native American than they are, Malcolm X." Runningstar scowled.

Evans laughed again, then turned to the pogue. "You buy us a beer when we get off this bus and we'll think about it."

The pogue nodded vigorously.

"If we're gonna have a drink together we should know each other's names," Morris said. "I'm Henry J, that's Jeb, he's

Chief, and Malcolm X is the dude said you gonna set us up at a bar. Who the fuck're you?''

The pogue stuck out his hand. "Lance Corporal Donnot. Humphry Donnot.''

The four exchanged glances. What kind of name for a Marine was "Humphry"? And was that last name dough-not or dough-nut? They shook their heads. "Pogue" was going to have to do for him.

Between the first and second beer, before agreeing to go to the off-limits place with Donnot, Morris asked, "What kind of shit might come down?''

Donnot leaned close to whisper, "MPs.''

The others whooped. "Shee-it, man, that all? No problem, we going with you.''

Twenty minutes later, when a patrolling MP was looking in another direction, Donnot ducked into an alleyway. The others followed. Before long they were walking through a shantytown slum. Scabrous children peeked at them from behind whatever barriers they could find. Sullen adults pretended not to notice the Marines. Old people turned their backs to the passing outsiders.

"Glad we got us a native guide,'' Morris said. "We'd need a long time to find our way through this shit alive.''

"Bet they all cousins to Charlie,'' Casebolt said.

"No, they ain't all,'' said Evans. "Half of 'em *be* Charlie.''

"Shut up and keep your fucking eyes open,'' Runningstar said. "No way I want to get ambushed in here.''

Donnot didn't say anything, he just kept moving forward.

A larger, stuccoed building the size of a two-bedroom rancher loomed suddenly on their right. Aside from a few Vietnamese words painted on its front, it was unmarked.

"Here we are.'' Donnot spoke for the first time since leaving the approved area.

"Where?''

"The place I told you about. This is it.'' He opened a door and walked in.

An area the size of a large living room spread before them. At one end of the room a chipped and scarred bar stood in front of a cracked mirror. Two bored Americans in civilian clothes slouched over drinks at the bar. The floor was an uneven, soft wood of some sort, splintering in places, and stained many colors from the countless drinks and body fluids that had spilled on it over the years. Fly-spattered red brocade paper was peeling from the walls. A few faded prints of Rubenesque nudes hung crookedly. Three smoke-stained fluorescent light fixtures were suspended from the ceiling—only one of the lights was lit.

At the end of the room opposite the bar was a small cluster of overstuffed chairs and settees badly in need of new upholstery. Six young Vietnamese women lounged on them. Their hair needed washing and some of them bore what the Americans called "gook sores." Four of them wore dirty, tattered nighties; the other two were garbed in half bras and bikini panties that hadn't seen detergent or water in recent memory. One of the women was busy picking her nose with an elongated pinky nail.

Donnot beamed. "What'd I say, ain't it great?"

Smiles spread across the others' faces. "Gonna get some," they said.

"First let's get a drink. Nobody in here talks to you until you've had a drink." Donnot led them to the small bar.

A sickly-looking Chinese man was the bartender. He wiped the back of his hand across his mouth and nose while opening their bottles of Ba Moui Ba. The Marines declined his offer of glasses.

Soon one of the women sauntered over to them. She wore the top of a baby-doll nightie. Placing a hand on Donnot's back, she straddled his thigh and pecked at his throat with a well-lipsticked mouth before grinding her pelvis against him. "Hey, Ma'deen, you want boom-boom? Ten dollah MPC. You buy rubber, one dollah more."

Donnot reached an arm half around her until his hand found and squeezed her small buttocks. "Ten dollars MPC and I got my own Trojans. Lead me astray, beautiful." He winked at his companions as he handed the boom-boom girl the Military Payment Certificates. "Take your choice, guys. They're all about as beautiful as this one. And they fuck like you wouldn't believe."

The boom-boom girl took Donnot's hand and led him through

a beaded curtain at the side of the room. He was clutching and rubbing his crotch before they reached the curtain.

At the other end of the room one of the women relaxed as though she had won a good poker hand. The other four were rising to their feet; their faces didn't quite hold expressions of distaste. Soon the bartender was alone in the big room with the two bored Americans and the last boom-boom girl.

Behind the beaded curtain was a smaller room with light seeping in through closed louvered windows. The room was divided into open-ended cubicles by eye-high split bamboo partitions. Inside each cubicle was a split bamboo bedstead padded with a straw-filled mattress cover. Morris's girl led him into one of the cubicles and gestured at him to drop his trousers. Cracking noises came from her panties as she peeled them off. Nude except for her half bra, she lay back on the mattress.

"The tit bag, too, honey," Morris said.

She looked at him quizzically, and he tugged at one bra cup. Shrugging, she rose slightly to unsnap the bra and slide it off. Laying back down, she spread her legs and said, "Come, boom-boom."

Morris noted an open sore on the inside of her thigh while rolling on his rubber and made a mental note to talk to a corpsman about it later.

The girl adjusted her position as he entered her and made very few more movements until she asked, "You through yet?" He was soon after that, and she pushed at his shoulders to make him get off.

The girls had other customers, and three more bored Americans were taking up bar space, so Donnot and his grunt friends relaxed in the boom-boom girls' chairs.

Donnot was saying, "Ain't it the greatest? Easy chairs, cold beer, and a great fuck," when a child rushed into the room and chattered something in Vietnamese.

The words energized the men at the bar, sending them out the door with Donnot right behind them. Cursing came from the boom-boom room. One voice gave an anguished cry, "But I ain't finished yet." Another voice answered, "You never will be, anyway. Let's split now." Six men emerged from the back room, buckling their belts, adjusting their uniforms, and left by the front door.

"What the fuck that all be about?" Evans asked.

"Donno," said Morris, "but maybe we ought to di-di our own fucking selves."

"Too late, Marine. You're under arrest for being in an off-limits establishment." An MP sergeant stood inside the door. Four more MPs were crowding in behind him. They wore helmets and carried M-16s.

"We got a problem," Casebolt said.

"Speak for yourself, paleface," Runningstar said, and bolted for the third room in the building.

Everyone followed him; three trying to escape, five trying to capture the escapees. A door in the third room opened outward to a blind alley. Evans, the last of the four, slammed the door into the pursuing MPs. Casebolt found a wood beam to wedge against it while Morris helped Evans hold the door against the pounding of the MPs. Then they ran after Runningstar, who had stopped to recon at an alley intersection.

"What way?"

"I don't know. Let's go left."

"Right."

They ran to the left with the noise of the door breaking open behind them. A few twists and turns and they began to think they had lost the MPs. Now, though, they had another problem.

"Where the fuck are we?"

"I don't know. I thought you did."

"No, I don't know where we are."

"But you said go left."

"I was picking an avenue of escape, not a route back."

"Oh."

Alone and unarmed in an off-limits part of the city, the four tried to remember what direction they had gone in to reach the place they escaped from. They decided on north, looked at the sky and started off toward what they hoped wasn't south. It was, but north was the wrong direction anyway. Before long they found themselves at the liberty bus stop. The nineteen hundred bus had left five minutes earlier.

"Shit. What do we do now?"

"Catch the next bus."

"Is there a next bus?"

"Says so right there on that schedule. Twenty hundred. Last bus for E-five and up."

"But we an E-three and three E-twos."

"One E-three and three E-twos adds up to E-nine. We're a sergeant major."

"Oh."

"Right."

They found a dark corner in a nearby bar and sat, nervously pulling on a few beers, until the bus came. The driver was bored and in a hurry to get back to base before the E-club closed. The MPs at the gate just wanted to get it closed and return to their card game. Everything was okay until they reached Lima Company's Quonset hut.

Staff Sergeant Ortega was waiting for them. "You missed roll call."

"Roll call? What roll call?"

"The roll call I held to make sure everyone had returned from shore liberty."

"We didn't know there was going to be a roll call."

"That's no excuse. You were supposed to come back on the nineteen hundred liberty bus. That would have had you here for the roll call."

"But we didn't know about the roll call."

"So we went to the E-club when we got off the bus."

"Before we came back here."

Ortega stared hard at them. They looked back at him blandly.

"I don't believe you. You had best hope I never find out you're lying to me."

"We aren't lying."

"We've been at the E-club for the last hour."

"The bartender'll tell you."

"If you weren't, your ass is mine. Dismissed." Ortega marched away, headed for the staff NCO quarters.

They walked down the center aisle of the Quonset hut to their squad's area.

"Hope he don't check at the E-club."

"Or ask the bus driver."

"He does, we fucked."

From the NCO area of the Quonset hut Sergeant Johnson told

them, "Don't worry about it. The company's down to half strength. He's not going to want to break anybody's balls for getting back an hour after curfew unless he absolutely has to."

"You sure?"

"He didn't report your absence to Lieutenant Haupt or the skipper. Don't sweat it. You're back and safe and that's all he cares about."

Brown Water, Brown Star

"I'VE BEEN TELLING YOU ALL KINDS OF WAR STORIES, SON, BUT Nutsy Nooncy was the only one I told you about got a medal. Don't want you to think my platoon was a bunch of jerkoffs didn't do no heroics, so I'm gonna tell you about how Mouse got himself a Bronze Star. But I'm gonna lead up to it by telling you what kind of crap we was doing at the end of the summer of 'sixty-six.

"Don't ask me what happened to Charlie and his big brother, the NVA, because I don't rightly know. Whatever it was, they were mostly leaving us alone. Best guess I got is he was licking his wounds and resupplying himself after the hurting got put on him on operations like Scythe and the defense of Hill 143. We were having companies get chopped up bad in late 'sixty-five and the first half of 'sixty-six, but Charlie was getting battalions and even whole regiments busted up even worse, though us grunts couldn't always see that from where we were trying so hard just to stay alive. Charlie was getting ready for the push he made up in the corner of South Vietnam near the DMZ and Laos border the next spring, I guess.

"We were mainly running company- and platoon-size patrols after we got back from that R and R in Da Nang. Night ambushes and some daytime squad patrols, too. Hot dry work with little to show for it, and it was boring as all get-out. There were

206

a few battalion operations but they didn't amount to much. Other battalions ran into some crap, but Three Fifteen didn't see much. Lima Company even sat a couple weeks guard duty around a Hawk antiaircraft battery on a big red hill outside Chu Lai. They had dogs there, that's something I got to tell you about, those dogs.

"These dogs weren't the curly-tailed little Vietnamese dogs that were in all the villages. These dogs were German shepherds, all of them weighed over a hundred pounds, and they were Marine war dogs. Marine war dogs are a lot different from guard dogs, don't care about capturing nobody. They're trained to kill. A lot of civilians think Marines are crazy because we act so bad and believe nobody can kick our ass. Most Marines think grunts are crazy. All grunts know dog handlers are crazy. Those people go way out ahead of the point of a column when they're on operations, alone except for their dog. And they go on patrol at night just armed with a forty-five and a K-bar knife—and that dog.

"Picture a hundred-and-thirty-pound German shepherd that don't do nothing except what his handler tells him to—unless the handler ain't around. Then he does whatever he wants to. Imagine that dog just laying there real quiet, just eyeballing you, seeing every move you make. And think about how only one person can touch that dog, his handler. They are even kept locked away from each other when they ain't being taken on patrol or being trained, because they're liable to kill each other if they ever get left alone together. Remember that Marine war dogs don't get retired from that Green Machine when the war's over; they get put to sleep because they can't be returned to civilian life. Marine war dogs are vicious, mean critters who want, really want, to kill you. And they will if they ever get the chance.

"What kind of men you think is gonna work with these dogs? Crazy men, that's what kind. Always going around with a kind of cockeyed smile on their faces, all the time wanting to show grunts how well-trained their dogs are. They do it by pointing the dog at the grunt and saying, 'Kill,' and you hope he's got a good grip on that dog's lead and the lead don't break. That damn dog tries with everything he's got to get away from his handler and kill you. Then the handler tells him, 'Down,' and the dog stops barking and struggling and just drops in place. Another thing they do is draw their forty-five and let the dog see them point it at you. Makes the dog think you're an enemy, and it tries to get to you until the handler says, 'Down.' Or maybe he'll have you point your rifle at him. Makes the dog go crazy trying to protect his handler.

"What kind of man gonna do that kind of crap with a dog that really wants to kill someone? Crazy man, that's what kind.

"When you're sitting in a fighting hole on a perimeter that's also being guarded by dogs, one of the last things you want to hear is fifty, a hundred meters away a dog acted like he heard something and his handler let him go to find it alone. You sit there afraid that damn dog ain't gonna find what he heard and is gonna come find you instead. A dog can walk quieter than any human, and when they get close enough to make their charge it's gonna be too late for you to line your piece on him. I'd rather get killed by a gook than chewed to death by a dog any day. End result's the same, but you probably suffer less when Charlie kills you.

"Dogs scare the piss out of everone except their handlers. They even scare the other handlers. Sometimes they even turn on their own man if they want to kill bad enough and ain't had enough chance, at least I heard that somewhere.

"Ain't much more to tell about. Of course, Mouse did threaten to kill Smiff because that big dude was getting on his case too much about his size. Lieutenant Haupt was transferred to regimental headquarters, which cost us a good grunt officer and made us have to break in a new brown bar. Johnny Johnson and Hernando Falalo rotated back to The World because their enlistments were up, and Buster Bahls became the squad leader. When we got enough new men to make more than two fire teams, I was made a team leader. But before that happened Mouse won his Bronze Star. Most of the time we were just hot, dirty, tired, and pissed off.

"We were out on day-long patrol that started an hour before daybreak. Someone at battalion got the bright idea Charlie had a hiding place somewheres a few klicks from our fire base. Thinking was, if we got an early start we could be deeper in

Indian Country than Charlie'd expect and have a better chance of catching him with his pants down.

"A half klick out of the fire base was a klick-wide paddy we had to cross. The point fire team didn't like it at all, but orders were to move quick as we could and get across the paddies before dawn. Point didn't like it because they didn't have a chance to look for booby traps that might have been set overnight. If there were any new booby traps, we didn't find them the hard way. And we were in the cane fields on the other side of the paddies when the sun came up.

"The day was gonna be a scorcher but it wasn't yet. May as well been, though. That cane field was dusty and the air was still, no breeze to evaporate sweat.

"We spent all day humping around without finding any sign of a Vee Cee camp in use. We saw a few farmers working in the paddies and a few kids herding buffalo back to the villes late in the day, but not one gook that was carrying any weapon or looked at us nasty like a Vee Cee might. We did find sign of a couple old campsites and some old fighting positions, but they didn't look like they been used recently. The only thing we found that looked suspicious was a deserted ville with one hootch that was patched and didn't have no dust on the floor. Wasn't nothing there, though. Maybe someone'd come through and gone on but they weren't there now and it didn't look like someone was planning on coming back right away.

"It'd been a long hard day and we were all about as tired and sweaty as we could get. The heat really got to us with the sun beating down on our helmets and no circulation getting through our flak jackets. Then it was time to head back to the fire base. We were crossing some paddies about a klick and a half from the base and had a stand of trees to cross through before we got in sight of the hill we were on, when it happened. The whole platoon was in the paddies heading for the trees when a twenty-millimeter cannon opened up on us from in the trees.

"The lieutenant and platoon sergeant and guide and squad leaders and everybody started yelling to hit the deck, get down behind the dikes and return fire. We were down with bullets zipping overhead trying to figure out where the Vee Cee was shooting from so our return fire'd mean something, and the cannon fire was coming so close we couldn't look or we'd get our heads blown off. All we could do was lay there in the water and stick our rifles over the top of the dikes and hope the bullets were going where they'd do some good. It was a bitch.

"That water'd been sitting in the sun too long and was stagnant. Mosquito eggs was laying on it in clumps and it was full of hungry leeches that ain't had a good blood meal in too long. Leeches ain't nice at all, son, got no respect for nothing, and they start off small enough they got no problem getting inside your clothes anyplace. Everyone hates them, and one thing about them scares every grunt is fear some leech gonna swim up his asshole or even worse, inside his cock and latch on there. Get a leech inside you, they say it can maybe kill. I don't know and never want to find out. Us jumping in the water like we did stirred up the muck on the bottom and made the parts we were in pretty muddy. The water was red in places, too, from the casualties we got when the fire opened up.

"So there we were, tired, dirty, suffering from heat, laying there in that warm, stagnant, muddy water with leeches sucking on us and twenty-millimeter cannon rounds zinging overhead like we knew the mosquitoes wanted to. This damn boot brown bar we got started yelling for first squad to go on a flanking maneuver. He picked on first squad because it was bringing up the rear of the column and there was brush cover on the hillside behind us. That got stopped in a hurry when first squad took three casualties soon as they started moving.

"One of the people who got taken out by the opening bursts was the platoon radioman. His prick twenty got shot to hell, too. This was the main hazard of being a radioman, that antenna makes you a prime target. Only communications we had left was the prick sixes each squad had, and they couldn't reach far enough to get through to the fire base to get us air or artillery support. It was a tight spot, especially if the Vee Cee had some riflemen that could flank us. Fortunately, there weren't any riflemen flanking us.

"Now the lieutenant started yelling at us to spread it out, so we give the gun a more dispersed target and put down a broader base of fire ourselves. Mouse was on the right flank, and only a few feet away was a dike going the same direction we was going in before we got stopped. He had to go over it if we was gonna be able to spread out any. He was so tired and wiped out from the heat he didn't give a damn no more, so he went over that dike and crawled through the stinking water all the way to the next dike. Next thing Mouse knew there weren't no Marines in the same paddy he was in because nobody else crossed that dike and that cannon wasn't shooting anywhere near him.

"He looked over the top of the dike and saw the rest of the platoon was pinned down bad by that cannon, which was ignoring him. Charlie didn't see him go over them dikes. That's when he knew he could do something better than what the lieutenant wanted first squad to do. He looked careful until he saw exactly where that cannon was and waited until it was putting out a heavy burst on the platoon, then he rolled over the dike in front of him. He kept going like that, roll over a dike, crawl through water in a paddy, wait until there was a heavy burst and go over another dike then, until he was one paddy away from where the cannon was.

"Then he jumped up and charged straight ahead firing from the hip. Startled the shit out of the Vee Cee crew on that gun. They tried to turn it on Mouse but he was so close and coming so fast they couldn't. A couple of them grabbed their rifles, but they didn't know how to aim at a moving target and they missed. The magazine in Mouse's M-14 was empty by the time he reached the cannon so he dropped it and pulled his bayonet out and jumped on the barrel of that cannon and slid down it with his bayonet stuck out in front. Killed the gunner that way, then he rolled off and killed the rest of the crew with his bayonet.

"Rest of the damn platoon'd been shooting at the cannon from behind the dikes. Their rounds were going so high the Vee Cee weren't in no danger from them. Mouse had to call cease fire instead of waving because nobody would of seen him if he'd have done that.

"Everybody was so impressed by what Mouse did they gave him a Bronze Star. He also got a Purple Heart because his chest and belly got burned when he slid down the hot barrel of that cannon. Hell, if he hadn't been so hot and tired he never would have gone over that first dike and wouldn't have been able to do it. Mouse used to like telling people they gave him that medal because he was suffering from heat exhaustion and deserved some sort of reward for going on anyway."

Chapter Eleven

RED HILL, HILL 138, HUNCHED ITS BACK OUT OF THE COASTAL plain two kilometers northwest of the air strip at Chu Lai. A Hawk antiaircraft battery was mounted on the hill's top. Security for the battery was provided by a grunt company that was rotated on a monthly basis, and by a war-dog platoon that was stationed wherever the battery went. Guard duty on Red Hill was considered choice duty for a grunt company that had seen too much action.

Cpl. Bart Teniel was a dog handler. He was one of the best and he knew it. Teniel's dog was a hundred-thirty-five-pound German shepherd named Tiger. Sometimes Teniel needed all of his two hundred pounds to control the big dog. Tiger was also one of the best, and Teniel knew that, too. Once, when he and Tiger were wandering some hundred meters or so ahead of the point on a battalion operation, the dog had sniffed out an NVA ambush. Together, the man and his dog assaulted the ambush's flank and killed seven men before help arrived in the form of the battalion's point platoon. By then the need for help was moot. The ferocity of the man-dog attack panicked the ambush and set the survivors fleeing.

Another time, on this very hill, Tiger smelled something and Teniel let him loose to check it out. A sapper squad was infiltrating the perimeter. Tiger found and killed three of the sappers. Most of the rest of the squad managed to escape alive without having done any of the damage they had planned.

But it had been more than a month since Tiger last tasted human blood. Teniel was beginning to get worried. That damn dog really enjoyed his job—Tiger liked to kill people, and he hadn't been able to kill anybody for too long. No one had tried to assault or infiltrate Red Hill in almost five weeks. Teniel was worried. It might have been just his imagination, but he didn't like the way his dog had been looking at *him* the last few days. The handler needed to find a way to get his dog's mind off his handler's blood. Maybe the new grunt company on the hill could give Tiger some distraction.

Every night the grunts put out two squad-size ambushes, and one platoon and the other squad from the ambush platoon sat in fighting holes around the barbed-wire perimeter. The rest of the company got to sleep and served as a reaction force. Every night four of the five dog teams quartered the perimeter and the fifth got to sleep. The fighting holes were a hundred meters apart around the fifteen-hundred-meter circumference of the hill. Each dog team patrolled a stretch of slightly more than a quarter mile. The handlers carried radios and talked to each other. That way none of them ever reached the edge of his area at the same time the team in the next quadrant reached the same edge. Dog teams meeting unexpectedly while on patrol at night could be very dangerous to each other.

Teniel, holding Tiger's lead firmly wrapped around his left arm, watched his dog and his footing moving upslope along the well-beaten path between watch posts Hotel and India. He didn't bother listening or watching for Charlie, that was Tiger's job. Teniel knew that it was more important for him to keep a sharp eye on his dog; just in case the killer turned.

Tiger tensed slightly at the scent of humans in the nearby India hole. Teniel firmed his grip on the lead. Can't afford to have him get away from me now, Teniel thought, dog's not supposed to kill Marines.

"Dog team coming up," Teniel called out softly. Can't afford to let some trigger-happy grunt shoot me 'cause he doesn't know it's me, he thought. Would give Tiger another chance to kill someone, though, get him off my case.

"What's the password, dog team?" came the challenge.

"Captain Blood."

"Errol Flynn," was the countersign. "Advance and be recognized, dog team. Whozat, Teniel?"

"You got it right the first time. Who's in the hole tonight?"

"Henry J and Jeb," said Morris.

Teniel and Tiger loomed out of the darkness alongside the fighting hole. "Sit, Tiger." Tongue lolling, the huge dog lowered his haunches to the ground at his master's command and sat with his eyes shifting between the two men in the hole. Teniel sat on the hole's lip and draped his arm over Tiger's shoulders.

"You got a good grip on that dog of yours?" Casebolt asked with a trace of tremor in his voice. "Them big fucking city dogs always scare me."

Teniel held up his arm to show the lead wrapped around it. "He ain't going nowhere I don't tell him. Long as this leather doesn't break, anyway." He ruffled the fur on his dog's chest. "But he ain't no city dog. Born and raised on a ranch in Utah."

Casebolt grunted, then the three men and dog sat quietly for a few minutes, the men watching and listening outward, the dog watching the two men in the hole.

After a while Morris asked, "You or Tiger hear anything yet tonight?"

"That's a negative. Been real quiet for a while. Ain't even had to let Tiger go on his own for more than a week." The dog's ears twitched when his master spoke his name. "Tiger, down." The dog lowered his elbows and chest to the ground. Teniel thumped Tiger's chest. "Good dog."

Silence returned to the hole. Tiger kept his eyes on Morris and Casebolt.

"Listen, you ever let that dog go, make sure it's not a night I'm in a hole," Casebolt said. "Or at least don't do it anywheres near the hole I'm in."

Teniel chuckled. "No sweat, Jeb. Dog's well-trained. He won't kill anyone unless I tell him to. And he'll stop soon's I say to."

"Right," Casebolt said. "He's gonna stop chewing on someone just because you tell him to stop. Uh-huh."

Besides being slightly nervous about his dog, Teniel was bored. "Watch this." He paused to check his grip on the lead then pointed at Casebolt and said, "Kill."

Instantly, Tiger was on his feet lunging at Casebolt, a deep growl rattling out of his throat. Casebolt flattened himself against the far side of the hole.

"Tiger, down!" Teniel snapped. The dog dropped to the ground, but continued to grumble in a low voice. "Quiet." Tiger's jaws clapped shut. "What'd I say? He'll stop when I tell him to."

"Hey, fucker, don't pull that kind'a shit with me," Casebolt stammered. "Blow you the fuck away, you do that again."

Teniel grinned unseen in the night. "Can't. Kill me and the dog is free to get your ass."

"Then I'll kill the fucking dog first."

"Can't do that, either. Point your weapon at me or at him and he'll attack."

"Bullshit."

"Try it." Teniel checked his grip again. "Turn your muzzle away when I tell you to."

Casebolt was holding his rifle across his lap. He started to point it in Tiger's direction, but before the muzzle completed half its arc, the dog was lunging maniacally at him again.

"Turn it away." As soon as Casebolt pulled his muzzle away, Teniel snapped, "Tiger, down!" and the dog dropped again. "I don't have to tell him to get someone. But he'll stop as soon as he hears me say 'down.' "

"But only if he hears you, right?" Morris laughed. He was enjoying Casebolt's discomfort and glad Teniel wasn't pointing Tiger at him.

"You know it."

"Point that dog someplace else, will you?"

"Okay. I'll show you something else he does." Teniel suddenly drew his forty-five and pointed it at Morris. Tiger lunged, almost pulling his master into the hole. "Tiger, down!" The dog dropped.

"Ain't so funny now, is it, Henry J?" said Casebolt.

"Shit, say something when you're going to do that, will you?" Morris said, shaken. "Man might do something to that dog he don't know what the fuck you're doing."

"He's a good boy." Teniel thumped Tiger's chest again. The dog rumbled deep in his chest. "Well, that's enough tricks for now. We've got more perimeter to cover." Teniel rose to his feet. "Heel," he said to Tiger. The large German shepherd stood by his left leg. "See you people next time I come around."

"That's an affirmative," Morris said.

"Don't hurry back on our account," Casebolt told the dog handler.

Walking along the well-used path, Tiger laid the side of his open mouth against Teniel's thigh.

"Good dog," Teniel murmured.

Tiger snapped his mouth shut and made a masticating motion with his jaws.

Maybe I shouldn't have shown those men how well-trained he is, Teniel thought nervously. He put his right hand under the flap of his holster and made sure the forty-five was loose in it.

On a rare, lazy afternoon when third platoon wasn't patrolling or on an ambush, Johnny Johnson, Buster Bahls, Smith, Henry J, Malcolm X, Mouse, and a couple of other men from the platoon were sitting in the shade of a grove about two hundred meters from their fire base. Smith was holding forth on how he had managed to grow to six-foot-four, two hundred forty pounds.

"Soon's I was big enough to pick it up, my daddy give me a hatchet and teached me how to chop wood. When I got strong enough to swing an axe, he put me to chopping down trees. 'Member, I lived in the deep woods and alla other boys was big. My daddy wanted me to be big and strong enough to kick anybody's ass instead of ever getting my own ass kicked, so he made me strong right from jump street. The main thing, though, was when I was a little baby, my momma tit-fed me. That's why I'm so big."

Mouse sat and stared at Smith for a moment. "You shitting me, Smiff?" he finally asked.

Smith leaned back, looking slightly offended. "I wouldn't shit you, Mouse. You're my favorite turd."

Mouse's hand didn't exactly move, his fingers just reoriented themselves so they pointed more toward his rifle. "One of these days, man, you gonna say that to someone and you gonna die."

Smith shrugged. "Okay, so you're not my favorite turd. Malcolm X is. He's more turd-colored than you are, anyhow." He looked closely at Evans. "Nah. You ain't turd-colored. More like baby-poo diarrhea."

Evans glared at Smith and rolled a grenade between his palms. Smith ignored him.

Mouse snorted. "You really think you're so big 'cause you was a tit-fed baby?"

"That's right."

Mouse screwed up his face. "Shit. I was a fucking bottle baby. God-fucking-damn. They's no way pasteurized cow milk is as good for a baby as mother's tit milk is. Shee-it! If my mama'd fed me tit milk instead of pasteurized cow milk, maybe I'd'a growed a bit. Jesus H fucking Christ, who knows, I might even be five-foot-six or something if my mama'd fed me tit milk instead of cow milk!"

Smith stared hard at Mouse before saying, "Mouse, you just about the right size."

"What the fuck you talking about?" Mouse's face was red, he almost looked like he wanted to cry.

"You know how big these goddam gooks is? They about five-foot tall. Some of 'em's even smaller'n that. Ain't hardly none of 'em is big as you. And they skinny." Smith hawked and spat before continuing. "You got any idea how good a shot or how dumb lucky you gotta be to shoot one them scrawny fuckers when he's scrambling through a cane field? It's hard. You know how hard it is to shoot my fucking ass when I'm doing the same thing? I make three times the size target he do." Smith leaned forward conspiratorially. "Mouse, you almost as hard to hit as that l'il fucker, and you bigger and stronger than he is so's you can kick his fucking l'il ass he ever gets that close to you." He clamped a huge hand on Mouse's shoulder. "Man, you the right size to fight this war."

Slowly at first, then more emphatically, Mouse nodded his agreement. "You right, Smiff. I'm just the right fucking size. Why, I'm almost small enough to make me wish I was even smaller—the Crotch wouldn't'a took me when I enlisted, I was any smaller." Then he stared into Smith's eyes. "But the next time you call me your favorite fucking turd, you sum-bitch, you don't live to see the sun come up."

Malcolm X guffawed and tossed his grenade aside.

* * *

"First squad, move it out." Staff Sergeant Ortega passed the word he had received from Lieutenant Wyman, third platoon's new officer. So far no one in the platoon knew or liked the young lieutenant. He had been commissioned less than three months earlier and this was his first command. Wyman would need to have more than one week of combat leadership experience before anyone would feel comfortable taking orders from him.

The point man stepped through the wire and the rest of the platoon followed. A machine-gun squad and 60mm mortar team reinforced the badly understrength unit. Moving almost at a forced-march pace under the stars, the platoon reached and crossed the nearby paddies and was under the cover of the trees on the distant hillside by the time the sun came up, nearly an hour after the platoon left the fire base.

Things had been very quiet in Three Fifteen's area of operation for a while, and someone had gotten the bright idea that the quietness was due to Charlie's using the area as a resting place, and he didn't want to rile up the Americans. Each of the battalion's companies sent a platoon out before dawn on this morning. Their mission was to locate possible VC hiding spots or base camps. The early start would have the platoons deeper into the bush earlier than Charlie had any right to expect.

So third platoon humped through the rising heat of the morning. Helmet, flak jacket, five hundred rounds, and four grenades per rifleman—fifteen hundred per machine gun and thirty rounds for the mortar—two C-ration meals, two quarts of water that would have to be replenished somewhere along the way, bayonet, first-aid kit. Weighted down just like on an operation. It was going to be a long, hard day. The landscape third platoon maneuvered through was slightly hilly and wound through with small streams. Cultivated cane fields and rice paddies were dotted wherever the lay of the land allowed.

"What'cha think, Jeb, we gonna find Charlie today?"

"Nah, Henry J. Charlie goan find us."

"Let's have some quiet up there, people." Sergeant Johnson's voice was soft but carried clearly to the talkers. "Charlie hears you, he's gonna know we're coming and we get our asses ambushed."

Morris and Casebolt fell silent and kept a sharp watch through the brush for the enemy.

The platoon humped carefully but quickly and managed to cover five kilometers before Wyman called a halt for noon chow. No one had been seen, not even farmers. Buffalo were absent from the fields and paddies. Other than insects, the only animal life any of the Marines saw was one ridge-backed hog so thin it looked emaciated. The inexperienced men in the platoon wondered where everybody was. The experienced men knew what the absence of people meant; they wondered when they were going to get hit. After eating, the platoon moved out again on a different tack.

Runningstar, on point, half turned his shoulders and held up the palm of his hand to the man behind him, then jabbed his rifle toward the brush to his front. He settled to one knee and waited for Johnson to come up.

"What you got, Chief?" Johnson asked, and dropped to his knee next to Runningstar.

"Ville." Runningstar nodded in the direction his eyes hadn't moved from since he stopped.

Seventy-five meters ahead a hedgerow was dimly visible through the brush. It was the kind of thick mass of trees and hedges that formed fences around so many Vietnamese villages.

"Three, this is Three Charlie," Johnson said into his radio. "Ville up seventy-five. Over."

"Stand by, Three Charlie," came the answer.

While he waited, Johnson deployed his squad across the axis of movement so it paralleled the hedgerow. Lieutenant Wyman and Sergeant Zimmerman joined him by the time his last man was in position. They dropped to one knee and peered through the brush.

"Take two men and recon the hedgerow," Wyman finally told Johnson.

"Aye aye." Johnson didn't like it, but couldn't think of a good argument for not going. He turned to his right and said, "Henry J, let's go. You too, Chief." He slapped Runningstar's shoulder.

On line, five meters apart, the three Marines slipped through

the brush toward the hedgerow. Wyman returned to his CP and
Zimmerman stayed up front, in command of third squad.

Skin prickled on the backs of the three Marines' necks and
their eyes dilated to take in more light as they neared the barrier.
The platoon wasn't far behind, but wouldn't be much help if VC
were waiting for them. The foliage of the hedgerow was too
dense to ease through, too thick to see more than glimpses of
rundown hootches. No sound came through the hedgerow and
no movement was seen on its other side. Johnson signaled Morris to move to his right then followed him. Twenty-five meters
farther was an opening in the fence. Morris carefully looked
around its edge, then pulled back to let Johnson see. The hamlet
appeared to be empty. With another hand motion, Johnson signaled them to return to the platoon, where he reported to Zimmerman what he had seen.

The platoon filed rapidly through the opening in the fence.
First squad moved through the hootches on the right, third
searched the ones on the left. Second formed a line inside the
opening to lay a base of fire if needed.

The base of fire wasn't needed. The residents of this small
hamlet had abandoned it some time in the past and taken all of
their belongings with them. Only one hootch showed any sign
of recent use, and that sign was a bareness of even the dust that
filled the others.

"Nobody's home," Wyman announced when the search was
finished. "First squad, take the point. Move it out."

An hour later Wyman called another chow break. When they
started out again, second squad had the point and there was
another course change. Third platoon started heading back toward its fire base. They still hadn't seen any sign of Charlie. All
they saw all day long was the one hog and the deserted ville.

Lieutenant Wyman didn't bother with any kind of recon or
consultation with his senior NCOs at the edge of the paddies
with a treeline on their far side. The platoon was four klicks
from the fire base. When second squad stopped at the foot of
the low hill for instructions, Wyman waved his arm in the air
and pointed forward. Ortega tried to say something to Wyman
about the wisdom of crossing the open paddies, but didn't push
the point when he saw the lieutenant didn't want to listen.

Smith shrugged. "Move it out, people," he said. He was hot

and tired and it was getting late. He didn't like going across the open paddies, but he wanted to get behind the barbed wire before dark, so he didn't argue with the order.

Second squad started across the paddies toward the trees on the other side. The long day had taken its toll. The platoon members were more than half exhausted from the long walk and the relentless heat. Everyone felt rushed by the approaching night. The column opened to fifteen-meter intervals on the dike. The Marines felt exposed and wanted to get out of the open as fast as possible.

After the last man entered the paddies, two machine guns opened fire from the trees and second squad crumbled. Mouse, on the point, took a burst full in the chest. The man in back of him died from the tail end of the burst that killed Mouse. Two other men in the squad pitched into the water with wounds. The second gun sighted on the antenna of the radio with the CP, shattering the radio and killing the man carrying it. The survivors dove into the paddies on both sides of the dike.

"Spread out along the dikes," Ortega yelled. "Get some fire out there." The squad leaders echoed him.

Men from second and third squads dragged themselves through the thigh-deep, stagnant water to the dikes between them and the guns. They didn't move by squads because some men from each squad went over one side of the dike and some went over the other side. First squad lined up along the dike the platoon had walked on—it was too far back to be able to fire.

Morris found himself on the right flank, in the corner of the paddy. He couldn't go any farther unless he went over the dike. Bullets sang overhead. Morris didn't want to put his head in their path, so he held his rifle above the dike and pulled the trigger. Ten meters away Salatu looked over the dike to aim. A burst from one of the guns tore his face off his head.

In ripples, the remaining men in the two squads fired over the dikes while keeping their heads down. None of them looked to see if their fire was having any effect.

"First squad, pull back onto the hill and flank those bastards," Wyman shouted. "Go right two hundred and cut across the paddies. The rest of the platoon'll cover you."

First squad didn't move. Wyman crossed three dikes getting back to them and nose to nose repeated the order to the squad leader. The squad leader "aye-ayed" and ordered his people to move. First squad lost three men before it reached the foot of the hill.

"First squad, hold up. Take cover," Wyman shouted when he saw his men getting hit. Scrambling, he returned to the CP and started screaming, "Spread it out! You're too bunched up. Spread it out!"

Morris looked up at the dike by his side. Over it? he thought through in a daze. And the thought was father to the action. Seconds later he had reached another paddy corner.

"Spread it out!" Wyman was still yelling.

Morris's fogged mind forced his tired body to obey.

Wyman kept yelling for second and third squads to spread out and use aimed fire. So Morris continued rolling over dikes. When he gathered himself to go over the fifth dike, Morris realized with a start that there was no firing near him. He looked to his left and saw he was alone in a paddy. No machine-gun fire whined overhead or dug into the other side of the dike he crouched behind. Raising his head and looking to his left, he saw a body collapsed on a dike three paddies over. There was no sign of anyone between him and that body. That was where the spread out had stopped. The VC didn't realize Morris had gone so far to the flank, and weren't firing at him.

Morris looked again and realized the body on the dike had to be Runningstar. "The fuckers killed Chief," he said to himself. "Someone gonna die for that."

Fueled by anger and too tired to care about danger, Morris crossed two more dikes before starting forward. Half crawling, half swimming, he waded toward the trees through the tepid, scummy water. At each dike he put a hand on top and heaved himself over it until he didn't drop into more water, but landed on grass. On hands and knees he scuttled into the cover of the trees.

The temperature was much lower in the shade. Morris lay quietly for a few moments gathering strength and clearing his mind in the relative coolness. Thinking only, The fuckers killed Chief, he rose to a crouch and trotted softly toward the sound of the nearer machine gun.

Behind a log barricade a uniformed Viet Cong squatted at the stock of a captured M-60 machine gun. A second VC lay at the gun's side feeding belts of ammunition into it. Another, watching over the barricade, directed the aim of the gunner. Morris lay down behind a tree less than five meters from the nest. He pulled a grenade from his pouch, pulled the pin, eased the spoon off and tossed it at the VC. The grenade landed two feet behind the gunner and exploded almost at the instant it hit the ground.

Shrapnel and slivers of the notched wire wrapped tightly around the explosive core of the grenade tore into the gunner and his assistant, killing them instantly. The spotter was partly shielded by the body of the gunner and received only minor leg wounds. Before the spotter could react to the attack and turn toward it, Morris was on his feet charging the position, firing into the bodies. The spotter died from a three-round burst in his chest. Morris ran to the other gun.

A log barricade similar to the first one gave protection to another gun team. Again Morris took cover behind a tree and popped the spoon from a grenade. He held this one a half second longer than the first one and lobbed it high into the air, hoping for an air burst. The grenade dropped into the circle formed by the gun team. They started to jump away but it was too late. The grenade went off and killed all three. Morris made sure by putting a burst from his M-14 into each of them.

In the paddies, third platoon was still firing. Everyone was down behind the dikes with only their weapons exposed. No one was shooting level, all of the platoon's return fire too high to be effective. None of them seemed to realize the guns had been silenced.

Morris stood behind the barricade and shouted, "Cease fire! Cease fire!" Either they didn't hear him or they thought it was a trick, so he called again, "Cease fire! Third platoon, cease fire. Hey, Lieutenant Wyman, it's Henry J. Stop shooting, I knocked the guns out."

In the paddies Wyman heard Morris and called for the platoon to cease fire. He raised his head over the dike and looked toward the trees. Morris was waving his arms and shouting that the VC were all dead.

Two med-evac birds lifted out Runningstar and the two wounded men from each of the other squads along with Salatu's body and Mouse and the other three dead men. It was too close to nightfall for the rest of the platoon to hump back to the fire base before dark, so they sat under the trees and waited. Battalion was going to try to get three more birds in to lift them out, but no guarantees. If air hadn't arrived by sunset, they would have to wait until dawn, then walk in. The helicopters came for them.

"I'm writing you up for a Navy Cross, Morris," Lieutenant Wyman said the next day. "What you did has got to be the ballsiest thing I've ever seen. Why did you go after them alone?"

"Thank you, sir," Morris answered. "I did it because I thought they killed Chief. Me and him been through too much shit together. I couldn't let the shitheads that killed him get away with it." Besides, he thought, they didn't know I was over there and I was too fucking tired to give a good goddam.

"Well, Runningstar isn't dead. He's out of the shit now, he's going home. That was still brave, Morris."

Recommended for a Navy Cross and awarded a Bronze Star. That's the way things went. A boot lieutenant's word wasn't enough to get Morris anything better.

"Gonna miss you people," Sergeant Johnson told the five men who remained from the squad he had started with the previous November. Four had died and two more had been wounded badly enough to be returned to The World. Now Johnson and Falalo were going home, to be released from active duty. Their enlistments were up.

"Bullshit." Falalo grinned. "We ain't gonna miss any of you turds. We going back to The World and drink so much cold beer, American whiskey, eat so much ice cream, and fuck so many round-eyes, we won't have time to think of any silly-assed grunts humping through the toolies."

"No, really," Johnson said. "We been through a lot of shit together, and I'm proud to have served with you men. You only have three more months to get through. Hideaway and me going now 'cause it's time for us to put the civvies back on. Keep your asses down."

Solemnly, Johnson and Falalo shook hands with Bahls, Morris, Evans, Casebolt, and Devoid. They boarded the waiting amtrack and rode toward battalion headquarters. From there they would get transport to Da Nang and board a civilian airliner for Okinawa and then on to California and freedom.

Welcome to Pleasantville

"YOU HEARD ABOUT THAT GUY IN THE ARMY, LIEUTENANT Calley, and how he was such a monster, killing all those people in that village. Well, I want to tell you, Calley wasn't the only one that did things like that. If the press didn't decide to make a big thing of it, nothing probably would have happened. Or maybe Calley pissed off someone and that someone wanted to hang his ass for it. I'm not gonna tell you what he did was being done all the time, but anybody who was in the grunts for any kind of time at all can tell you a similar story. Not as bad a massacre, but civilians getting killed in cold blood.

"The way we saw it, we were over in Vietnam fighting a war for the Vietnamese to keep them free from communism. Even those of us who didn't know why we were there knew we were fighting the Vietnamese's war for them. We expected them to cooperate with us. If they didn't, they had to be on the other side, and that meant they were the enemy and whatever you do to the enemy in war is legal. When you're out there and your buddies are getting their asses shot up or killed and little yellow people who you can't see are trying to kill you, you can get powerful pissed. Next little yellow sum-bitch you see that ain't being real nice and helpful is someone you want to kill for revenge. It's like we always said, 'Payback is a motherfucker.'

"I knew some Marines—good people, mind you—who blew

227

away unarmed civilians deliberately. Some of them did it on their own account, some of them because an officer or staff NCO told them to. Ain't nice, but anybody says war is nice don't know diddly-squat about combat. One day third platoon walked into a village that had maybe thirty people in it. When we left, twenty of them had to bury the other ten.

"Before I tell you about that, though, let me tell you about the new men we got in the squad.

"Third squad was down to seven men—the five originals who were left after Johnny Johnson and Hernando Falalo rotated back to CONUS plus Gant and Hunter. A big replacement draft come in and we got four new men in the squad. One of them was this big bull of a corporal name of Durham. Naturally, we called him Bull. Bull'd been in the Corps for three years. He was with the Ninth Marines on Oki, then wore a pogie rope with the Fifth Marines at Lejeune in North Carolina for a while before going home on an emergency leave and missing his battalion going to Veeceeland. They stuck his ass at Twentynine Palms for a few months before cutting him orders to go to war.

"The other three, one was a big blond, PFC Thorsfinni. Thorsfinni was Norwegian and always said how he wanted to be a Viking but had to settle for being a Marine because that was the closest thing in the twentieth century. He already started growing what was to become the biggest damn blond mustache I ever saw. The other two were privates Anderson and Zwang, who were good buddies with each other from boot camp. Bull started calling them 'Alpha and Omega' when he found out they were buddies, but that was too intellectual for most of us, so it never caught on.

"Buster Bahls was made squad leader and got his third stripe. Bull Durham was made first fire-team leader. I got a promotion and the second fire team, and Malcolm X also made corporal and got third fire team. Devoid was now the blooperman. Jeb and Gant went to Bull's team, Malcolm X got Hunter and Anderson. That left me with Thorsfinni and Zwang. I bitched to Buster about getting stuck with two boots, but he said the men he had, somebody was gonna get two boots and he thought I could handle it. Maybe I could handle it, but I didn't have to like it.

"But you want to know about the day third platoon walked

into a village that had thirty people in it when we got there and only twenty living when we left, don't you? I thought so, son. You didn't seem to be paying much attention when I was telling you about the new men. Just hold your pants on and I'll tell you about it.

"It was about three weeks after the new men came to us. We spent a week of that time guarding the perimeter at, I think it was, Dong Ha and went on a battalion operation in sight of the DMZ. Don't know how we managed to luck out, but with rockets coming into Dong Ha every night and all the mortar fire we took from the other side of the DMZ on that operation, third platoon didn't get any casualties.

"Goddam that DMZ. The NVA could cross it whenever they wanted to, or they could sit over there on the other side and fire at us, but we couldn't cross it to find their asses or shoot over it at them, though once in a while our artillery got permission to fire back.

"The fire fights third platoon was in didn't get any of us wounded or killed, either. Now we were on a fire base doing platoon patrols. Three weeks and we ain't been hurt except for all the new men dropping from the heat and Thorsfinni and Anderson having to be med-evacked because of it on that operation. Then we ran this patrol and the shit hit the fan all over us.

"We were humping over hills covered with low brush, scrub trees, and stayawhile vines. This day we were supposed to go west three klicks, arch to the south for a couple more, then swing east and come back in south of the fire base. Everything was going smooth for the first three hours we were out there. We moved slow, about a mile an hour, so three hours took us almost to where we were to turn back east. But there was a ville on our route we were supposed to check out. Some of the people who lived in it'd been relocated to what they called a 'Freedom Village.'

"Most of us thought those farmers lived like animals out in the boonies in their thatch hootches, drinking warm tea made from well water that had typhus, typhoid, cholera, and who knows what else kind of bugs in it, and crapping onto the river bank for the people downstream to ignore. But them villes *were* old and well tended, even looked like some of the South Seas villages you see in the movies. Real pretty, sort of. Those 'Freedom Villages' were worse. They were grass hootches with tin roofs lined up in rows and there weren't any shade trees nowhere. Trenches were dug around them and filled with pointy stakes and they had barbed-wire fences around them. Looked like prisons is what they looked like. The people in the regular villages looked suspicious of us, but the ones in the 'Freedom Villages' looked like they hated us. Can't say I blamed them for that but, hell, those damn places weren't our idea.

"Anyway, we walked in and the place looked empty, like everybody had all of a sudden decided to go on a picnic or something. At some time this ville had been shelled by artillery, and there were big holes broken in the hedgerow around it. We were supposed to look for any sign of Vee Cee hanging around; maybe living here, storing weapons, getting food from these people. They were. We found that out soon as the point squad was all the way inside. And we found out why nobody seemed to be at home. First squad had the point, followed by second, and third was bringing up the rear.

"First squad was pulling into line along one side of the place and second was gonna line up on the other side. Third would be the cover and reaction unit. Before second squad could get in, a machine gun and an RPG opened up on first squad. Everbody hit the deck and first squad tried to return fire. The ones that still could. Smiff started maneuvering second squad to get inside the ville and help out first. Then there was another machine gun and some automatic weapons firing at second squad, too. Lieutenant Wyman was trying to yell orders, get information about what was happening, and talk on the radio all at the same time. First and second squads were pinned down real good. They couldn't move for nothing. Third was just sitting tight waiting to be told what to do.

"In a little bit, two gunships on their way back from somewhere else came by and shot all the rockets and machine-gun ammo they had left into the ville. That quieted down the Vee Cee fire for a bit, but when they started up again, it was as bad as before. We couldn't tell where they were shooting at us from. While the Vee Cee weren't firing as much, first squad had a chance to drag out its casualties where they could be taken care of by corpsmen and for both squads to get better positions in the ville. Second also had two men down, but they weren't hit bad and stuck compress bandages on their ownselfs so they could keep fighting. Once the five wounded from first were patched up as good as they could be, Wyman had third carry them to an LZ he set a couple hundred meters back behind a bend in the hill where they wouldn't get hit again, and we waited with them for the med-evac birds to come.

"After the med-evac, Wyman had third squad go along the left side of the ville to try and flank the Vee Cee. Would have been a great idea except Charlie expected us to do that.

"Thorsfinni fixed a bayonet and charged along the hedgerow looking like the Viking he said he wanted to be—if you can imagine a Viking looking like a combat Marine, that is. Good thing he was moving fast at first, because twenty meters along he ran smack into three Vee Cee coming out of the hedgerow. Surprised the hell out of him. Fortunately they were even more surprised than he was. Thorsfinni had his M-14 set on full auto and opened up before they did. He zapped two of the little buggers before his weapon jammed, and then gutted the third one with his bayonet. After that we all moved more carefully. Thirty meters farther and Thorsfinni almost got taken out again. A machine gun was hidden in the hedgerow and opened up on him. Buster Bahls had Devoid pop a few grenades up high hoping they'd drop down into the hedgerow where the gun was, but Devoid did it all by guesswork and the gun kept shooting.

"Then Bull Durham crawled out in the open to where he could see where the gun was and tried to throw a hand grenade at it. But someone else inside the ville saw him and put a bullet through his chest before he could get it thrown and it went off in his hand. Then for some reason we never did learn, the gun ignored us and we were able to keep moving.

"Finally we were parallel to where the Vee Cee shooting was coming from and fired on it. Then everthing stopped. Ain't had no idea at the time where the Vee Cee went to, but they bugged. This is broad daylight, remember. So far the only Vee Cee we had seen was the three Thorsfinni killed. The enemy fire ceased and stayed ceased. When we searched we found tunnel openings and spider-trap covers where Charlie'd been shooting at us from, but didn't find any of him. Couple splashes of blood, but that was it. We had nine casualties, four dead and five wounded, and couldn't find none of the gooks that did it. The tunnel complex under that ville was too complex for us to search more than a small part of it. We suspected there were escape tunnels that came out someplace far from there.

"Even if we couldn't find any Vee Cee in those tunnels, we found something else, people, about thirty of 'em. These people were women, children, and old men. We figured the younger men must all be Vee Cee and all bugged out of there. Those people sure didn't like seeing us. They looked at us mean, the ones that wasn't crying and wailing, afraid we was going to kill them all, the same as they knew their men did when they took a ville against resistance. We did a good job of searching that ville while Wyman and Ortega tried questioning the people. They didn't get any information, but we found enough rice and dried fish to feed two hundred men for the best part of a year. Best things we found, though, were a tommy gun, a BAR, and four hundred rounds of ammunition.

"Now, there ain't no statute of limitations on murder, and some people would say what came next was murder, so I ain't gonna say who did what, except for one thing about Wyman and one about Ortega. The man who found the tommy gun was just about through searching one of the hootches when he heard the old mama-san who lived there sigh. He said it sounded like relief. Real quick, before she looked away from it, he saw her glancing at a rice-filled basket he checked out without finding anything. The basket was about three foot high and he hadn't searched all the way to its bottom. Now he did. He checked it by knocking it over and dumping the rice out. In the bottom, wrapped in plastic to keep rice dust out, was a pouch with nearly two hundred rounds of forty-five-caliber ammo. Just before he found that, he found a hole in the dirt floor under it. In the hole was the tommy gun wrapped in plastic. When this Marine tried to ask the mama-san whose gun it was, she tried to act surprised like she never saw it before. He said it was a Vee Cee weapon and called her Vee Cee. She kept saying, 'No Vee Cee, no Vee Cee.' So he balled up his fist and hit that old woman in the face. She flew back a few feet into a wall post and you could hear the crack her neck made when it broke just like an old dry stick. Then she fell down, dead.

"Someone else found the BAR in another hootch. A young

woman who was watching the search ran when it was found. Another Marine searching the hootch pulled his M-14 to his shoulder and put a round into her back. He walked to her and kicked her onto her back. Looking into her dead, staring eyes, he said, 'It's too goddam bad you're a Vee Cee. You look almost pretty enough to fuck, you goddam gook.'

"When Wyman found out about the weapons and the gooks who'd been killed he declared the ville a Vee Cee village. The next gook who tried to act innocent and ignorant with him, he said to a rifleman standing by him, 'Kill him' and that old papa-san died. Everybody still tried looking like they didn't know anything about Vee Cee, but we knew better. The lieutenant got the village headman and blew out the back of his head with his forty-five. Next Ortega lined up a bunch of people and we killed them.

"They were Vee Cee. They knew it and they knew we knew it. But they wouldn't talk to us, wouldn't tell us anything that'd help us stay alive and win that war. They were only lucky we didn't kill them all like we should have. We let them go after burning down half the hootches in that ville.

"I ain't gonna say what we did was right and I ain't gonna say it was wrong. It was war and we'd just been ambushed and had four men killed and five more wounded. We were pissed and upset and someone had to pay for it. Those gooks were Vee Cee. They paid. Even if they weren't wearing uniforms or shooting at us, they paid. That's the way war is sometimes. Civilians in the wrong place or doing the wrong thing at the wrong time die.''

Chapter Twelve

TOO MANY MEN HAD DIED OR BEEN WOUNDED TOO BADLY TO return. Sergeant Johnson and Corporal Falalo lived out their service as Marines, and Wegener and Salatu had long since been killed. Third squad was down to half strength, seven men. It didn't stay at seven for long, though. More Marines came to help fight the war. A salty peacetime grunt corporal, one bad-assed boot PFC, and two brand-new privates made third squad just big enough to form three understrength fire teams.

Lieutenant Wyman wanted to assign all of his people into their new positions within the platoon.

"Never mind, sir, I'll do it," Staff Sergeant Ortega told him. "The lieutenant has more important things to do with his time." Wyman hadn't been with the platoon long enough to earn the men's respect. None of them trusted him yet, and Ortega knew if he made the assignments morale would suffer.

Then he said to the squad leaders, "Here's your new men. Rearrange your squads and let me know how you've assigned your people. If I agree with what you did, I'll pass it on to the lieutenant. If I don't, then you gotta do it all over again, so get it right the first time."

Naturally, there was a lot of grumbling in the platoon when experienced men were assigned to be with new men, and friends were split into different fire teams. But there was less unhappi-

ness because the squad leaders made the assignments than there
would have been if the assignments had been made by higher-
ups. Corporal Morris may have been the most unhappy. He was
made second fire-team leader; he wanted first fire team because
that would have made him the de facto assistant squad leader.
The more senior corporal, Bull Durham, had no combat experience. Worse, Morris's two men were a loud-mouthed boot
PFC who wanted to be a Viking, and a private so green Morris
wasn't sure he could blow his nose by himself.

C'est la guerre. Buster Bahls had full confidence in Morris's
ability to handle two boots and wouldn't accept any arguments.
At least that's what he said.

In the stifling heat of just past noon, the members of third
platoon tried to keep the tops of the sparse trees between them
and the sun's burning rays. They had been humping through the
brush for five hours looking for Charlie. All they had seen other
than insects were abandoned rice paddies and cane fields. Now
they approached an equally abandoned village. Abandoned because it was in VC territory and the inhabitants had been relocated to a Freedom Village. The platoon's assignment was to
search the ville for sign of enemy use.

The ville's hedgerow fence was partly overgrown from lack
of care, partly blown out by a few artillery barrages and air
strikes laid on shortly after its abandonment to convince Charlie
he really shouldn't use it now that there weren't any civilians
around for him to hide behind.

First squad, leading the platoon, could see through the entrance to the ville and gaps in the hedgerow that most of the
hootches in it were damaged and either collapsing or completely
down. The ville looked like it would be easy to search. When
the pointman was within seventy-five meters of the hedgerow,
Wyman halted the platoon to give himself a chance to eyeball
the situation and issue orders.

"Squad leaders up." The word passed back along the column
from where Wyman, Ortega, and the platoon's radioman squatted in the grass near the point team. The three sergeants joined
them.

"First squad, see those two breaks in the hedge to the right
of the gate?" First squad leader nodded. "Send one fire team

through each of them and your third fire team through the gate.
Get on line and sweep through, check out all the hootches to
the right of the main path. Sergeant Smith, send half of your
squad through the gate after first has cleared it and the other half
through that break on the left. Get on line and search the hootches
on that side of the path. Sergeant Bahls, third squad stands by
for use as fire base, reaction team, or anything else we need
going through there." He looked each man in the eyes. "Questions?"

The three sergeants eyed the broken hedgerow and collapsing
hootches beyond it.

"Safeties on or off?" one of them asked.

"Lock and load," Wyman replied. Round in the chamber,
bolt closed, safety off.

The others nodded.

"First squad, move out in—" Wyman checked his watch.
"—five minutes."

First squad leader looked at his watch and nodded.

"Second, move out when first is twenty-five meters ahead of
this position. Third, move to this position when second has
passed it. Do this thing."

The squad leaders rose to crouches and returned to relay the
orders to their team leaders.

At the end of the five minutes, first squad moved out on a
ragged line. Second followed twenty-five meters to its left and
rear. Wyman moved twenty-five meters behind second with his
command unit. Third moved to the line of departure.

In three bunches first squad passed through the hedgerow.
Second was starting to move through when the matted foliage
among the hootches roared its displeasure at first squad with the
rattle of machine guns and burps of rocket-propelled grenades.

First squad hit the deck—some men diving, others dropping.
The divers rolled and crawled to what cover they could find and
returned fire at the unseen enemy. Those who dropped stayed
where they were, some writhing, others still. Smith screamed
for second squad to get through and take cover. Their weapons
added to the cacophony of death in the ville.

Wyman rushed his CP to the concealment of the hedgerow.
"Where are they?" he yelled at the men inside. "How many
are there?"

His only answer was enemy machine-gun fire coming in his general direction and Marine fire going the other way.

"Get the Six on the horn," he shouted at his radioman. "Tell him we're at Tuan Hua and taking fire from unknowns." Twisting around, he called back to third squad. "Move up to here," he shouted, indicating the hedgerow and pumping his arm up and down, telling them to run. He turned back to the radioman. "Got the Six yet?"

An unexpected voice answered the radioman; it was a gunship pilot. Two gunships were nearby on the way back to their base and had some ordnance remaining. They'd be more than happy to dump it any place Wyman wanted it—and Wyman was more than happy to accept the offer.

The two helicopters swung down and fired their rockets at the smoke grenades third platoon put out to mark where they thought the VC were. The rockets were followed by machine-gun fire. Too soon for the Marines on the ground to feel much comfort, the birds were emptied and flew off. Maybe others would come to give more help.

The gunships' fire depressed the VC enough for first squad to drag its casualties out of the ville, then first and second squads took better positions in it.

"Third squad, move those wounded back about a hundred meters, where the corpsmen can patch 'em up," Wyman ordered. "I'm calling for a med-evac."

Staying low, third squad ran the wounded back behind a low rise, where they'd have some protection from the fire, and stood guard over them while the corpsmen worked. Slowly, the fire from inside the ville regained its previous volume.

"Third squad up," came the radioed order. "Come to the hedgerow."

"On line, people," Bahls shouted. "Keep it low and fast. Let's go. Move it, move it, move it!"

Spread out wide, third squad ducked low and ran for the hedgerow. They reached it and hid behind what cover they could find.

On the left flank with Morris, Private Zwang discovered a trench running parallel to the outside of the hedgerow. Ortega and Bahls crab-scuttled to Zwang's side. A trench, five feet deep and three wide, zigzagged away from them.

"Bet we could flank them dinks from here," Thorsfinni volunteered.

Morris nodded agreement.

"I'll tell the lieutenant," Ortega said. "You probably gonna go down that sucker." He left Bahls with Morris and scuttled back to the CP.

Ortega was back in little more than a minute. "Me and my big fucking mouth. The lieutenant wants third squad to go in that trench and I'm going with you." He looked blank-eyed at Bahls. "Tell your fire-team leaders, then move it out."

Bahls crawled to Durham and Evans, telling them about the trench, then signaled Morris to move his men into it. Morris started to send Zwang in first but Thorsfinni pushed past him with fixed bayonet.

"Odin!" the big blond shouted, plunging into the trench. Holding his M-14 slightly ahead of him in one hand, with the fixed bayonet jutting before it, Thorsfinni did resemble a Viking with long sword at the ready. "Odin!" he shouted again and ran full tilt, crouched so his helmet was barely below the top of the trench.

Morris ran hard behind the big man, swearing at him to slow down and look before taking corners. Thorsfinni ignored him, having already slammed around the first bend. The rest of the squad pounded behind them.

Thorsfinni took the second turn and crashed into three VC running the other way. His extended bayonet skewered the first man, and he fired a burst to knock the VC off it. The momentum of the two bowled the other two VC off their feet. Thorsfinni fired a burst into one of them, but his rifle jammed before he could shoot the last one, so he plunged his bayonet into him before the VC had time to react.

Struggling to clear the jam, Thorsfinni grinned back at Morris. "That's why I'm going so fast," he said. "Catch the little fuckers by surprise and knock 'em over before they can do anything."

"Zwang, take the point," Morris ordered, glaring at the blond. "You get that fucking jam cleared and go at my pace, boot. Understand?"

"Shit, man, you just ain't no fun." Thorsfinni was still grinning.

"I said, understand?"

"Got'cha, Honcho." Still working on the jam, Thorsfinni fell in behind Morris.

The pace was slower now. Zwang saw the three Viet Cong Thorsfinni killed and was terrified he'd run into some who would be ready for him. He looked to Morris for direction before turning any corners. After Zwang edged around the first bend, Morris showed him how to turn the next one. Back pressed to the dirt wall, rifle across his body, Morris suddenly threw himself at the opposite wall around the bend and pointed his rifle down the trench. Then he waved Zwang on. The private took the next corner the way Morris demonstrated.

Thorsfinni clapped a hand on Morris's shoulder. "Come on, Honcho, let me have the point again."

Zwang looked back hopefully.

Morris shook his head. "All right, Thor. But remember you ain't John fucking Wayne."

"You numbah fucking one, Honcho." The big man was still grinning. So far, he liked combat.

"Man must think he's fucking Nutsy Nooncy," Bahls muttered at Morris.

"I do believe he does," Morris muttered back before following Thorsfinni past Zwang.

Bahls motioned Zwang to follow his fire-team leader.

First, back against the wall like Morris had done, Thorsfinni threw himself at the opposite wall, then plunged down the length of the trench to the next turn. He spun past it and flung himself backward, gaining the cover of the corner at the instant a long machine-gun burst split the air where he had been.

"I saw the fucker before he saw me." Thorsfinni grinned at Morris.

The gun was silent for a few seconds then let loose with another stream of bullets over the top of the trench. That was followed by a series of two- to three-second bursts followed by five-second pauses. The squad was pinned down.

"How far back is he!" Bahls yelled at Thorsfinni.

"Right at the edge of the trees, on a straight line with the next leg of the trench."

"Empty Nick, keep your stupid head down and try to pop an HE on his ass," Bahls told the blooperman.

Devoid fired a few 40mm grenade rounds toward the gun position but couldn't come near it without looking. So he looked. The next burst would have taken his head off if he hadn't ducked immediately.

"Fuck this shit," Durham swore, and hauled himself out of the trench on the village side. He rolled to the concealment of the hedgerow and crawled toward the gun. He stopped ten meters from it and pulled the pin from a grenade. In order to throw over the mass of fallen trees he was behind, Durham had to rise to his knees. Someone in the ville must have seen him rise. A bullet slammed into Durham's chest. He dropped the grenade when he fell. The grenade exploded next to his body.

Two more gunships arrived on station and rained rockets and machine-gun fire into the ville. The gun covering the trench stopped shooting when a brace of rockets hit it, and third squad was able to resume moving. They reached a place where Ortega and Bahls agreed they were flanking the Viet Cong positions in the ville. The only fire they could hear now came from their own platoon and the two gunships. Looking over the lip of the trench, third squad couldn't see anything, either.

When he realized the VC had bugged out, Ortega boomed out, "Cease fire! Cease fire!" at full voice.

Slowly, the Marines and their gunships stopped firing. Silence settled on the ville. The acrid smell of cordite eddied in the air and the background hum of insects returned. There were no other sounds except for those made by the Marines.

"Third squad, check it out," Wyman yelled. "Look for bodies, spider traps, and tunnel mouths. Staff Sergeant Ortega, take 'em through."

Helping each other, the men of third squad climbed out of the trench and carefully picked their way through the ville. Tunnel openings were found under piles of brush and debris. Two were located inside half-collapsed hootches. Spent brass was scattered on the ground around many of the holes, but no bodies—alive or dead—were found.

Wyman had the remaining wounded and dead gathered outside the ville. Another med-evac chopper touched down and lifted them out. Two volunteers went into the tunnels with flashlights and forty-fives. They found scrapings that looked like the movement of many men, and a few dark, wet spots that might have been blood, but no bodies. The scrapings all led to a long, straight tunnel that seemed to lead to the river, a couple of hundred meters distant. Neither volunteer followed that tunnel.

Third platoon settled on the upland side of the village and watched while a flight of two A-4 Skyhawks flew low and dropped napalm on it. They were angry and frustrated. First squad had lost two men killed and three wounded, second had one killed and two wounded. Bull Durham was dead. "Looks like you gonna get to be first fire-team leader after all," Buster Bahls said to Morris. Morris grunted. Thorsfinni had killed three VC in the trench and saw another with a machine gun in the hedgerow. No one else had seen the enemy or knew he killed one of them. The burning of the village was an emotionally satisfying sight. The word they received about an engineer platoon coming to blow the tunnels was also satisfying. But no one was sated. Anger still seethed beneath the surface.

Third platoon hadn't made anybody pay. But they would. "Payback is a motherfucker," they said. And, "Somebody gonna pay for this, cocksucker."

"Third platoon, saddle up," Ortega shouted.

"Saddle up! Saddle up! Saddle up!" the order was echoed by the squad leaders. Fire fight or not, nine dead and wounded or none, the patrol had to be completed, and enough men remained to complete it.

Grumbling, the twenty-odd men remaining in the platoon rose to their feet, shrugged their packs back onto weary backs, adjusted their cartridge belts and bandoleers, checked that they had everything, worked the action of their weapons, formed into a staggered column. Wyman raised his arm toward the sky and let it fall. Third squad led off, followed by second. Badly hurt, first squad brought up the rear.

"I wanna kill me somebody," the muttering started.

"Charlie gonna pay for this," it continued.

"Next fucking gook I see gets certified as a Vee Cee. Certified by six rounds of seven-sixty-deuce in his scrawny ass." The susurration flowed to and fro along the column.

Little more than a kilometer from the abandoned ville, third platoon entered a populated village. Elderly men and women stared blankly at the Marines from holes carved in the mahogany masks of their faces. They did not grin around the blackened stumps of their teeth. Middle-aged women went about their business as though no strangers had appeared in their midst. Young women skillfully maintained a distance from the Americans. Children hid from them. Shirt-clad boy toddlers and shorts-clad girl toddlers took refuge behind their mothers. Hostility peered from shadows, lurked in the trees, behind doorways, around the corners of the hootches.

"Where the fuck the men at? They all in the Arvins or sompin'?" someone asked.

"Shit no," he was answered. "The mans is all Vee Cees."

"The ones that ambushed us," a third man said.

"Spread it out, people," Wyman ordered. "Round 'em up and bring 'em all to the square." The village square was a small open area in the center of the village where a flagpole stood. The flagpole was supposed to fly the red-banded yellow banner of South Vietnam. It stood flagless.

Third platoon divided into fire teams and gathered the villagers, about thirty people, in the square. The seven survivors in first squad circled the villagers while Wyman and Ortega questioned them in broken Vietnamese. Second and third squads searched the hootches. The village headman managed to express concern to Wyman that the Marines might steal or break things if they were allowed into the hootches without anyone to watch them. Wyman agreed to let one person who lived in each hootch watch its search.

"Shit, Henry J," Thorsfinni said, "ain't nothing in this fucking little hut can do any harm to nobody."

Morris and Thorsfinni were in a one-room hootch along with Zwang and Casebolt. After Durham's death the squad had been reformed into two fire teams. The hootch's single room held a three-by-five-foot sleeping pallet, a small table with two chairs under one of its two windows, a storage chest containing clothes and cooking utensils, and five large rice-storage baskets. The hard-packed dirt floor was meticulously swept.

"Think so?" Morris asked. "Then why the fuck's this old mama-san got all this rice?" His sweeping arm indicated the five woven baskets, each filled with more than two hundred pounds of rice. "You think she's gonna eat all this shit her ownself?'' He turned to her to ask, ''You gonna eat it all your own-self, old woman?'' but didn't.

The old woman jerked her eyes away from one of the baskets when Morris looked her way.

''What you saying, mama-san? You saying I missed some-thing?'' Morris had earlier stuck his arm into the baskets and felt around them, but hadn't dug very deep. ''I'm gonna take another look.'' He grasped the lip of the basket and pulled it over, spilling rice on the floor.

The woman's face remained expressionless as she edged to-ward the door.

Morris upended the basket and heard a muffled clank. Toss-ing the container aside, he saw the four plastic bags that fell out of it. They were filled with forty-five caliber bullets. Where the basket had stood was a wooden cover set in the floor. Morris lifted it aside. An elongated plastic bag was in a hole underneath the cover. The bag held a well-oiled Thompson submachine gun.

''No harm, Thor?'' Morris held the tommy gun out to him.

''Goddam.'' Thorsfinni took the offered weapon. ''Watch,'' he shouted, because the old woman looked like she was about to bolt.

Morris took a step toward her. ''You Vee Cee,'' he accused.

''No Vee Cee,'' she shook her head. ''No Vee Cee.'' She remained expressionless.

''Yes, you Vee Cee,'' Morris insisted. The old woman started to run toward the door. Morris lashed out an arm, grabbed her by the arm and threw her against the wall. She crumbled to the ground looking like a pile of sticks loosely wrapped in shiny black silk. Her head hung at an odd angle.

Morris knelt by the body and checked for a pulse. Finding none, he shook his head. He heard bone ends grinding against each other.

''She's fucking dead,'' he announced. ''I broke her goddam gook neck.''

In another hootch Evans was directing his men in their search. This hootch had a back door leading to a small courtyard. Three other hootches backed on to the courtyard, and the spaces be-tween the hootches were blocked off with thatch walls, completely enclosing the small courtyard. A ground-level well with a wooden lid was in the middle of the courtyard. The Marines were being watched by a young woman, probably not much past her teens. She wore a tight white tunic top and baggy black pants. Her feet were bare.

Gant earlier had looked her over like a side of beef. "Too bad for you all the men in this ville Vee Cee, girlie," he had said. "By the time any of 'em get back to marry you, you gonna be an old, old, dried-out old woman with your teeth rotted away and their stumps black from that fucking betel nut." She had looked at him with uncomprehending eyes.

"Check out the well, Anderson," Evans said. "Sometimes they be hiding stuff in 'em, all the way down in the water."

Anderson pulled the wooden cover aside and peered down the well shaft. "Don't see nothing," he said. He looked at his fire-team leader. "Malcolm X, how the fuck they gonna get something out of there if they put it down in the water?"

"Lay down and feel along the wall far down as you can reach. If there's anything down there it's probably tied to a camouflaged cord so we can't see it."

Belly down, Anderson stuck his arm in the well and started crawling around it. He had almost described a full circle when his hand found something. "What's this?" He rose to his knees and started pulling up. A thick cord, carefully mottled to match the pattern of the well side, was in his hands. With a last jerk he flipped an elongated plastic bag over the lip of the well. His questioning eyes looked to Evans for instructions.

"Open it," Evans said.

A much-used Browning Automatic Rifle emerged from the bag.

"Halt!" Gant's warning was almost drowned out by a burst from his M-14. The young woman pitched forward onto the path she had run to. The back of her shirt spread with red.

Evans ducked through the hootch out to the body. He shoved the toe of his boot under the woman's shoulder and kicked her onto her back. The woman's dead eyes stared past Evans's left shoulder. She looked surprised. "Too goddam bad you a dead fucking Vee Cee," he said. "You look almost clean enough for a man to fuck without worrying about getting a disease."

* * *

The tommy gun, BAR, and ammunition were stacked on the ground next to the flagpole. The two bodies lay on the other side of the pole. All the Marines were present; the search was over. Wyman stood questioning an old man. The officer's foot was touching the pile of munitions.

"No Vee Cee, no Vee Cee," the old man stammered. The fear in his eyes was the first living emotion the Marines had seen or heard in this village.

Disgusted, Wyman turned his head to a rifleman standing a few feet away. "Kill him."

The Marine shrugged, clamped the stock of his rifle to his side with his elbow, and pulled the trigger. The old man jerked like a puppet and toppled backward.

"Bring me the headman," Wyman snapped.

A burly Marine roughly grabbed the village chief and shoved him to the lieutenant.

Wyman stared down into the old man's face. "You Vee Cee. Vee Cee kill boo-coo Marine. Vee Cee die." He drew his forty-five, flicked off the safety, lay the muzzle forward of the headman's ear and pulled the trigger. Amazement flickered across the man's face in the instant of his death.

In that same instant Wyman gained some respect from the men of his platoon. He was taking the war and their lives seriously.

Ortega stormed through the group of villagers. "You're Vee Cee, all of you," he shouted at them. "I'll show you what we do to fucking Vee Cee." He started grabbing people not quite at random and throwing them out of the group. One old man and an old woman. A middle-aged woman and a young one. A boy child and a girl. He stood them in a line at the side of the square.

Ortega spun away and stalked ten meters toward the Marines. "I want every swinging dick in this platoon lost a buddy today to line up in front of me."

First squad came to Ortega. Half of second squad joined them. Bull Durham had died without making any friends in third squad. Twelve men stood in a row in front of the platoon sergeant. They were facing the civilians he had lined up.

"Fucking Vee Cee killed your buddies today," Ortega shouted. "You people want payback? These people are Vee Cee.

They're the families of the fucking Vee Cee killed your buddies. Payback is a motherfucker.''

The men who came to Ortega looked at each other uncertainly for a moment. Then one of them repeated, ''Payback is a motherfucker,'' and leveled his rifle at the line of people. The other Marines leveled theirs and someone said, ''Fire.'' A hundred bullets burst from twelve muzzles, and six civilian lives shattered into death.

Wyman stared at the twenty remaining villagers. ''They Vee Cee,'' he told them. ''Vee Cee die. You no Vee Cee, you no die.'' He turned to his men. ''Third platoon, saddle up. Second squad on the point, first bring up the rear. Move it out. We've got a patrol to finish.'' Someone tapped an open but unlit Zippo against two thatch hootches as he walked by them.

In a staggered line, third platoon walked out of the village, blood lust sated. Someone had paid for their losses. It could have been anybody, but it was the civilians of this small village that paid. They were civilians who may, or may not, have been the families of the VC who ambushed the platoon. But that's the way it is. You get in the way of a war, you pay the price.

Over the Hill and Into the Trees

"THERE'S ONE THING THAT TORQUES MY JIBS EVERY TIME I really think about it, son, and that's vertical assault. You see, the Marines have been working with helicopters since Korea, where they used them for med-evac same as in Vietnam. In the early sixties, or maybe even earlier than that, the Marines were developing tactics for making assault by helicopter. The men in my squad who had been in the Corps before Vietnam, men like Johnny Johnson, Buster Bahls, Hernando Falalo—and Corporal Doyle, while he was with us—they talked about how they were doing vertical assaults on operations on Okinawa, in Hawaii, at Twentynine Palms, and at Lejeune. Then in Veeceeland we didn't have enough birds to really do what Marines were training for earlier.

"When the Army's First Cav got to the Central Highlands in the summer of 'sixty-five, they had all the Hueys they needed, and the Green Machine didn't have any Hueys. Not sure that was too big a loss, though. The Army had lots of problems with the Hueys because of the weather; they weren't designed to fly in that kind of heat. Anyway, the Army was still developing their vertical-assault tactics, things the Marines already did. Outfits like the First Cav and the American Division didn't have forward fire bases like the Marines did, they had 'Landing Zones.' To the Marines a landing zone was anyplace a bird went down to drop troops or supplies. Nowadays people hear 'vertical assault' they think Army, because they did most of it in the war. If us jolly green giants had more of them birds, we could have made more air assaults, covered more territory, and kicked more ass. Also, we wouldn't have been so tired when the shooting started. I guess what I'm saying here is, we developed it, we should have been the ones to use it the most and get the credit for it.

"I've already told you about how we a lot of times used those forward fire bases so we could be close enough to where Charlie was we could hump to a fight. Most of the time we either humped to those places we then made into fire bases or we were trucked to them. But we didn't always hump. Lots of times we flew in on an operation like we did on Abilene Run. That was a cold LZ—nobody there to shoot at us when we were coming in.

"Operation Rockledge Manor was my last combat operation. It started almost a year to the day after I'd arrived in-country. Second year in a row we had a major operation start a few days after Thanksgiving. Three Fifteen flew in on Sea Knights for that one, big birds that had a rotor at each end and could carry seventeen fully-equipped Marines at a time. We were going in where we could look to the west and see the mountains of Laos. Word was an NVA regiment was in that area. We were supposed to find and neutralize it. We found it, all right. We landed right in the middle of it. In the beginning of the landing they gave us some sniper fire—just enough to let us know someone was already there. They let half the battalion land before they really hit us. The battalion was pinned down for two days before reinforcements that landed out of the heat could reach us and bust up the ambush we were in. Next day another NVA regiment came into the area and then we were in an even deeper hole.

"But I'm getting ahead of myself. Let me tell you about Rockledge Manor from jump street, just the way it happened.

"About a week after third platoon killed those civilians, the battalion got pulled back to Da Nang and put on a fire base and guarded it for a couple of weeks. This was pretty slack time, because Charlie wasn't doing too much around there then. We were running daytime patrols and night ambushes, but the important stuff was we got to take showers and rest for a while without having to worry too much about getting hit. We even saw some movies and drank some cold beer.

"Then we got trucked up to this hill maybe fifteen miles west of Dong Ha, where we set in for the night. In the morning choppers came and got us and we flew west. Kilo Company was the battalion reserve for Rockledge Manor. Mike Company went in first to secure the LZ. India Company followed next and enlarged the perimeter. It was when Lima started coming in that the shit hit the fan. The actual LZ was only big enough for one platoon to set down in at a time.

"Four birds were coming down fast to drop off a platoon and eight more were circling, waiting for their turn, when the NVA opened up like they meant it. Mike Company came under fire from what seemed like a whole battalion, and India—on the other side—started taking heavy incoming, too. The NVA had some rockets and fifty-caliber machine guns they were shooting at the birds with. About fifty feet from the ground one of those birds got hit by a rocket and sort of disintegrated in the air. Grady Zimmerman was on that bird and got killed with everbody on it. Most of the other choppers took hits from fifties, and a few men in them got wounded before they even reached the ground.

"Those three birds had their ramps already down when they hit the LZ, and everbody scrambled off and headed for cover most ricky-tick. The other birds with the rest of the company in them went back up out of range to wait until the LZ cooled a skosh bit. On the ground it seemed like most of that NVA regiment was hitting India and Mike companies and the one platoon from Lima that made it down. Good thing Mike and India had time to set in first. Most of them had some cover and concealment, so they weren't getting hit with too many casualties. Lima's platoon, though, was in the open and had to scramble like crazy to find any cover. The two corpsmen with the platoon and a couple other Marines tried to save some of the men from the bird that got hit by a rocket, but it wasn't any good—they were all blown to hell.

"The battalion CO was three klicks up in his command bird and he called for artillery to come in on the NVA. When they got the word on the ground he was doing this, the FOs started calling in coordinates and the spotter rounds started coming in until they were hitting where they were supposed to, then all hell broke loose on where the NVA were shooting from. Some of the Marines in the fight started whooping about this, saying how nobody could live through that fire, but then someone else wanted to know who was shooting if nobody could live through it. Then everybody just settled in and waited for the barrage to end.

"Artillery came in for about three hours before the NVA fire slacked off to next to nothing and the CO called the big guns off. Next he wanted some air strikes, and a squadron of F-4 Phantoms came and dropped everthing they had where the big guns already hit. When they flew away the sky was filled with helicopter gunships to cover our movement, and the rest of Lima came in then, too, and the rest of the casualties were med-evacked.

"The CO figured we knew where that NVA regiment was so we didn't have to go looking for them. Mike pulled tighter around the LZ to keep it secure and India moved three-quarters of a klick in one direction to another hill and Lima went a half klick in a different direction to a third hill. Now all we had to do was figure out how much of that regiment was still out there, where they were, and how to get to them. It was easier than anybody thought it would be; they hit India and Lima before we finished digging in.

"Two companies tried to overrun us. They snooped and pooped in the brush on the sides of that hill until they were less than fifty meters from where we were digging in, and next thing we knew there were all these gooks yelling and screaming and shooting and running up the hill at us. Half of us were digging and the other half were watching. The half watching started shooting immediately, the other half took a second to put down entrenching tools and picks and pick up rifles, bloopers, or machine guns. We was all blasting away at them before they got ten more meters up the hill, but that made them only forty meters away. Twenty more and they started throwing grenades at us. But we already started chucking grenades down at them.

"Our fire was too heavy and some of the gunships were able to come down real close to the lines, so even though they broke through in a couple of places, we were able to kick them back off of the hill. Two NVA companies ain't enough men to overrun a Marine company in the daylight. Then the gunships chased them right into the heavy brush at the bottom of the hill. Just about the same thing happened to India Company. Those gooks took one hell of an ass-kicking.

"We was kind of shaken up, too, so the three companies settled in for the night and sat tight. Dinks must have been licking their wounds, 'cause all we got that night was some sniper fire and a few mortar rounds coming in. They didn't even send anyone to probe our lines. We didn't hardly have to return any fire from our hilltops, but there was more H and I fire from the guns than usual. In the morning we were feeling kind of good because we figured we put a real hurting on Charlie the day before. But he didn't seem to think the same way we did about it.

"We were eating our morning Cs when they hit us again. This time they tried to prep us with a heavy mortar barrage, but I guess they didn't have enough tubes to do a real good job because it seemed like they were hitting each company with only two or three sixty-ones. We stayed down deep in our holes and they didn't do much damage except where a round dropped into a hole with a couple of Marines. Good thing that didn't happen too often.

"About a minute after the barrage lifted they came charging up the hills again. This time a couple hundred gooks hit one side of each of our perimeters. This give them something like four- or five-to-one odds in each assault. But our mortars were registered by now and started dropping rounds right into their middle and busted them up something fierce. Come noon the hills were starting to stink pretty bad because of all the dead gooks on the slopes were swelling up and rotting. We thought this was a shitty thing for them to do to us. Hell, if they'd come unarmed and under a white flag we would have let them pick up their dead. Wouldn't have blown them away until they picked up the bodies.

"All that afternoon they dropped mortar rounds on us and kept us ringed around with lots of snipers so we couldn't really move. Lots of gunships were flying around doing their thing, but those gooks were too well dispersed and hidden for the gunships to do much good. And they were all the time moving their mortars so we could never get a fix on them to tell the gunships or big guns where to hit. Something different needed to be done to get them off our backs good enough we could go after them.

"That something else was Kilo Company. The colonel had them dropped six klicks away, where the NVA weren't, and they humped almost in a forced march to where we were. Would have been better for Kilo if they'd humped a bit slower because they got a bunch of heat casualties and half-a-dozen point men ran into booby traps and got taken out before they reached us. But those gooks didn't think the grunts from the birds they knew came down where they did would go that far that fast, and they weren't looking to get hit from outside their ring around us.

"Kilo came drifting up behind the companies snipping at India, found their gook asses and just plain busted the hell out of them. That happened and all of those little buggers di-di'ed out of there—they didn't know what was happening or who else was coming. We spent the few hours we had left before night looking for bodies and getting a count. Our confirmed count was more than three hundred and fifty. Figure an NVA regiment had anywhere from twelve to fifteen hundred men in it. We had less than five hundred Marines come in the first day, and Kilo made us maybe six hundred and fifty. Our whole casualties, including Kilo Company's heat victims, were about one hundred and twenty-five. We lost almost one man out of five. They had more than one out of four, maybe even more than one out of three. Most of our wounded were med-evacked and could be saved. Lots of Vee Cee and NVA died because they couldn't get to a modern hospital. We put a heavy-duty hurting on that regiment.

"Kilo Company dug in on another hill so the four of our companies formed sort of a square, and we sat there for the night. Gooks didn't hardly try to bother us that night—just a few mortar rounds and a few sniper rounds was all.

"Next morning we moved down off those hills and went hunting for Charlie. All day long we had small skirmishes with him, but nothing big. They dinged a few of us and we found a shitload of blood trails, but they didn't put a real hurting on us and we never found many of them at one time. Around noon we stopped for some chow, then broke down into platoons to keep hunting. The platoons found the same kind of action the companies did in the morning—small skirmishes, but no big actions. We took a few more casualties and found more blood trails, but that was it.

"Then we pulled onto more hills for the night and dug in. Sure glad we dug the holes, 'cause the mortars and snipers were heavier than the night before. The only casualties we had in Lima was one man got out of his hole to take a shit. Mortar shrapnel hit him in the ass right next to his bunghole. Don't know how he shat for a couple weeks after that, but he sure didn't do it sitting down.

"Next day was samee-same. Platoon patrols and small fire fights. But that night battalion changed the rules to give us a better chance of catching what they thought was the remnants of a busted-up regiment. Each company put two platoons on ambushes in the low brush while the other platoon dug in on top of a hill with the mortars and CP unit. Each platoon had two machine guns with it. Third platoon's ambush site was a place the mortar section used as a registration point, so we could give them good directions if we needed them. We did need the mortars that night, too. Even had the chance to call in the big guns. Believe me, son, ain't no fun having your own one-fifty-fives coming down less than a hundred meters in front of you.

"Would have been less fun if we didn't have the guns come in so close, though. That night everything changed on Operation Rockledge Manor. Must have been Uncle Ho didn't like the way we were kicking his boys' asses, and he sent in a second regiment to help out the first one. From here on, Rockledge Manor was different from the way it was."

Chapter Thirteen

THE FEW DAYS FOLLOWING THANKSGIVING WERE WET AND overcast. Dawn seeped through the clouds and slowly lifted the darkness. The morning was chill and damp. Rain had fallen lightly all night, stopping shortly before the barely seen sunrise. Everyone was wet in this empty place somewhere west of Dong Ha, and no one had dry uniforms to change into. Mike Company was barely given enough time to heat a C-ration meal and bolt it down before the first waves of CH-46 Sea Knight helicopters landed to take them within sight of the mountains of eastern Laos. Three-quarters of an hour later more waves came to lift India Company out. By the time Lima started flying toward the distant landing zone, Mike had already established a secure perimeter around it and India was circling preparatory to touching down. So far the landing had been quiet, without even sniper fire to bother it, and the NVA regiment reported in the area remained only a rumor.

"Man, I hate this shit," someone was heard to mutter as the helicopters circled lower to pick up the waiting Marines. "I hate going on fucking operations."

"You, me, and the horse the Skipper rode in on," someone else answered.

"Gonna get us some," another Marine said.

"They gonna get some, too," said one more.

254

Nobody spoke loudly, no Marine looked at another Marine when he said anything. The few voices that were heard showed tremors of nervousness. Mostly the Marines remained silent, kept their thoughts to themselves, within themselves. Often the wait for the lift-off before an operation was worse than the landing or the actual combat.

Anderson and Zwang watched the circling helicopters sink toward the waiting earth.

"We're going into Indian Country," said Anderson.

"Yeah," Zwang agreed, "*deep* into Indian Country."

"Real deep. Deeper than we ever been before." Anderson worked his jaws. "Wonder why I'm thinking the colonel's name should be Custer?"

Zwang kept his eyes on the descending helicopters. "Don't know, but if the colonel's name is Custer, I hope to shit the skipper changed his name to Reno."

"Reno? That's a gambling town. Why should he change his name to Reno?"

"Custer sent Captain Reno on a different route to double his chance of catching the Indians. Reno didn't get to the big fight until it was over. He buried Custer and didn't get any casualties of his own."

"Sure hope the skipper changed his name." Anderson shuddered and spat.

The Sea Knights touched down, their rear ramps already lowered. Crouched over, third platoon ran toward the birds' waiting maws. Before the last men were settled into their web seats, the birds lifted off and the flight into Operation Rockledge Manor was begun.

Mike and India companies enlarged the secured LZ, waiting for Lima to arrive before they moved out on their assigned searches. Their landings had been quiet, and the only fire was from their own gunships. The only heat they encountered was the climatic kind. Charlie had decided to wait for the next wave of aircraft before he hit.

The helicopters carrying third platoon dipped toward the cleared LZ and dropped down to it fast. The men riding them tensed and glanced with nervous eyes at each other. Suddenly they heard the metallic tings of bullets hitting the aircraft. Next to Morris, Anderson sagged in the web seating and leaned forward against the restraining strap. He coughed once and flecks of bloody froth bubbled from his mouth.

"Oh, shit. Corpsman!" Morris shouted.

Morris's voice couldn't be heard above the roar of the engines, but a corpsman saw him shove Anderson back up and noted Anderson's fixed stare and lolling head. The corpsman jumped across, looked into Anderson's eyes, felt his neck for a pulse, hurriedly examined him for wounds.

Morris put his mouth next to the corpsman's ear and shouted, "How is he, Doc?"

The corpsman shook his head, looked at Anderson's dog tags, and started writing on a tag. Third platoon had suffered its first KIA of Rockledge Manor.

Guess the skipper didn't change his name to Reno, Zwang thought. He shivered.

The back ramp dropped so no time would be wasted in unloading the troops when the Sea Knight landed. This close to landing, the Marines were even prepared to jump out above ground and move.

The Sea Knights hovered just above the field and the Marines ran off them, scattering, running away in ragged lines. The helicopters were down for less than ten seconds before lifting off with the last Marines jumping to the ground. Now third platoon could hear the fire Mike and India companies were taking.

One of the helicopters that dropped third platoon was hit by a rocket before it cleared the trees on its way out and fell back into the landing zone, blocking it for other helicopters. The birds carrying Lima Company's first and second platoons withdrew to allow artillery to fire support and to give the men on the ground time to clear the broken bird out of their way. They would come back when the enemy fire slackened.

In Hanoi, General Giap was under pressure to produce a victory. The American people didn't seem to understand that they were winning the war, though nearly every time they met the Viet Cong or the North Vietnamese Army units fighting in the South, the Americans won the battle.

The pressure General Giap was under came from Uncle Ho, who needed to show the people that the Americans weren't invincible. It came from the Russians, who were supplying the North with money and weapons. Pressure came from the Chinese, who wanted to send troops into the fight, or at least take over its leadership. The internationals, who saw a socialist movement being beaten by imperialists, screamed for a victory.

So General Giap selected an area that would be easy to re-supply and reinforce—an area the Americans would find inaccessible. He sent his crack 97th Regiment into the area of the Rockpile, Hill 881, Khe Sanh. He hoped to lure an American battalion into the area. When the American battalion came, he would unleash the 154th Regiment to join forces with the 97th and destroy the Americans. This would be a victory that even Lyndon Johnson and General Westmoreland would have to publicly admit.

Neither General Giap nor the Americans could know it at the time, but this was to be the first action in a series of battles that would last until the spring of 1968. The final battle in the series, the siege of Khe Sanh, would be one of the most crushing defeats the North Vietnamese suffered on the battlefield. It would also signal the beginning of their final victory, because the American people would not understand the battle was a victory for their side.

It defied belief, but the Americans never did seem to understand when they had beaten the Viet Cong or the NVA.

Artillery rounds crashed and boomed into the hills surrounding the two companies and third platoon. The explosions raised an acrid curtain of smoke and dust. The noise deafened them and the very earth shook to its roots. The Marines held onto the ground to keep from being thrown off it. The fertile land became the face of the moon.

After what seemed an eternity, the rolling barrages stopped. The NVA no longer fired. The men on the ground pushed the broken helicopter aside and the rest of Lima Company came in with no opposition.

"Saddle up, people," the platoon sergeants roared.

"Saddle up! Saddle up! Saddle up!" the squad leaders echoed them.

The three companies moved down off the hill in different directions, over the next hills to other hills where they would dig in for the night. The hills they moved to had been bombarded by artillery and air. The Marines could dig their fighting holes in the craters. They had to hurry if they wanted to be settled by nightfall.

"Spread 'em out," the platoon leaders told their squad leaders. "Ten meters between holes, two men to a hole. We start off with a fifty-percent watch and be prepared to go to one hundred percent. If the big guns didn't wipe them out, we can expect the gooks to hit us tonight. The platoon sergeant will set the machine guns."

"Dig them holes in deeper, people," Bahls shouted at his men. "Henry J, you've done this before, show all the boots in the squad how it's done. I'm gonna be between first and second teams with Groton." Lance Corporal Groton was a new man in the squad; he had joined it a few days earlier from service with the 8th Marines in North Carolina, and Bahls had given him the M-79 grenade launcher.

"One man in each hole keeps his pot on his head and his rifle in his hands, pointing downhill." Morris went from hole to hole giving instructions. "Keep your eyes where your muzzles are pointed. The gooks might decide to hit us while we're digging in. Other man, dig. Use that E-tool like your life depends on it, because it does."

Two ridges ran fingerlike from the bottom up to the top of the hill. One of the ridges came straight at third platoon's positions. Broken brush, shattered by the artillery rounds, covered the slopes. The craters were bare patches, and the brush thrown out from them made the surrounding brush denser.

Lieutenant Wyman and Sergeant Zimmerman started checking the platoon's positions, making sure the holes were properly spaced and dug deep enough. They asked the men about their interlocking fields of fire. Zimmerman saw to it that everyone had enough ammunition and grenades. Third platoon was ready for the enemy.

Wyman, Ortega, Zimmerman, and the radioman settled in the platoon's CP. Everything was quiet on the hill. Even the men who had something to say to their teammates spoke softly in voices that wouldn't carry. The sun sank toward the no longer distant mountains. Nervously, the Marines of Lima Company

ate their C-rations. They knew Mister Charles would hit them
that night. He had to hit them.

The light dimmed and night fell. Two four-man listening posts
left the perimeter. They went a hundred fifty meters down each
of the ridges.

An hour after sunset both listening posts reported movement
on the slopes below them. Mortars were fired and their aim
adjusted according to directions from the two LPs. The sounds
of movement ended for a half hour. More movement was reported and the mortars fired again. Another half hour and a trip
flare set by one of the LPs was set off. Both LPs were called in
and the line went to one-hundred-percent alert.

"Think they're out there, Henry J?" Thorsfinni whispered to
Morris.

"I know they are, Thor. Keep your ears and nose open. We'll
be able to hear 'em and smell 'em before we can see 'em."

Tensely, the company waited. The only questions the Marines
on the hills had about the coming assault were when and how
many. Then a trip flare was set off outside third platoon's line
and the approaching NVA were only thirty meters away from
the fighting holes. The mortars popped illumination rounds into
the air and everyone opened fire.

"Goddam, they're close," Thorsfinni swore. His first burst
knocked an NVA down. Next to him, Morris took rapid aim at
the approaching line and started pulling the trigger. Half of the
first wave of attackers fell under the Marines' fire, then the other
half dropped to return fire. A second wave swept through the
first one.

"Thor, fire to your right!" Morris shouted, to be heard above
the battle's din.

The automatic rifleman shifted his aim to a bunched-up NVA
squad running toward the hole Hunter and Zwang were in. Several pith-helmeted men fell to his fire.

"Grenades, throw grenades," Bahls screamed from his position in the middle of the squad's line.

Automatic rifles and machine guns kept firing, but the other
Marines started pulling grenade pins and throwing downhill as
quickly as they could. Screaming, the NVA continued their mad
rush up the hill. In seconds they were too close for the Marines

to use grenades. Many of them met the Marines in hand-to-hand combat.

A charging NVA soldier with fixed bayonet came straight at Morris. Morris swiveled to the side, picked up his rifle, and slammed its butt plate into the man's face, but the NVA's bayonet slashed him along his upper back, under the shoulder. Thorsfinni swung his entrenching tool in a wide arc at the belly of another NVA. The man fell screaming, disemboweled.

"So that's why you told me to sharpen my E-tool," Thorsfinni grunted at Morris.

A few NVA managed to break through the line in scattered places, but they were all killed before they could wipe out any command post or the mortars. Then the rest of them pulled back. Two of the company's mortars continued putting out flares; the others pursued the NVA with high-explosive rounds.

"Squad leaders report!" The cries came from platoon CPs. "Fire-team leaders report," the squad leaders called out.

Before the fire-team leaders could check all their men, whistles were heard on the hillsides. The mortars popped more illumination, showing the NVA charging again. Many of the advancing enemy were shot down by the Marines, and the others dropped to fire back. The whistles brought them back to their feet to close with the Marines. Again they were knocked down and again the whistles sent them a few meters closer. And a third time and a fourth time before the survivors finally broke and ran.

Once more the fleeing enemy was pursued by mortar fire, and artillery was called in on their likely escape routes as well. The crashing roar of the exploding 155s washed over the hilltop in waves. When it ended, the fire-team leaders could finally check their men.

"You okay, Thor?" Morris asked. The big man nodded. "Hunter, how you doing?" he called out. No answer. "Hunter, answer me." Morris half stood in his hole and looked to his right. "Hunter, Zwang, sound off."

Farther to the right Bahls looked to the hole on his left. Neither he nor Morris saw any sign of movement in the hole between them.

"Check it out, Henry J," Bahls shouted.

Morris scooted to the hole. Four men were piled unmoving

on its bottom. "Corpsman up," he screamed and dropped into the hole. He threw one NVA out of it and grabbed the other one. The body wouldn't lift out. Hunter's dead hands were clamped around its throat.

Zwang moaned.

"Corpsman up!" Morris screamed again.

Pounding feet arrived. "Anybody breathing, Henry J?" the corpsman asked.

"Zwang is. Hunter feels like he's wasted."

The corpsman helped Morris peel Hunter's hands off the NVA and heave the body away. A quick look by the glow from a cigarette lighter into the glazed eyes, and a feel for a pulse on Hunter's neck, and the corpsman turned to Zwang. "Hunter's dead," the Doc said to Morris.

Morris felt numb. He wanted to sit on the edge of the hole and cry or wait for the war to end, or get to his feet and walk back to The World. Hunter had been through hell with him for eight months, even though they weren't in the same fire team for most of that time. When Anderson got killed on the helicopter, all that meant was one less Marine in the fight. Hunter was more of a friend. But Morris didn't do any of the things he felt like doing.

"First fire team, Hunter wasted," he reported to Bahls. Because Casebolt was on the other end of the line and couldn't make this report himself, he added, "Third fire team, Zwang wounded."

Bahls ran over to the hole.

The corpsman looked up at him. "Buster, we need a medevac. Zwang'll make it, but we have to get him out of here most ricky-tick."

Carefully they lifted Zwang out of the hole and laid him on a poncho.

"Take him to the CP," Bahls said to them. "When you get back, Henry J, I'll get somebody to carry Hunter's body over there."

"Grady's gone," Ortega told Morris at the CP.

"Say what?" Morris asked, startled.

"One'a them little fuckers made it to the CP and killed Grady."

"Oh, goddam."

Eventually Morris remembered he had been wounded during the attack. Thinking about Zimmerman, Hunter, and Zwang, he almost didn't go for medical attention.

The med-evac birds came in and carried out the wounded and dead. Lima lost fifteen men to the NVA assault plus six more earlier in the landing. They counted sixty-seven NVA bodies on the hilltop and the near slopes.

"We keep killing 'em like that, how long can they keep coming at us?" Morris asked Bahls.

"Until they run out'a men." Bahls swallowed. "Then they'll send the old folks and the women and the baby-sans at us." His eyes scanned the darkness in front of their positions. "They ain't like us, Henry J, life don't mean the same thing to them it means to us. They gonna keep coming till they all dead or we go away."

General Giap studied the situation-report maps in his command room. The reports, culled from intercepted American radio transmissions and Russian intelligence reports as well as NVA sources, were incomplete. Added up they indicated either confusion as to what was actually happening—or the Americans were doing considerable damage to his army.

On the scene the colonel commanding the 97th Regiment felt great concern. His battalions had each attacked an American company and been repelled with severe casualties. He would spend the second day pounding the American positions with mortars and very heavy sniper fire, try to keep the imperialists in place while he regrouped his infantry for another attempt. The mortars and snipers would have to be in continual motion in order to prevent the Americans from bringing artillery or air strikes in on them.

Night came to the hill like a striking cat. Third platoon rose silently from its positions and slipped in a snaky line down the hillside. The rest of Lima shifted to close the ring around the hill's top. An artillery observer went on the ambush with third platoon.

Using hand signals and touches on the arms, Wyman and Ortega settled the thirty men of third platoon into an L-shaped ambush three hundred meters from the base of the hill. If Charlie came, this was probably the route he would use. No one in third platoon would sleep on this night.

Thorsfinni touched Morris on the shoulder some time after midnight. "Hear anything?" he whispered.

They were on the far left of the long leg of the ambush, providing flank security for the machine gun on that end. The other gun was on the short leg with a fire team protecting it.

Morris listened closely for a moment. The insects and night callers had started their noises again after the platoon settled in its position. Now they had silenced again. "Not a damn fucking thing," he whispered back and moved a few feet to his right. "Stand tight," he whispered to the assistant gunner. "Company's coming, pass it."

Quick tension rippled along the ambush line. Everyone tried to sink into the ground.

A piece of shadow detached itself from the darkness to Morris's left and edged forward, darting slightly from side to side. Another piece of shadow followed it. And another. And another.

Morris counted the shadows and depressed the button on his radio with each count. He had reached twenty when there was a shout from the other end of the ambush and the gun on the short leg opened fire. The point man in the NVA column had run into the machine gun at the other end of the ambush. The fight was on, and third platoon didn't know how large a force it was facing.

"That way!" Morris slapped Thorsfinni's shoulder and pointed him at the shadows the NVA were coming from. The heavy booming of Morris's M-14 joined the rattle of Thorsfinni's automatic.

Whistles, screams, and shouts came from the area they were firing at. The sounds of running and bodies crashing through brush came from that side.

"Whoa, shit," Morris shouted. "Gun, fire on the flank! They gonna try'n flank us."

Gunfire started from where they could still hear people maneuvering. Before they could get organized, the machine gun moved to the side and added its voice to the weapons of Thorsfinni and Morris.

"This is a big one," Morris said into his radio. "They trying'a flank us over here."

"Bahls, get your squad over there," Wyman shouted. "Cut off their flank movement."

"Malcolm X, Jeb, get over to Henry J's left," Bahls shouted. "Let's go!"

Bahls and his remaining five men scrambled to Morris's flank and opened up on the muzzle flashes coming from that side. Wyman sent first squad to check the NVA bodies in the killing zone before moving the rest of the platoon to meet the threat from the side. At the same time he directed mortars from the company's hill onto the NVA force.

The NVA fire gradually built up until the Marines knew they were facing a much larger force—at least a company, not counting the ones that had been caught and killed in the initial ambush.

They were right about at least a company. The same battalion that had ringed Lima's hill for its assault the night before was coming back for another try. Only this time it divided into two groups. Each section would attack along one of the ridges. Fewer than forty men in third platoon's ambush were facing more than a hundred fifty crack NVA soldiers. Fortunately, the Marines' fire at first was heavy enough that the major in charge of this assault force didn't realize he was opposed by such a small unit, or he would have charged third platoon as soon as enough of his men were on line.

"FO," Wyman said to the artillery observer, "get us some help. There's too damn many of them for us and the mortars to deal with. Get those guns in here now."

The FO radioed in the numbers that would tell the battery where he was and where he wanted the first spotter round to land. In little more than a minute a white phosphorous round blossomed brightly to the right rear of the NVA.

"On my azimuth, right one hundred, down one hundred. Fire for effect!" the FO shouted into his radio. Half a minute later six 155mm high-explosive rounds landed among the NVA.

On the line the squad leaders were screaming at their men to fire slowly, to conserve their ammunition for the expected charge. "Pick your targets," they yelled, "fire at muzzle flashes." Riflemen slowed their rate of fire to make a full magazine last almost two minutes. Automatic riflemen slowed their fire; some of them switched to semiautomatic. The machine gunners let their barrels cool slightly between bursts.

Every thirty seconds six more rounds of 155mm high-explosive slammed into the NVA. Screams came from their area as men were hit. Their fire slowed and some of them tried to run. Wyman called for the mortars to drop a flare over them, but all the blue light showed was brush. The NVA were concealed from sight. Still, both sides kept up their fire—a hail of bullets flew in each direction.

"Keep your fire low, people," Bahls called out to his squad. "The gooks are under the bushes, not up in 'em."

"Low and slow, Thor," Morris said. Evans and Casebolt gave their men the same instruction.

Sweat poured off Morris's face and the palms of his hands were slick with perspiration. A muzzle flash lit a small portion of brush seventy-five meters to his front. Half blind in the night, he sighted in on where he thought it was and waited for it to repeat. When it did he adjusted his aim and fired three rapid rounds at it. The flash didn't come again.

Whistles sounded in the brush and voices rose above the gunfire. Suddenly the NVA were on their feet, charging the Marines. Rapidly moving shadows flitted through the darkness, highlighted by muzzle flashes. The Marines had clear targets and the volume of their fire grew. The NVA charge wilted, bent, broke. The remnants of this part of the 97th Regiment turned and ran. They reached their previous position at the same time as the next barrage of 155s hit it.

Now that their battle was over, third platoon could hear fire on their hill. The other assault force had made it to the top and was breaking itself on the rest of the company.

There were a few cries of "Corpsman up" in the platoon, but the artillery had been so effective that the NVA hadn't been able to do much damage to the Marines. One of the wounded was Cpl. Malcolm Evans.

"Shit, Buster," he swore. "Piss me the fuck off. I been in this stinking gook country for a year, only got one goddam more month to go before I rotates, and I gets shot."

"Why's that piss you the fuck off, Malcolm X?"

"Piss me the fuck off 'cause the fucking wound not be bad enough to get me out'a the fucking bush, that's why."

Bahls laughed. "You gonna be all right, Malcolm X. You gonna be all right."

"Third platoon, saddle up," Wyman called out. "We're going back topside."

The men rose to their feet, picked up their dead and the few wounded who couldn't walk, and started back toward the ridge. Fewer than forty Marines had surprised and beaten a force four times their strength. They hooted and hollered all the way to the top of the hill. Not even ten wounded and six dead could dampen their spirits.

In the North, on the morning of the third day of Three Fifteen's Operation Rockledge Manor, General Giap pondered the fragmentary casualty figures he had received. If they were accurate, his 97th Regiment had severely damaged the 3rd Battalion of the American 15th Marines. Unfortunately, the 97th Regiment had suffered so many casualties that it was no longer effective as a combat unit.

After midnight on December first, the fourth day of the Americans' Operation Rockledge Manor, the 154th Regiment of the North Vietnamese Army entered the ring. A fresh regiment, to be reinforced by the remnants of a broken one, would try to kill an injured American Marine battalion.

No, No! Not the Briar Patch!

"I'VE BEEN THINKING ABOUT THIS FIGHT REAL HARD. THESE next few days are kind of fuzzy in my mind. Lots of crap I don't like to remember happened on this operation. Rockledge Manor was a real tough operation. Lots of people that I lived and fought with for a boo-coo long time got hurt or killed on the second half of that op, and I came damn close to getting killed my ownself more than once. The next few days are kind'a blurry in my mind, son, but I'll tell it to you close as I can to the way things happened. Leastways, close as I can remember, but don't hold it against me if I ain't got everything exactly right.

"There we was, after two days and two nights of fighting we knew had put a bad hurting on Mister Charles. Our own casualties were on the heavy side—third platoon had nine men dead and a bunch more wounded, but some of the wounded were able to stay, so we were still about thirty men, including the gun squad we had with us. Low as our strength was, we knew outnumbered the gooks in the area, so when the company-size patrols couldn't find anybody to kick ass with, we didn't mind too much going on platoon and squad patrols. Hunting parties, we called them. And we had a bunch of ambushes out every night, too. Maybe half of the company sat on the hill at night guarding the CP. The rest of us was in the brush waiting for the NVA to walk into our ambushes and get killed.

"Then some platoons started going out on two-day patrols with overnight ambushes a day's hump away from the company CP. It was on one of them all hell broke loose and third platoon almost got itself wiped out.

"First we was moving the company bases deeper into the hills until we reached what was almost jungle and running into small bunches of NVA. Might have been the second morning after we busted the crap out of that NVA battalion on that ambush. Lima was moving in platoon columns through the trees. Third squad was on the point for third platoon when Empty Nick saw something he didn't like. We stopped at the edge of a grassy clearing and everybody that could get close to it looked. Nobody else could see what Empty Nick saw. But when a man's been in the bush for a year, you listen to him when he says something is wrong. Buster asked which way we should go around, and Nick led us around to the left side of the clearing.

"That was exactly the wrong way to go. Mister Charles had that side of the clearing booby-trapped and was set up in an ambush on the other side. Nick stepped right into a trip wire and pulled a grenade out of a tin can. He heard it soon as the spoon popped off and tried to jump out of the way, but the bush was too thick and he got a foot blown off. Almost bled to death before a corpsman could get to him with a tourniquet. That grenade going off was the signal to set off the ambush. Must have been a whole company opened up on us. We just hit the deck and gave what return fire we could.

"Lieutenant Wyman got on the horn and called in mortars and artillery, but those gooks had us pinned down real good. We couldn't do much more than lay on the ground like we were making love to it and try to shoot without raising our shoulders or heads. After a while the artillery and mortars stopped and a half-dozen helicopter gunships came in and laid everything they had on that ambush. That must have done the trick, 'cause Mister Charles stopped shooting at us and we were able to take care of our wounded.

"It was real tough. Thor was dead. Groton got shot up real bad. Gangland had to be med-evacked. Only four of us left now. Hell, we were a fire team with a squad leader in charge. Buster took the blooper for himself, and Malcolm X, Jeb, and me all had automatics. Wasn't many of us, but we were real well-armed. Way we looked and felt, you could have called us a Death's Head squad. Lots of our buddies had been shot and we was gonna make Mister Charles pay. Or we'd die trying. There're times even a sane man goes crazy for a while; that was one of them.

"That night the platoon set in on top of this ridgeline in a thin jungle. We were down to half strength—including the gun squad, there were maybe twenty of us sitting there. What we didn't learn until later was a new NVA regiment came into the area that day. We were up against new troops and they had us outnumbered something fierce. All during the night we were getting probed by those new NVA. The constant probing kept most all of us from getting any sleep that night. We had good fire discipline and didn't give away our positions by shooting at them. What we did was roll grenades down the ridge at their noises. Zapped a bunch, too.

"About oh-four-hundred, or maybe a half hour later, must have been two platoons came up those slopes at us. They didn't use any mortars to prep us with and they snooped and pooped real quiet getting close, so we didn't have any warning they was there until they just up and started shooting and screaming at us. This is when staying awake paid off for us. We might have been only twenty men strong, but we had two machine guns, nine automatic rifles, and three bloopers. Even the lieutenant and Ortega was shooting M-14s instead of their forty-fives.

"By the time those two platoons reached our line we had already wiped out a third of them. They came charging into our lines with fixed bayonets, but we had our bayonets fixed, too, and one Marine was generally about twice the size of one of them and four times as strong. They were worn out from running uphill, and we just stood up and started swinging our blades and butts just like we learned with pugil sticks in boot camp and them little buggers started dying at our feet. An M-14's a mite longer than an AK. Between that and our longer arms, we were usually able to put them down before they could get close enough to stick us with their blades.

Good thing, because we were still outnumbered about two to one when they got to us.

"The ones we didn't kill at our positions ran all the way to the top of the ridge and turned around to shoot downhill. Figured anybody below them on the slopes was us, I guess. Their mistake was, this put them on the skyline and we had good shots at them. Not many of them lived long enough to figure out that mistake and make their way back down and past us.

"When the sun rose we were able to take stock. We found close to forty dead NVA soldiers on that ridge and a bunch more blood trails where wounded ones dragged themselves away or their buddies dragged bodies off. The bad news was, we had fifty-percent casualties our ownselves. The med-evac birds came in and flew off with four more dead and a couple that were wounded so bad they couldn't stay anymore. Jeb Casebolt got a leg wound from a bayonet, but he stayed. Buster Bahls was banged upside the gourd bad enough to get a Purple Heart out of it—he felt kind of dizzy—but he stayed, too.

"We pulled down off of that ridge and set an ambush along a trail we felt sure Mister Charles would use that night. Only fifteen of us now, but everyone except the machine gunners was armed with an automatic—even the men carrying the bloopers was carrying M-14s. Anything less than a company walking into our ambush that night was gonna meet a wall of fire that'd tear it apart. And if a company did walk in, the fifteenth man we had was an artillery observer the med-evac dropped off along with more ammo and grenades.

"That night we had a chance to both use that artillery FO and raise a wall of fire. We were sitting on a ridge something like fifty meters above the bottom of a broad gully that had a trail alongside the small stream in its middle. Little after midnight a big supply train come humping along that trail. The FO called in some spotter rounds during the day, so the battery he was in contact with was registered in our area. The FO had a Starlight scope he used to watch the trail and he saw the gooks coming. Every third man in the column was standing upright with a rifle in his hands—the rest of them were bent double carrying heavy-assed packs. There was near a hundred and fifty men in that column. The FO called his big guns in and that supply train got itself blown all to hell. We didn't fire our ownselves, so Mister Charles didn't have any idea where the observer was and couldn't do jack shit about it.

"Hour or so later, a platoon came sweeping along the side of the ridge we were on, looking for our observation post. They must have thought we had a Force Recon patrol out there, and all we had to do was shift our positions a skosh bit. We killed most of the thirty men in that platoon and they didn't manage to put any kind of hurting on us at all. Of course, we did have to move after that because Mister Charles knew where we were at.

"We were one happy squad-size platoon when the sun came up. We were dirty, stinking, tired, and bloody, but we were responsible for at least a hundred, maybe close to two hundred NVA getting killed, and we didn't get any casualties of our own. Besides, a couple birds came in and lifted us out of there and back to the company CP where a hot meal was waiting for us. A hot meal in the field. That was something most of us had never seen, though what I hear is the First Cav and other air-mobile Army units got one or two almost every day. That's because they had enough choppers to do it with and the Marines didn't.

"I know, it sounds unbelievable. So far on this operation third platoon claimed credit for killing maybe two, three hundred NVA. And we lost only twenty men of our own. That's one bodacious kill ratio. But what most people don't understand is we really were a whole lot better fighters than the gooks we were up against. Not usually that much better, but we were definitely better. If the Army brass and the press had just stood out of the way and let the Marines fight that war the way we wanted, we would have won it.

"Couple of hours rest and we got sent out on another patrol, but it was a short one. Malcolm X had the point and walked smack into a pungee stake trap. It was an old one, though, and he didn't get hurt real bad. Just enough to have to be evacced out after we carried him back to the company CP.

"Hold on a minute there, son.

"What's that you say, dear? Yes, he's here with me. You want him right now? All right, I'll send him to you.

"Sorry, son, but we got to stop for now. Your mama wants you. Go see what she wants and I'll finish this story for you when your mama's done with you. Go ahead, the rest of this can wait until you get back. Then I'll tell you about how we found the main NVA base camp and what we did to it."

Chapter Fourteen

KILO COMPANY JOINED THE THREE ALREADY IN THE BUSH FOR the hunt. Together, the four companies of Three Fifteen rapidly swept deeper into the hills, looking for the survivors of the NVA regiment. The companies were on a line of platoon columns that covered a swath of light jungle two and a half miles wide. If Mister Charles was foolish enough to stand and fight, he would die.

Sergeant Bahls listened to his radio, then called ahead, "Step it out faster, Henry J, Wyman wants us on that ridge up ahead in a half hour." He picked up his own pace to urge the men in front of him to move faster.

"Pick up your pace, Thor," Corporal Morris said to the broad back five meters to his front.

The big blond man turned his head to look at his fire-team leader. "You mean I get to go as fast as I want for a change?" His grinning teeth barely showed beneath his sweeping mustache.

Morris's return grin more resembled a Death's Head mask. "Not that fast, Thor," he said. "We gotta take a half hour to get there."

"Shit, man, you ain't no fucking fun a-tall," Thorsfinni said cheerfully, and turned his attention back to the game track he was following.

Tree branches intermingled overhead and would have formed a tunnel if the game track had been wide enough to be called a path. Little direct sunlight managed to filter through to the ground; it was slightly brighter than twilight under the trees. Unless the NVA had set an ambush, the greatest danger was from hard-to-spot booby traps the rapidly walking point man couldn't spot.

Few insects buzzed, fewer birds sang, as Thorsfinni lowered his shoulders and pushed his body through the thin brush along the track. The big man's blue eyes flickered everywhere—he was sure he'd be able to spot an ambush or a booby trap in time to keep from being killed by it. Behind him, Morris felt less certain. Gangland Gant nervously watched the trees to both sides of Morris's back. Bahls, fourth in line, wished the lieutenant wasn't in such a hurry to get on top of the ridge. Groton hadn't been in-country long enough to know how slowly jungle patrols normally moved. Malcolm Evans, lower left arm throbbing from the bullet crease it suffered the night before, wanted to walk slower to ease the pain in his arm. Nick Devoid and Jeb Casebolt, bringing up the rear, hoped Thorsfinni's eyes were as good as he claimed, but mostly they were glad they weren't on the point.

Thorsfinni froze, then almost without motion, stepped backward.

Morris eased up to Thorsfinni. "What'cha got, Thor?" he whispered into his ear.

"*Nuoc mam*, Honcho," Thorsfinni whispered back.

Morris sniffed. The distinctive rotten-fish aroma of the universal Vietnamese fish sauce drifted through the air. Morris slowly pivoted his head, trying to determine the direction the smell was coming from. He nodded, then turned to report back to his squad leader.

The Marines double-checked that their rifle bolts were closed, safeties off, and magazines well seated. The smell of *nuoc mam* had to mean enemy—any civilians had certainly cleared out of this area by now.

"Think we're in it, pano?" Devoid whispered over his shoulder to Evans. They were two of only five men in the squad who had survived a year of combat.

Evans shook his head. "Can't be," he whispered back.

"Dinks dinged me yesterday. Ain't time again yet."

Devoid snorted softly. "Zips already zinged me twice. Gimme your Purple Heart. I need a third one to go home."

"Bullshit. You be a short-timer. You going home 'long with me in a month, anyways."

Devoid worked up some saliva and swallowed. "Think this is the last time we gotta go into the bush?"

"I do believe so."

Bahls put his radio aside and signaled them and Casebolt forward. "We're gonna get on line and move through that area there." He swept his arm to the right of the track. "If Mister Charles been eating, maybe he's taking an after-chow nap and we can catch him sleeping. Let's move."

The eight Marines formed a line and crept forward. Large-leaved and small-leaved bushes parted easily at their passing, closed softly behind them, leaving no trace of their passage. The damp earth had no dry sticks covering it for their footfalls to snap. Third squad came upon the NVA squad undetected.

Six North Vietnamese soldiers sat eating in a small clearing formed when a medium-size tree toppled in a storm. The Marines froze in place.

Bahls slowly swiveled his head, listening for any sound made by unseen enemy. His eyes swept the surrounding jungle, seeing nothing but trees and undergrowth. To his right Morris did the same, as did Evans on his left. Morris and Evans exchanged nods with their squad leader, who held up a grenade and one finger. The two fire-team leaders also readied a grenade and signaled their men to get down and be prepared to fire. Bahls pulled the pin from his grenade and eased the spoon off; the other two did the same.

"One thousand one, one thousand two," Bahls counted to himself, "one thousand three." He tossed the grenade and dropped to the ground. Morris and Evans did the same.

The three one-pound packages of explosives, wrapped with notched steel wire, sheathed in steel sheet, landed among the startled NVA. The enemy soldiers hardly had time to start jumping out of the way when the grenades went off.

"Fire!" Bahls screamed, and opened up on the leaping enemy. So did the other six Marines with rifles. They were too close for Groton to fire his M-79 so the grenadier used his forty-five.

The fire fight was over almost before it began. The six NVA sprawled dead in the clearing, two of them killed by the grenades, the others wounded in the explosions and killed by rifle fire before they could respond with their own weapons.

"Henry J, get your people to the other side of the clearing and set up security for us," Bahls ordered. "Malcolm X, check the bodies for documents."

Morris, Thorsfinni, and Gant rushed across the small open space and into the brush on its other side. Evans, Devoid, and Casebolt started going through the dead men's packs and pockets.

One corpse gave up a wallet that contained a photograph of a pretty young Vietnamese woman—a wife or girlfriend. Casebolt studied the photo for a moment before pocketing it. "Wonder what your name is, girlie," he said to it first.

Another dead man surrendered a small pornography collection. Devoid flipped quickly through the grainy photos and licked his lips before putting them back in their waterproof plastic case and slipping the case into the inside pocket of his shirt. "Gonna save you for after this op," he said, patting his belly where the pocket was.

The third NVA yielded a packet of American ID cards. One carried several handwritten letters with the ink starting to run. Three sheets of paper that looked like official documents came from another. The last man had a small North Vietnamese flag covered with signatures and slogans—this soldier's family's and friends' best wishes for success in battle and a long life in an afterward that he would never see.

Bahls collected the letters and documents to pass over to the lieutenant for whatever intelligence value they might have, and let his men keep the photos and flag.

"Why for first team don't get any souvenirs?" Morris asked when the body search was finished.

"You want a souvenir, Henry J?" Bahls asked. "Take this." He sailed a blood-spattered pith helmet to Morris.

Morris knocked his steel pot from his head and perched the NVA helmet on top of his crown. "Better watch out, Mister Charles," he grinned, "here comes the 'Phantom Gook' after your ass. You gonna die, hoss.'' He crouched over and made jerky hop-steps around the clearing, poking his rifle at the bodies.

Evans's fire team moved into the brush to watch for anyone coming while Thorsfinni and Gant looked the bodies over for souvenirs.

"This is a nice pack you don't need anymore," Thorsfinni said to one of the dead. He stripped off the pack and dumped its contents onto the ground, then removed the contents of his own pack to the larger, more comfortable NVA pack and put it on his back.

"You're mine now, baby," Gant said, and picked up an AK-47 and its ammunition. "I'm shipping you home. Gonna go deer hunting with you when I get back to The World."

Wyman and Ortega joined them in the clearing. Sergeant Smith set up his second squad for security on its far side.

Wyman looked around. "Gather any weapons and ammunition nobody wants to souvenir into a pile," he told Bahls. "We'll thermite them when we move out."

"Aye aye," Bahls answered.

Morris's team quickly gathered the munitions into a small stack. When they were all together, Wyman gave the order to continue on to the ridge.

Ortega and a man from first squad stayed behind in the clearing until the rest of the platoon was three minutes ahead of them. Then Ortega placed a steel-melting thermite grenade on top of the stack of weapons and ammunition and pulled the pin. He and the other man ran as fast as they could to get as far as possible before the heat and melting metal set off any of the bullets or grenades in the pile.

The 97th Infantry Regiment was dead as a fighting unit. Its few survivors were scattered in pairs and small groups simply trying to survive. The Marines didn't know it, but they were about to meet the vanguard of the fresh 154th Regiment.

Night fell before the battalion stopped. Each of the battalion's twelve platoons formed its own perimeter and set security for itself. There was no chance to dig in; every man found what cover he could in the earth and trees. C-ration cans were opened as quietly as possible and the food eaten cold. Watch rotations were set.

Near two A.M. a jolt of tension coursed through Thorsfinni's body. He touched Morris lightly on the shoulder. Morris's eyes snapped open. He was awake instantly, but no other part of his body moved.

"What?" he whispered.

"Movement." The big man pointed to his left front.

Morris listened intently. The sound came again, a slight rustling in the brush. Morris tapped Gant's shoulder and put his finger to his lips. Gant changed from asleep to alert.

Ten meters to their left Groton trembled at the sound and woke Bahls. The movement was directly to their front. Ten meters farther along Evans woke Casebolt and Devoid. Third squad was ready, but the men in the three positions couldn't communicate with each other because the noise would pinpoint their positions to the prober.

Bahls picked up a grenade, held the spoon tightly with his fingers, pulled the pin and waited for the rustling to sound again. When he heard it he rose to hands and knees, eased the spoon off the grenade, and tossed it in the direction of the sound. He dropped back to the ground and hugged it, waiting for the explosion. The grenade went off and Bahls was rewarded by the scream of an injured man and the noise the wounded prober made running away through the brush.

"Hold your fire," Bahls hastily called out in a low voice. The muzzle flashes would give their positions away. The NVA now knew the Marines were on the ridge, but they didn't know how many or exactly where. He wanted to keep it that way.

Grenades were thrown at other points around the platoon's perimeter as more probers came. Most of the other platoons in the battalion's line were also being probed. Most of the Marines threw grenades at the sounds—only a few fired their rifles. There was no return fire from the probing elements.

A tense hour passed without more probing. By three-thirty half of the Marines were sleeping again. Thinking that the probers were the remnants of the destroyed NVA regiment slipping through in an escape attempt, the others were starting to ease the degree of their alertness.

Shortly before four in the morning, anyone who thought the

probers had been stragglers found out how wrong he had been. Whistles sounded and the darkness of the thin jungle surrounding third platoon was abruptly lit by muzzle flashes as the platoon was hit from all sides. They were completely ringed, as were eight of the other eleven platoons.

"Control your fire," Bahls yelled over the noise of the fire fight. "Aim at muzzle flashes."

The other squad leaders screamed the same order to their men. The commands were echoed from the middle of the platoon circle as Wyman and Ortega called to the squad leaders. The squad leaders were thinking ahead of them. The rate of fire from the ridge top was already slowing.

"What the fuck is going on down there?" Morris asked. "They aren't charging us."

That was true. The NVA were prone, firing uphill from behind what cover they could find. They wanted to know where the Marine positions were before advancing into their fire. Not all of the attackers were shooting; most of them were waiting for orders to start crawling up the ridge.

"Grenades, throw grenades down at them," Bahls shouted.

Third squad's rate of fire slowed further as the men started tossing grenades, usually toward where they had seen muzzle flashes. Screams also came from places none of the Marines had seen muzzle flashes. The timing was perfect; the grenades were landing among the NVA who had just gotten the order to crawl up the ridge while the Marines were shooting at the men who were shooting. More whistles sounded and, screaming battle cries, the NVA all charged upward.

Heavy fire from the machine guns, rifles, and M-79s—and more grenades—met the assault, bent it, tore rents in it, sent it reeling backward. The attacking company hadn't expected that much instant resistance from the platoon they wanted to overrun. The NVA regrouped, gathered into two sections and started crawling back up the sides of the ridge. This time they wouldn't hit the entire platoon, only its down-ridge sides. This time they got closer to the Marines before the fire fight started.

But the Marines were waiting with grenades which they rolled or threw down at their attackers. Scrambling along the steep slopes, in some places the NVA had to grasp tree branches and bushes to haul themselves up. Their ability to fight was severely reduced by the steepness of the ridge, and they were beaten back again. This time they pulled back from the ridge. Dawn was coming anyway, it was too late to continue trying to overrun the Marine position.

"Henry J, Malcolm X, report," Bahls ordered. The other squad leaders gave the same order to their team leaders.

Morris checked his men. Thorsfinni was all right, but Gant was unconscious. "I got a casualty," Morris reported, "Gangland's been hit. Corpsman up!"

"Corpsman up!" Evans shouted. "Empty Nick be down."

The two corpsmen were suddenly very busy. Every squad had casualties. So did one of the gun teams and the command post.

"Bring your casualties to the CP," Wyman ordered the squad leaders. "We'll establish a med station here." The corpsmen could treat all of the wounded more quickly if they were gathered in one place than if the corpsmen had to go from squad to squad. In the CP they would triage, treating first the men who had the best chance of surviving their wounds if given quick treatment.

At dawn the platoon cleared a landing zone for the med-evac helicopters. Four men had been killed during the night and six others wounded—two of the six had to be evacuated for treatment. Some of the other platoons were in better shape, some were in worse. One had been overrun and almost completely wiped out.

Evans stood looking down at Devoid's body, the pain in his arm forgotten in the greater pain of losing a man he had fought alongside, eaten and slept with for a year.

"The other night Empty Nick said he wanted the Heart I got for my arm," he said. "With three Hearts he'd get to go back to The World. Now he's got his third Heart and he be going home. Shit. Fucking short-timer. He lived through this operation, he be going back in a couple weeks anyhow."

Casebolt knelt beside Devoid's body and reached inside the bloody shirt. His hand drew out the waterproof case with the pornographic pictures. There was a bullet hole in the case. Blood dripped out of the hole when the case was tipped.

"Fuck," Casebolt said. "He wanted to save these for after this op. He never had a chance to use 'em, and now nobody else can use 'em either." He opened the case and looked at the blood-soaked pictures with the hole through them. "Nobody can use 'em ever again." He shook his head and threw the pictures and their case over the side of the ridge.

A few feet away Morris sat next to Gant. "You know, Gangland, this is a bitch," he said to the wounded man. "I've been here three months longer'n you, and you going back to The World before I do. That's a fucking bitch."

"Man, I ain't going back to no World." Gant grinned weakly. "I'm going to a hospital in Japan." His right shoulder and his head were wrapped in battle dressings.

Morris slapped his uninjured shoulder. "Japan." He nodded. "That's good duty. Boom-boom a geisha for me."

"I'll do that, Honcho." Gant's grin widened. "After I boom-boom a whole shitload of geishas for *me*."

The *whumpa-whumpa* of a descending helicopter made everyone duck. The med-evac bird set down and the dead and wounded were quickly boarded on it. Then it lifted off and flew away, leaving a smaller platoon on the hill.

Bahls looked at his men. "A Marine rifle squad has fourteen men," he said to them. "We got six of us. Gonna have to reorganize again." He shook his head and spat into the dirt. "Unless squads get combined and we gotta do something else, Jeb, you come with me and Groton for the first team. Henry J, you got Malcolm X and Thor for the second team." He turned and walked toward the platoon CP, muttering, "Shee-it, man. How in'a hell am I supposed to run a squad when I only got six men including my own damn self?"

"Today we have an easy hump," Lieutenant Wyman said to his squad leaders. "We only have to go three klicks to another ridge. Mister Charles probably won't be out looking for us. The best bet is he's hiding during the day. Questions?" As usual, there were none. "All right, then get your people ready. Staff Sergeant Ortega will issue ammo and rations. We move out in twenty minutes." He turned from them to prepare himself for the short hump.

"Third squad, saddle up," Bahls called when he reached his squad. The other squad leaders did the same. "We move out in less than twenty minutes." The big sergeant checked his pack and made sure his rifle was ready and that he had all his ammunition. Then he checked his men. Third squad was ready for another day. What there was of third squad, anyway.

Three klicks. Sounded like an easy hump. But that was three kilometers on the map. The actual walk was more like eight kilometers. There were three ridges that had to be climbed and other terrain that needed to be gone around. The low ground and ridges were covered with more of the thin jungle and undergrown with dense brush and stayawhile vines. A trail had to be cut through some places because of the thickness of the brush. Some booby traps were found and disarmed, others were marked. None of them were found the hard way.

It took third platoon five hours to cover the distance. Then they had to dig in for the night. Twenty men to hold a ridge against whatever force the NVA might attack with.

"You say this is a suicide mission, Buster?"

"Nah, this ain't a suicide mission, Henry J. We is bait."

"When the fish comes to take the bait, who's gonna set the hook and haul that sucker in?"

"We is, Henry J, we is."

"You saying we're both the bait and the fisherman?"

"Give the man a cee-gar."

"What's the difference between being bait and being a suicide mission?"

"Ain't none."

But the digging was wasted effort and the bait wasn't to be used. A patrol from the 1st Recon Company had found an NVA battalion camp a klick and a half from third platoon's ridge. Mike Company was assigned to be the blocking unit for the assault the Marines would make on that camp. Lima Company would make the actual assault. First, Lima and Mike would position themselves three and five hundred meters respectively from the camp. Then it would be heavily bombarded by artillery. The recon patrol had established an artillery observation post on a nearby ridge. Two A-4s and a half-dozen helicopter gunships would be on station for air support during and after the assault.

Wyman briefed the squad leaders on the mission, then asked, "Questions?"

"Yes, sir, I have one."

"Speak up, Sergeant Smith."

"Is the rest of the company in as bad shape as we are?"

"I don't believe so."

"But you don't know so, sir."

Wyman shook his head. "I don't know so, but I believe the other platoons are in better shape than we are."

"Hope you're right, sir."

"So do I, Sergeant Smith." Wyman looked at the squad leaders for other questions, but Smith had asked the one that was on everyone's mind. "Brief your men and saddle up. We move out in fifteen minutes."

"No shit. We're going to where Mister Charles is trying to get some sleep," Thorsfinni said, wild-eyed. "Hot damn, we gonna kick some ass."

"You a crazy fucker, Thor," Morris said. "If the whole company's like this platoon, its gonna be less'n a hundred Marines jumping on five, six hundred hardcase NVA."

The big blond grinned. "Any time one Marine can't kick ass on a half dozen of these little fucking people, it's time for that Marine to get out and become a sloppy civilian."

"Sloppy civilian. I like the way that sounds. Think in a couple weeks I'm gonna turn myself into one."

"No can do, Henry J," Casebolt said. "You're like me. You got two and a half more years in this Green Machine."

"Me, too," Evans said. "This war lasts that long, before next year's over we gonna be back here to kick some more ass."

"Or get ours kicked."

"Whatever. Maybe when we come back again we be having the M-16 like the Army does."

Thorsfinni's eyes glowed. "Maybe we'll even have them Huey birds. We might even have enough of 'em we can fly everywhere like the Army does instead of having to hump."

"Never happen," Evans said. "Why you think we be called grunts? It's 'cause'a the grunting we do every time we take a step. And you know we take a lot'a them."

The march to the place where Lima Company would wait out the artillery bombardment took two hours. The closer the Marines got to the NVA camp the slower and more cautiously the point moved. They expected to find more booby traps as they neared the camp, and they did. Then they pulled into position and the captain reported their position to battalion, who relayed it to the recon patrol. Mike Company was already in its blocking position on the other side of the campsite. The first barrage of 105mm and 155mm rounds landed in the NVA camp five minutes later.

The recon OP moved the barrages around the NVA camp from one end to the other. They shifted the target areas in a seemingly random manner so the NVA couldn't pick up any pattern other than every fifteen seconds, six rounds would land in the camp. In minutes everything in the camp standing above ground level was broken or destroyed.

The crashing explosions rolled over the Marines like the rhythmic thunder of a maniac storm. They huddled, hugging the ground, hoping no rounds fell short or long, wishing for every shell to hit its assigned target. In Lima Company they wanted the bombardment to kill every human being in the bombardment zone.

In the waning moments of the artillery attack, Lima Company rose and rushed forward in a column that made a ninety-degree turn and became a line thirty meters from the edge of the camp. No concern for quiet now—the artillery would cover the noise of their approach. Just watch out for the booby traps, that's all.

Sudden silence filled the air. The artillery's part of the battle was over. A thin keening attempted to fill the sound void left in the artillery's wake as wounded NVA gave voice to their hurt.

Now it was up to the grunts. Screaming, they charged into the camp, firing from the hip. Shattered trees lay broken on the ground. No longer identifiable containers and clothing were strewn about. Scraps of bloody flesh and shards of crushed bone were evidence of the death borne on the artillery shells.

''Bunkers. Look for bunkers and spider traps,'' Bahls shouted. ''Frag the bunkers and shoot into the spider traps.''

Third squad ran forward in a crouch. Groton saw the embrasure of a bunker and fired a white phosphorus round from his M-79 into it. Morris ran to the rear of another and slammed a grenade through the entrance. Evans fired three bursts from his automatic into the lid of a spider trap. Casebolt fired his automatic into the embrasure of another bunker, covering Thorsfinni

while he ran up to it and threw a grenade through the opening.
No one took the time to allow anyone to surrender. In this war
the enemy preferred to fight to the death.

The company had moved halfway across the camp before fire
started coming from bunkers they hadn't reached. At first all the
enemy fire did was tell the Marines which bunkers to be sure
they threw grenades into. Abruptly, soldiers started bolting from
the bunkers and ran away from the Marines, many falling to the
Marines' fire.

"Turkey shoot!" Thorsfinni shouted, and threw his M-14 to
his shoulder.

Then the only sound in the camp was the Marines' fire.

"Cease fire! Cease fire!" Wyman and Ortega ordered. Third
platoon's fire slackened and died as the squad leaders repeated
the order.

"Let's check out those bunkers, people. Make sure there's
nobody alive and in a fighting mood in 'em."

Carefully, throwing grenades in first, third platoon inspected
all the bunkers in their area. First and second platoons did the
same. Every bunker had dead men in it. The dead and their
weapons were left for later. The few wounded found were
dragged from the bunkers, disarmed, and watched.

Heavy fire could be heard half a kilometer from the camp. It
was Mike Company ambushing the survivors from this battalion
camp. However many NVA were present in the camp when the
bombardment started, the battalion was wiped out.

"Hoo-ee, man, we kicked some ass." Thorsfinni grinned.

"Thinks he's fucking Nutsy Nooncy," Morris muttered from
a few feet away.

"Sure talks like it," Bahls agreed. He was standing near
Morris.

"Man gonna get hisself shot to shit one a these days." Casebolt joined them.

"Who's Nutsy Nooncy?" Groton asked as he walked up to
the group. The four Marines stood near a few wounded NVA,
watching Malcolm Evans search a body for documents or souvenirs.

Evans was unaware of their scrutiny.

"You say I'm gonna get the shit shot out'a me?" Thorsfinni,
still grinning, called over to the group. "Look at you. One gre-

nade could get you all.'' The grin vanished from his face and he swung his rifle up, yelling, ''Grenade.''

The four stood watching him until he pulled the trigger. They turned to see what he shot at and saw a wounded NVA flip back dead. Then they saw the grenade he had rolled toward them.

''Grenade!'' they shouted and dived away. But it was too late for them to escape the explosion.

Just as the third squad of the third platoon of Company L, 3rd Battalion, 15th Marines was no longer an effective fighting unit—with only one man unwounded and one wounded but able to continue—so was the 154th Infantry Regiment of the North Vietnamese Army no longer functional. Operation Rockledge Manor was a vicious series of battles, large and small. Hundreds of men on both sides were killed, more hundreds were wounded. Two NVA regiments and one Marine battalion were reduced to less than functional strength.

In Hanoi, General Giap informed Ho Chi Minh that a Marine battalion was knocked out of the field. Then he told him the cost. Two regiments—one had died on the battlefield and the other was so badly wounded it might never return to combat. Uncle Ho needed badly to have a victory to report to his people in the North and to his Russian supporters. In his report of Rockledge Manor he exaggerated, but only slightly, the damage to Three Fifteen. Uncle Ho did not tell them the extent of injury to the NVA units that did the fighting.

''Man, were we dumb or what?'' Bahls asked. His head was wound with gauze and tape.

''Way my leg feels, we was lucky,'' Casebolt answered. ''Could'a lost the sucker.''

Morris considered the broad bandages wrapping his side and the tubes sticking into his arms. ''Dumb lucky,'' he said. ''Dumb for not moving when Thor yelled, lucky to be alive.''

Groton looked at the massive cast encasing his left arm. ''Going back to The World. This might not be bad enough to get me out'a the Crotch, but it's sure as shit getting me back to The World. No fucking way I'm ever getting near a war again.''

They were aboard a C-130 cargo plane outfitted for hospital duty, on their way to Japan for further treatment before transshipment back to the United States. All four had survived the grenade. They had survived the war and wouldn't have to return to it.

"Think we'll see Gangland there?" Casebolt asked.

"If we do, I bet he can tell us where the best nooky is," Morris answered.

"Man can't have been there for more'n one day," Bahls said.

"Fast worker," Morris said.

"You better believe it," Casebolt said. "He got in-country after we did, used up his thirteen months, and left before us."

Groton laughed. "I'm even faster," he said. "I used my thirteen months up in less than two weeks."

The others stared at him.

"Fucking boot," Bahls said after a few silent moments passed. "We spend a whole fucking year and then some in that goddam place, and this goddam boot, less than two weeks in-country, goes back to The World same time as we do. Shee-it."

Morris grew solemn. "Could be worse," he said. "We could be going back like Grady did. Or Frenchy, or the Samoan."

"Or Empty Nick, or Wegener, or Kim Chang, or Mouse," Casebolt added.

"Amen, Brothers," Bahls said softly.

Silence returned to the group, and the aircraft soared farther from the war.

The End—
and the Beginning

"I WAS IN THE HOSPITAL IN JAPAN FOR A WEEK OR SO UNTIL the doctors were satisfied I was all stabilized. Then they flew me back to the Valley Forge Army hospital and they kept me in a ward there for a couple months more. What with my Purple Heart and me being a good storyteller and all, instead of sending me back for a second tour like so many other Marines got, they gave me training duty in Okinawa, where I helped teach Marines how to survive in that war. Only time I got scared was during the Tet Offensive. The Fifth Marines took a lot of casualties kicking hell out of those gooks that tried to take Hue, and I thought maybe they'd use me as a replacement. But by the time the NVA hit Hue I only had three months left on that overseas tour, so they left me where I was and sent other Marines who hadn't done any fighting yet to take their turn.

"By the time I come back from Oki I was a sergeant and was sent to Camp Lejeune in North Carolina for the rest of my four years and served as a military policeman. When I got out I hurried home and married your mama, who was my high school sweetheart. Ahem. We started fucking enough to make up for the last four years and forget the war.

"Ah, son, you ever tell your mama I said her and me spent most of our time fucking our brains out right after we got mar-

288

ried, you're gonna hope you get to go to a war you don't come home from.

"Anyhow, one time my bullets hit her target and nine months later you popped out. So here we are today, eighteen years after your birth, and I'm telling you about how you've got a family tradition to carry on. It's time for the next war now.

"That's the way it is, son. I spent a year in an overheated country where you couldn't drink the water and if you trusted any of the people, you did it at your own risk. A bunch of my buddies got killed and more got wounded—hell, I got zapped that one time there at the end myself. But what with us getting our brains half fried from the heat and going half crazy in the godawful monsoons and getting sliced up by elephant grass and having leeches trying to drink us dry like they was Dracula and having these strange little people running around trying to kill us, I'm proud to be able to say I was good enough to be a Marine and go off to fight in that crazy Asian war. Just like my daddy before me and his daddy before him and on and on all the way back to the American Revolution. We all did it and it's your turn now.

"If you have trouble believing me when I say it's time for another war, read your American history, son. It's there. One generation goes off to fight a war and its sons go off to fight the next war. The generations in between are peaceable. The ones in between don't generally do much fighting. Other countries might have different rhythms, but in America we have this cycle of the men born during or right after a war go off to fight in the next one. This cycle started with the Revolution when we broke off from England. I was born at the end of World War Two, you were born near the end of the Vietnam war. Some time soon, maybe the next year or two, there's gonna be another war. Fits our cycle. It's your turn to go fight.

"Oh, and don't try to say that the War of 1812 and Korea broke the cycle. The men who fought in those wars were the younger brothers of the men who fought in the previous wars."

About the Author

David Sherman served as a Marine in Vietnam in 1966, stationed, among other places, in a CAP unit on Ky Hoa Island. He holds the Combat Action Ribbon, Presidential Unit Citation, Navy Unit Commendation, Vietnamese Cross of Gallantry, and the Vietnamese Civic Action Unit Citation. He left the Marines a corporal, and after his return to The World, worked as a library clerk, antiquarian bookstore retail manager, deputy director of a federally funded community crime-prevention program, manager of the University of Pennsylvania's Mail Service Department, and a sculptor.